THE COSMO CHRONICLES:
THE WELLS OF YGGDRASIL

Chloe Louise Yelland

THE BOOK:

Haley harboured cosmic magic abilities since the day she was born. Raised by her brother and sister, her questions about her past and heritage are soon answered on her eighteenth birthday upon the appearance of the Aurora Eclipse: she is the crown princess of Asgard and a descendent of the Thunder God. After learning the truth about her powers, she must now embrace her destiny in becoming the true heir to the throne and seek out the hidden pieces of the most powerful weapon in the universe: Mjolnir. But in the wake of her quest, her family's enemies have discovered her existence and will stop at nothing to ensure she does not succeed.

THE AUTHOR:

I grew up mostly within the arts, including art and literature. It was not until I was fifteen years old that I started drafting out The Cosmo Chronicles and, through episodes of writer's block and education, developed it into a full-length novel, filled with epic magic and wonder.

My writing consists of epic fantasy aimed for young adults or above.

Some of my favourite things are: reading, writing, drawing, painting, musicals, running, dancing and spending time with friends and family.

THE COSMO CHRONICLES: THE WELLS OF YGGDRASIL

by

Chloe Louise Yelland

Papyrus Author, Inc. - Virginia Beach

1. Edition, 2020

Papyrus Author, Inc. - Virginia Beach

CHAPTER 1: PROLOGUE

I was born on one world, and raised on another.

In legends, the branches of the World's Tree, Yggdrasil, link the Nine Realms of the Cosmos. For thousands of years, our civilization spread out through the stars.

The Nine Realms saw my birth as a blessing: a child born of all Realms...An Asgardian Princess, heir to the throne and new owner of Mjolnir...

Now, I am returning to my home after eighteen years of living amongst the humans...to fight for the worlds of our universe...for love, honor and freedom...

This is my story...

My name...Princess Halena Thora Antoinette, loved daughter and sister, descendent of the thunder god...

A child of the Universe...

Our universe has millions of stars and galaxies. Many believe there are other worlds outside the Solar System, inhabited by various forms of life like our Earth being the world of humanity. But the theoretical existence of these worlds was dismissed as a near-impossible fact but praised as a fascinating legend. Before the universe, everything was a naked blanket of darkness with no burning sun. Until a sudden explosion of intense heat as hot as a supernova took place billions of years ago, creating an expansion of space conquering the darkness, and giving birth to light itself. The many atoms and rocks scattered in the explosion's aftermath were soon gravitationally pulled together, like being drawn together by a powerful magnet. That was how our universe was born.

Many stories then began to unfold over the centuries about the legends of the universe, about how ancient civilizations looked to the stars, worshipping them as gods for guidance.

While the universe was in formation, a peculiar sequence of stars, rocks and cosmic storms circled the Earth like our planets orbit the Sun, becoming the glue that held the universe together. The civilizations identified these as the Nine Realms.

These nine realms were linked together by the cosmic silhouette of a giant tree with roots and branches of ever-sparkling stars, comets and galaxies. Like the other eight realms, one of these starry branches surrounded the Earth encasing it with cosmic magic. It was said that the three wells drank the waters of the home worlds: the very sacred waters of wisdom, understanding and destiny.

The people of Earth saw it as nothing more than a large group of stars, but really it is an open pathway leading to another world.

The Nine Worlds - home of the Cosmos Beings born with magical gifts passed down from their ancestors, their worlds spiritually linked by the tree of life, Yggdrasil. In ancient times, inhabitants born within the Cosmos named Earth, Midgard; the remaining realms being Asgard, Vanaheim, Jotunheim, Nifheim, Muspelheim, Alfheim, Svartalfheim and Hel. But they were not the only worlds out there, for they had enemies in the universe, most of which could determine the fate of the Cosmos.

Perhaps this fate laid in the hands of a young girl: a girl whose destiny was written long before her birth…a child destined to bring about a golden age and become a symbol of hope for the first time in over three thousand years.

CHAPTER 2: THE BIRTH

It began on Asgard, one of the Nine Realms, one of the most beautiful kingdoms in the universe. The roses in the gardens were multiple colours for every Asgardian to appreciate the realm's radiant, undying beauty. Within the kingdom's walls were the most powerful warriors, training in every form of combat and teaching the Asgardian children how to control their magic abilities. The rulers of the magnificent Asgard were King Darius and his beloved wife and queen, Antoinette with her two eldest children, twins Eric and Arianna from her first marriage, which ended tragically. Since then, Darius adopted the twins and raised them as his own. The queen was now eight months pregnant with her third child, and the king's soon-to-be firstborn heir. According to the Mermaid Clan of Prophecy, the child would be a girl.

While the king and queen attended to royal affairs with the High Council of the Nine Realms, Eric and Arianna were out on the fields teaching the children how to control their magical gifts. Eric was an attractive, brown-haired young man with gray eyes in a shade of blue. He had a lean athletic physique under his Asgardian armor baring the Asgardian symbol, complete with two katana swords attached to his back. Arianna also wore battle armor, a sword attached to her waist. Her long, dark brunette hair was half-clipped back while the rest flowed freely. Her rouged lips were pure, her cheeks rosy against her fairly toned skin; and her blue-green eyes shone against the sun's rays.

The children watched Arianna fire an arrow towards a Glasir Tree. As soon as it hit the golden brown bark, it transformed into a fully bloomed rose. 'Your power comes from within you', Arianna addressed to the awestruck children. 'It is not just about harnessing the magic. It is about focusing on what would give you the strength to channel that power. For my brother and I, we value the wellbeing and love of our family and friends above all else'.

She turned to Eric with a nod, which he returned. Everyone watched as he closed his eyes and entered a meditation mode of deep concentration, withdrawing one of his katana swords pointing to the sky. The children looked up with innocent curiosity. Sure enough, a single black cloud appeared above Eric while the rest of Asgard remain illuminated in the spring sunlight. The cloud grew blacker, until finally a flashing bolt of lightning emerged touching the shining metal of the katana sword in Eric's hands, glowing white. The children sat amazed by this powerful form of magic.

'Our ancestors, the gods, could control certain elements, the notable being thunder and lightning', he explained, as he rechanneled the power through his body. 'They performed magic through nature and created auroras and eclipses, specifically for our ancient rituals and ceremonies: the most rare astronomical powers for a child of the Cosmos to be born with. To this day, no one within the Worlds has inherited or used these gifts for thousands of years'.

'It is true. No child was seen with such powers, not since the centuries when the people of Earth worshipped the stars as their protectors', Arianna pointed out. 'And not since the Norns hid Mjolnir at the furthest points of the universe'.

'Do you think someone will have these powers again?' a five-year-old boy asked. Eric and Arianna gave the boy a simple smile.

'We think of it as a possibility, young one', Arianna explained. 'However, there have been prophecies about a child born of all Worlds, destined to do great things for our worlds'. Indeed, the children were told tales about the Great Gods, Yggdrasil and Mjolnir; of how the thunder god would conjure up lightning bolts as the ultimate weapon, vaporizing anything in its path.

Before the twins could continue with the lessons, a set of hooves was heard on the stone pathway behind them. It was a knight of Asgard on his horse. He had dark hair and wore similar metallic armor to Eric with a cloak baring the Asgardian symbol. He dismounted his horse and stepped forward with an urgent look. 'My Lord Eric, my Lady Arianna, I bring news from the palace', he addressed them. 'The queen is in labor, and is to give birth this evening'.

Reality hit them like a flood. The new princess was coming…

'Sir Darien, you will take charge of the children's training while we tend to our family', Eric ordered. 'We shall resume our sessions with them, as soon as the child is presented to the people'.

The knight named Sir Darien gave a nod and slight bow, before turning towards the children to demonstrate his ability to manipulate the earth. Eric and Arianna mounted their horses they left on the fencing beside the Glasir Tree and raced to the entrance of the palace, their minds focused on the birth of their sister. As they reached the palace doors, they noticed storm clouds coming over Asgard, even though the Oracle of Asgard predicted sunlight over the course of the month.

'The sky has not been like this for three millennia', Arianna proclaimed.

'No, it has not', Eric replied. 'But it means only one thing, sister…' Arianna turned to her brother, as he turned to look at her with a slight smile. '…It is a sign from the gods: that what is happening right now is a very special birth'.

Another bolt of lightning then flashed across the sky.

Using their telepathy, they pushed past the numerous voices within the palace until they heard the labored breathing coming from their mother, and the voices of the maids and ladies-in-waiting. In the main hallway on the third floor, leading to the royal chambers, they saw King Darius anxiously pacing, awaiting the new arrival, while the king's best friend, King Elwood of Alfheim and his four-year-old son, Aeolus and nine-year-old son, Silas stood in front of a large painting of a mountain. Their hearts leapt, as the queen let out a painful scream. The king wanted to be at Antoinette's side, but the maids repeatedly said it was against traditions for the father to be in the room.

'She will be alright, Sire', Arianna reassured the king, holding his hand with comfort. 'She is strong. Have faith, and she and the child will be well',

With every minute that went by, the thunderstorms outside grew more intense. The twins kept a firm grip of each other's hands, trying to block out the deafening roars of thunder and flashes of lightning, while they attempted to calm their father from hearing Antoinette's cries…

Then after what seemed like an eternity for them, the screams stopped along with the storm outside. There was silence…until finally they heard the sweetest sound in the universe: the cries of a newborn baby. They all stood, as the doors opened and a handmaiden came out with a reassuring smile on her petite face.

'My king, you are blessed with a beautiful baby girl', she announced. The whole family let out a sigh of relief at the news, happiness brewing in their eyes.

'Praise the Gods', Elwood rejoiced with a smile, patting his friend on the shoulder.

The king replied to the maiden. 'Thank you, Sula. I am forever grateful for your services'.

Sula curtseyed and stepped aside to allow the royals to enter the room.

Queen Antoinette was propped up against two layers of pillows on a four-poster bed in a fresh white nightgown. Her long brunette hair was tied back in a side plait; despite feeling tired from the effects of childbirth, she wore a beautiful, glowing smile on her face with joyful tears in her electric indigo eyes as she stared at the little bundle wrapped in blankets safely in her arms. There were two more women in the room gathered around the bed, clearing away blankets and pillows: Queen Amara, Elwood's wife and Lady Orla, the leader of the prophetic mermaid clan and Antoinette's best friend, who took human form whenever she came on land.

Upon seeing them, Antoinette beckoned them to come over, Darius going first and kissing her forehead tenderly before having a look at his newborn daughter. Having come a month early, she was very little with a small button nose and rosy cheeks. The tuft of hair on the baby's oval-shaped head matched Antoinette's colour. She was almost asleep, letting out a little yawn, but her family could see the bright blue in her eyes. What was the most intriguing about them was that they had a continuous sparkle against the sun and moonlight. Along her right collarbone was a birthmark shaped like a cloud.

'She is truly a beauty as bright as the stars, my love', Darius declared softly. Antoinette smiled, bringing her beloved husband into a loving kiss.

'What are we to name her?' she asked.

The king went into deep thought. 'We should name her after your mother', he recommended.

'Halena', the queen said thoughtfully, strongly agreeing to it without a second thought.

Eric and Arianna looked at the baby with pure love and admiration, their eyes lighting up at the thought of their grandmother's name being passed down to their little sister.

'She will no doubt be a fine warrior, and a wise queen', Eric said.

Arianna smiled. 'Truly, we can feel the pure strength within her'.

Antoinette nodded in agreement, as Darius affectionately put his arm around his wife while stroking the baby's cheeks. King Elwood stood at the edge of the bed, with Queen Amara taking a hold of his hand. Aeolus and Silas climbed on the bed to get a closer look at the baby, while her tiny hand flexed around Aeolus's forefinger. Antoinette looked up at the sky now alit with the lights of an Aurora Eclipse, shining alongside the sun's rays and moonlight. She remembered feeling the energy of the thunder surging through her body, as it encircled the womb carrying her child.

'She needs a second name too', Antoinette suggested. The rest of the family listened intently. Antoinette smiled knowingly, having thought of the answer as she gazed at the last of the thunderclouds in the distance. 'Thora'.

Darius returned the smile. 'It is perfect', he said lovingly.

*

During the sixth month, the people of the Nine Realms were gathered in Valhalla to hold a christening ceremony for Halena. The family approached the statues of the gods, where the High Priests and Priestesses stood with Lady Orla. Halena was nestled in Antoinette's arms, her open eyes curiously looking around. Lady Orla stepped forward, as the hymns ended. Her silver blonde hair was styled into a braided bun with light blue highlights. She wore an off-shoulder turquoise shimmering dress with open sleeves that touched the foot of the gown, with silver crystal earrings, two rings on the fingers of her right hand, and a necklace baring her clan's crest. The king and queen stepped towards her while Eric and Arianna bowed their heads. Antoinette handed Halena to Orla, who carried her to the stone basin in front of the gods.

'Today, we are all gathered together to bless into the Cosmos: a daughter. A daughter of the Nine Realms, a daughter of the gods, a daughter of the universe', she declared, as she reached into the basin and dipped her fingers in fresh water, tracing them across Halena's forehead in the sequence of a cross. 'On this day, I declare her with the name, Princess Halena Thora Antoinette, daughter of Darius and Antoinette of Asgard: born at the final hour of sunset on the twentieth day of the fifth month. Distant daughter of the Lord of Thunder, princess of the Worlds: may the gods forever smile on you, may our magic protect you, and may the light of an aurora forever bless you with guidance'.

At this, the priests and priestesses raised their hands, palms up towards the open ceiling showing the starry night, and began chanting in the Asgardian language:

Legendary lights, we call upon your guidance and your blessing
Shine your light upon this child and bathe her in your lighting

As they chanted, their hands began to glow in dancing, colourful lights. Lady Orla carefully lifted the baby up towards the open ceiling, the temple hall becoming illuminated with mixes of blue, orange and green lights. The people bowed their heads and looked up at the sky, where they saw the beautiful Aurora Eclipse. The moon moved in front of the sun, and the Northern Lights became surrounded by both sunlight and moonlight. Every single vibrant light touched every part of the temple, but they were only their brightest when they touched baby Halena, blessing her in purity.

Suddenly, Lady Orla's eyes widened, while holding Halena, everyone else realizing she was having a vision, their smiles turning upside down replaced by a worrisome look.

Before either could react, the ground rumbled beneath their feet like an earthquake...

All the knights and nobles unsheathed their swords, searching for the source of the attack. The queen quickly went to Orla, who broke out of her trance; and took the now crying Halena. The king, Eric and Arianna unveiled their swords and bows from underneath their ceremonial robes, and moved into battle formation to protect the queen and princess. Joining them were King Elwood and the queen's brother and sister-in-law, King Alexander and Queen Elena of Vanaheim. Orla called upon her tribe of mer-people, commanding them to form a circle around the royal family, chanting in MerTongue. They soon conjured up light blue energy using their palms and elevated it into a protective sphere, encasing themselves, Halena and her family, narrowly avoiding the debris and stain glass window fragments from the walls and the ceiling. The impact seemed to have an effect on the mer-people and Orla as they let out low groans of pain.

The shaking stopped, much to everyone's relief. But it did not last long, as all looked through the smoke...To their horror, they saw thirty to forty monstrous figures coming through the smoke at the hall entrance and twenty more floating down through the ceiling, surrounding the people. Their faces were human, except for the red-yellow eyes, pale skin with black tattoo markings and scars and sharp pearly white teeth, wearing black metal armor, armed with black bows and arrows, and swords crafted with fatal poison.

Antoinette looked down at her daughter, whose eyes still tear-streamed were calmer now, and then at Darius, as realization dawned upon them because of the recognition of these creatures.

'Nebulans', they both said, as a menacing laugh came from above, with one more lone figure floating down. The man had jet-black hair, dressed in dark velvet robes, with black boots and a sword. His eyes were a menacing dark reddish-brown.

'Vladimir!' Darius whispered in shock. The man's thin mouth curved into an evil smile.

'The one and only, dear brother', he replied arrogantly

Darius' eyes became filled with anger that he very nearly advanced forward ready to withdraw his sword. Elwood grabbed him to hold him back, telepathically reminding him to focus on protecting Halena. 'If I remember correctly, you stopped being my brother the moment you murdered those three families in cold blood', he said firmly, struggling to calm down.

Vladimir just smirked at the comment.

'And did you really think I would miss my own niece's christening?' His eyes moved towards the baby in Antoinette's arms, as she kept a tight hold of her.

'She is quite a beauty, Darius', he sneered. He stepped forward, his eyes locked on Halena. Antoinette's eyes grew fearful, as Darius kept a firm grip on his sword with an angry expression. Eric and Arianna moved directly in front of the three of them: Arianna drawing back her bow and arrow ready to fire, and Eric keeping a strong hold on his katana sword.

'My children. How you have grown', Vladimir said mockingly, with a smile.

Eric too became fuelled with anger.

'We are not your children', he hissed. 'You lost the right to call us that the moment you betrayed our mother and all the Realms'.

'Darius may not be our biological father, but he helped Mother raise us and has shown us nothing but love', Arianna said proudly. 'That is what a father does for his children'.

Vladimir just let out a low laugh, looking towards Antoinette. 'Ah yes, your Mother: the woman who would not commit to me, the woman who betrayed me for my own brother'.

Antoinette found the courage to speak up.

'I did not betray you, Vladimir', she proclaimed with such strength. 'I was in love with Darius, long before I married you. I was just too blind to realize it sooner. At first, I thought I was doing it, because I loved you and as my duty as a princess would. But I was wrong…marrying you was the worst decision I have ever made. You think you know love, Vladimir? You know nothing of it!'

Vladimir let out a howl of rage and unleashed a ball of deadly red lightning and fire aiming it at the mer-people's sphere. The two collided against each other, the mer-people their eyes clenched shut at the impact, blood coming out of their ears and noses, as they struggled to harness more of their power with Elena and Amara stepping in to assist them. Arianna fired her Arrows of Nature at any advancing Nebulans, while Eric channeled his power over the elements towards his katana swords. Darius, Alexander and Elwood battled Vladimir, but his swordsmanship equaled theirs, in turn receiving deep gashes.

Their strength was fading…

Halena seemed to sense their distress and pain, and her crying filled the room combined with the loud bangs and battle cries, while her mother tried to comfort her. An extra sound soon came from above. Halena looked up to the sky with teary eyes and saw a giant thundercloud overhead. The rest of the family and their subjects looked up, even the Nebulans.

What happened next shocked everyone.

Halena let out one last cry and as it happened, a large bolt of lightning came crashing through the open ceiling, aimed towards Vladimir and the Nebulans. The lightning's electrifying sparks destroyed the last energy ball Victor created, and vaporized any Nebulans moving towards the family or other citizens. The shock wave the lightning strikes created sent people flying backwards, but the royal family was still safe from harm thanks to the sphere, which broke down, and the mer-people, Lady Orla, Queen Elena and Queen Amara collapsed from exhaustion. Eric and Arianna scrambled to their feet to tend to Orla and her people, while Alexander healed his wife's wound from a shard of glass. Aeolus and Silas came running from behind one of the pillars towards their exhausted mother and their father with a broken left arm, while Darius went to embrace his wife and Halena, relieved to see them safe.

Both wondered how Halena managed to demonstrate such an extraordinary power, before being interrupted by the sight of Vladimir, who struggled to his feet one half of his face now scarred from the lightning. Shocked by what he had just witnessed, he looked at Halena who stared back with nothing but innocence.

He regained his balance and waved his right arm to signal the remaining Nebulans to retreat.

'I swear to you, my vengeance will come about', he threatened as he continued to eye the innocent little baby. 'If that child is a proven threat, I will find her and I will make sure she will never see the light of the sun again'.

'Consider this my christening gift to you, dear brother. You and your precious little princess…for you will finally know what it means to lose someone you love…and that is a promise!' With that, he and the Nebulans disappeared in the black smoke his menacing laugh echoing throughout the city.

*

The king and queen sent scouts to the outcasts of Yggdrasil to keep a close watch on any activity occurring on Nebula. Groups of their best men were slaughtered, when they got too close to the world's borders. Darius suspected Vladimir put watch posts along cosmic passageways in case they attempted to thwart whatever his plans were. Still haunted by Vladimir's vengeful words, Darius and Antoinette went down to the lake chambers beneath the temple to find Lady Orla in need of her console. There they found her in mermaid form, sitting on a large rock tracing finger patterns in a rock pool, while performing incantations in MerTongue.

Sensing their presence, she stopped her chanting. 'You have come, my lord and lady', she said. 'You are here about young Halena, I imagine?'

The queen stepped closer towards her friend. 'Ever since Halena's christening, Vladimir's words have been consuming our dreams', she explained. 'Every night, it is the same dream. We saw Halena unleashing thunder and lightning on a battlefield with remarkable strength, and we cannot neglect the feeling that she is now in even more danger'.

Lady Orla removed her mermaid tail from the water, transforming into her human legs, followed by the magical appearance of a beautiful flowing blue gown. She stood and turned to face Darius and Antoinette. 'It is true: Halena has the power to control thunder and lightning, but I sense she has other powerful gifts that have not yet emerged. While you were in labor, Antoinette, the thunderstorms spread across Asgard. Like you, I felt its power and it only grew stronger as Halena became closer to drawing her first breath. When she was born, the power within her was something I have not felt in any child of the Cosmos for thousands of years'.

'When the Nebulans attacked, I connected to her mind. I saw brightness in her future: pure and peaceful. But there were also moments of darkness: I heard eerie screams and victorious shouts. And then, the vision changed...I saw her on a battlefield, facing enemies. She wielded a very powerful weapon in her hand. And it ended there'.

The king and queen looked at each other, unsure what to think.

'Did you ever contemplate a solution about ending my brother's reign?' Darius asked, mentioning his half-brother with combined determination, sadness and anger.

'The power within Nebula is indeed growing, my lord', Lady Orla said. 'Your brother was once of Asgard, but his heart has blackened. I am certain he was one of the enemies in my vision. From what I have seen, the only way to defeat him is for the mighty weapon to be found and re-forged'.

'As for Halena, I believe she is the One destined to vanquish the second apocalypse'.

Their hearts sank. Realization dawned upon them, as Orla spoke these words to them. Antoinette let out a light gasp, putting her hand over her mouth in shock and her eyes whirled with tears of worry.

Darius closed his eyes; unable to believe this one fact...

Halena was the Child.

'But she cannot be', Antoinette uttered. 'She is only an innocent baby. I am aware of the great power she now possesses from it being passed down from generations, but she cannot be The One'.

'And you said it was near impossible to see a child's future at an early age', Darius pointed out.

'Not unless a child can possess powerful magic', Lady Orla explained. 'Indeed, young Halena's mind is very delicate. But what I saw was the beginning of her destiny. Your daughter's gifts came about when she was just four weeks old, the earliest age for a child of the Cosmos. You saw her create animal avatars with cosmic elements of lightning, water, ice and wind. It will only grow as she matures. I sensed it as she was being blessed under the lights of the Aurora Eclipse. She will face many dangers and have enemies like the shadows in the vision, but her heart is pure. That will be her greatest strength'.

'Vladimir and many who stand against us will not hesitate to destroy her', Orla warned the king and queen.

Darius and Antoinette at this point realized they were faced with a tough choice.

'What would you do?' Antoinette asked.

'I would do what I have to do to protect her', Orla answered.

*

A long debate went on for months until they agreed that the best way to protect Halena was to put her into hiding on another world, and leave Vladimir under the belief that she died from an incurable illness. The High Council suggested Earth, where she could easily blend in with the humans. Eric and Arianna volunteered to take guardianship over Halena until she turned eighteen. A young man and woman honorably volunteered, much to the twins' sad reluctance, to stage their deaths.

In the middle of December, as snowflakes came down from the sky flawlessly landing on the rainbow bridge, everyone gathered at the end of the bridge to say goodbye to Halena. The family took a moment alone with Halena, who was nestled asleep in her mother's arms wrapped around her red velvet cloak, dressed in a small hat and white silver baby dress complete with sky blue shoulder shrug. Each family member and friend held her and kissed her forehead, before baring the little girl with a gift: her aunt and uncle, Alexander and Elena a ring forged from a burning star; Elwood, Amara, Aeolus and Silas a Valkyrie dagger and an Elven moonstone dream-catcher; and her parents a silver pendant enchanted to keep her hidden from the Nebulans and a music box baring the Asgardian symbol, with a letter for her to read when she was eighteen.

The baby was passed back to the queen, who looked at her with such sadness in her eyes refusing to let her go, remembering her own mother's words when she was a child that *'a mother's love for her children was as strong as the love for her beloved...'*

'Antoinette, she will be safe', the king reassured her, wiping away a lone tear on her cheek. 'When the time is right, she will return to us'.

The queen nodded, more tears streaming down her face. She and Darius gave Halena one last kiss and passed her over to Arianna.

'Keep her safe', she instructed to her son and daughter, squeezing their hands lightly. 'She will need your guidance as she grows'.

Eric and Arianna nodded.

'You have our word, Mother', Arianna replied comfortingly, and gave Darius a one-arm hug, careful not to wake Halena. 'You as well, Father'.

Darius gave her a kiss on the cheek, and went to hug his son.

'No harm will come to her, my lord and lady', Eric said. 'You have our promise'.

The siblings made their way to the bridge's gateway, gazing out over the endless lake of stars. Alerting the gatekeeper, he opened the gateway with his magic. Within seconds, pure light matter as bright as the Northern Lights appeared creating a reflection of the destination like a mirror. As soon as it opened up, Eric with Arianna carrying Halena stepped into the gateway, and then they were gone.

CHAPTER 3: THE UNUSUAL

'Fulfill your destiny', the voice called out.

The girl who dreamt the dream woke suddenly upon hearing the disembodied voice. She lay on a single bed in navy blue pyjamas, her long brunette hair tied back in a side plait and her bright blue eyes wide with mixed emotions, as a flash ignited in them. Her hands were shaking, and beads of sweat coated her oval-shaped face.

Her name was Haley Freeman.

She lived in a three-bedroom beach house in Cornwall, with her twin brother and sister. It was very close to the ocean, something she was very grateful for, because every morning she would wake up early to go surfing or running along the beach. At times, she would just sit on the sand and listen to the many sounds around her: the sounds of the waves, children laughing and playing each other, others playing volleyball, couples walking hand-in-hand, the seagulls flying around looking for food, the sounds of babies giggling in the sand, as their parents made them laugh. It felt normal for Haley.

Except one thing…

Haley had this unshakable feeling that she was different from other people.

Even normal cannot be a word to describe her life experiences.

Taking slow deep breaths, she fell back on her bed, briefly eyeing the crystal dream-catcher above her bed; the string beautifully crafted in Celtic pattern. She just awoke from a very strange dream. But the funny thing was that she wasn't sure whether it was a dream, a vision or an event from a distant timeline: like it was a scene being brought to life from a fantasy novel.

Since she was little, she had had dreams of seeing what lies beyond the stars: dreams where she was flying gracefully through the night, wearing a flawless blue and gold gown, her eyes sparkling at the beauty of the universe. She saw billions of stars and the planets orbiting the sun, until she caught sight of something: other worlds, orbiting the Earth. Impossible, yet familiar to her: it was as if she had seen this before. The scene then changed to her sitting on a soft blanket with toys made out of wood in the royal nursery of a palace, manipulating lightning into a phoenix and a dragon.

What an extraordinary thing to do, Haley thought. While she was playing with her magic, she saw people who loved and adored her dearly. Next came an eclipse dancing around the Northern Lights, the glow touching her like a blessing. She then saw a powerful lightning bolt, just as she cried out in fear for the lives of innocent people. It then switched to a conversation between the baby's parents and another lady. They talked about the king and queen's infant daughter, her foretold destiny and her magical gifts. Two other people she saw wore body armor like warriors from ancient times. All had love in their eyes, as they gazed upon her. But there was something else: sadness towards the fact that they had no choice but to send the child somewhere safe…

And then came a blinding light. That was when Haley woke up. Next thing she heard was the gentle voice in her head, awakening a strange power deep within her that she had since she could remember, creating a bolt of lightning across the sky, despite there being no clouds about.

It took Haley by surprise. Although something about thunderstorms made her feel at ease. But why did it feel like she was causing it every time she woke from a dream? It was like something within her caused it, through her emotions.

After a moment, Haley's alarm clock went off. It read half past six. Haley sat up at the edge of the bed, took another deep breath, and walked past her easel and abstract sky paintings toward the glass balcony doors to draw the cream curtains back.

It was a beautiful spring day, the sunrise reflecting off the sea. The beach was quiet, except for early morning surfers and runners. The warmth of the sun touched Haley's skin, and the cool breeze lightly blew through her hair. On her left of the balcony stood a mint green lounger with cream cushions and blanket laid out on top. In front of it was a silver telescope given to her by her brother and sister on her sixteenth birthday. There was an Old Norse inscription engraved on, translated as:

To our little sister…Love, your brother and sister.

What amazed Haley was how quick they noticed the way her eyes sparkled with enthusiastic excitement every time she looked at the stars, even painted them out on a blank canvas so that they were not forgotten from her memory. With that very thought, Haley observed the sky and saw that there were still at least eight stars twinkling brightly – even remembering one of her sky abstracts bore the exact same details. Haley's eyes brightened at their beauty. She caught sight of her reflection in the glass to see the blue in her eyes was brighter than the day before, something she always took great care noticing. She then ran her fingers over the cloud-shaped birthmark across her right shoulder. It was strange, as she somehow felt connected to these stars. She just didn't know how…

'Haley!' a girl's voice called, interrupting her thoughts. 'Hey, Earth to Haley!'

Haley looked down and saw that it was her best friend, Kelly Miller. She stood at the foot of the balcony gate, her wavy, blonde hair blowing lightly through the wind and her grey-blue eyes in shades of light turquoise buzzing with excitement. She wore a black and blue swimsuit, complete with swim shorts decorated in blue and white flowers, and was carrying her light blue surfboard.

'Come on! It's time for our morning surf!' she exclaimed eagerly.

Haley just smiled and let out a small laugh, as she ran back into her room.

'Just coming, Kelly!' she shouted in reply.

She quickly changed into a red and black swimsuit, with matching swim shorts, before heading into the kitchen to make a protein smoothie. Humming to herself, Haley started making her way back to her room humming to herself.

No more deteriorating thoughts of the dream, she thought. Just her looking forward to going on her daily morning surf with her best friend…

But as she walked towards the door to her room, she heard two voices coming from the living room. She just shrugged, as it was only her brother and sister considering they were usually up before her. But as she got closer to her room, she couldn't help herself as she eavesdropped on her siblings' conversation.

Her brother, Eric let out a very deep sigh.

'They telepathically contacted us, without being detected, thanks to the cloaking spell', he said. 'Like us, they sensed her powers are growing. There were moments where she could control elements cosmically. It is only when she turns eighteen, will she learn who she really is'.

'But you and I have seen what she can do, brother', her sister, Amy pointed out. 'They are unintentionally triggered by emotion. When she wakes from a dream or if she senses something, lightning flashes across the sky. It's fear and anger. The people share our concern: if she does not control them, they fear he will be able to fine her sooner than we think'.

Haley moved closer, careful not to alert them to her presence.

'Orla looked through the Mirror of Prophecy', Amy continued. 'The princess is the only one who can conquer the darkness that threatens to destroy us and other species across the universe. When the time is right, she will need to be ready'.

'You are right, sister', Eric said. 'She is the light and the hope of all'.

Haley quickly dashed back to her room before her brother and sister noticed her presence, absorbing what she just eavesdropped on. Why were they talking like they were from different time? And who was this so-called princess they were referring? They both sounded indifferent, like they were hiding something.

Throughout her childhood, Haley questioned why she was so different which her brother and sister always dodged. She even didn't understand the reasons behind the occurrences of elemental activity in the places she goes to. Like when they saw the sparkle shining in her eyes like a fire waiting to burn. Or when they watched her spin around in the falling snowflakes ten years previously, and the snowflakes would spiral around her in a twister formation, like she was commanding them to. It frustrated Haley to the core, because of how secretive they were being...

Haley felt the steady rhythm of her heartbeat, while playing with the necklace around her neck. It was something she wore since she was a child, for it was a gift from her parents before they *passed away* when she was a few months old; and she swore to herself that she would never take it off because it was the only connection she had to them.

The necklace was hand-crafted from pure metallic silver. The charm on the simple silver chain was a pattern of a trefoil knot shaped as the triquetra sign from Norse Mythology. In the center of the knotted symbol was a silver crystal. On the perfectly crafted knot were engraved black etchings of ancient letters. Haley analyzed the symbols carefully and using what she learnt from studying the Ancient Celtic language in her History classes, was able to translate it in less than a minute:

"To our dearest daughter. May you forever be adored and protected.
Love now and always"

Haley's heart warmed every time she read the message, bringing a tear in her eye - the words a parent would say to their child. Haley wondered what her parents were like. Were they compassionate and loving? Did her parents always think about her?

No, it was just a dream, Haley told herself. She blocked out the remaining thoughts putting a big smile on her face, as she looked outside at the ocean waves at least fifty yards away. Thanks to the increased breeze, the surf picked up more now. Haley headed down the balcony staircase, where her white surfboard with a calligraphic flower patterning imprinted along the left edge of it stood. Kelly sat on the sand admiring the beautiful beach view, her surfboard upright in the ground to hold it secure. Haley smirked. Her board tucked underneath her right arm, she tiptoed towards her. As soon as she got close enough, she went –

'KELLY!' she yelled, grabbing her shoulder and laughing.

Kelly yelped, jumping out of her skin and laughed.

'Gotcha!' Haley exclaimed, in a fit of giggles.

Kelly took a moment to catch her breath, before calming down looking like she caught a stitch in her stomach from her uncontrollable laughter.

'That you did, Hales', she said jokingly. 'What took you so long anyway?'

Her face went from giggling to interested.

'Just my brother annoying me again and constantly reminding me about my archery training next week', she lied, despite it being half-true.

Kelly raised her eyebrows.

'You make it sound like they're training you for the Olympics', she proclaimed.

Haley just laughed. 'Sure as hell feels like that sometimes…I just wish they would at least tell me why I need to up myself to more advanced levels. I mean, don't get me wrong…I love them but at times I just don't understand my own brother and sister'.

'Do you think they're…keeping something from you?' Kelly asked.

Haley thought back to the times when she noticed something off about Eric and Amy. Once, she was keen to know more about her family history, whether she was of a specific descent. She even researched any relatives under the surname *Freeman* whenever she went to the school library to study, but it led to a dead end.

Another strange circumstance was that her siblings still seemed to be bore the physical appearance of a twenty-one-year-old, since Haley was five, and she wondered whether it was one of the reasons why they moved from town to town every four to five years.

Everyone must think they followed a healthy diet and workout regimen, Haley thought.

'I don't know', Haley answered. 'The only thing they really answered was that our parents died in a climbing accident when I was a baby but I can't shake this feeling that there's more to this that meets the eye'.

Kelly let out a deep sigh and put a comforting hand on Haley's shoulder, as they slowly began to walk toward the shore.

'You deserve the chance to know', she advised. 'Let them know that. I'm sure they'll understand'.

Haley knew Kelly was right.

Whether Haley wanted to find out more about her original family and the secrets her brother and sister or not, it was entirely her decision, not theirs to make.

'Anyway, you looking forward your birthday party next week?' Kelly asked. 'We've got it all planned out for you. It's on the beach and it'll have a great view when the eclipse comes'.

Haley shook her head lightly laughing, upon realizing what Samantha said on the last sentence.

'Definitely', she replied with a grin. 'And that *eclipse* is called the Aurora Eclipse. Remember, we did a group essay on it, about how it's supposed to appear once every eighteen years; and it's a lunar eclipse with a combination of the Northern Lights'.

'Right, I got you', Kelly said, arching her eyebrow. 'Just out of curiosity, how is it that you know so much about it?'

The question caught Haley slightly off guard. At school, people including Kelly complimented her about her strong awareness and intelligence. She once named over fifty artists and one hundred important figures in history in under a minute, identified all the star patterns resembling mythological creatures and faces, and even translated the ancient languages from Old Celtic and Ancient Greece. To everyone, it was an inspiring accomplishment, but to Haley it was an unusual fact.

Like her mind was allowing her to multi-task between four or five different activities.

'There's a simple fact, Kelly', Haley answered. 'It's called studying'.

Kelly just rolled her eyes with a smile.

'Right there as well. Now, let's see how athletic you are when we catch that first wave', she exclaimed, and just as she finished the sentence, she began running towards the ocean.

Haley laughed as she ran after her, keeping her surfboard secure under her arm.

Reaching the edge of the water, Haley once again took in the magnificent view of the ocean. She saw three more surfers catching an incoming wave. The feel of the water on her feet felt soothing against the spring heat. Haley then ran forward into the water alongside Kelly. Once they were deep enough with the water at their knees, they launched off their feet and onto their boards paddling over several waves, before coming across a four-foot wave. As soon as it touched the fronts of their surfboards, they duck-dove underneath the wave, re-surfacing a moment later.

Feeling her surfer instinct kicking in, Haley felt the sensation of the water run from her fingertips to her toes and sure enough as if she was timing it, she spotted another forming wave. As quick as she could, she turned and began paddling hard and fast towards the shore ignoring the burning in her muscles. After about five seconds, Haley stood up onto her board, taking a sharp turn off the top, followed by an up and down carving movement, before the wave came into a semi-crest. She bent down, riding along the edge of the curving wave feeling the water's rippling pulse on her fingers.

She emerged from under the wave at incredible speed, coming off her board and landing in the water gracefully. The other three surfers cheered at the moves she just pulled off.

'Hey, nice moves!' a boy around her age shouted, winking at her.

She smiled, blushing.

'Thank you!' she replied back with a quick and friendly wave, as she got back on her board. Haley then spotted Kelly catching another four-foot wave, attempting a fade and floater before perfecting a tube-ridding move underneath the curling wave at almost the same speed as Haley.

Haley smiled and cheered, clapping her hands.

While Kelly went to catch a second wave, Haley laid down on her board relaxing in the sun. She let out a short breath, sharing at the water. Her impulse soon got the better of her, as she dipped her hand in. She felt something oddly familiar: something she had experienced many times when she was young…a soft tingle travelling up her spine towards her arm…a sequence of unexpected, powerful channeling from air to ground, from earth to water, from head to toe…the cosmic magic of elemental occurrences within pulsing through the blood in her veins…

The water rippled and swirled around until it took the formation of a whirlpool. Haley remained transfixed on what she created with her bare hands, that she scooped it up the way a person would hold a tennis ball. Floating an inch above Haley's hand, the little whirlpool then morphed into a ball-like shape, still swirling around.

Suddenly, Haley's eyes became cold.

At the same time, the whirlpool ball turned to ice. Haley stared at it in wonder, taking in the beautiful structure of it like an ice sculpture from an art exhibit. The sunrays shone off the surface of the frozen ball, casting a series of reflective colorful lights.

SPLASH!

The sudden force of seawater hit Haley, causing her to drop the ice ball and fall off her surfboard. Haley went underwater and she could just see through her little blurred vision that the ball slowly melted upon loss of contact. Did that really just happen? Did she actually manipulate a whirlpool of water into a sphere, before channeling a different kind of energy? As she resurfaced, another wave came hurdling towards Haley, smacking her hard in the face sending her under. Her concentration motivated her to now focus on making her way back to the surface, but the impacting force of the waves dragged her further down to the ocean floor. Her foot became detached from the leg rope. Her lungs were beginning to burn from the conserving of oxygen…she had to find the strength to keep swimming and push past the powerful waves.

Haley came to a midway stop.

Looking around, she saw the ocean darkened and a fish colony swam in opposite directions. Surfers were paddling fearlessly back to the beach. For some reason, Haley knew she wanted to help them get away from wherever was happening. As that very thought occurred to her, she looked beyond the water surface.

What she saw answered her question about the blackened manifestation.

Above the water, storm clouds were forming. She tilted her head to one side, eyes fixated on them. Suddenly, she felt a familiar burning feeling behind her pupils. It was the same feeling she had when she turned the water ball into ice. The sensation only grew stronger forcing her to forget about the water filling her lungs and lost all control of her mind and body, as the strange power channeled through her, like an electric shock flowing through her veins.

Claps of thunder and lightning bolts travelled across the sky, Haley letting a silent whimper as if it sensed her distress. She squeezed her eyes tightly shut, holding her head in her hands trying to control the sensation and the power the lightning seemed to have over her. The power journeyed through her, until it reached her right shoulder where her birthmark laid. Haley felt it burn, like a scorching fire. She shut her eyes, keeping her breath contained, trying to cease the burning.

All of a sudden, Haley swiftly caught her right arm on a sharp rock on the underwater reef, causing her to let out a silent yelp of pain. Her blood conquered the black and blue water, and another bolt of lightning came at the exact moment she let out the quiet scream. She soon drew her last breath of air, her vision fading and her arms and legs going limp no longer having the strength to make her way to the surface, or channel any more energy, or feel the need to hold onto hope that someone will find her drowning...

As she fell into unconsciousness, she spotted a human-like figure swimming toward her...

One thing she was not aware of, as her eyes closed: the necklace around her neck began to glow...

*

'Come on, Haley! Breathe! Breathe!' one muffled voice yelled.

A set of strong hands being pressed into her chest making her heart beat again, as air slowly filled her lungs...Hearing the voices of numerous worried people...

'Come on, sister! Wake up!' another one shouted with worry.

And then came another like an echo.

A beautiful, disembodied voice; the rush of dancing lights, as bright as the sun and the moon, guiding her back to the world of the living...

'HALENA!! WAKE UP!!'

Haley's eyes popped open, as she shot upright spitting out the remainder of seawater blocking her airway, coughing and choking, her head still thumping and ears ringing. Through her still-blurred vision, she saw brightness around her and she figured the sun was out again.

'Haley, Haley, can you hear me?' she heard a male voice ask.

She took slow, deep breaths, blinking her eyes until she could see more clearly. She looked around and saw at least five people standing over her, one of them being a very worried Kelly, and the three fellow surfers. The other two were her moderately distressed brother and sister, kneeling in front of her letting out sighs of relief embracing her. Haley assumed Kelly ran up to the house to get them, while the surfers performed CPR on her.

Eric was an athletically-built young man, aged twenty-something, confirming Haley's suspicions about their aging. He had brunette hair and gray eyes in a shade of blue. He wore a pair of black jeans and white polo shirt with trainers. Like her twin brother, Amy was a beautiful twenty-something woman, athletic and smart like her twin brother. Her brunette hair was tied back in a low pony-tail, and she had blue eyes the same shade as Eric's. She wore a pair of jeans and a long periwinkle-blue blouse, with a pair of worn black flats.

Haley glanced up to take in her surroundings.

Much to her surprise and everyone's astonishment, the ocean was calm again returning to its original deep blue it was when she got out of bed, and the remainder of the storm was quickly and gradually clearing away. Her vision went blurry again, as she remembered holding a ball of ice, before dropping it in the water because of being hit by a wave and being dragged further underwater, as the powerful thunderstorm appeared out of nowhere halting her struggle to return to the surface, putting herself into a coma before being rescued.

Haley's eyes popped open, as she remembered cutting her right forearm on the rocky reef. But as she looked down, she saw much to her own confusion no cut: no open wound, no blood pouring out of her. Nothing. Like it was never there. She ran her fingers over the spot where she cut herself. She recalled the sharp rock penetrating her skin, and the pain she felt as she placed her hand over it, applying pressure to stop the bleeding. She didn't remember her body healing itself. Could it be another power she did not know she had? Was she able to harness energy within her to allow her to mend any wounds or injuries she received? Or better yet, could she do that to other people? Was this a similar experience like when she was ten years old, when she injured her elbow after receiving her black belt in martial arts and three days later, it was back in place perfectly healed?

Now, here she was back on dry land, the storm completely cleared, wondering what on earth happened, while she was in a temporary lapse of limbo.

'Haley?' her sister asked, gently shaking her shoulders. 'Haley, are you alright?'

Haley ignored her words, remaining unresponsive towards the actions going on around her. She just stared blankly out at the ocean, as her brother and sister eyed her with concern. Around her, all she could see were shapes and shadows and the only sounds she heard were the gentle crashing of the waves and the steady rhythm of her heartbeat, thumping through her ears until –

'It is almost time'. A voice spoke, making her heart flip and skip several more beats. It wasn't her sister and it certainly was not Kelly. It was another woman's voice. It sounded desperately encouraging, but it was also very angelic and beautiful. It was the same voice she heard, as she woke up, the one that called another name. Halena…why did that name sound so familiar to her? What was this undeniable connection she had to the disembodied voice?

'Haley? Haley!' a male voice called out to her.

This time, Haley listened to her brother's voice rather than shut down further. She blinked twice, her vision returning quicker than she realized, focusing in on her brother and sister, who stared at her with concerned suspicion.

Kelly, still shaken up by the ordeal Haley went through, let out a sigh of relief.

'Are you alright, little sister?' Eric asked, like Amy did. 'Are you hurt?'

Haley just shook her head, still shaken up. Kelly put a towel over her shoulders, noticing her shivering.

'What happened?' Haley asked, pretending she didn't know.

One of the surfers named James stepped forward. Haley recognized him as one of her next-door neighbors. He had good physique from surfing since childhood. He was twenty-four years old with bronze hair and compassionate bluish-grey eyes filled with reassurance. The other two surfers were his older brother Matthew and his fiancé, Emilie. Matthew was three years older, bearing a similar physique to his younger brother, bronze hair and blue eyes. Emilie had a petite but athletic figure. Her shoulder-length hair was highlighted in blonde and brown, and she had aquamarine-blue eyes.

'You didn't paddle back to shore, when that storm hit', he explained. 'When you were nowhere to be seen, we paddled out to find you while Sam ran up to your house to get your brother and sister'.

'Thankfully, the storm cleared once you were rescued. You was still unconscious though', Matthew pointed out.

'How long exactly was I out for?' she asked, confusingly.

Before he could speak, Emilie got there first. 'You were out for about an hour'.

'WHAT?' Haley yelped.

'You had a pulse, though it took a while for you to get oxygen back into your system, as we performed CPR', James proclaimed.

Haley ran her hand over the place where she cut her arm on the underwater rocky reef, skin smooth with no open wound or heavy bleeding.

'I-I thought I cut myself on the reef', she pointed out sheepishly, ignoring the brief wave of nausea and the unreadable looks of her brother and sister. James with his medical training from the army closely examined her checking her heart rate and any injuries, including her right arm where the deep gash originally was.

'You seem to be okay, Haley', James explained. 'Aside from the nausea and dizziness, I couldn't find any broken or dislocated bones, or deep wounds'.

Haley's eyebrows narrowed, her eyes bewildered, as she flexed and twisted her fully healed arm exposing her toned muscle to more of the yellow sunlight.

'But I cut myself on the reef', she replied shakily.

She was on the verge of letting out a few tears, quietly begging everyone to believe her. Even as she looked at the unreadable expressions of her brother and sister, Haley felt helpless. She took a few more deep breaths, preventing herself from hyperventilating.

'*Help us, daughter*', she heard another voice calling out to her.

This time, it was a man's voice: serious but just as encouraging as the woman's voice. Haley squeezed her eyes tightly shut and shook it from side to side. What did these voices want with her? The male voice called her *daughter*. Was this her father? Haley opened her eyes, blinking several times to see if there was an invisible someone watching her unusual actions, reading her emotions.

Nothing.

'*Our darling, please help us*', the woman and the man's voices pleaded together. '*We are waiting for you. Only you can defeat the darkness*'.

Haley tried to pull through the overwhelming episodes. She took five deep breaths to provide herself from unleashing another immense magic trick. Eventually, she was able to let in the real-life voices of her friends, blocking out the disembodied voices inside her head. Deep down, Haley was afraid of being taken to the hospital for a blood test, and the doctors discovering her ability to heal quicker than others. Who knows what they would do to her, upon that alleged discovery?

'Haley's clearly still shaken up', Eric proclaimed as if sensing her frightened emotions. 'She probably just needs to get some rest'.

Haley smiled on the inside in relief, as it saved her a trip from the hospital. It was another odd fact she added. The last time she went to the hospital was before she moved to Cornwall. She and her siblings lived in a small town in Bournemouth. She was five years old and contracted tuberculosis, which the doctors believed she would recover from in one week, but it ended up being three days.

'Maybe I'll take the rest of the morning off from surfing', she eventually said, wanting to get away from the wondering eyes.

Kelly gave her a sympathetic look.

'As long as you're sure, Hales', she said. 'If you're feeling better, we can try surfing tomorrow'.

As if asking for permission, Haley looked at her siblings. They just smiled, taking it as a yes.

'Yeah, I'll definitely be fine by morning', she uttered feeling the fire she had inside her when she went to catch the waves return. Amy helped her to her feet while Eric picked up her surfboard, which washed ashore, with Kelly trailing behind making sure Haley didn't have another fainting episode.

'Wait, who pulled me out of the water?' Haley asked the others.

James shrugged. 'I don't know...a boy around your age saw the whole thing, and dove in', he answered. 'As soon as you were out and on the shore, he was gone'.

Who pulled her out? And why couldn't she see his face out of the humanoid figures she spotted underwater? She wished she knew.

After thanking James, Matthew and Emilie, Haley became dazed in thought walking back up towards the house keeping the blanket Kelly gave her wrapped on her shoulders, and Amy gently supporting her weight. Her thoughts flickered between her regular morning surf and her coming close to death's door.

Once they reached the house, Haley said goodbye to Kelly who headed back to her black Volvo.

'What really happened, Haley?' Amy asked. There was nothing but disbelief on Haley's face at the fact that whenever something unusual happened out of the ordinary, her brother and sister felt the need to ask, like they needed an incident report.

'I already told you and the others', she answered, leaving out the part about the storm coming at the same time she went underwater, 'I was relaxing on my surfboard, and then got hit by a wave, and dragged down, because of the storm'.

'Haley, you said you cut yourself on the reef. Are you absolutely sure that was what happened?' Eric asked, closely eyeing the arm she supposedly cut. Again, Haley tried to recall everything that happened. All she saw were the bright white flashes from the lightning of the thirty-second thunderstorm.

'Honestly, I don't really know or understand what happened. Somehow, the storm made me feel at ease. I just kept looking at it like I always did, when I was little. You know how much I love watching thunderstorms'.

'But the cut though?' Eric asked again.

'I-I don't know', she muttered shakily.

Haley's eyes watered again, feeling as if Eric and Amy knew she could do the impossible.

'If you don't mind, I want to take a nap. Sleep off the whole thing', Haley excused herself, shrugging her shoulders.

Eric and Amy just nodded, despite the conversation not being over. They would probably end up asking more questions, making it a topic over a dinner conversation. The thought remained in Haley's head, as she walked up the staircase to her balcony and closed the glass doors, leaning back against it breathing deeply and closing her eyes. She looked out the window at the blue sky and saw the same eight stars shining, as she always saw them.

CHAPTER 4: A CHILDHOOD STORY

The rest of the week passed by steadily. Haley was in her bedroom, standing in front of her easel having been awake since eight o'clock producing a starry night painting for a university application to study fine art at the Falmouth School of Art. Another was of a stormy cyclone protecting an island on the sea, inspired by one of her dreams, which she couldn't explain the meaning of – just that it was a story she needed to tell.

Three days ago, flashbacks of the dreams haunted Haley, as she became drawn to the recurring voices, as if they knew her every move and where she was, choosing an appropriate time to convince Haley to help them with whatever it was they were dealing with. Somehow, the memory of her flying through the night sky became the biggest inspiration to the latest painting in front of her. The next thing she added was a girl with an elegant gown, flying towards something invisible to the naked eye, even Haley's own eyes.

But what could it be? If only she knew the answer…

Haley's brother and sister seemed to be keeping too many secrets from her: secrets she was too stubborn to avoid. Their expressions made her think they had in fact seen her do something inhumanly unusual. At the time, Haley had been trying to coax Eric and Amy into talking to her about what was happening to her, about why she was so drawn to the thunderstorms; even asking them more questions about her parents. Every single one they dodged them yet again. The stressful situation left her with the repeats of the dreams, which left faint grey circles under her eyes. She moved past the frustration, by continuing her five-deep-breaths techniques, in an attempt to block out the recurring images and voices. Following this, Haley's emotions went to full determination mode, baring the smallest glimmer of hope. The only positive outcome since the whole incident was that she was having less dreams about other worlds and extraterrestrial beings that looked like humans thanks to the dream-catcher.

She looked out the window. The sky was blue, only small white clouds about. Though it still bore the same remarkably beautiful eight stars. She smiled at their timeless beauty, as bright as the sun, astounded by the fact that other people didn't seem to notice these particular stars.

She shrugged the feeling off and went back to her night painting made from liquid acrylics.

After another half hour, a gentle knock came at the door followed by the creaky opening of it as Haley lifted her head up to face it. Eric and Amy were still in their pyjamas, Eric in a tank top and sweatpants, and Amy in some grey and white check pyjamas. They were carrying a food tray, and three presents.

'Happy birthday, Haley!' they chimed together.

Haley stopped painting and smiled amusingly. She promised herself she put aside the search for answers for this day.

'What is all this?' Haley asked, sitting down on the bed, her expression clouded with curious excitement.

Eric and Amy just smiled.

'It's your birthday breakfast', Amy said. 'And you know, it is family tradition when you open three presents in the morning, before receiving your main ones later'.

'Yeah, I remember: at the stroke of sunset'. She spread her smile more. 'And the Aurora Eclipse is supposed to show at six. I can't wait to see it. I know it's going to be a beautiful phenomenon to see'.

It was true. Ever since studying it in science class, Haley prepared herself for the astronomical event sitting on the edge of her seat wishing those three years would go by quickly just so that she could see the vibrant dancing lights of the Aurora Borealis surround the lunar eclipse.

Her words brought bigger smiles to her siblings, though she could have sworn she saw a tiny hint of concern behind their eyes. She simply brushed it off, putting herself in denial and reminding herself that her mission was on hold for the day.

'Well, we know how much you've been looking forward to it, Haley', Eric nodded. 'You should know this event was very important on your birthday eighteen years ago'.

Haley arched her eyebrow.

'Really?' she asked hopefully. 'How so?'

'You remember the story we told you when you were little?' Amy replied, handing Haley her tray of breakfast food: smoked salmon on toast with watermelon and cucumber water.

'You mean the one about Mani and the Valkyries?' Haley asked, her eyes lighting up at the mention of it.

'Yes'.

Haley took a bite of her toast, as her brother and sister sat down with her.

'Do you remember what we told you in the story?' Eric asked.

'Of course', Haley replied, putting her toast down. 'It started with the same story in Norse Mythology. Mani was the personification of the moon, making him the son of Murdilfari, the god of the fire giants on Muspelheim, and the brother of Sol, the goddess of the sun. Every night, he rode a chariot pulled by horses through the sky carrying the moon with him. But one night, he was chased by a wolf in the formation of stars called Hati'.

'After some time, Hati finally caught the moon in his mouth and a lunar eclipse occurred. It lasted for no more than thirty minutes, until the wolf was chased away by the sounds people made'.

Eric and Amy nodded in agreement.

'And what about the Valkyries?' Amy asked eagerly.

Haley's eyebrows arched yet again, but she continued.

'The Valkyries were a host of female immortal warriors who rode across the sky, in chariots pulled by horses, and chose who would be taken in Odin's temple, Valhalla to be blessed with the afterlife. They worn special armour, which shone with reflections of beautiful, colorful lights, believed to be the Northern Lights. People saw these lights as a blessing, believed to be associated with the miracle of life, as the Valkyries brought less pain for the mother blessing herself and the child'.

As she reflected on her strong knowledge about Norse Mythology, Haley returned her siblings' smiles. There were so many stories and legends about how the universe works, but it was this specific mythology she appeared more drawn to. Was it all part of her family history descent? Did she have some Norse blood in her?

'Could you remind me of how Mani and one of the Valkyries met and fell in love?' she asked, feeling relaxed but anxious to know more.

Eric and Amy acknowledged Haley's request, for Haley knew they were better at describing these fairytales than she was, even though she could explain the mythology.

'Very well then', Eric sighed. 'You know the facts but not the whole story',

'As you know, Mani was known as the Master of the Moon, gifted with the power to control the moonlight and manipulate eclipses, once the wolf moved him in front of the sun. And according to the legend, the Valkyries were immortal female warriors, blessed with the power to generate the natural lights of the Aurora Borealis through the reflective metal on their armour. They use this gift to guide the fallen warriors to Valhalla, the temple of Odin'.

'One day, Mani came across the Valkyries and they watched as the wolf, Hati made the gruesome choice to devour both him and the Moon, after seeing his eclipse power grow stronger than his own. Therefore, he wanted to spread more fear into the people who frightened him each time he was close to making that accomplishment'.

Amy continued the story. 'Fortunately, one particular Valkyrie fought the wolf off with great courage and skill, and then cursed Hati to an eternity of never harming any being within the cosmic universe; and healed Mani's wounds'.

'Once Mani recovered, she was the first face he saw upon awakening. He found out her name was Raven. He told her she was beautiful, strong, kind and brave: everything he ever dreamed in a woman. It was love at first sight'.

Haley's heart soared, hearing these words about two people from different worlds falling in love, after escaping dire peril at the claws of an ancient mystical creature.

She eagerly awaited the continuation of the story.

'Mani recovered within a week', Amy explained. 'And since then, he and Raven began to spend more time together. They would go to the outskirts of the cosmos, and ride their chariots of horses side-by-side, laughing and enjoying each other's company, falling even more in love'.

'Until one day, a society called the High Council of the Nine Realms approached Mani and Raven after witnessing the power they demonstrate together', Eric pointed out. 'Seeing how powerful their love was, it was decreed that they would be promised to each other in marriage. The ceremony took place at the last hour of sunset on this very date. Through the marriage, their gifts were combined together to form a legendary phenomenon, which would become known as the Aurora Eclipse'.

Haley went on to finish the story.

'And because of how specially rare the moon manipulation, lunar generation and aurora manipulation powers were, Mani and Raven made an agreement with the Council to have the Aurora Eclipse symbolize the birth of a child born with the most extraordinary gifts', she proclaimed in deep thought.

Eric and Amy responded with another nod.

'I know it's a fairytale, but don't you think it is weird how the eclipse takes place once every eighteen years on the exact same time and date as my birthday?' Haley asked. It was yet another suspicious fact she stored for safe keeping in her mind-forged list.

'It's probably just a coincidence, Haley', Eric replied offering her consideration. 'Doesn't mean these stories are real'.

'Hmm, I suppose you're right. I just had a feeling, that's all', Haley shrugged her shoulders, sighing and feeling her determination going up to at least seventy percent accuracy, as she was unable to shake the slight seriousness in Eric's tone.

From what she heard, her two siblings sounded very shifty as if they were indeed hiding something and wanted to protect Haley from that something.

Amy took a hold of Haley's hand comfortingly.

'We know you want to know more about what is happening to you', she explained. 'But it will have to wait until after your birthday party and when the Aurora Eclipse have finished'.

'But why?' Haley swallowed. 'What is exactly so special about our family, when I'm pretty much the only one who can do things other people can't?

Eric and Amy simply gave her a sympathetic look.

Of course, they would know about the elemental occurrences having watched her control these. Heat rushed to her face and hands, as her emotions clouded over and the familiar tingling signaled to her that she was about to unleash another power like a crazy lunatic. She managed to tell herself she could control this, and the tingling stopped.

'When the eclipse occurs, you will not only see it. You will feel it', Amy smiled.

'Feel what exactly?' Haley asked suspiciously. It was like they were engaged in the speech from another time. It only made the entire conversation more questionable.

'You will see when it is over', Eric replied.

The statement was confusing, but warmed Haley's heart when she received the realization that she was finally going to learn more about her family heritage.

She just sighed and said, 'If you say so'. And the conversation ended there.

Haley then opened the three presents her brother and sister brought in with her breakfast. She was bewildered, but amazed by what she received.

The first gift was a beautifully crafted silver dagger, which according to Eric once belonged to a family friend. Its blade was pure metal steel, sharp enough to draw blood. Woven down the center of it was an ancient scroll patterning. The handle of the dagger was beautifully detailed in gold trim and scrollwork. Still, Haley did not understand why she would receive a dagger as a birthday present until Eric explained to her that she would need something to defend herself with now that she was eighteen. The second present was a silver bracelet, with two charms attached to the chain, the charms being an ancient Norse symbol translated as the letter H for Haley's name, and a blue sapphire crystal. And the third present was a simple silver ring braid in a knot style, formulated into a Celtic pattern. In the base was a blue garnet gem.

Everything about these three gifts caused Haley to play with her triquetra necklace, wondering if it was somehow connected to the dagger, the ring and the charm bracelet.

CHAPTER 5: THE AURORA ECLIPSE

Haley, Eric and Amy spent the next part of her birthday on the beach with Kelly and her aunt, Serena, a naturally toned woman in her late thirties with flowing brown hair; and her eyes in different colours: one was blue and one was green, identified as heterochromia, with a neat shade of turquoise similar to Kelly's. She wore a simple maxi dress of Aztec patterns. The five of them were playing volleyball and surfing, having sandwiches, salad and fruit. Haley felt relaxed now that she did not worry about her impulse habit taking control like it did that day, when she created the ice ball out of a seawater whirlpool and the near-violent thunderstorm. Like a shield was placed over the source where her elemental magic emerged.

And what exactly did her brother and sister mean when they said she would feel something after the eclipse?

Only later, Haley thought.

Haley and Kelly laughed, as they caught the waves even falling into the water on purpose while Eric, Amy and Serena joined in the laughter, splashing them. The picnic lasted until three o'clock, when it was introduced it was time to get ready for the party. Everyone packed up, with Amy carrying the picnic blanket and Eric the food basket. Haley and Kelly carried their surfboards under their arms; Serena, a photographer, went through the photos she took. Walking back, Haley looked up at the clear blue sky seeing the familiar eight stars shining almost as bright as the day as before. Her curiosity increased to the point where she thought her brain might explode from this unstoppable thinking.

Until –

'*We are here, sweetheart. Your time is near*', the woman's voice called out.

Haley let out a slight gasp. She turned around to see if someone was behind her, whispering this but there was no one except a few passers-by going for their afternoon walks. She gave a peculiar look at this odd occurrence and shook her head.

'Haley, come on!' Kelly called her.

'Coming!' she replied back and ran to the balcony steps, while Eric, Amy and Serena went into the downstairs room.

The outside was decked with a blue, gold, white and purple *Happy Birthday* banner above the entrance to the basement lounge area with matching balloons. There stood a long table covered in a white tablecloth, with paper plates and blue plastic cups.

When Haley was in the shower, the warm water poured onto her skin like she just stepped under a light waterfall. She stared at the droplets on her fingertips and watched as they levitated an inch away from her skin. The water was still unlike the swirling whirlpool ball she produced; you would mistake these little droplet balls as the silver balls you would put on a cake, or just bubbles. Each water droplet displayed a small spark like a tiny surge of electricity in the center of them, remembering the lightning she would wake up to after her dreams. Haley let the water drop back onto her skin and turned off the shower, stepping out to grab a towel from the cupboard. She wrapped it around her hair, put on her dressing gown and then headed back to her room.

Kelly was already there, applying some light makeup, in her extra leggings and button-up shirt.

'Ah, Haley! You're out!' she said excitedly, as she stood up out of the stall in front of Haley's white dressing table. 'Come on, let's get you ready'.

Smiling, Haley sat down. Kelly began working on her hair, applying the coconut-scented hair mousse, and tying it up into a tight bun to leave for five minutes as instructed on the bottle. While waiting, she did Haley's makeup, consisting of light pink lipstick and matching blush, finishing with black eyeliner and mascara.

Kelly stepped back to look at her handy work and clapped her hands together, signaling the first part completed.

'It's looking good', she said, handing Haley the mirror on the dressing table so that she check it.

She gave a nod and a grin, hinting that she liked it.

The five minutes were up, when the alarm on Kelly's phone went off, and she let loose the hair-tie holding Haley's hair, blow-drying it with a hairdryer and styling it into elegant bouncy curls.

'It's great. Thank you, Kelly', she said with a slight smile.

'You're welcome. I knew you'd like it', Kelly replied, giving her a hug from behind.

Haley's eyes suddenly widened, the moment she felt a strong burst of cosmic energy pass through her from Kelly's touch, sensing something within her, something familiar and magical. Her eyes lit like a burning fire and the world around her faded, becoming replaced with images of dark figures surrounding a circle of people during a bloody-red sunset. She was drawn back to reality, as the vision ended. She stood up to turn and look at Kelly, her expression mirroring Haley's.

'Did-did you feel that?' Haley asked. Kelly was in shock from the electric sensation to answer.

Haley carefully stepped forward. 'You have something, don't you?' she questioned hopefully. 'Just like I do'.

Kelly tried to act disbelieving.

'Haley, it was probably just an electric shock', she said. 'You know, we get those cases of static electricity. So why don't we go -?'

'Don't deny it', Haley interrupted seriously. 'I know you felt that little jolt pass through me. It was the first time I felt something like this'.

She looked out the corner of her eye and spotted thunderclouds in the distance over the open ocean, possibly triggered by her slight outburst of desperation.

'Please, Kelly. Just tell me', she pleaded in an attempt to tone things down. The clouds faded as quickly as they appeared.

Kelly bit her lip, seemingly unable to deny Haley's request.

'All right, I'll tell you. But what I am about to show you, Haley, may change your view of me', she uttered reluctantly. 'It is dangerous to know these things before the Aurora Eclipse. Your brother and sister can't know, for it goes against everything I was instructed with'.

Haley felt puzzled by this statement.

'Dangerous?' she questioned, as her determination level went up to eighty percent.

'Let's just say there are bad people out there who know and see everything, except what you do at this very moment because you are concealed from them'. The answer made no sense whatsoever to Haley, like it was a messed up answer to the wrong question on an exam paper.

'Please promise not to tell', Kelly begged with a whisper. 'Otherwise, I'll be the one at the end of a debate of whether to keep what I have'.

Seeing how serious she actually was, Haley replied. 'I promise'.

But what did Kelly mean by it being dangerous to know some things before the eclipse? Was it because of how cosmically pure this magic was, the recent one now being able to sense unusual things within people, like super-humans or witches?

Perhaps she would know the true reason after this.

Haley observed Kelly's actions, as she pulled the towel off her head and pulled her hair up into a ponytail. She picked up a matchbox from Haley's dressing table, taking out a matchstick. Lighting it, she kept her eye on the small orange flame without blinking out water, like when you cut onions. She then did an astounding movement: she touched the flame with her fingertip.

Shocked, Haley almost gasped fighting the urge to pull Kelly's hand away from the flame to prevent her from burning herself. Her best friend had to be insane, pulling this little stunt with one little flame! But then again, what was the most bizarre stunt with a supernatural entity: manipulating fire with your bare hands; making an ice ball out of ocean water; or sensing the pulse of a lightning bolt? Her thoughts shifted back to Kelly who began playing with the flame. It divided into five, moving across Kelly's fingers each flame balancing on one, her face in deep concentration, like being connected to the fire element.

Then, much to Haley's amazement, it did an extraordinary thing reverting from yellow and orange to a pure rainbow fire, changing to swirling water, but keeping to the rainbow.

'You know my secret now', Kelly said, extinguishing the flame, leaving Haley in shear shock, after witnessing her best friend manipulate the impossible.

'But-but how?' Haley stuttered, lost for words. 'How come you never told me? If I'd have known or felt something like this, I would have not been the only one knowing I could do magic'.

'Believe me: I wanted to so many times, Haley', Kelly said guiltily. 'But I swore an oath to protect you from the truth and to honor the word of your family'.

'Protect me?' Haley questioned. 'From what? And what do you mean by the word of my family?'

Pregnant pause.

She tried to solve the riddle behind Kelly's words still taking in the whole ordeal, maintaining her feelings of wonder and hurt: wonder from being a witness to a beautiful supernatural power, and hurt from the fact that something like this was kept from her.

There was only one guess as to who would instruct Kelly to do this.

'My brother and sister?' Haley asked. Tears filled her eyes, but she detained them like prisoners fighting to escape.

'Yes', Kelly replied.

'I knew there was something odd about their behavior. I just couldn't put my finger out. But you…you were always so normal. I didn't sense anything'.

'You only know one side of the story', Kelly proclaimed. 'That is about you and you're now learning to gain control your abilities'.

'But what's the other side?' Haley asked.

Just as Kelly opened her mouth to speak, there was a knock on Haley's bedroom door and Kelly's aunt, Serena's voice called out from the other side.

'Haley, Kelly!' she called. 'Eric and Amy said the party guests will be here in about half an hour, so be ready by four sharp'.

Haley's frustration came about. Guess answers would have to wait until later after all, she thought.

She and Kelly went back to getting ready, without so much as uttering another word to each other about the circumstances of their conversation. Haley touched up her makeup, while Kelly wavered her hair pinning half of it back and applied some lip balm, with pale pink blusher from a clam-shell compact mirror, mascara and eyeliner. By quarter to four, they were ready. Haley wore a black floral dress with ankle boots, also wearing her triquetra necklace, charm bracelet and a pair of crystal ear-studs Kelly got her as a present. Kelly chose a blue butterfly print wrap dress with mid-heeled boots, alongside a charm necklace (the charm being a hippocampus) and a golden intertwined bracelet.

As they headed towards the door, Haley broke the silence between herself and Kelly – to reassure her, but also remind her of the things she was now aware of, even though it was an unexpected thing to stumble across.

'Kelly', she muttered, grabbing her arm and making her turn around to face her. 'I want you to know that what you've shown me is still a lot to take in. I'm just sorry to drag you into this, but please…promise me I will get those answers by the end of today'

Kelly's eyes softened and gave Haley's hand a light comforting squeeze, as a reassuring gesture of friendship. 'Haley, you must understand that that decision is down to the word of your family', she replied. 'But I promise you: by the end of tonight, you will know'.

She smiled, pulling her into a hug, which Haley gladly returned.

'Now, come on, Guests are waiting', Kelly grinned.

*

At the party, music was coming out of the radio speakers, numerous people on the dance floor outside the basement doors, disco lights illuminating the sand, other guests playing volleyball and others going surfing on the water wearing glow sticks. A lot of people came up to wish Haley a happy birthday. The large table was stocked with party food and drink: chicken drumsticks and wings, green salad, tomatoes, cucumber, carrots, chipped potatoes, spiced whitebait, vintage cupcakes and cookies, wine, lemonade and coke. The birthday cake was a three tier white floral cake from *Little Cow Creative Cakes*.

Haley thought for one split moment that her brother, sister and Kelly would go over the top after hearing them brag about the whole planning which had been going on since her sixteenth birthday. It was on that birthday when while on a surprise surf trip in Hawaii, she discovered she could morph an ice cube into a cube of swirling water, and then into a lightning ball. Haley clenched her first to cloud out the memory and ease off the tingling through her veins. She would not risk exposing herself to her friends, otherwise who knows what the reaction would be like?

'Haley?' Kelly asked, grabbing her wrist. Haley blinked twice, before turning to her. 'Don't let your emotions cloud you. You're immersed with cosmic energy, constantly channeling through you'.

Haley just nodded, breathing calmly yet slowly, until the last of the tingling was gone. It worked. Kelly's advice actually worked. Proud of herself, she gave her best friend's hand a gentle squeeze.

'Thank you', she said appreciatively with a smile. 'I don't know how you dealt with it every day. I found it hard'. Her expression changed. 'I still don't get why you never told me. I'm your best friend, and we share each other's secrets no matter how crazy they are'.

Despite feeling relieved that she was not the only one with magic, the betrayal was still there.

'As I said before, I wanted to, but I couldn't', Kelly said. 'As for how I was taught, well…all I can say is that it was all about focusing on things I hold dear. The reason you found it difficult was because your magic is powerful, more powerful than my own'.

Haley raised her eyebrows.

'Even if it's true, it still doesn't explain why my brother and sister were so secretive. I mean, you told me that they know about what I have', she said.

'Yes, I did. But I'm afraid I can't be much help right now, at least until the eclipse is over'.

Haley let out a deep sigh but managed a reluctant smile. Kelly closed her hand over Haley's shoulder and pulled her into a quick hug, despite the disappointment of waiting more.

She then went over to the buffet table with Kelly to grab some food and drink. Once there, James, Matthew and Emilie, having a conversation with Eric, Amy and Serena laughing, greeted them. Serena wore the same maxi dress from the picnic, in touched-up makeup. Amy had clipped half her hair up with the rest flowing freely, and the dress she was wearing was a simple navy blue with matching wedge heels. Emilie went with a dark red maxi dress, matching the lipstick she was wearing, and silver sandals; her hair perfectly straightened. The boys were in button-up short-sleeved shirts; Eric in pale blue, and James and Matthew in white, all three of them wearing trousers or jeans.

'Haley! Happy birthday', Emilie said, giving Haley a peck on the cheek and a hug. The boys did the same gesture.

'Thank you', Haley smiled. 'So glad you could make it'.

'Of course', Matthew replied. 'You only turn eighteen once, after all'.

Haley let out a slight laugh.

'The party looks amazing as well, thanks to Kelly and her party planning', she said, as she pulled Kelly into a playful bear hug.

Both girls let out giggles.

'Oh come on, I'm not that good at organization', Kelly replied.

'Hey, you're the one who prints out itineraries for the both of us', Haley reminded her, smiling even more, with the other joining the laughter.

'Well, you're lucky to have her as a friend', James pointed out.

Haley collected her plate of food, while she chatted more with James, Matthew and Emilie. Serena whispered something to Eric and Amy, before approaching Kelly. Kelly's expression changed worry, as she excused herself. Haley however eyed her siblings, watching their eyes shift to Kelly. She hid the emotions she was feeling towards this, coating it with the happiness and excitement she felt. Did they know about what Kelly told her? What was going to happen to Kelly now? Was she going to get a telling-off or a warning, until it reached the three-strike mark? No, that won't happen. Kelly was going to be fine...she was going to tell the next part of the story and everything would be okay.

Eric looked at his watch, gesturing five fingers to Haley signaling five minutes before the big astronomical event. He and Amy went to the DJ to turn the music down.

'Hello everyone, may we have your attention please?' Eric's voice bellowed out of the microphone. 'Thank you everyone for coming. As you know, today is Haley's eighteenth birthday.

The guests cheered, making Haley blush.

'Our sister is someone very dear to us', Amy continued. 'She is the most beautiful, kindest, sweetest, and let's not forget, feisty and sometimes headstrong young woman and we're very lucky to have her as a sister, because she is someone very special. And here we are, as today we celebrate her day, and remain hopeful of what the future holds for her'.

'To Haley!' both Eric and Amy rejoiced.

Everyone raised his or her drinks. 'To Haley!' they repeated.

Haley gave a slight smile at the heartwarming speech, taking sip of her wine. Some of the boys winked at her, causing her to stare at the ground blushing even more. She instead pecked out of the corner of her eye and saw the ground began to blacken at a slow pace.

'And now, observe the rare astronomical phenomenon that occurred on this very day eighteen years ago', Eric announced gesturing up to the sky.

Everyone followed the direction of Eric's gesture, the early evening sky now on the verge of the blue hour the indirect sunlight against the predominant blue becoming blocked by the slow movement of the moon.

They and Haley watched as the white yellow lighting of the sun encircling the eclipse changed dramatically, like a supernova explosion colliding with a comet. Within seconds, vibrant colours conquered the white. Haley became transfixed by the incredible beauty of the Aurora Borealis, remembering the eclipse as referenced in her childhood story about Mani and Raven displaying this Aurora Eclipse as a symbol of love. They shone as bright as the rainbow, but they were different: more powerful, brighter than any light on Earth or in the universe.

It was the most beautiful sight she had ever seen.

Suddenly, the pulsing tingle she experienced as a child came about. This time, it was a hundred times stronger, her muscles building up and her eyes burning like a white-hot fire ignited by a highly flammable substance. Haley saw through the whiteness the times she manipulated lightning, ice, snow and water into animal avatars and shapes, and realized she was having flashbacks as if it was sending her reminder of what she could do. Then came the visions…the burial of an ancient king…his weapon divided into pieces…a mystical kingdom surrounded by stars…the birth of a child during a thunderstorm…that child being blessed by the lights of the Aurora Eclipse…the horrifying, unexpected attack on the temple as the child's family did everything in their power to protect her…a deadly lightning bolt just as the baby let out a cry, sensing the danger…the baby being sent away to another world, as the family said their goodbyes to her.

The blurry figures holding the baby became clearer…their faces shocked Haley to the core…recognition kicking her in the stomach, next to a feeling of overwhelming shock…

Eric and Amy!

Brightness flashed…

Lightning.

And not just one, but two…three…four…five bolts bonded with the Northern Lights spreading across the sky, its illumination reflecting off the ocean water; surrounding the eclipse as the moon moved away from the sun. The overwhelming sensation caused Haley to start hyperventilating, herself having repeats of the elemental occurrences and visions of a past life, followed by a war, knights fighting for their homes and their people. Her birthmark burnt, as she reached to touch her necklace.

Party guests gasped at the newest addition to the Aurora Eclipse.

'*Whoa, that's new*', a seventeen-year-old girl named Quinn said. But her mouth wasn't moving.

'*I've never seen any thing like it*', the girl's boyfriend pointed out. His mouth didn't move either.

Haley's eyes widened.

That moment, she realized that she was hearing people's thoughts.

Eric and Amy were right about one thing: she would feel something phenomenal, something she had never felt before, like it changed the nature of Haley's powers drastically. Speaking of Eric and Amy, Haley turned her desperate, tear-filled eyes towards them, their smiles slowly fading; her mind becoming more overwhelmed with the recurring thoughts and voices of the people around her, as they complimented about the eclipse and wondered why thunder suddenly appeared.

'*Haley, can you hear us?*' two more voices asked through the powerful sequence of voiceovers. It was Eric and Amy. Haley locked her eyes to them, their eyes full of wisdom and guidance, but Haley's filled with confusion as it pulsed through her veins.

She just nodded.

'*What you are hearing is beginning to overwhelm your mind*', Eric's voice spoke. '*Drown them out. Focus our voices*'.

Through the constant whispering, Haley found the strength to break through by replying. '*What was that I just felt?*'

'*We will explain in a moment, sister*', Amy said next. '*Just listen to our voices*'.

Following their instruction, Haley closed her eyes and focused on rebuilding her mind barrier that broke down when she unexpectedly harnessed the streams of colourful energy from the Aurora Eclipse, as if it blessed her with even more mysteries. The more Haley concentrated, the quieter the voices got, like pressing the mute button on the remote control.

'*Now, come upstairs to the spare bedroom*', Amy said. '*We have a lot to talk about*'.

Haley saw that they were serious. At this point, she realized the answers she was hopefully getting were lurking upon the faces of her siblings. Excusing herself from Matthew, Emilie and James, Haley made her way across the dance floor watching as everyone gave a round of applause indicating the eclipse was wearing its end, though the colours of the Northern Lights continued to shine brightly.

As she edged towards the glass doors, she caught a glimpse of her reflection and saw that the sparkly blue colour in her eyes was brighter than ever.

Chapter 6: The Music Box and the Letter

Haley took a detour through the basement living room, and up the spiral staircase leading to the top floor, while everyone went back to dancing and chatting about how astronomically beautiful the eclipse was. In all honesty, Haley really wanted a few minutes by her self while still taking in what she witnessed inside her head, before she received these so-called life-changing news. Whatever power she felt during the Aurora Eclipse still pulsed through her blood. She made her way across the open area towards the bedroom hallway. One door stood ajar and out came some whispered chatter. She edged closer and heard it was Kelly and Serena, Eric and Amy having a debate type argument.

'You know you were not supposed to tell her who she is yet', Amy argued. 'Why would you risk it and your gifts?'

'Because I saw it in her eyes', Kelly argued back. 'There was no anger, but there was wonder and betrayal. I couldn't keep lying to her, even after feeling that power flow'.

'Keilantra, you know how dangerous it is', Eric contended. 'The king and queen have informed us through their telepathy that the cloaking spell has begun to weaken, after the Aurora Eclipse's return, which even your own mother was unable to predict'.

'Look, I do not care what the High Council does to me, or my gifts; and I am aware of the risks my mother contemplated, but Haley deserves to know. Even before the eclipse, you knew as much as I did that she was old enough to be told the truth about her past'.

Serena sighed deeply.

'We know you meant well, dear niece', she proclaimed. 'But need I remind you that I swore an oath from your mother to ensure I carry out her teachings for only you, and Eric and Arianna for Halena, to avoid exposure to the Nebulans'.

Haley tried to recall a time where Kelly or her aunt behaved oddly secretive in the same manner as Eric and Amy, but found nothing. She had to hand it to them though: they were very good at hiding whatever it was they were hiding. And why did Eric all of a sudden start calling Kelly by another name, Keilantra?

Unable to hear anymore of this disagreement between the four, Haley pushed open the door quickly without knocking. All four sets of eyes turned to her, emotions automatically changing to the same astonishing wonder. Either that, or they noticed the brilliant brightness of the sparkle in her eyes, possibly enhanced from the effects of the apparent magic of the Aurora Eclipse.

'No more secrets and no more lies', she pointed out. 'You're going to tell me why I have these powers, and why I felt a strong pulse you said I would feel during and after the eclipse. And about why I saw you, Eric and Amy in a vision. And one more thing: Kelly telling me about what she could do was entirely my decision. She had nothing to do it, so don't put the blame on her'.

Eric and Amy attempted to speak up, but Haley wouldn't let them – not this time…

'Everyday, I've kept what I have hidden from everyone else. But I can't do this anymore', she begged. 'So please, tell me what is going on and how I am able to do this'. And she gestured toward a vase of water with no flowers in it, channeling her energy, picturing the shape the water would morph into. The water formulated into a hippocampus, like the charm on Kelly's necklace.

Everyone watched knee-deep in awe at this astounding phenomenon Haley demonstrated. Although from the exchanging looks, they were aware this would happen. She herself grew more determined for answers, involving her controlling elements, channeling energy from the Aurora Eclipse, hearing voices, sensing others like her and so forth.

'And why did you call Kelly Keilantra?' she asked. Judging by Kelly's guilty expression, everyone knew there was no more hiding any more secrets from Haley.

'Because it is my birth name', she answered slowly. 'Kelly Miller is my Earth alias'.

Haley became bewildered by this answer, making her heart beat faster.

'What do you mean by during your time on Earth?' she demanded.

Kelly just gazed down at the floor with an even more guilty expression, unable to bring herself to answer the question, Haley now torn between repeating the question and keeping quiet, wondering if it would only make things worse.

'She means she is not of this world', Amy eventually said. 'And neither is Serena, nor Eric and I...and you are not either, Haley'. Both siblings contradicted movements with their hands. The gestures were swiftly quick and gestured, that as soon as they started something appeared right in forward of Haley's very eyes and floated toward her, as if it sensed the magic within her.

Haley reached out and took the object out of the air.

It was a music box. Haley examined it running her fingertips over every detail delicately like an antique, making sure she did not break it or scratch marks on it. It was a beautifully crafted box, made out of birch wood, the surface of it smooth and glazed that the setting sun and the last of the aurora lights shone against it. The hand pyrographed pattern on the lid was a tree Haley recognized as the Tree of Life symbol, baring the same triquetra on each corner.

On each side of the lock at the front were ancient runes in the Norse language translated as *The Light* and *The Hope.*

'You – you can do magic as well?' Haley stuttered, looking at Eric and Amy.

'Yes', Eric replied. 'Like you, we were born with abilities beyond your imagination'.

Haley shifted her eyes back to the elegant patterned music box

'The answers you seek lie within that music box', Amy claimed.

Mixed emotions washed over Haley, as her eyes shifted back to the elegant patterned music box. She waited about five seconds, before clicking the golden lock and slowly with trembling hands, opened the box. Her emotions immediately diverted back to astounding wonder, in reaction to what she saw and heard next: a soft melody

Then, a glowing orb of white and gold shimmering magic levitated out of the box, slowly transforming into the same tree pattern from on the lid in shining gold, with green crystals as the leaves. The beautiful humming of ancient hymns followed with the miniature tree structure gradually turning in a circle.

Haley's eyes filled with tears, as the music played.

'It was a gift from our parents', Eric explained, Haley looking up as a lone tear streaked down her cheek. She did not realize Serena and Kelly had left the room, perhaps to continue to host the party in their absence.

Amy continued. 'The box was handcrafted from the wood of an ancient tree with its natural magic, blessing it with the powers of the Tree of Life. The continuous loop of hymning enchanted with the incantation of the magic...'

'Like – like the kind of recording you hear on a radio?' Haley asked, realizing the close comparison between both subjects. It was indeed like hearing a successful number one song on repeat on the radio, as there was no turning key required to restart the music, humbling Haley. All of because even though there were overwhelming tears, the hymn brought to her, for a nameless reason, a small burst of easing happiness.

'Yes, I suppose you could say that', Amy replied with slight amusement.

Haley ran her hands over the smooth, shining gold of the tree structure as it got to the middle of the hymn. Then, something happened.

Haley's body went rigid, her eyes widened, her vision clouded with a blurry visions, the blood in her veins replaced by the magic channelling...the shadowy shapes of people in a temple...a giant bolt of lightning striking a dangerous enemy, and badly disfigured their leader giving him a blind eye and burnt scars...and the constant whispering.

'Thora...because she was born under the strongest thunderstorm in centuries...'

'You stopped being my brother the moment you murdered those three families in cold blood...'

'She will never see the light of the sun...'

'The only way to defeat him is for the mighty weapon to be found and re-forged...'

'What she was born with is very rare...'

'She will return to us. We will one day see her again...'

'Keep her safe...She will need your guidance, as she grows...'

'A daughter of the Nine Realms, a daughter of the gods, a daughter of the universe...distant daughter of the Lord of Thunder, may our voices protect you, and may the light of the aurora forever bless you with guidance...'

The blinding colourful lights drew Haley out of the vision, as she began to breath heavily now on the verge of hyperventilating from the overwhelming shock of witnessing what looked to be a distant past, exactly like the dream. She remembered having this reaction whenever she woke up from a dream, only this reaction was hundred times stronger. The same reaction she had to whenever she was cosmically connected to the magic elements. Haley closed the music box quickly, the melody stopping and the tree fading away into silver gold magic dust as the sounds of thunder rang through her ears; though silent in the distance of the ocean, it was louder inside her head.

A pair of hands gently shook her shoulders, her vision clearing as she saw the hands were Eric's.

'Haley', Eric said with a comforting expression. 'Control your emotions'.

And thanks to the maintaining of focus and breathing exercises, that relaxation monument was enough to bring herself back to a reality where she was not enduring mental emotion torture and powerful magic, or suffering anxiety attacks.

'What was that?' she asked, her voice shaking as she struggled to find the right words. Her eyes looked between Eric and Amy, the latter of whom was now holding a folded piece of paper.

'What did you see, Haley?' Amy asked.

Haley took slow breaths, before speaking.

'When I touched the tree, I saw images. Like my dream, only this time it was…so real. I heard voices. I couldn't the first time round. They weren't just desperate voices, they were voices speaking in the speech of noble blood. And I saw lightning coming through a temple, and lights bright like the Northern Lights that I nearly blacked out'.

The two elder siblings sighed.

'Haley', Eric said. 'What you saw was more than just a dream. It was a vision of your past, when you were just a baby'.

'Your memories are different, compared to humans', Amy answered, before Haley could ask the question. 'They are stronger and more delicate, but the majority of them were blocked out by the continued usage of your abilities. That was why all you saw were blurred figures…Until you turned eighteen and the power of the Aurora Eclipse surged through you, it being the first trigger, with the touch of Yggdrasil from the music box'.

'Yggdrasil', she whispered, knowing the name of the World's Tree from Norse Mythology came up in history classes. The realization was close to bringing back her frustration. 'You know, in almost every conversation we had or every story you told me when I was little, that name came up. Why?'

Seeing Haley's pleading eyes, Amy handed over the still white, perfectly folded parchment. Haley saw a name in perfect italic writing on the front: a name she recognized from the disembodied voices inside her head.

Suspicion changed to astonishment.

Halena.

Disturbed by this new information, Haley turned her widened eyes back to Eric and Amy.

'Open it', Eric encouraged gently.

Haley blinked twice, taking a deep breath, before lowering her eyes back to the letter. Very carefully with shaking hands, she unfolded the paper and opened it, and saw that it was a letter written in very elegant italic writing much like the name on the front, the ink a perfect dark indigo not a smudge or faded quality to it.

To our dearest daughter,

Happy birthday. If you are reading this letter, then you have reached the age where you are now old enough to know the truth about the abilities you were born with. These abilities were given to you for a reason and because of how specially rare and powerful they were, it was part of that reason we were forced to send you away.

And because of who you really are…

Your name is not Haley Freeman…your real name is Halena Thora Antoinette: princess of Asgard and a distant daughter of the Lord of Thunder. You were born and blessed with the powers of thunder and lightning, which you have been drawn to since birth, because of a prophesied enchantment cast by the thunder god and the Norns of Yggdrasil. You can not only control them, but you are connected to them for when you feel danger, it feels danger. When you are in pain, it senses your pain.

Know that sending you away was the hardest and most difficult thing we had to ever do, but it was also the right thing to do. Our enemies have sensed the incredible power within you and has been plotting ways to overthrow our kingdom and destroy you and the royal bloodline, for you have a great destiny which was prophesied three thousand years before your birth.

We love you dearly, our sweet Halena. Even if you couldn't see us, we have been watching over you. And every day, we hold onto the hope that you would one day return to us and take your rightful place as a child of all of the realms.

That time will come soon, as you grow with your gifts, and you will receive more answers.

With all our love,

Your mother and father, Darius and Antoinette

King and Queen of Asgard

Haley re-read the letter over and over again, her eyes scanning every detail like she was saving it into a memory drive projected inside her head. The warmth in her heart gradually changed to shock upon reading the first paragraph about being a princess from a foreign world of ancient cosmology, and then actual disbelief that this was a touching letter left by her parents, before they supposedly died.

And the name from the second paragraph…

Halena Thora Antoinette.

So royal and fitting for a princess with the middle name meaning thunder and lightning in honour of Thor, the thunder god from the Norse legends. And Asgard…the name of one of the Nine Worlds located somewhere in the sky. Now after reading this unexpected letter, everything became more jumbled like millions of pieces of a jigsaw puzzle that remained unfinished since Haley's birth.

'My-my parents', Haley stammered tearfully. 'They're-they're alive?'

Eric and Amy nodded. 'Yes', Amy muttered.

'Everything you heard about other worlds is true', Eric continued. 'Everything your mother and father said about being of royal blood and having special powers…also true. It is the reason you grew up not knowing your actual origins…you are a princess of Asgard: a child of the Nine Realms'.

Haley was unable to find the words, still speechless. She always imagined her brother and sister telling her amazing stories about her parents; of how it warmed her heart they loved her dearly and would do anything to keep her safe as any parent would for their child. But this…this came out differently upon opening that letter. Even more betrayal bubbled up and coursed through Haley's veins, her eyes watering, as she shrugged Amy's hands off her shoulders.

'How could you not tell me?' she muttered angrily, as she struggled to maintain the cosmic energy pulse in her system. 'You lied to me my whole life. Didn't you think I had the right to know?'

Eric and Amy's guilt grew, as they tried to figure out a way to help Haley control her uprising anger, if even the slightest hint of magic emerged. 'We wanted to, but we feared it would be too dangerous and that you would be discovered', Eric proclaimed, as he moved next to Amy giving her a brotherly squeeze on her shoulder.

'By who?' Haley asked, her anger threatening to rise.

'Our enemies…as told in the letter. You have a powerful gift, and – '

Haley let out a short, sarcastic sneer.

'Gift? If it's a gift, or better yet, if what you're saying is true, then why does it feel like since I was a baby I've been cursed by something paranormal?'

The thunder above the lowering sunset came back as if it was becoming in sync with her anger.

'There were times when I thought what I could do was a blessing, being drawn to the elements of the earth and sensing other things around me. But now…now I'm not so sure anymore!' Haley turned her back on her brother and sister not wanting to direct more of her anger towards their guilt, and began to head towards the door, but a gentle grip of her brother's hand held her back.

'Haley, believe me when I say we're sorry', he said sadly.

Unable to hear anymore, Haley pulled her arm away.

'If you don't mind, I want to be alone', she said directing her disappointment in them, wiping away a single tear and quickly walking out of the door.

She considered going back to the party, needing a distraction, but went against it due not only being unable to face Serena or Kelly, but also to her fear of her emotions mentally unleashing her magic and hurting someone she cared about. Realizing something like that could happen caused Haley's heart to skip three beats, as she envisioned that possibility once she was out the front door, after managing to sneak past the remaining party guests. She ran along the sunset-kissed sand dunes, the long grass tickling her fingertips; and her mind projecting endless images of her formulating elements into various shapes, including the ice-ball, the twister of snowflakes and the bolts of lightning, all of which allowing her to finally understand that these activities were connected to her past. And now that the truth was out, she was more uncertain whether to accept it as a beautiful thing or a curse.

Minutes went by, until Haley tripped and fell in a small clearing. She brought her knees to her chest as more tears trickled down her face, continuously haunted by the memories filled with magic and wonder, but the deepest suspicion about the unimaginable occurrences. Haley's lingering thoughts became overcast by the channeling of a breeze coursing through her veins, like the gentle touch of a temperature between ten and fifteen degrees in weather conditions. Pushed by her impulses, she raised her right hand above a small mountain of sand, and the crystallized sand-grains formed into a perfect twister. She slightly smiled, relaxing herself. The sand twister morphed into a striking resemblance pattern of the Northern Lights, the first thing she thought of on her list of most beautiful occurrences to lay eyes upon. Glimmering against the last streaks of sunlight, the glittering sand mirrored the Lights' movements.

Suddenly, everything changed drastically as the sand dropped to the ground, forcing Haley to lose focus. An eerie coldness swept over her skin. Darkness befell the dunes. She sensed something similar to what she felt in Kelly; only this presence was all consuming darkness, which frightened her to the core. A low rumble beneath her feet, like the shift of the earth's crust came. Haley fell onto her side, as she tried to get up and run home to help the others find cover. She made a second attempt to scramble to her feet against the likely to be nine-point-something earthquake, but to no vain.

The last thing she heard was a storm and loud roars and evil laughter as if it was close by, before unconsciousness overwhelmed her.

CHAPTER 7: THE FIRST ENCOUNTER

Uncontrollable shaking, screams and shouts, a smoky smell…all three brought Haley out of her unconscious state. Haley reached for her head. A trickle of blood streaked down it. She must have hit her head on a rock when she passed out. She felt around for a cut, but there was nothing there: also remembering she could heal faster. As her vision cleared, Haley took in her surroundings. The branches of some near trees were blown away and thousands of millions sand grains coated so much of the grass, the short remaining tufts sticking out. The sand covered much of Haley's clothing and stuck most of to the blood on the side of her head. She quickly shook it off.

Haley's eyes widened in horror, realizing they were not deceiving her by judgment of what she saw. The sky was now bloody red, a sign of something devastating. Black smoke rose near her house. Nausea turned her stomach inside out at its smell travelling across the beach. But what was worse was that there were at least fifty or sixty figures emerging from the smoke, surrounding every remaining party member on the beach. Haley flinched, as she doubled over in pain. She realized that she was in connection with people's emotions near her. She felt fear, her friends' fear and her own fear of them dying. But she felt a sense of relief when she reached into the minds of her brother and sister forgetting her anger towards them, feeling their unexpected bravery and will; the same for Kelly and Serena, somehow knowing they would protect them and themselves.

Her one thought was to rush back and help her friends escape whatever was taking them hostage.

But moments were spoken too soon. Haley's magical, but still questionable senses suddenly washed over her entire body. She reached into the thoughts of the dark figures, and gasped the deeper she went. For all she saw and felt was the consuming darkness of powerful evil magic. Another silent gasp escaped her mouth at the sound of heavy footsteps walking over crunching brunches, motivating her to get down onto her stomach, hiding herself behind the tall grass of the highest dune slope. Keeping herself completely hidden, Haley peered through the long grass just enough to learn everything she could about who or what was coming after her.

There were at least four figures in black velvet clothing with hoods over their heads, most of their facial features concealed, but Haley could just make out the pale skin baring still-open blotches and faint scars which made her stomach turn over again. Their poorly manicured nails on their hands were long but stubby. Haley was thankful the hoods concealed their eyes, as she did not want to see how allegedly scary they looked. Their lips were chapped with formulated smirks and sneers. It dawned upon Haley in seconds that these unknown figures was not of Earth, and with no pure light presence flowing through blackened souls.

Their heads turned in Haley's direction, leaving Haley with only one second to lower her head and lie on her back, her heart hammering against her ribcage. She placed her hand over her mouth to regulate her petrified breathing.

One of the human-like figures spoke. A man, or so Haley thought...

'Spread out. Search every area of the dunes', the humanoid man hissed. 'Find her... and remember: the High Lord wants her alive'.

Haley's eyes widened. Peering back through the grass, she watched as the group began to spread out among the sand dunes. The tallest figure was coming up slightly on her left. Haley closed her eyes, held her breath and prayed he wouldn't feel her presence. If he spotted her, it was over for her even though they said they wanted her supposedly alive for whomever their master, this High Lord was. If she put up a fight against the other minion, she was outnumbered either way...

If only there was something she could use to get them away from her...

Then, as if sensing that very thought, Haley felt something cold and delicate appear between her fingers. She opened her eyes, and saw there in her hands was the dagger with the golden trim and beautiful scrollwork. How on earth did it get here? Haley thought to herself, with raised eyebrows.

'*It came in your time of need*', a woman's voice came, answering the rhetorical question. Haley resisted looking around to find the source of the voice. '*There is no time for answers, young one. Use the dagger. Use what you have been taught against the enemy*'.

By enemy, she assumed the four stalking figures. An idea she found to be completely crazy. No way would she be able to go up against these creatures, yet alone kill them even though they were evil. That was not the person she was. And who knows what tricks they had up their sleeves? Haley looked between the hooded man, who stood ten metres away from her, and at the dagger, remembering how, after unwrapping it, entranced she was when she laid eyes on it for the first time.

Still hesitant, Haley unsheathed the dagger, ready to strike, waiting for the right moment. She looked around and much to her relief, the other three creatures disappeared behind the higher sand dune hills. She brought her eyes back to the lone figure, standing with his back turned to her, meaning he would hopefully not see what Haley was about to do coming. She then reevaluated her surroundings again to see what else she could use besides the dagger, spotting broken branches spread out from the earthquake and strong winds. Closing her eyes but keeping to her knees, Haley focused on the image she projected in her mind feeling the elemental magic channel through her as she held her open palm out her hand facing upwards, but kept in the direction of the branches. She opened her eyes to see if the channeling worked.

Sure enough, the branches slowly rose from the ground, and spun and twirled in various directions, formulating into shapes: the same shapes Haley imagined they would take on, as she unleashed the wind magic. The branches began to change. Some broke up into smaller pieces, while others grew out to larger scales, large enough for a dog to carry in its mouth. Haley spied the figure scowling suspiciously at the twister of windswept branches, as they took on the shapes of small birds and bees, like they were remotely programmed to leave a grandfather clock. Energy left her fingertips, the wind coming back stronger than when it first came, and did the unexpected.

The branch tornado attacked the figure, the birds pecking at his exposed skin and the bees crawling and buzzing all over him, as he attempted to attack them with his sword. Haley watched in awe at the actions of the birds and bees. Seeing that the hooded man was still unaware of her presence, Haley got to her feet and, taking careful aim like in her martial arts training, threw the dagger point-blank into the man's back, causing him to let out a yell of pain.

An unexpected fire ignited in her eyes, and the next thing she knew, she was running up to the figure full speed; and jumped onto his back, twisting the dagger deeper into his skin. Blood spilled out and not red blood, but blackened oozing blood like that of a demon. The deeper the blade went, the painful it became for the man. His yelps were a mixture of pain and anger, a determination to bring down his enemy. Haley was his enemy. He refused to be defeated and would continue fighting to the death, even in pain. Sensing his anger building up, Haley suddenly felt the sharp nails of his hand dig deep into her leg, sending a jolt of agony up her spine, but that pain went away when her leg healed by itself. The man finally dropped to his knees and fell onto his stomach, more and more blood spilling out. Haley figured it was a penetration of an artery near the heart, followed by heavy breathing from both the man and Haley…him from dying slowly from severe blood loss and heart failure…Haley from struggling to catch her breath and controlling her mixed emotions towards herself having just unleashed a killing blow for the first time in her life.

She let out one last deep breath to calm herself down and stepped forward to her opponent, a reason deep within her telling her she needed to look this man in the eyes, as his spirit left his body. Haley knelt down, mentally and physically preparing herself for a surprise attack having her dagger ready, and hovered her hand over the man's right shoulder, as she went through a brief phase between considering and reconsidering seeing his face.

Eventually, she found the courage to remove the hood and turn the man over, avoiding his low grunts of pain.

Her emotions changed when she set eyes on the man's now revealed face. She tried her best to display bravery, but underneath it all, she was scared. The man's emotionless face looked like he lost every shred of humanity, displaying pearly white teeth against the chapped lips. The same blotches and faint scars on his pale-skinned face looked like they were faded third degree burns and cuts from a really bad accident. The most haunting feature was the eyes; they were a glowing red with black pupils, filled with nothing but arrogance, hatred and evil.

Haley truly felt nothing towards this man, except hatred and pity. Without any straight thinking, she roughly grabbed his collar with all her strength. Strangely enough, he was lighter in her grip. Either this was down to the amount of weight lifting she did, or this was another supernatural power that emerged within her when the Aurora Eclipse passed by.

'Who the hell are you?' she asked the man with aggression she had never felt before.

The man only answered back a slight chuckling smirk. 'You know. You have known your whole life...Princess Halena'. His blackened blood stained his sharp teeth, as he began to choke on it.

The tightness in Haley's chest increased at the recognition of the name. Anger and hatred towards this man overtook her fear, as she held the dagger to his throat.

'I'll ask you again', she sneered. 'Who are you? And what do you want with me?'

Again, another low cackle escaped the man's mouth, finding Haley's visible threat amusing.

'All...Hail...Nebula', he stated, coughing up more blood. The pupils in his eyes dilated as a blank expression permanently imprinted on his face. Haley checked his pulse...He was dead.

Her hands shook. The man's lifeless eyes would forever cloud her memory. Never in her life had she killed anything, except a spider she found crawling up her arm, while packing up her things before her big move to Cornwall. But a being with a physical resemblance to humans...

She was torn between feeling anguishing guilt and sheer hatred, as she continued to stare into the man's empty red devil-like eyes, dissatisfied with the information she tried to force out of him. What motivated her carry out an interrogation of this kind anyway? Her mind, body and voice were all of a sudden essentially between it being she, and not being she. And why did the man say that statement, before dying?

All...Hail...Nebula...

What did he mean? Did he mean something was coming? The need for answers came to a halt, when Haley heard another shout, this time from a woman with what sounded like an East-European accent.

'There she is! She murdered the captain!' she shouted furiously.

Emotionally terrified, Haley remained rooted to the spot struggling to retain the bravery within her. The same dark magic flowed through the woman like it did with their captain. Haley did not dare look at their faces to compare.

'Halena, have courage...' the angelic woman's voice came again.

As strange as it was, those simple words were enough for Haley to realize she was not going to let herself and her family and friends down.

They needed her help, no matter what the cost.

Moving away from the body, Haley placed her hand firmly on the ground, keeping her magical senses in tact. From what she observed, the woman and the other creatures were five yards away, but their footsteps were hammering loudly in her ears like she was in a locked room and they were trying so hard to break down.

With her hand still its place, Haley reached deep within herself, channeling every element she interacted with: water, wind, thunder, earth, sky, ice. She pictured the formation they would take if combined together. As this happened, the adrenaline pulsed through her veins faster as electricity passed through her body to her fingertips, her heart on the verge of exploding out of her chest. Feeling her fiery eyes glow a brighter blue, she looked up at the sky. Dark clouds rapidly rolled in during the silent incantation, the deep rumble of thunder surging overhead. Haley stood up, slowly turning around to face the figures, as they each surrounded her. She had her dagger withdrawn, the thunder, earth and rain beside her as her allies.

She stared each of them down, waiting for something to happen.

'Take her!' the woman sneered. And the three of them charged forward.

Out of the corner of her eye, Haley spotted the first three drops of rain and pictured them expanding to a larger size together. And with the flick of her hand, the giant water ball swirled into a six-foot tall wave and upon touching the creatures, froze them solid like ice statues for a museum display. Knowing the ice would melt, setting the creatures free, Haley moved her eyes to the thunderclouds above, and envisioned the pain the lightning would cause these figures. Projecting a second incantation, Haley summoned the electric charge exiting her fingertips, producing a lightning bolt and directed it towards the three creatures whose pupils widened in fear. The three flashing sparks of the lightning bolt staked their hearts, but the powerful electricity shattered them into a dozen ice cubes.

Haley's head pounded for a second and a numb-ness tickled her muscles. She assumed it was because of the adrenaline rush. Re-enhancing her focus, Haley turned her attention back to her house, one reason being unable to look at the statue-like icicle pieces of the creatures.

Closing her eyes, Haley tried once again to reach into the minds of the hostages and other hooded creatures. The first attempt was just muffled thoughts that she could not read or understand, but on the second attempt she did not expect to unintentionally break through the surface, and the designation of the words between both parties.

'Eric, Amy: what are they on about?' James' voice came, sounding both suspicious and scared.

'We already told you: she is not here', Eric said, ignoring him, and addressing one of the creatures. 'She died of an incurable illness as an infant. Now, let the hostages go. They have done nothing to you'.

A man's voice came, seemingly ignoring Eric's request to free the others.

'If she is dead, how is it that we can sense her magic?' a man sneered with impatience. 'My master uncovered a mysterious cosmic disturbance occurring on this very world, the same magic that occurred on the day of that child's birth and christening!'

Silence fell.

With no other way, Haley began running over the hills of the sand dunes back towards her house, keeping her mind connected to the others' minds.

'Tell me: son and daughter of Vladimir and –'

'HE IS NOT OUR FATHER!' Amy shouted angrily. But the sound of a flat palm colliding with her face hard stopped her. Haley flinched in anger, as she heard and felt her sister's pain of being slapped. Then, came Eric's enraged shout and the sickening sound of bones breaking, telling Haley that one of the hooded creatures broke one of his arms or legs, or both. At that point, she ran faster infuriated by the torturous methods the captors were carrying out on both her siblings and her friends.

'Son and daughter of Vladimir and Antoinette', the man sniggered, making it quite clear to Eric and Amy threateningly. 'If you value the lives of your friends and family, you will tell me where the girl is'.

'You'll kill us anyway', Eric said, coughing up blood after being punched in the face and having his arm or leg broken. 'We will never tell you where she is'.

The man let out another low growling sneer. 'Then, your little friends will suffer, until you reveal her location!'

Terror mixed with her anger, upon hearing the slow, painful screams. Her running changed to a full-length sprint, the cosmic magic channeling through her body once again. Only a few seconds passed, when her eyes burnt like a roaring fire, her hands tingled as a breeze pulsed towards her palms. What happened next was something Haley did not know she could control, at not at her own record in her sense.

As soon as the creatures came into full view, she lifted her arms high above her head, some of them turning their heads in her direction, arrogant recognition shining their eyes as they locked eyes with Haley's. Like the three she confronted on the dunes, the fifty or so were cloaked in black robes, with pale white skin, poorly manicured nails and dark facial expressions, and red eyes.

Haley half-expected herself to be scared, but all fear extinguished upon laying eyes on the remaining hostages: Eric, Arianna, James, Emilie, Matthew, Serena, Kelly and four of her friends from school.

Just as the creatures opened an attack upon her, with their swords drawn and glowing menacing eyes, Haley felt the draw of dark energy, blackening the atmosphere, between herself and the hostages with Eric and Arianna's eyes widening with worry, begging her to run.

'*Haley, no! Get out of here!*' their voices shouted inside her head. But she would not hear a word of it, not when their lives were in dangers.

Ignoring the pleads, Haley slammed her hands together with strength she did not know she possessed, compared to all the times during her training sessions. With the power of that strength followed a vibration of sonic boom, closely matching to that of a frequency to a loud explosion. The force of it sent the creatures nearest to Haley's location flying over forty feet towards the thundery sky. Then, out of nowhere, the largest lightning bolts collided with them, practically causing them pain so intense that Haley felt it and heard their horrific, dying screams, until they finally vaporized into ash and dust, coming down like snowflakes, the very thought of which made Haley's skin crawl. It touched her skin, as she remembered to her own horror that the ash used to be people. She couldn't help but feel anguishing guilt towards the fact that she killed more, even though she classed it as self-defense. A sudden wave of dizziness caused her to sway and she looked around, blinking multiple times to clear the blurry spectrums in her vision line.

She fell on her hands and knees.

The sound of calm footsteps approaching caught her attention. Haley slowly lifted her head, struggling to avoid the supposed side effects from using her magic. Though she still had a foggy vision, Haley could tell that they were the only creatures left standing.

'So…this is supposed to be the descendent of the thunder god', a man's deep voice hissed. 'Not so strong now, is she?' The other creatures laughed, mentally agreeing with him.

Haley was too exhausted to stand, realizing although she just mysteriously vaporized numerous supernatural creatures with elemental magic, whatever was going to happen next, she was going to lose for sure if she didn't find a way to recover.

The man's rough, blotched hand grabbed her by the chin, forcing her to look him in the eyes and stay awake, pushing the drowsiness to one side.

'Well, little princess', he hissed. 'You have shown tremendous strength, coming to your family's aid…But after what you just did to our fellow comrades, you are too dangerous and a threat to our kind and our master'.

Haley's fearful eyes wondered who this master of theirs was and why he considered her a threat because of her powers. Through her slightly cleared vision, she saw the man and his followers a state of meditation, their eyes closed, their posture still as the three others who were turned into icicles. It reminded her of a movie scene she watched where a mystical trial took place for bad witches or wizards, and the good witches mentally decided the best form of justice.

But there was no crime Haley committed, she thought to herself. Aside from defending herself from an attack she was still confused about and why she was the target.

After a minute or two, the creatures exited their meditation and turned back to Haley with arrogant smirks. Frightened, Haley looked behind them and saw Eric and Amy defending themselves against the remaining creatures, shouting for everyone to run for cover, and trying to rush her aid.

'Any last words…little princess', the man sneered, holding the tip of his sword to her heart.

Haley simply just stared into his eyes, trying to show she can be brave. The sword's point gave her a sharp poke, just enough to draw blood, causing Haley to let out a small hiss of pain.

'Go…to…hell', she said through gritted teeth.

The corner of the man's lip turned upright, as he raised his sword above his head playing judge, jury and now executor. Haley closed her eyes, no longer able to stay awake or keep them open to watch everyone unfold. For at least ten seconds, she awaited her quick and painful death.

Nothing came.

Something sudden happened to replace that feeling of death on her shoulders. She saw the darkness behind her eyes, being replaced by something unexpectedly bright and powerful. Opening one eye, she saw the creatures look towards the commotion.

Haley saw up in the sky a stream of bright light in the formation of a tornado funnel, opening up wonders of the night. Its brightest colors were the greens, blues, indigos, and violets, a pure representation of the Aurora Eclipse, Haley guessed. Even from this distance, Haley felt a sea of grateful warmth crawl up and down her skin, praying that God or whatever savior of the universe would protect her family and her friends. Sure enough, out of the swirling gateway came at least ten figures who looked to be assisting Eric and Amy with finger movements conjuring up magic forms, and withdrawing of swords, and bows and arrows.

Now was her chance.

Feeling a burst of strength return to her, Haley clenched her fists together harnessing the little magic energy she had left bringing them to close her face right in front of her eyes. White energy began bursting one of the palms of her hands, and the fearless sounds of thunder and lightning once again could be heard above, growing louder and stronger in sequence with the white light.

It reached its peak and Haley, ignoring the pain she was experiencing and the blood dripping out of her nose, opened her hands as the creatures turned back towards her having noticed the bright whiteness behind them. As the white magic burst into a giant, shimmering ball of light, it knocked them backwards with the lightning bolts vaporizing them into dust.

After that, Haley's energy no longer flowed through her body, and she collapsed onto the soft sand in exhaustion. As she closed her eyes, clouded figures approached her, one of them lifting her into their arms.

CHAPTER 8: ASGARD

Never had Haley experienced a far worse splitting headache until this moment. She thought she had the craziest dream about Eric and Amy revealing that she was a princess from another world, which she reacted to in utter disbelief. Next thing she knew: she was using elemental magic, notably thunder and lightning to fight off scary-looking creatures, who were trying to kill her. Despite feeling oddly peculiar about the whole episode, Haley was relieved to be in bed. Except it did not feel like her bed at all. The sheets were like silk. Thankfully, the clustering headaches settled down enough for her to sit up on her elbows. That was until she noticed what she was wearing.

It was a periwinkle blue dress, the inner skirt being made of satin and the outer skirt coating it with a see-through silk embroidered with an endless Celtic patterning of gold reaching from the shoulder straps to the waist area.

Haley touched her neck and chest, relieved to find the triquetra pendent still there, the only connection to her parents, along with the charm bracelet and Celtic-knotted ring.

She then looked around at the bedroom.

Imprinted on the domed ceiling were paintings showcasing people worshipping an ancient king wielding a hammer, a crystal chandelier hung from the middle; opposite the balcony doors and windows was a henna-styled engraving double door. The curtains were a silky golden silver of crystallized material; the tiny specs representing distant stars. Haley eyed the large circular bed she was on, admiring the soft silk covers and pillows in shimmering gold and white. On each side of the bed was a polished bedside table: one had a small pile of three books, her dagger on top, and the other a bronze vase of white roses. She studied the rest of the bedroom and saw there was a beautifully detailed floral and vine designed dressing table, complete with one large mirror and a smaller mirror on either side, along with a stool baring a similar design to the table. There was a decorative double wardrobe with a similar pattern as both the dressing table and the chest of drawers.

After a long while, Haley swung her body over the edge of the bed not without noticing the low-heeled gold shoes she had on her feet. She stood up, the echoes of her footsteps in sequence with the singing birds from outside one of the already open windows. She walked up to the dressing table, picked up one of the ornamental bottles on the dressing table, took the lid and sniffed it. Rose, her favorite scent: but how did whoever lived in this building know this?

Speaking of which, she still needed to figure out where she was.

Slowly and hesitantly, Haley picked up a shoulder wrap on the stool chair and wrapped it around her shoulders, before heading to the balcony door. Outside, Haley could see mountains and hills, and parts of what appeared to be a very large city, definitely not a city like London, Paris or New York. Without question, Haley slowly gripped the door handle and pushed the doors open. At first, all Haley saw was bright sunlight.

Eventually, the reflective coloring cleared upon stepping onto the balcony.

'Wow', Haley muttered under her breath at the sight in front of her.

Outside was the most enchanting kingdom she had ever seen. Everything from the palace she was in to the town below was like every fairytale she read as a child coming to life. It was majestically enchanting from marble stone to stained glass window, built on a mountain-surrounding land, buildings with domed roofs of stain glass designs baring Norse inspirations around ancient imagery, completely unlike any other palace. Magical with ancient statues of gods and goddesses; and the pale golden marble breathtaking fountain, standing in front of the large gateway to a bridge. Haley spotted the rose gardens and hedges constructed in a miniature labyrinth, leading to the statue of a goddess. One plain green field Haley saw had what appeared to be knights practicing sword-fighting and teaching children to use magic. Beyond the gateway stood a large city, most definitely unlike any city she visited; but beautifully made up of solid marble stone in pure grey and pale gold, the rooftops domed and red. Haley could see citizens of the city; walking around running errands. What was odd about these citizens was their clothing, consisting of robes and dresses from an ancient time.

Haley's eyes shifted up to the sky. Electric blue with small white clouds swaying by, but the most intriguing about it was the billions of stars, passing comets and moons were visible enough for her to quickly identify by name; like the Pole Star, Comet Hale-Bopp and the brightest star in Earth's night sky, Sirius. All she saw through her telescope all those years ago, all she pictured and painted on her blank canvases, capturing them in a special moment.

Three knocks at the door interrupted the peaceful silence. Haley gasped, fear coursing through her veins. She stumbled back into the bedroom, making a quick debate whether or not to hide her dagger behind her back.

Unexplained warrior instinct, Haley thought.

'C-come in?' she said in questionable confusion.

The double door opened and in walked a young maiden. She was pretty with a petite figure fitting perfectly around the lilac dress she wore. She appeared older than Haley, possibly in her late twenties. Her long brown hair was tied into a simple plait reaching down to her waist, and her eyes an emerald green. She carried a tray of food and drink. Haley eyed the tray, taking in the bronze plate of strawberries, blueberries and melon, with crusty bread and honey, and a goblet of fresh water.

'Ah, good to see you are awake, My Lady', she said with a cheery voice, bowing her head slightly. 'I was instructed to bring you some breakfast'.

Suspicious, Haley looked directly into the girl's eyes.

'Umm…w-who are you?' she asked, stuttering.

'My name is Angela', the girl answered, putting the tray down onto another table close to the bed. Haley hesitantly grabbed a blueberry, but just played with it in her hand. 'I am your handmaiden, and your physician'.

'My physician?' Haley questioned.

'You were unconscious for some time, my lady. Myself and other healers examined you and saw you used an immense amount of magic. It exhausted your mind and body. If you'd have kept it up without recovery, it would have overwhelmed you completely'.

A shiver travelled down Haley's spine at the ending of that last sentence.

'Y-you mean it would have killed me?' she muttered, knowing the possible outcome. Angela did not need to nod or shake her head, or say yes or no. Haley saw it in her eyes, confirming the answer.

She let out a shuddering breath, sitting back down on the bed.

'I must be dreaming', Haley mumbled stubbornly. 'How else would I suddenly be in the bedroom in a kingdom, in a dress like this?' She gestured to the princess dress she had on, reminiscing about all the times she played dress up with her school friends.

Another knock at the door prevented Haley from theorizing any further. It obviously wasn't Angela's place to say, Haley thought. Both girls looked to the door. Haley put her hand on her dagger. Angela seemed to take note of this.

Suddenly, Haley began to hear Angela's voice inside her head.

'*The princess would like to know who comes*', she said.

Another voice broke through the barriers of her mind: it was Kelly. '*Tell her it is the Lady Keilantra*', she proclaimed.

Keilantra, Haley thought to herself. The name meaning magical princess of the night sky, the name that Haley was told was Kelly's original name…Will this dream ever end? How much more fairytale-turned-reality facets could Haley take, with the fifty-fifty chance of this all being a dream? Then again, knowing it was Kelly relaxed her and she focused her mind to try and send a response.

'*You may come in*', she echoed.

Worked like a charm, Haley thought.

The bedroom double door opened, revealing Kelly. Except she was nothing like the Kelly Miller Haley practically grew up with. In fact, she was more like a noblewoman who just stepped out of a children's storybook. She was in a strapped, off-the-shoulder blue flowing dress, and the inner skirt silver. The waviness in her blonde hair was now curled and clipped back into a plaited crown and light blue highlights mixed in her layers, which Haley found to be an odd feature for her best friend, as she had never seen her with colored highlights.

'Kelly?' Haley uttered in disbelief.

Shaking it off, she immediately rushed over to Kelly and hugged her.

'Thank goodness, you're alright', Kelly whispered.

Haley smiled and said, 'Me too'. They pulled away. 'I-I don't even understand what's happening. I-I keep saying that what I saw was a dream'.

'I'm afraid it was not a dream', Kelly answered, upon hearing those words. 'Everything that happened on Midgard was real'.

Haley's eyes widened, remembering the earthquake, the arrival of those creatures and –

Her friends, her family!

'They're dead, aren't they?' she gasped, a tear streaming down her face. The likely deaths of Eric, Amy, Matthew, Emilie, James, Serena and all her friends hit her like a full-forced tidal wave. She was alone, no one to turn to except her best friend and a total stranger.

'No, My Lady', Angela reassured her. 'Your brother and sister are alright, but they needed to recuperate from injuries they received during the battle'.

'They-they were hurt?' Haley became scared.

'And they will recover in no time. They are stronger than you think'.

'And-and w-what about m-my friends?' Haley asked, shakily. 'P-please...please tell me they're alright too'.

Kelly, or rather Keilantra sat down next to Haley and took a hold of her hand comfortingly. 'I promise you, they're alive and safe, Halena', she reassured her. And that weight on Haley's shoulders was lifted. 'But all they witnessed has been forgotten'.

'What do you mean?' she asked, putting aside her relief.

'Their memories were erased of the whole encounter'.

'Erased?'

Keilantra pursed her lips together. 'Your brother and sister have the ability to manipulate minds, so they can compel people to forget certain events'.

'Manipulate minds?' she repeated, still in disbelief through narrowed lips.

She smoothed her nightdress, feeling more awkward by the material.

'Every Cosmos Being, especially the Royal Family, was born with the gift of mind manipulation', Keilantra explained. 'The mind manipulation works only if we project the memory spell in our own minds to erase the memories of a being, or give them alternative memories completely different to the originals'.

'What did you do then?' Haley repeated the question.

'They made them believe that you went away for a three-month summer art programme'.

'And you have that power too, Halena', Keilantra proclaimed. 'Every being within the Cosmos has it, but only use it when it is absolutely necessary to protect their loved ones'.

Haley's breathing heaved. 'Every being in the Cosmos" she questioned. 'I'm in one of the places...aren't I? This is the place where I was born, wasn't it?'

'Yes', Keilantra smiled. 'This is Asgard...Welcome home, Halena'.

Her brief moment of clarity became a moment of awe, Haley looking back towards the still-open balcony doors at the enchanting kingdom of Asgard: the name as beautiful as when she heard and read about it in school textbooks, even repeating it in her head over and over again after reading her parents' letter. Her astonishment increased, the realization reaching its peak.

'Oh my goodness!' she said, letting out a small laugh of wonder which caused Keilantra and Angela to jump out of their skin. 'Asgard: one of the Nine Realms connected to the branches of Yggdrasil the Tree of Life, the centre of the Cosmos! The tree holding the universe together, with three sacred wells…the tree that has animals inhabiting it: a dragon, a hawk and an unnamed eagle, a squirrel who delivers messages, and four stags named Douinn, Dvalinn, Duneyrr and Durapror'.

Haley stopped her incredulous babbling, frozen in utter bewilderment.

'What just happened there?' she asked the two girls, who displayed recognition towards the newly cultivated characteristic. Sure, she read about the Nine Worlds in her A-Level history classes, but what she just blundered out sounded above and beyond.

'It is the All-Knowledge', Angela explained. 'It activates when a being of the Cosmos, including humans, journeys to the other worlds, by passing through the Bifrost gateway, blessing them with heightened intelligence and knowledge of all stories told in Norse Legends'.

'How come this All-Knowledge activated, when my memories as a baby started to come back after the Aurora Eclipse?' Haley asked.

'You were raised amongst the humans', Keilantra answered. 'At the time, you were unfamiliar with the Nine Realms' cultures, but the magic of the Aurora Eclipse sensed your magic. And also, because your memory is so powerful and highly valuable, that most of it became blocked. It would not have been aware to you until you were eighteen'.

'I remember bits and pieces, where my family, including Eric and Amy, were looking down at me', Haley gave a small smile, recapping the memory. 'Two other people were there…a man and a woman. There was love in their eyes, so pure and eternal…' Realization dawned upon her. 'They were my parents, weren't they?'

'Yes', Keilantra said. 'And they are waiting for you in the Hall of Glaosheimr as we speak, for they are anxiously overjoyed to see you'.

Haley's knee buckled. 'They are?' she asked rhetorically. 'But…but what do I say to them? I…I don't know how I feel about all this. I haven't even had time to process all of this'.

Sensing her anxiety growing, Keilantra stepped forward to bring Haley into another comforting hug. But it did not stop Haley's heart pump blood and magic through her veins.

'Everything will be alright, Halena', she said compassionately. 'Your brother and sister will be there, and once you get to know your mother and father, you will see how much they truly love you'.

'But…but how will I know?' she asked, trembling.

'You will know it and feel it', Angela stated, a hopeful twinkle in her eye. Haley just gave a reluctant smile, wishing she felt the same way. For now, she had to push it aside and remain focused on her next task: to get more answers and find out why she just stepped inside a fairytale storybook.

*

Haley was grateful they gave her an hour to gather her thoughts and have her breakfast – the most delicious breakfast she had ever tasted – and get ready for her big meet-the-parents entrance. She sat still on the stool at the dressing table, while Angela touched up her hair and applied light makeup on her face and the rose perfume. Keilantra stood to one side waiting patiently. During the remainder of this hour, Haley mentally campaigned to herself whether to start another polite conversation. At the same time struggling psychologically with the surreal fact that she was of royal blood.

She maintained her calm tranquility, deciding to make polite conversation to Angela who had done nothing but be nice to her. 'So', she paused with a nervous smile, fidgeting with her fingernails, fighting the urge to bite. 'I take it you know my parents very well?'

Angela smiled brightly. 'Yes, my lady. Through my mother, Sula at least…She was there, the day you were born'.

Haley thought, upon hearing those words, she had a brief flashback of a queen giving birth to a daughter. 'She was?' was all she could get out.

'Yes. She told me from the moment Aurora Eclipse blessed you, she knew there was a strong bond between yourself and the queen, and you have the purest heart'.

Haley wondered what this strong bond meant and why it was cosmically connected to herself, and an astronomical phenomenon like the Aurora Eclipse.

'Could you just call me Haley, please?' the sudden out-of-the-blue question slipped out at her impulse. Deep silence filled the room, until Keilantra approached,

Haley preparing herself another lecture like she was a young child needing guidance on how to behave.

'Halena, I don't think it's proper to –' Angela began, before Keilantra speak, but Haley cut her off secretly exasperating all the interferences she put up with for eighteen years.

'Look, I appreciated what you are doing for me…but I don't want to be treated like royalty', Haley explained. 'It's just too complicated. And being called by another name is one. To me, I'm still Haley, the girl who loves art, who loves surfing…'

The words drifted away, as she dazed deep into thought.

She thought the water in her goblet rippled, slowly rising to form the shape of a hilltop. It became still as quickly as it appeared. Keilantra and Angela exchanged glances, coordinating a telepathic conversation. Haley remembered when those monstrous creatures entered a deep meditation. The flashback of the sword blade raised above her head drew her out of it.

'From what your brother and sister said, your artistry is something else', Angela complimented. 'If it means that much to you, then yes', Angela said. 'We will call you Haley'.

Haley smiled. 'Thank you', she replied, relieved that they understood her feelings at this point, minus the many hundreds of currently unanswered questions swarming around in her head. 'I'll show you what I draw and paint when I get the time.

Angela smiled. 'I would like that, my lady – I mean – Haley'.

A knock at the door caused both girls to whirl around. Keilantra called for whoever was on the other side. There stood two men and judging by their appearance, they were guards or rather knights each baring an athletic physique underneath the gold silver metallic armour they wore with a navy blue cloak baring the triquetra symbol, the Asgardian crest Haley guessed, very much like the charm on her necklace. One had dark hair and intense blue-grey eyes while the other had blondish brown and blue eyes, with a scruff of a beard. Although there was something about the handsome dark-haired one that caught Haley's attention in an electrifying way, but she shrugged it off.

'It is time, my dear best friend', Keilantra said compassionately.

The blondish guard bowed to Haley. 'My lady, we are here to escort you to the king and queen'.

Haley's stomach turned over, the butterflies flying around, but she kept the nausea down. It would have been embarrassing, if she threw up in front of her parents, who are not only her parents, but the king and queen of Asgard! She swallowed hard and just looked down at the floor delivering a simple nod, not without glancing at the dark-haired boy again, who winked at her with a smile, making her blush. Robotically, Haley dragged her feet forward into the long hallway feeling slightly awkward in the dress she wore.

The hallway pillars were made up of open gaps leading out onto a longer balcony, the warm summer breeze touching Haley's skin. Everything was pale gold and grey, pure marble stone, clear and polished. Haley examined the artifacts: a large Celtic-patterned vase containing more white roses on a navy blue cloth draped over a small table, an assorted number of paintings of past kings and queens, one of which featured gods and goddesses being worshipped by people, and Celtic-patterned candle stands.

Everything looked antique, but also brand-new. Either they were enchanted to remain this unique, or the servants of the royal household took their duties seriously. On the ceiling were four crystal chandeliers, very much like the one on the domed ceiling in Haley's new bedroom.

The knights led Haley and the two girls down a flight of stairs, and that was when it hit her like a giant wave…the all-too-familiar trigger of memories arranged on a card full of images, until one dominated to the top: one of a woman breathing and screaming, bringing her child into the world, followed by the deafening echoes of thunder and swift flashes of lightning. Haley suddenly realized it was a flashback of the day of her birth. It fast-tracked before her eyes like a big movie sequence.

Keilantra squeezed her hand.

'*It was the day of my birth*', she uttered telepathically, before her best friend could even ask. '*There was so much thunder and lightning that day, that it pushed me to enter the world…And my mother: she felt it too, like it was encircling the womb to brand me with its power…as if I was destined to inherit it…or something*'.

'*As we said before, you have a very powerful memory*', Keilantra replied back. '*Because of your growing connection to Asgard, it is starting to come back to you*'.

'*I don't understand*', Haley pointed out.

'I mean, because you were raised among humans, you had zero contact with the Realms, aside from myself and your brother and sister, until the passing of the Aurora Eclipse. That was when your earliest memories as an infant started to come back to you'.

They walked along a patio by a perfect turquoise blue lake – Haley thought she saw mermaids swimming, which she believed didn't exist. Maybe she had been reading too fairytales, but this mystifyingly beautiful kingdom casted doubts over her mind, especially with its beauty shining upon the sun's rays and the everlasting moonlight, and stars.

Haley telepathically spoke to Keilantra and Angela, preoccupying herself. *'So…what are they like?'* she asked out of curiosity. *'My parents?'*

'Fearless…and kind', Angela replied. *'A lot like you'*.

The two girls smiled underneath their unreadable expressions, but Haley on the other hand had a sense of uncertainty. Yes, what she saw in the visions was perhaps the ultimate love and strength in families, but her deepest concern was not fitting into this supposedly extraordinary civilization, after being kept in the dark for the past eighteen years. Minutes passed, until the knights came to a halt in front of another double door, carved in an ancient pattern of flower vines, birds and butterflies. It swung open as if they sensed their presence. What sort of magic was this? Haley thought.

She dragged her feet forward, astounded all she was seeing around her.

The Hall of Glaosheimr resembled the inside of an ancient temple, with at least ten marble stone pillars on one side with olden statues, one in between two of each. Behind each was an open gap, showing another breath-taking view of the city that she began to compare it to Mount Olympus. Haley then reviewed the longest painting she had ever seen. It featured noble and handsome knights in battle, queens and ladies of court being a symbol of radiant beauty, wisdom and elegance. In the central part of the painting was a hammer-wielding god on a mountaintop, fighting off giants. At the very end of the hall stood a set of two large thrones, each with a red cushion attached to the seat – thanks to the All-Knowledge, Haley identified it as Hlidskjalf, the high seat designed for the rulers of Asgard to see all Realms. Three smaller throne-like chairs stood on the middle platform, Haley assumed were Eric's Amy's…and hers. Two guards stood next to the thrones, straight and noble. In front of the thrones were five other people having what appeared to be an important discussion. Three of whom were Eric, Amy and Serena, whose usual brown hair now had caramel highlights against blue and green: a perfect counterpart to her heterochromia eyes, alongside the green and silver off-the-shoulder dress with long open sleeves; the other two, a man and woman Haley did not recognize with their backs turned. The brunette haired woman held the man's hand lovingly.

Haley guessed that they were her parents.

'…now he, along with his many followers, grow stronger', Eric said. 'We can no longer keep her hidden, now that we are on the verge of discovering the true extent of her powers'.

'Your children speak the truth', Selena spoke. 'They have done all they can to protect and guide her, but the time has come for her to be taught to gain full control and fight with us'.

The man and woman looked at each other for a moment. 'Very well', they replied to all parties.

Eric and Amy were the first to notice Haley, who was taken aback yet again, as they were nothing like the brother and sister who raised her.

She laughed on the inside when she thought they stepped through a time portal, coming out dressed differently but keeping the same personalities. Eric was wearing dark blue robes and black boots. His right arm was bandaged up, being the one Haley heard snap in two. Attached to the black Celtic-patterned belt around his waist was a sword, which Haley could just see from inside the sheath was silver, glinting against the sunlight coming through the open gaps. Amy's appearance was dissimilar from her in-house image of jeans, t-shirts and blouses. She was wearing a long one-shoulder robed dress of turquoise blue silk material held by a golden Celtic-patterned waistband. Her hair, tied up an elegantly plaited fishtail style, shone lightly alongside the sparkle on her gold earrings. Her left wrist was also bandaged from a broken wrist.

Relief washed over Haley at the sight of them being alive, but at the same time she could not ignore the wondering astonishment and slight betrayal of seeing them like this. Despite it, she immediately rushed forward and hugged both of them.

'It's so good to see you, little sister', Eric whispered in her ear.

'We were so worried', Amy muttered in happiness. 'We thought you would never wake up'.

Haley broke away from them to closely examine their injuries.

'When Kelly – I mean Keilantra', she corrected not quite used to it yet. 'When she told me you were hurt, I-I was so scared'.

Amy caressed her cheek, while Eric took hold of her hand.

'You need not worry, Halena', she said comfortingly. 'The Nebulans struck us badly, but we had the best healers in Asgard. But you…you were so brave on that beach'.

Haley sighed, and sobbed under her breath.

'Halena?' Amy asked worriedly.

'It's just - ', Haley paused, all the anger about the lies gone. 'I thought you were dead'.

She pulled them both into another hug, praying and hoping they were actually alive and not ghosts. The small reunion was only interrupted when Haley locked eyes with the king and queen of Asgard, her parents, for the first time in forever.

There they stood, her long-lost parents, a glimpse in their eyes hoping that seeing their long-lost daughter wasn't an illusion. Memories rushed back to Haley of her parents and her as a baby, while she took in their appearances, her feelings conflicted.

Her mother, the queen's beauty, stunned Haley, especially given the resemblance she shared with her. She looked to be in her late-thirties, though mentally older by hundreds or even thousands of years. Her flowing brunette hair travelled down to her waist, some of it in a half-up crown braid, clipped in place by sterling silver clips. Her eyes, kind and filled with wisdom, were electric indigo in a shade of aqua blue, her delicately smooth skin displaying her exquisite cheekbones and rouged lips. She wore a flawless blue gown with a matching roped cloak over her shoulders, held by a buckle baring the triquetra symbol. Her father, the king was a tall, broad-shouldered man, wearing armour and navy blue robes. Judging by his age, he was in his mid-forties, mentally the same as the queen. He had darkish-brown hair contrasting against his small struff of a beard, with blue eyes very much like Haley's.

Out of the corner of Haley's eye, Keilantra dropped down into a low curtsey. 'My lord and lady', Keilantra pronounced clearly. 'May I present your daughter…Princess Halena'.

With a look of guidance, Keilantra turned to her ever so slightly and nodded. Haley lowered herself into an awkward curtsey, like weights were suddenly dragged her down on invisible chains. By the time she stood back up, her parents were about two to three feet from her, allowing her to look deeper beyond their appearances. Though there was nothing but pure wisdom, compassion and love, there was also sadness having overrun all those happy emotions, probably ever since they sent her away. As they edged closer, Haley considered taking a step back but her mind and body kept her glued to the spot, her parents still looking as though they couldn't believe their eyes.

A single tear streamed down the queen's cheek as she displayed a smile and gently caressed Haley's cheeks to make sure she was physically real. The feeling of warmth in her mother's palms was unlike any warmth Haley felt in her life. It was the warmth of longing love a mother would give to her child, something Haley never experienced before, something she longed for. Her father had a gaze of overjoyed proudness, after being apart from her for so long.

Her bottom lip quivering, Haley mirrored their expressions, tears filling her eyes as more images flashed past her by that one single touch; images of her letting out little giggles, as her parents smiled at her joyously watching her play with the elements. It was not how she imagined meeting her parents, but none of it mattered. All the shuddering anger she showed towards all the secrecy she tolerated since childhood melted away upon connecting with them in one simple look. Keilantra was indeed right about knowing, seeing and feeling this, she thought.

'Halena', her mother whispered, her voice as angelic as when Haley first heard it in the disembodied form; and her indigo eyes glistening in unshed tears. 'It is her, my love. Our beautiful Halena'.

Haley looked towards her father again.

'Halena', he muttered emotionally. 'Our angel of the stars'.

As they hugged her, the warmth became stronger, her father gently stroking her hair, her mother holding her never wanting to let her go. Haley, with minor hesitance, returned the hug holding them for exactly twenty seconds before pulling away slowly, taking a precise moment to retain the thousands of questions she had buzzing around in her head. She stood frozen on the spot, silent as a mouse, still processing this new revelation; awkward in her princess dress, looking between her parents, siblings, Keilantra, Serena and the knights.

'Halena, our parents', Amy declared. 'King Darius and Queen Antoinette of Asgard'.

Hearing those names sounded like they were the perfect match – a mysterious, but epic love: gracefully kind and everlasting.

'H-hello', Haley stuttered.

Antoinette caressed her cheeks again. 'Welcome home...our dearest daughter', her mother said, her smile never leaving her face.

'We cannot tell you how long we have dreamt of this moment', her father voiced with pure emotion. 'We have thought of you everyday'.

'Umm...thank you', Haley replied, feeling skeptical about the whole scene unfolding.

Her parents turned towards Eric and Amy.

'And thank you once again, Eric and Arianna, for taking care of her', Darius said. 'We cannot tell you how contented we are to finally have our three children back'.

'Wait', Haley interrupted, with a quizzing stare as everyone turned to her. 'Eric and Arianna? Not Eric and Amy?' It wasn't hard for Haley to notice the glinting guilt behind these smiles.

'Lord Eric', Eric declared.

'And Lady Arianna', Amy pronounced, as Haley eyed her more than Eric.

'Arianna?' she asked. 'Your real name is...Arianna?'

Her sister nodded.

'So...all those times I overheard those conversations between you two...when Eric called you by that name, they weren't my imagination', Haley implied.

'No, they weren't', Arianna answered. 'Like Keilantra, I too adopted an alias as Eric and I agreed on taking the surname Freeman to be more human'.

'And that meant forging our own life records, including your birth, Halena. Even compelling people to believe our stories about you and ourselves', Eric explained.

Haley thought back to the times she accidently eavesdropped on Eric and Arianna, even remembering the look of wonder in their faces, whenever they saw her do something supernaturally inhuman, her healing herself included.

'Kelly – sorry I mean – Keilantra', Haley corrected herself again. 'She told me you erased my friends' memories of what happened on the beach'.

'You are correct, little sister', Eric replied. 'As Keilantra made you aware, yes…they were compelled to ensure their safety. And for the sake of the Nine Realms…'

'Why?'

'Because we have enemies, who are now becoming aware of your existence', King Darius proclaimed. 'Enemies who are presumably willing to target you and anyone close to you'.

Another feeling sunk to the pit of her stomach. Who could possibly want to destroy her and the people she cares about? Was it linked to her past, and this so-called enemy who sent those red-eyed creatures with dark magic after her?

'So, it's my fault then', she blunted out. The family and the knights looked at her in disbelief. Her mother, Queen Antoinette stepped forward to place her hands on Haley's shoulders, Haley torn between flinching and accepting this motherly comfort.

'Of course not, dear daughter', she said. 'Do not think like that. None of what happened is your fault. You must understand that everything Eric and Arianna did was to keep you safe'.

'Then please…please explain it to me', Haley begged, fidgeting with her fingers to keep her elemental magic channeling in check. 'I have been lied to for the past eighteen years, and now I'm hearing that I'm a princess of Asgard, with magical powers. Then, the next thing I know I'm fighting those monsters, who attacked me and my family.

'I killed them…I killed them which I still feel guilty about, but at the same time I shouldn't be! I don't even know if this is a dream I'm not waking up from!'

Electricity pulsed through her veins, feeling and hearing the surge of thunder and lightning. The magic only settled down, when she closed her eyes and thought of her happy memories on Earth.

'We will explain everything to you, Halena', Darius promised, interrupting her moment's peace. 'But first tell us…what do you remember?'

Haley bit her lip as she recalled unforeseen encounter over and over again on a continuous loop.

'There was an earthquake, so strong that I passed out', she answered, her glass eyes on nothing but her fidgety fingers, bracelet and ring. 'I remember feeling this darkness around me, as if I was standing right next to it, and heard these voices in my head: some filled with fear and suffering, some evil. Then, I...I heard footsteps and there were these creatures with white, stone-cold skin and deep unhealed scars. And I...I killed them. When I ran across the beach, I-I unleashed a shock wave, striking those monsters with lightning. After that, I felt exhausted...like my body was dying'.

'Your gifts are so powerful, that your mind and body at this stage are not yet trained enough to create magic on an indefinite loop', Antoinette explained. 'But once you are capably strong enough, you will be able to do so without...without killing yourself in the process'. The five-second pause between her mother's words told Haley that her parents would have faced a reality of losing her a second time, despite just getting her back. She sympathized them for that, but retained her focus unwilling to let herself be distracted by these mind-crossing thoughts.

'Guess that explains why I felt dizzy and weak, with a nose bleed like I was suffering a cerebral hemorrhage', Haley mumbled. All, except her family, and Serena and Keilantra, raised their eyebrows, another indication of them having lesser knowledge about Earth's modern cultures. Had they ever visited Earth at all? Haley thought to herself.

'Bleeding in the brain, causing severe headaches, seizures and fainting spells?' she tried to give a alternative answer. They nodded, satisfied. 'But it doesn't explain why those creatures came after me'.

'You have rare gifts, due to you being a very powerful descendent of the Thunder God, that they now consider you a threat', Darius stated. Haley eyed the painting of the thunder god, Thor on the mountaintop with a magical hammer.

'Who am I threatening?' she questioned, determined to know who this individual was.

'Many who seek control of the universe, including...' Darius struggled to say the name out loud. 'Including my half-brother...Vladimir. The Lord of Nebula'.

CHAPTER 9: THE TALE OF VLADIMIR

A chill slithered down Haley's spine, upon hearing that name. Her uncle: a family member who was most likely disowned and banished from Asgard. Judging by everyone's looks, it was for an unforgivable reason. A name they, even Darius were reluctant to speak of. Haley had friends on Earth, who disowned or are not on relative speaking terms with a parent or sibling.

Except this seemed to be different.

'He is five years younger than me', Darius explained. 'After my mother died from disease, my father, Leon remarried to a noble maiden, Elvira. Unknown to him, she was an exiled witch queen from a coven located on the outskirts of Niflheim. The High Council secretly discovered that she used dark magic to cast a powerful enchantment over my father to make him fall in love with her, so she would have some claim to the throne. She fell pregnant with Vladimir five months into the marriage'.

'What happened?' Haley asked out of curiosity.

'Her plan was to murder my father and myself, and take the throne with Vladimir to bring about a dark age over Asgard', Darius answered. 'It failed when the Gods cursed her to die in childbirth, in order to break the spell'.

' *"In order to give life, another must be taken"* ', Haley paraphrased this curse as a likely option.

'Yes', Darius confirmed. 'The side effect from the enchantment was my father had no memory of Elvira, except their first meeting. From that moment, a dark fog clouded his mind, unable to recall any events. Upon laying eyes on Vladimir, he could not bring himself to dispose of him. He saw him as an innocent child and decreed he would become the second prince of Asgard. Due to the possibility of him inheriting his mother's dark magic, a number of High Council members voted against it, but my father believed he could be spared from the consuming darkness with the right teachings toward the light side of magic. I too tutored him and tried to be a good older brother'.

Haley caught the sad tone in his voice, feeling sympathetic pity towards both him and her uncle.

'Vladimir', she said to herself. 'I heard that name before'.

'From your dreams?' Darius asked.

No. Not from the dreams', Haley replied, turning to Eric and Arianna. 'When I connected with your minds, one of those creatures called you *son and daughter of Vladimir and Antoinette*'.

Eric and Arianna were just as disinclined as Darius, wanting absolutely nothing to do with that name. What caused both sides to develop an intense hatred towards one another? Eric, after encouragement from Antoinette through obvious telepathy, let out a deep sigh.

'Vladimir is our biological father', he reluctantly answered.

An aftershock comparable to an earthquake rumbled inside Haley, her heart beating faster, as she wrestled with allowing this dubious information to sink in. Did she even hear that correctly?

'And my first husband', Antoinette spoke out.

Like a brewing content, more and more questions brewed inside Haley's head after hearing this new concealed secret.

She turned to Keilantra and Serena. 'You knew', she stated. Their nods only confirmed it. 'Why didn't you mention that my own uncle was the enemy referred to in the letter?' On queue came the slow re-emerging of the projective magical channeling in her blood from her brief anger, before calming down.

'Because since being consumed by the dark magic, he has now become one of the most dangerous beings in the universe', Antoinette answered.

'But if he…Vladimir is dangerous, why did you marry him?' Haley asked, until she saw the look in her mother's eyes as if she was reliving a bad dream. Her father placed his hand in her mother's as a sign of comfort, reminding Antoinette that she was a strong and wise queen. 'Why didn't you marry Darius to begin with?'

Antoinette gestured Haley to follow them. Haley felt uneasy at first, but her siblings nodded to her. Everyone went in pursuit, aware of what was about to happen next, Haley wondering whether they too could see the future. They walked out onto the balcony, overlooking the city, the bridge to the Bifrost gateway central to Haley's point-of-view, and Comet Hale-Bopp completely visible to all Cosmos Beings, its icy colours brighter against the sun's rays.

'I was the princess of Vanaheim', Antoinette explained, pointing out Vanaheim in the sky, foggy against the whiteness of the sky, although Haley managed to spot the shades of green land and blue waters, with grey and white shapes, which can only be tall hills and mountains. 'My brother, your other uncle, Alexander was the crown prince and heir to the Vanir throne'.

'When I was sixteen, I went into the woods to pick flowers for my mother who was taken ill. I was making my way back, when a group of bandits revealed themselves. They had a plan to hold me to ransom, after I read their minds. I unleashed my powers of nature onto them. I exhausted so much energy to the point of collapse, leaving myself defenseless. Until - '

'Until?' Haley asked.

'Until two brothers came to my rescue. Both handsome, young princes with powerful warrior skills...they fought off the bandits', Antoinette continued. 'I was so impressed by their strength and will, even my own strength returned to me and I assisted. As soon as the bandits retreated, the brothers introduced themselves as Princes Darius and Vladimir. We became instant friends. We spent time together, fought together and then I fell in love...'

'With Darius?' Haley asked hopefully.

'No', Antoinette replied. 'With Vladimir'.

Haley's heart sank. Unbelievable, she thought. Here she was hoping what her mother and father was a magically epic love story, like the ones she read in Nicholas Sparks novels, but finding this out had her thinking: how can the kind-hearted woman fall in love with the bad boy?

'But...how could you have fallen in love with him?' she asked. 'From what you told me so far, he's...evil'.

Antoinette went into deep thought.

'He wasn't always evil', she clarified. 'He was a gentleman: strong-headed, polite, charming, intimidating. It was arranged that we would marry. For a long time, I was happy and the twins were conceived. But after they were born, Vladimir began to change. Somehow, he found and read his mother's journal shortly after he passed away and through that, he found out about his heritage. He unknowingly channeled the dark magic of Niflheim in his anger, taking it out on me. He apologized. As his wife, I supported him through the revelation, but over time we started to grow apart: him needing to know more about the dark magic he inherited; and me realizing I had unspoken feelings for Darius. I confided in him about my marriage problems, about how I grew afraid every day of Vladimir's anger and corruption, about how distant he became to my children and I'.

'During those months, we became lovers', she said. 'Our love grew stronger; overriding even the love I once had for Vladimir. In that moment, I realized Darius was the love of my life standing right in front of me, even while I was married to Vladimir. It was a selfish act, I know, but Darius and I do not regret every moment we spent together. We decided to elope and tell Vladimir about the relationship in person. But…' She paused.

Haley didn't know what else to say or think, other than feel pity and relief towards this situation between her parents and Vladimir. From her mother failing to recognize her unresolved feelings for her father, to when she decided to leave Vladimir, after watching him slowly become a monster.

'But what?' she questioned, needing to know more.

'He found out before we could tell him', Antoinette replied. 'He unleashed his rage in his ever-growing dark magic, intent on destroying us. He…He brutally beat me to the verge of death'.

Haley all of a sudden put herself in her mother's shoes, gasping and projecting a relatable memory of the blunt force from Vladimir's hands and the darkness of his magic striking her mother. The more she imagined the pain and suffering Antoinette endured, the more it felt like she was actually there and even felt an intense hatred towards her uncle. It was dark and consuming. A fair warning that the universe did indeed have a dark side…

'So what happened next?' Haley asked.

'Darius found me and used his healing powers to save me', Antoinette continued. 'But then, two knights of Asgard informed us that Vladimir went on a rampage and…and he – he ~ '. She paused, unable to continue. Haley suddenly felt guilty for pushing her mother into telling the rest of the story. She did not know how hard it was for her until up to this point.

'He murdered three families in cold blood', Darius took over, finishing the sentence. 'All three had children no older than six or seven years. Our theory, according to the High Council was that he targeted these families, because the mothers resembled Antoinette, and the children had very powerful light magic, which he considered a threat'.

Haley's visionary prospects switched dramatically to an incarnation of Vladimir murdering those three families. Innocent people with innocent children! Those poor children, Haley thought, tears threatening to spill out again. And they never got the chance to grow up, live their lives, explore the worlds and the magic they were born with. In the new vision, she saw fire and blood, heard the horrifying screams of the tortured families and the blackened heart of a man, choosing to become a remorseless killer. A man who was once an Asgardian with a heart as pure and strong as Darius'…

'Was he brought to…' Haley began to ask, subconsciously choosing the right words in terms of Asgardian communication. '…Was he brought to trial at Gilitnir?'

Brief amazement emerged in her parents' eyes towards Haley's still-growing knowledge of the Nine Worlds. Haley lost count of the number of places she started to mention facts about from the olden myths she had not even studied at school. If only the All-Knowledge was a real person and she could thank them in person for this unexpected gift.

'That was the original council decision', Darius answered. 'We were to bring him to the hall of law and justice, Glitnir and call upon the god, Forseti to decide his fate. Unfortunately, he escaped captivity before the trial. He swore he would be one of many to bring about the Second Ragnarok'.

'You mean…he seeks to destroy all life in the Cosmos?' Haley asked, another chill snaking down her back hearing the word, Ragnarok: *the end of all things*.

'Yes', Darius muttered.

'But there was only one positive outcome', Antoinette reassured her. 'Eric and Arianna…After Vladimir fled Yggdrasil, my little children were fatherless, left traumatized by Vladimir's actions and the abuse they suffered of him trying to force them to embrace the darkness they would have inherited from him. They would not speak, except to myself. It took a while, but Darius earned their trust after they saw he had shown them nothing but compassion and love. After I remarried to Darius, he adopted them and raised them as his own'.

'And then, you came along, Halena. You have been the greatest gift to our family, since the ordeal we endured under Vladimir's hands'.

It was a touching, but sad story, Haley thought. She gazed at Eric and Arianna. 'I'm so sorry', she said, compassionately, 'If I'd have known…I-I can't imagine what you went through'.

'Do not worry, little sister', Eric said. 'Darius was the one who saved us from Vladimir's dark magic, teaching us how to counteract it with light magic, potentially ending his bloodline mystically, when Darius adopted us'.

Haley smiled for the first time, since entering the throne room.

'So where is Vladimir now?' she asked the dreaded question. 'And what were those creatures? Where did they come from? And what the hell did their attack have to do me?'

She was afraid what she blundered out was improper…she was supposed to be a princess for crying out loud!

All her mother did was raise her hand to the sky, drawing out an invisible anti-clockwise circle, a stream of blue and white gleaming light shaping the circle. A section of cloud cleared, the blue sky opening up another distant part of the universe. It was like looking through a magic mirror. A swiping wave of cold darkness washed over Haley. Through the sky's opening, she spotted a blackened form of land as flat as a giant disc, reaffirming scholars' written theories about a flat Earth. The land was surrounded by a cosmic storm of dark energy and lightning flashes. Very few stars were visible, lifeless with no purity.

'What am I seeing?' Haley asked.

'This is Nebula', Antoinette explained without an ounce of fear. 'A world Vladimir created using his dark magic – one with a harsher environment that that of the Nine. The same way Earth was created by the Big Bang, only with a far dense atmosphere breathable only to himself and his followers'.

'After his escape, Vladimir began to gather a group of followers', Darius continued. 'Traitors, criminals, anyone who corrupts, branding them with the same dark magic he was born with, changing their appearance completely. With all humanity gone, they became the Nebulans'.

'Nebulans', Haley whispered to herself, remembering something. 'When I…I interrogated that creature, he said *All Hail Nebula* before he…died'.

Antoinette acknowledged Darius, Eric and Arianna, with a look, which told Haley she heard those very words from a Nebulan during an encounter coincidentally similar to Haley's.

'Along with others, they seek to conquer the universe, and create more dark worlds', Darius explained. 'And that includes making new species much like the Nebulans to pass that power onto the imprisoned Ragnarok. The more they feed Ragnarok their power, the closer it'll come to returning'.

'By the time Nebula formed, Vladimir and his new followers performed a forbidden blood ritual using the mythical substance known as Eitr, to instead of giving life resurrect the darkest, evil souls of men and women'.

The gruesome imagination of thousands, perhaps millions of decaying bodies, all of whom were condemned for committing unforgivable crimes…it sickened Haley. Everything about their resurrection: from the desiccated skin and bone reconstructing to full flesh, to their features transforming into the pale skin, murderous red eyes, scars and deep blotches from where the dead skin used to be.

One more lingering question reached Haley.

'What does all of this have to do with me then?' she asked, as her mother closed the portal, the sky and cloud returning to its original form.

'When you were born, Halena, the Oracle of Asgard saw you had a destiny', Antoinette struggled to get the words out, reminiscing about something. Haley's heart hammered against her chest on the very last word.

'What destiny?' she asked.

'One that was written three thousands years before your birth…written in an ancient prophecy, foretold by the gods', Darius proclaimed.

Haley bit her lip. 'Is this…prophecy to do with why I'm a descendent of the God of Thunder? And also why I was sent away?'

'Yes', Antoinette said.

'And this Oracle of Asgard…where can I find her?' Haley asked with unexpected determination.

Her parents seemed hesitant, like they somehow knew that this so-called prophecy, whatever it was, was one that Haley could not escape from. Then again, what choice did they have when Vladimir could very well be planning his next potentially unpredictable move?

'Halena - ', her father began to say.

'Please, if I have whatever destiny you speak of, I need to know. From what you said, the Oracle of Asgard has the answers. I need to know what this…this prophecy is, and then I'll decide what to do from there'.

'You can't escape something like this, sister', Eric pointed out.

'I know, but what I do is not up to you or any God', she said, no longer allowing them to make decisions for her like they did for the past eighteen years. She turned to her parents. 'Please…let me speak to her'.

Darius and Antoinette held their gaze in place of hers. Haley refused to blink, avoiding the salty stinging of water filling her eyes. They entered a meditation state, echoing whispers in each other's minds, blocked from everyone. Even Haley couldn't break through the psychic barrier, it being almost as hard as steel.

'Very well', Darius finally said. 'You may see the Oracle'.

'So, where is she?' Haley replied, happy she accomplished something.

'You will find her in Odin's hall, Valhalla', Antoinette exclaimed, gesturing to the large distant temple across a plain of meadows to the east, shining underneath the sun. 'One of the High Priests will be expecting you'.

'But you may go as long as you are escorted', Darius stated.

'Escorted? You mean…have bodyguards?'

Her parents nodded.

'But I can take care of myself', Haley said stubbornly.

Darius and Antoinette just smiled, even though they were serious.

'We know. We have seen it when we were watching over you', Darius said. 'But we do not know what the Nebulans' next plan is. They are an unpredictable race. We cannot leave you unprotected, now that they know you are alive'.

'And we have only just got you back, dear daughter', Antoinette expressed, caressing Haley's cheeks again. 'We are not taking any chances'.

Haley sighed, secretly wishing she could go alone. After all, she had the intelligent guidance of the All-Knowledge, meaning she sure as hell could cross a beautiful open meadow of grass, flowers and surrounding mountains.

'If you wish', she said reluctantly.

'Very good', Antoinette smiled. 'You will be escorted by Lady Keilantra and one of the finest warriors in the Cosmos'.

'Who?'

'Me', a man's voice came. Haley turned around: it was the handsome brown-haired knight.

'Halena, this is Aeolus: prince of Alfheim', Darius said.

A prince? Why didn't she see it? He looked like any knight would: honourable, noble, strong-willed...handsome. Haley flinched on the inside for thinking that word in her timid mind, startled by Aeolus' handsomeness. Especially when he kissed her hand, holding his gaze with hers. His eyes were emotionless, like he held a grudge against someone or something – Haley immediately guessed the Nebulans. But there was also a flicker of light magic underneath the toned skin of his hand.

'You're the prince of Alfheim?' she questioned, raising her eyebrow. 'And a knight of Asgard?'

'Technically, the second-born prince of Alfheim', Aeolus replied. 'I became a knight of the Cosmos, four years ago when I turned eighteen'. Next, she couldn't help but glance at his ears. Human ears. She expected them to be pointy, considering he comes from an elven race, living in a woodland kingdom filled with light and hope.

'And I'm half-human, as is my brother, Silas', Aeolus said with zero emotion, leaving Haley with the conclusion that something traumatic changed him. Haley blushed, embarrassed that she forgot about her mind barrier. It must have broken down, when she was taken by this mysterious, handsome young prince standing right in front of her.

'Come, Halena', Keilantra said, breaking the awkward silence. 'Let us fetch your horse'.

'We're going to be riding there?' she asked, excitement boiling in her blood, recalling all the horse riding she did at Pony Club Camp.

'But what about my dress?' she asked, running her hands over the smooth material.

'I can fix that', Angela said right away. She wavered her hands, gold magic dust materializing from out of nowhere, hovering in Haley's direction. Much to her bewilderment, Haley became encased in the expanding dust like a glowing cocoon. The flow in her dress vanished, her legs now coated, her feet sinking into low heels. Haley emerged from the magical chrysalis, looked down and saw her dress was replaced with riding breeches: black legging trousers with matching lace-up boats, a long tunic shirt of ivory flower patterning with a dark grey undershirt and a navy blue robe with the Triquetra crest as the buckle.

Haley also saw that Keilantra too magically changed into similar riding breeches.

'Well, that's sorted', Haley mumbled in amusement. 'Thank you'.

'Return before sunset', her father ordered gently. 'The Nebulans intend to patrol the pathways through Yggdrasil, before dark'.

Haley simply nodded, before gesturing the same action to Aeolus and Keilantra signaling to them that she was ready to go, but not before getting something else off the plate.

'Hang on', she started. 'If the Nebulans weren't able to find me as a child, how were they able to find me yesterday?'

Her mother pursed her lips.

'Before you were sent away, the High Priests and Priestesses cast a spell over Yggdrasil to conceal your presence, as well as Eric and Arianna, who were chosen to be your guardians', Antoinette explained. 'During the outbreak of the spell, Vladimir received false visions of you dying from incurable illness as an infant, and Eric and Arianna's deaths which were staged using decoys, who bravely and willingly volunteered'.

She then pointed at Haley's chest, where her necklace charm laid. 'A concealing enchantment was also placed upon your necklace to keep you hidden. But we did not realize the enchantment would in time be overrun by your growing power', she explained.

Haley played with her necklace again. Was she really so powerful that she could override any form of enchantment, like the one on her necklace? She considered for a split second ripping it off, unable to bare another lie, but she felt held back by the memories of overpowering love from each member of her newfound family and it has been one of her most prized possessions since birth.

'Hence why they showed up?' Haley questioned. Her parents nodded.

'Now, that is all we are able to tell', Darius said. 'Go now, the Oracle awaits you'.

CHAPTER 10: THE PROPHECY

There was something peaceful about riding on horseback across a plain of meadows to reach an ancient temple, the calm wind sweeping through your hair, admiring the breath-taking beauty surrounding the meadows. Another reason was to get away from all the attention directed to Haley. While walking to the stables with Aeolus and Keilantra, Haley half-hoped the townsfolk would at least treat her as a normal person, but seeing their wondrous gaze changed that. They greeted her with a bow or curtsey as they would a princess; worshipping her like the Gods were worshipped many thousands of years ago. All Haley did was timidly smile before pulling the hood of her robe over her head to conceal herself from any on-lookers. Now here she was riding alongside Aeolus and Keilantra on the most beautiful stallion she had ever seen. White with shimmering silver-gold mane and tail, compared to Keilantra's pure white horse and Aeolus' brown horse with darker mane.

'His name is Gullfaxi', Keilantra said.

'Meaning *Golden mane?*' she asked, recognizing the name from an old folk tale she read about. She petted the horse gently and he neighed like he was singing in response. 'Wasn't he the horse originally owned by the jotunn, Hrungnir who in the end was slain by the God of Thunder?' For a second, Haley wondered whether it was her own intellect or the All-Knowledge taking control. Again, Keilantra nodded in confirmation.

'I thought Gullfaxi was given to Magni as a gift from Thor as a reward for lifting the leg of Hrungir off his father', Haley pointed out, petting Gullfaxi. 'And how is he alive today then?'

'The horses are immortal', Keilantra added. 'All Cosmos Beings have a slow aging prowess. When we reach the age of twenty-one, the aging prowess slows down us living three to five thousand years'.

'The Gods were the original keepers of specific horses', Aeolus continued. 'When the descendent of a specific God is born, the horse senses the magic the

Being inherited, identifying them as that descendent and they become their new owner and their new owner alone'.

'As for your answer to your first question', Keilantra said. 'Gullfaxi was returned to Asgard by Thor's son, Magni a thousand years ago to redeem his father and any future bloodline'.

'I read Odin said he did wrong giving away the horse to the son of a giantess', Haley pointed out.

'What would you expect?' Aeolus asked flatly. 'The Giants were at war with the Aesir and Vanir, until they reached a truce. That war will be nothing compared to what the Nebulans will bring'.

Haley found his sudden careless voice appalling.

'How can you say that?' she asked, keeping her voice genuine. 'People die in so many wars, people even lose loved ones: wives, husbands, sons, daughters – innocent people. Why do you think this war will be worse? Do you even care about those lives at all, because it sure as hell doesn't look like you do?'

Aeolus' icy emotionless eyes, though still beautifully light, met Haley's and she looked away, worried if what she said was spoken out of turn.

'Caring will not save the people, my lady', he eventually answered. 'It will be a distraction in battle. I am not prepared to make that mistake a second time'. He then galloped ahead, saying he would scout out anything peculiar.

'What's up with Aeolus?' Haley asked, as soon as he was out of earshot. 'He's acting like he doesn't care about anything or anyone'.

Keilantra sighed.

'Aeolus was one of the kindest, strongest, most honourable men in Yggdrasil', she replied. 'His ability is manipulation of the Seven Cosmic Elements of the Universe: earth, fire, water, wind, holy, thunder and ice. I've known him since we started our schoolings. We grew up together. He's like an older brother to me'.

Haley imagined an innocent little boy running around playing with a wooden sword and shield, and manipulating every single elemental power into something supernatural. She imagined him flashing a radiant, handsome smile drawing the noble ladies' attention…a thought Haley couldn't help but feel jealous about for some reason.

'It's to do with Vladimir…isn't it?' Haley asked.

Keilantra sighed, threading telling the story.

'It happened two years ago', she explained. 'Vladimir and his followers found a pathway into Alfheim, launching an attack. The light elves were unprepared. Many lives were lost... including Aeolus and his brother, Silas' father, King Elwood, who was also your father's best friend'.

Haley's heart dropped, looking ahead at Aeolus' turned back. She did not understand how it felt to lose a parent up until this precise moment. She lost her parents, so she thought. Aeolus lost his father. The only difference was that she had an unexpected miracle. She got her parents back, but Aeolus however would never see his father again.

'He must have been very close to King Elwood', she said sympathetically.

'More than that', Keilantra pointed out. 'He admired, respected and loved him...looked up to him, as did his brother, like any son would for their father. He was a great ruler. By the time his death and funeral passed, Aeolus entered a dark place, while Silas was crowned the new king of Alfheim, after their mother, Queen Amara, stepped down to serve as Royal Advisor and an open member of the High Council of the Nine Realms'.

'Why did she step down?' Haley asked. 'Why not remain as Queen Regent?'.

'That would have been a possibility', Keilantra replied sadly. 'However, it was her choice to reject it. She believed Silas, being the first-born prince and heir apparent, was ready to be king and Aeolus to be the commander of the armies of Alfheim'.

'You said Aeolus was in a dark place, when his father died', Haley pointed out.

'He shut off all emotion except for the focus on his duty to serve the Realms as a loyal prince and soldier, and his sheer hatred for Vladimir and the Nebulans', Keilantra continued. 'He pushed his swordsmen and archers to great extremes, perfecting their warrior skills and magic abilities. During training, he channeled his ability through hatred and anger, something his mother, Lady Amara and Silas observed. They tried to help, but even now he still refuses to listen. The sweet, kind prince he grew up to be seemed to have gone'.

Keilantra poured her heart out in the words. Haley mentally painted a picture of a young boy in a loving family. A whole family love, as pure as her parents' love, fractured in half upon one's death. That poor boy, Haley thought. He went through so much that she couldn't help but feel responsible in a way, because of an unexplained mystical link to a so-called prophecy. Perhaps this Oracle of Asgard would provide more insight and Haley could help find a way to make Aeolus whole again.

'Someone once said the darkness doesn't hold the answers', Haley said as they rode past some farmers harvesting crops. 'Maybe Aeolus just needs, as you say, guidance back to the light'.

Keilantra appeared impressed by Haley's unexpected wise words. Even Haley felt the same: maybe it was the princess within reigniting like an eighteen-year-old extinguished fire.

'Perhaps you're right', Keilantra replied. 'But all we can do is hope'.

Another pause came, until the telepathic connection opened up.

'*He saved your life*', Keilantra continued. '*Twice*'.

Haley turned her head back to Keilantra, as she channeled her telepathy.

'*When?*' she asked surprised.

The look on Keilantra's face said it all. Haley shuddered at the thought of thinking back to the previous day, but the moment she collapsed was the same moment she spotted shadowy figures walking towards her, as she closed her eyes, one of those figures lifting her gently into her arms.

'*Yesterday...*' Haley reached the instant realization. '*He was the one who took me here, wasn't it?*'

'*That, and there was the first time round, when you nearly drowned*'.

'*That was Aeolus?*' Haley asked telepathically, staring at Aeolus' back.

Keilantra nodded. '*If that was not the act of the Asgardian princess' protector, I don't know what was. But I know his actions on those days showed he was honorable and deep down, he too cared about you as much as the rest of the Realms*'.

Another memory jog pierced Haley like a needle as the day of her birth rushed back to her. She saw her parents...her brother and sister...then two boys, eager to take a closer look at her. One of them, a dark haired boy no older than four, had his finger wrapped around her tiny little hand. It was not hard to identify him as Aeolus. Haley kept the details to herself, blocking it with her mind barrier.

She didn't even notice Aeolus turned his horse to go back to walking alongside the pair of them.

'The skies and Yggdrasil's hidden pathways are all clear', he said emotionlessly.

He nodded ahead. 'Valhalla'.

All three halted their horses, Haley immediately captivated by Odin's temple, Valhalla, the said location for travelling spirits of warriors who died in combat. Compared to pictures of ones she saw on historic school trips or read about in numerous ancient myths, only this one was pure marble stone and pale gold: ageless and forever standing on the cliff edges of the open ocean. As they dismounted their horses and walked across the moat bridge to the marble pillared open entrance, the next thing Haley took in was the rest of the surroundings. Nearby stood a tree of gold, green and red leaves, which Haley recognized as the Glesir Tree – as sacredly beautiful as the magically animated version in her music box. Stood next to it was a white stag, easily identified as Eikpymir to Haley. Eikpymir halted on his hooves from walking, making eye contact with Haley. He tilted his head curiously. He was a beautiful stag, that she ended up thinking about quietly approaching him and giving him a friendly stroke. But her mind and body pushed her more towards the temple, drawn to the magic within it.

As soon as she, Aeolus and Keilantra reached the entrance, the double door opened telekinetically upon their approach. Haley studied the architectural details starting with the marble stone pillars embroidering Celtic carved patterns around the bottom edges. The entire main hall was majestic like that of a chapel hall. At the very end, there stood three bronze statues forty feet high. Haley eyed the three runic inspirations at the base of them and translated them in seconds: Thor, Odin, Frig – all three of her ancestors, the two gods and the one goddess…Thor carrying a hammer and a shield, Odin stood proudly as the most complex god with his Gungnir spear; and his wife, Frig eternally beautiful. Above the statues was a large, circular open gap in the ceiling, showing the sky at night with the Northern Lights dancing across the stars, astonishing Haley. Looking at it reminded her of the looking glass Alice stepped through.

Haley spotted priests, kneeling before the statues.

'What are they doing?' she asked. 'Those priests?'

'Whenever the Northern Lights appear during their prayers, they sing to honor their ancestors', Aeolus answered.

The low hymn really moved her, the purest memories of the Great Gods and their descended children sweeping over her. She stared at the dancing structure of the aurora in awe, before eyeing Aeolus out of the corner of her eye. Perhaps starting up a conversation with him might sway him out of his emotionless state, she wondered.

'You know, I read a lot of legends about the Aurora Borealis', she explained. 'It was said that the lights represented the spirits of departed friends and relatives trying to communicate with those they left behind upon death. Many tribes performed a sacred fire ritual to call upon the lights to connect with their loved ones in spiritual visions'.

Aeolus turned his head slightly in Haley's direction. Haley took it as a sign of getting through to him, breaking down the darkness surrounding his heart. She continued. 'And in the Old Norse stories, the Valkyries' armour shed a flickering light which flashes across the Northern Sky, becoming named Aurora Borealis'. Haley sighed deeply.

Aeolus curved his lip into an almost smile. Either he was impressed by Haley's vast knowledge of ancient myths and legends about the stars she grew up reading about, or he was fooling her into thinking he felt something besides rage towards Vladimir – he was practically unreadable, Haley thought. Haley, on the other hand, could have sworn she sensed a surge of light energy pulse through him while describing the story to him. It was small but brief, leading her to the conclusion that perhaps there was hope for Aeolus after all.

Haley was dragged away from her thoughts, when she noticed the streams of sunlight disappeared as the priests' hymn continued. She watched through the circular opening, as an eclipse collided with the aurora creating an Aurora Eclipse, reminding Haley of the story of Mani and the Valkyries.

'The Aurora Eclipse only appears at a significant time, ordinarily during a hymn in honour of our ancestor', Keilantra clarified. 'Even you, Halena...on your birthday, even when you were gone, the High Priests and Priestesses call upon the Eclipse to honour the day of your birth. Everyone never forgot, nor lost hope'. Haley blinked twice at that statement. Never has anything been done in her honour, before all this happened – unless you count winning a special prize in an art competition, or winning a major school sporting event.

She stopped dead in her tracks when she came across something which sent another shuddering chill down her spine – at least forty blackened markings, resembling the outlines of people. The sight of it created another memory trigger...the screams of innocent people and the horror on their faces as they watched the Nebulans emerge…her uncle, Vladimir with a menacing look, as he dueled Darius and several others…baby Haley crying as lightning bolts vaporized her family's enemies. The notable feature was that the outlines were almost coated neatly with swords and shields to hide the dark shadow the Nebulans cast that day. It could be mistaken for a collaged work of art, but not easily fooled by the Cosmos Beings who saw nothing but a harbinger of evil.

The Aurora Eclipse and night sky slowly changed back to the sunny, mid-afternoon sky, the stars still visible. Soon, the sound of footsteps caused Haley to look away from the ceiling to see a High Priest approach them. He passed as a man in his mid-sixties, but the wisdom in his eyes told Haley he could be over a thousand years old. His robes were cream and off-white held together by a navy blue waistband. As he approached, his eyes locked with Haley's before switching his view to her necklace, recognition in them as if he too sensed her familiar magic, forcing Haley to question again whether she was indeed a very powerful Being.

'My Lady Keilantra, my Lord Aeolus', he greeted them with a bow, before turning back to Haley. 'And Princess Halena…it is an honour. You have grown into a fair, young woman'.

'Umm, thank you. And please just call me Haley', Haley said shyly, with a small but polite smile. The priest gave a nod, signaling to Haley that he understood her reasons. At least another person did, Haley thought. Aeolus rolled his eyes, seemingly misunderstanding about the modern culture Haley was raised under, even though he knew she was previously unaware of her Asgardian heritage. For all Haley knew, he could be manifesting that emotion to cover up that flickering light.

'My name is Markus, High Priest of Valhalla, the priest proclaimed. 'You wish to see the Oracle?'

His expression confirmed to Haley that they knew they were coming.

'Yes', Haley answered. 'My…parents said she has the answers I seek about a prophecy I'm apparently involved in'.

Markus gave a knowing smile. 'She is expecting for you', he proclaimed. 'Follow me'.

He began leading them to a door, located behind the statues. Haley stopped to glance at them, particularly the God of Thunder, having seen different versions of him in mythological texts and sculptures in art and history museums, more drawn to the emerging reality of being his descendent.

'Haley?' Keilantra called, upon noticing she fell behind. Haley caught up with them just as Markus opened the door. Although dark, Haley saw through her advanced peripheral vision that they were standing in a small stone room, the far wall baring a handprint with the triquetra symbol in the centre, leaving Haley puzzled.

'I drew something like this before', Haley recalled from a sketch she did in the past, amongst many other runes and symbols constantly flowing around in her hard-wired head.

'In order to enter the water chambers of the Oracle, you must have a reason to allow the gateway to open', Markus explained. He withdraw a dagger from under his robes, alarming Haley leaving her tempted withdraw her own. 'That reason must be channeled from the magic in your blood'.

'How so?' Haley asked, keeping somewhat connected to the symbol on the handprint.

'The Oracle senses the magic in any Being of the Nine Realms, as much as the gatekeeper of the Bifrost sees and hears billions of souls from considerable distances', Markus continued.

'Is the gatekeeper a descendent of Heimdell, the original gatekeeper?' Haley asked, intrigued.

'Yes', Markus answered. 'Optimus has been guarding the gateway of the Bifrost, since coming-of-age five years ago'.

'So, Heimdall's powers were passed to him? The fore-knowledge, the keen eyesight, the super-hearing...everything?'

'They were passed down through generations', Keilantra replied. 'All down to the predictions of the Oracle, who also foresees who will inherit the power of the gods'.

The questions stopped there, when Markus asked for Haley's hand, which she reluctantly offered to him. He carved the triquetra sign into her hand. What amazed Haley was she felt little pain unlike the deep cut from the sharp rock during the unintentional thunderstorm, or the scratch marks on her leg from the first Nebulan she killed. Then again, that pointed more to the near fact that she was a princess descended from the Norse Gods and Goddesses. Markus placed her hand on the symbolic handprint, central to the design. It felt warm to the touch.

After the gradual passing of a whole minute, Haley removed her hand as it healed itself, the scarring disappearing completely. Her eyes switched back to the wall. Her blood circulated around the symbol…until finally, the symbol glowed a light blue and turned anti-clockwise. The wall opened like a sliding door. Haley looked beyond and spotted a stone spiral staircase leading downwards, bluebell flamed torches illuminating the second room. Taking a deep breath, Haley stepped into the room with Keilantra and Aeolus, following Markus. On the way down, she started counting the steps in an attempt to ease off the butterflies in her stomach.

'*Get a grip, Haley*', she muttered to herself telepathically, ensuring that the others were out of earshot thanks to the mind barrier. '*You can do this, relax*'.

They soon reached flat ground. In total, Haley counted one hundred and fifty steps. The crackling sound of the dancing bluebell flames became replaced by the sound of rushing water. What Haley saw as she looked everywhere at every angle, was definitely a sight to behold, equal to the Asgardian scenery on the outside. It was a very large cave, the only source of light being the glow-worms on the cavern ceiling, some of which had wings. As one of them came up close to Haley's face, she saw they were not glow-worms – they were fairies…glowing fairies, with pixie faces displaying beauty like that of miniature human noblewomen and flowing blonde hair. They had tails. Mermaid tails. Though they had no speech, they let out pretty singing squeaks. From the gaze in their eyes, either they were intrigued about having a new visitor, or they knew who Haley was and felt her magic.

The little mermaid fairies flew back up to the ceiling, where the rest of their colony resided, reigniting the glow in their wings.

'Beautiful, aren't they?' Keilantra asked rhetorically, taking notice of Haley's wondrous gaze.

Haley just nodded. 'I never knew fairies existed', she whispered. 'I mean, I've seen them in the pictures of storybooks, but I never imagined what it would like to actually see a real one up close'.

'They're Mer-Faeries', Keilantra explained. 'The guardians of the Prophetic Caves, and water entities of Aegir'.

'The jotunn god of the oceans', Haley proclaimed, the faeries' enchanting beauty touching every square inch of the caves, their glow casting light over the shadows. Instinctively, Haley remembered another painting she did of some starlit caverns.

Now, she knew that they weren't stars. They were these faeries and their glowing wings.

Markus stepped forth, alongside Haley as the ocean crashed against the rocks.

'After Ragnarok and the reconstruction of the Nine Realms, the third king and queen of Asgard, your great-grandparents, Freydis and Mikkel, named the ocean after Aegir', he explained. 'The spiritual entities of Aegir and his beloved wife, Ran bonded with the waters. Now, they dwell in the Realms' oceans, journeying through concealed pathways of Yggdrasil, animating their powers over the water taking many forms'.

Suddenly, something broke the water's surface leaping out. Haley jumped back, nearly stumbling a large rock and falling backwards into Aeolus, something she felt embarrassed thinking about because she really wanted to, so she could feel his hidden warmth underneath his build muscles. She quickly shook that thought off to avoid further distraction to observe the leaping creatures more closely. They were scaly like fish, only what was different was that the upper body was that of a horse, the lower part the fins of a fish: a hippocampus.

'The hippocampus colony are their loyal friends', Markus continued. 'They too patrol the waters alongside Aegir and Ran's nine daughters to protect the realms from mystical threats who dare attempt an attack through these pathways'.

'I thought hippocampus colonies were only seen in Greek myths', Haley proclaimed watching the beautiful creatures roam freely and gracefully through the waters.

'They are', Keilantra said. 'To this day, the people of Midgard still believe that. During the ancient times, magic and creatures like the hippocampus colonies roamed the earth and across the stars. People worshipped them through their cultural religions. Even the Gods turned to them selecting specific ones as their guides and avatars. It was a story the Oracle told me as a child'.

'How do you know the Oracle?' Haley asked.

The water's surface broke yet again, this time not from a hippocampus or a wave, but from a woman with platinum blonde hair and light blue highlights. Haley looked beneath the reflective water to see that the woman bore a blue-green scaly tail. Haley gasped. The woman was a mermaid. She swam up to the stone steps, bathed in a circle of white-blue light, her tail now replaced with elegant shimmering turquoise sequin dress, the inner skirt a satin white and long open off-shoulder dress.

'Halena', Keilantra pronounced. 'Meet the Oracle of Asgard, Lady Orla, leader of the Mermaid Clan of Prophecy…and my mother'.

Haley's mouth hung open.

'Your – your mother's a mermaid', Haley muttered, speechless in utter disbelief to the fact that the woman standing right in front of her was a mythological creature she read about in storybooks. 'Wait…does that mean that you're one as well?'

'Not entirely', Keilantra replied. 'I am a half-breed. My mother is complete mermaid, while my father was an Asgardian soldier'.

'Aside from having the ability to manipulate rainbow fire, my Keilantra also has the abilities consistant to that of a mermaid', Lady Orla suddenly spoke as angelically as her mother. 'Enhanced hearing and strength, even the ability to breathe underwater'.

Orla's eyes locked with Haley's, every now and then gazing at her necklace and birthmark.

'Halena, it is so good to see you all grown up', she said taking hold of Haley's hands as a welcoming gesture. 'The last time I saw you were only five months old'.

Haley blushed. 'People say how much I look like my mother', she replied, forwarding that startling fact since meeting Darius and Antoinette.

'Indeed, you are', Lady Orla said. 'You are graced with the same beauty as your mother, except you have your father's eyes…only as bright as the average star in the sky'.

Haley returned a slight smile at the statement, blushing even more in the same shyness as when she made direct eye contact with Aeolus, who couldn't seem to stop looking at her, Haley feeling his gaze upon her.

'Keilantra: my lily flower, so good to see you again', Lady Orla said, hugging Keilantra.

'You only saw me yesterday evening, mother', Keilantra reminded her with a low laugh, but continued to mirror Lady Orla's smile.

Definite family resemblance, Haley thought.

'I know, but it has been four years since you and Serena went to Midgard, and need I also remind you that I too almost lost you yesterday', Lady Orla pointed out. 'I do not wish for that to happen again'.

Haley observed the interaction between mother and daughter, wondering whether herself and her mother could effectively have that. After all, Antoinette had great kindness within her, not to mention the sky manipulation ability: part of which Haley may have inherited from her to harass the advanced juncture of her own thunder power. Could that be it? Could it be that her powers from the thunder god were as much a part of her parents as it was a part of her? Bonded eternally to the flesh and bone, mind, body and soul?

'And thank you, Markus for your service', Lady Orla addressed the High Priest, before switching her vision to Aeolus. 'You too, Prince Aeolus for bringing Halena here with my daughter'.

'I am at your service, My Lady', he said, bowing his head.

Markus then spoke. 'Halena wishes to know more about her heritage and destiny'.

'Of course', Orla said. 'This way, my child'. She directed Haley towards a door across a set of stepping-stones. It was purely polished ageless wood with no handles, except for a circular crest baring a hippocampus encircling two people – Aegir and Ran – Haley guessing the crest was a representative symbol of the Mermaid Clan.

As Haley moved forward to follow Lady Orla, who was already across the stream, she noticed that Keilantra, Aeolus and Markus did not follow. 'You're not coming?' Haley questioned.

'This is something you must do alone, Halena', Markus explained. 'It was your reason alone, which summoned the Oracle'.

Haley ran her hand over the healed spot on her hand, where the knife penetrated her skin and Markus carved the triquetra.

'We'll be right here, Haley', Keilantra smiled encouragingly, before acknowledging her mother with an admired nod. Haley just returned the mirroring smile, and turned back to the first stepping-stone. Feeling opposed, Haley balanced herself on the stones, gradually moving along to the second, third, fourth and so on. Thank goodness all those dance lessons paid off, Haley thought.

By the time she reached the shore on the other side, Lady Orla touched her necklace baring the exact same crest. It glowed white, illuminating the door's symbol. Seconds later, the hidden dead locks clicked, rock against a concealed metal key. Lady Orla stepped through the open door, but Haley lingered behind looking back at the others. Their gazes put her more at ease, reminding her she came to the Asgardian Caves for a reason and that reason laid behind whatever was on the other side of this door. Not knowing what to expect, she gripped the sheath of her Valkyrie dagger. The long stone corridor seemed to go on for miles. Despite the warmth of the bluebell flamed torches, it still felt cold to Haley. Lady Orla did not appear to be affected by it, Haley guessed because of mermaids being more warm-blooded. Every step Haley took towards whatever was down this corridor, her heart hammered against her chest her magical senses activating a surge of energy lingering amongst every scaled angle of solid rock.

Unable to bare another awkward silence, Haley decided it was time for more questions. 'Where are we going, Lady Orla?' she asked.

'All will be revealed in a moment's time, dear child', Lady Orla replied.

Haley sighed, dissatisfied by the answer. She wanted it to be over and done with, so why not tell her now? Did this so-called prophecy harbor a deep secret that could only be revealed to Haley?

'Are you friends with my mother?' Haley asked, experiencing another brief memory trigger involving her parents and Lady Orla in the process. 'Sorry I didn't mean to be inquisitive or anything'. She silenced herself before her babbling got out of control. Relief reached her in the form of Lady Orla's hand squeezing her shoulder in reassurance.

'You do indeed have a curious mind, Halena', she smiled. 'Do not be ashamed of the person you are becoming. And to answer your question, your mother and I have been very close friends, since she first came to Asgard. During her marriage to Vladimir, she too came to me for my counsel about handling the situation involving Vladimir's growing dark power. By the time your parents' love was exposed, my people and myself swore an oath to protect them, the Nine Realms, and its oceans from dark beings'.

'Like the Nebulans?' Haley pointed out.

'Yes', Lady Orla replied.

The two took a right at the far corner of the corridor, heading towards an opening. Another sound reached Haley's ears: waterfalls. It was not a room at all: it was a large cavern, a lake structured around the entity of the area. Haley assumed they must be deep beneath Asgard now, in accordance to the gigantic hole in the cave ceiling, where a waterfall flowed down into the crystalline blue waters of the lakes. Must be above the Aegir Ocean, Haley thought. Except no smell of salt water travelled up Haley's nose: it was just a calm and gracefully crystallized waterfall. A concrete-platform bridge stood on the lake, a circular section in the very middle where there stood a stone basin; a sphere floating inches above it, glowing like a crystal ball leaving Haley marveling over whether it was an actual fortune-telling crystal ball.

'What is this place?' Haley asked.

'It is the Lake of Fortune', Lady Orla explained. 'The Norns created it after Ragnarok to envision specific prophecies involving a Cosmos Being's past, present and future'.

'The same Norns from the legends?' Haley questioned. 'The guardians of Yggdrasil's Wells?'

Lady Orla's eyes twinkled proudly. 'I see the All-Knowledge has worked for you. And yes, the Norns guard the Wells of Yggdrasil and have been since the dawn of time. They, like the spirits of Gods, are very much immortal and ensured that the survival and rebirth of the Nine Realms were forthcoming'.

'The waters of this lake travel through three tunnels'. Lady Orla pointed out the three cavern holes wide open in the rock walls – one on the left, one on the right and one behind the crystal sphere and basin. 'Once they purify, they journey to the three sacred wells: Urd, Hvergelmir and Mimir. The Norns branded them with their powers to foresee all visions, to overlook possible prophecies and destinies'.

'Like mine?' Haley asked nervously, unable to believe that the next few minutes were about to change.

Lady Orla walked towards the stone-platform bridge, Haley following in pursuit.

'Our destinies are entwined with the magic we are born with', Lady Orla explained. 'Whether we are born naturally with it, or by inheritance from the Gods'. They came to a halt in front of the sphere, which from up close swirled around like the gaseous storms of Jupiter. 'But you, Halena…Your destiny is different'.

'How so?' Haley asked.

'Written over three thousand years ago, it is unlike any prophesied story ever written', Lady Orla answered. 'More than a story…more than just one going down into legend'.

Upon the last word, Lady Orla twirled her fingers extending them on angled sides above the sphere, the invisible magic she conjured up telekinetically animating the swirls to move around faster, until it glowed brighter in white; and levitating streams of light in homage to the Northern Lights slithered through the open air. One stream glided towards Haley, as she narrowed her eyes in fascination, another minor phenomenon cosmically drawn to her power. The energy travelled through every part of Haley's body, like it was carrying out a mystical analysis of her magic to better coordinate what was about to be revealed. Did this source of light need a part of Haley's power as the main ingredient? And why did Haley have a half-feeling of wonder but frustration that she felt like a lab rat for something which involved harvesting some of her magic?

'The sphere needs to retain a pure connection to your magic to foretell the prophecy to yourself, as it is the only link to your ancestor', Lady Orla reassured her, Haley forcing herself to relax ever so slightly while the white stream of light completed its journey and shimmered across the lake waters alongside the other light streams.

The water rippled into the flat circular formulation of a developing whirlpool, blackness against the blue until it grew misty, and soon images appeared like the moving pictures of a silent movie on an old-fashioned film reel. The first image showed a banquet and dance between Cosmos Beings, smiling at their loved ones, and to the rulers of the Nine Realms in attendance: the Gods and Goddesses…their ancestors…Haley's ancestor.

It was not until when the second image replaced the first that the wave of light and happiness vanished, a sweeping darkness taking its place that even Haley felt it, not just where she stood, but from every corner of the lake, sending multiple chills down her spine. The second image was a great battle between armies each of over ten thousand men and humanoid creatures: a dragon flying overhead breathing out fire...and a giant scaly serpent with blue and yellow eyes battling against a god wielding a hammer.

'Three thousand years ago, it was a time of peace', Lady Orla said. 'The war between Asgard and Vanaheim ended after a brutal conflict and interminable negotiations. All the Gods and Cosmos Beings ever wanted was peace, and Odin who was king of Asgard at the time established a treaty with the people of Vanaheim...'

A third image of a dark, blackened entity resembling a face in deadly smoke emerged in the mirror lake, consuming every life-form in its sight...many innocent people. Not just soldiers...women and children...horrifying Haley to the core in the inside. 'Until a dark deity emerged from the darkest part of the universe, and bonded with the roots of Yggdrasil, bringing a mass destruction with natural disasters, and a great battle took place between the Gods and the followers of the deity, who also killed any other inhabitants of the World's Tree', Lady Orla continued. 'Every knight and soldier fought valiantly, but the gods – Odin, Thor, Tyr, Freyr, Heimdall and Loki – were left in the end and mortally wounded. The dark deity becoming known as Ragnarok began to transform the Nine Realms into barren wastelands. And all Cosmos Beings were too helpless to stop it'.

'My parents said my...uncle is one of these followers', Haley enquired.

Lady Orla pressed her lips. 'It is true. Some followers became extinct, but new ones are taking their place, partly due to their legacies and because there are those who possess dark magic capable of resurrecting Ragnarok. Like Vladimir, whose magic was passed down through his mother...' Her face went sad. '...Now it is too late for him'.

Both Haley and Lady Orla wanted the subject reverted back to the story.

'So what happened after the battle?' Haley asked.

'Though wounded, Odin managed to convince Thor to harness more of his power', Lady Orla answered. 'With the last of his strength, he unleashed the full power of thunder and lightning to vanquish the humanoid followers, and banish Ragnarok back into the dark abyss, and its followers either perished, remained in dormant or ultimately became extinct...But though the victory was profound, there came a price. Many of the gods were dead, and Thor was wounded and weakened from the amount of power he used up'.

'On his deathbed, he called upon the Norns and the High Council. Together, they linked his spirit to his future bloodline so that his powers could be passed down through generations. But no descendent could fully tap into his power, and the prophecy which was created was all but forgotten'.

Haley bit her lip. 'Until me', she muttered rhetorically.

'You were born during the most powerful thunderstorm in over three thousand years', Lady Orla proclaimed. 'Something which had not happened since the Lord of Thunder himself. It meant only one thing'. She turned her hopeful gaze to Haley. 'You, Halena, are Thor's heir'.

Haley's heart pounded against her chest, as the swirling white mist of the orb slowed down to a gentler pace, like the movement of clouds swiping slowly across the sky. Then came a dying man's voice, but it sounded soft and genuine against the low chanting in the background.

In three thousand millennia, let thy spirit and power live on in The One
The One born of all the Worlds
The One born with the powers of the Thunder God
The One born with the heart of the warrior
The One born to be the next worthy wielder
The One destined to destroy the re-born Evil
And bind the Cosmos into eternal peace.

Haley remained too transfixed on the voice exiting the orb, failing to notice the lake mirror transforming back into the original elegant turquoise. Secretly, she preferred watching the images like a slideshow than listening to the mystical audio recording of the man's voice, claiming this was a so-called inescapable prophecy she was somehow linked to through a spiritual bloodline.

'It was foretold that The One was destined to vanquish all Evils', Lady Orla explained.

The more she took it in word for word between both Lady Orla and the man's voice in the mystical orb, the more stronger the sensational triggering of the uncontrolled nature in her magic became, as it channeled through her veins.

'And you think it's me?' she asked with utter disbelief.

'We don't think...we know so', Lady Orla replied with a smile and ignited hope in her eyes. 'You have been blessed with the reborn spirit of the Thunder God, now running solely through your veins; and the Aurora Eclipse, the spirit of our ancestors, and Mani and Raven's sacred power, were able to identify your birth as the moment every Cosmos Being across the universe waited for, for three thousand years'.

All Haley did was let out a low, shallow breath and a non-smiling laugh. 'But...but there has to be a mistake', she muttered reluctantly.

'There is certainly no mistake', Lady Orla said. 'Prophecies never lie. In the eyes of the Gods, you are The One and it is your destiny as heir to the throne and to the Lord of Thunder...to stop Vladimir from plunging Yggdrasil back into darkness, along with every other Dark Being who threatens your existence and the existence of others'.

'So...all the elemental occurrences, that was all me because of the Thunder God's spirit...merged with mine', she confirmed to herself, once again relieved she was not crazy, but remained knee deep in shock following this entire revelation. 'And all the training sessions...my brother and sister were – were preparing me...for moments like yesterday. And I thought they were a bunch of interests I willingly picked up upon'. She went through a brief phrase of resentment towards her siblings for making her believe this was a personality intact she developed like any other human being on Earth. Just a simple piece of normality she half-hoped to cling onto for the remainder of her life...

'Every recurring moment you spent harassing your power, every moment in which an answer drew you closer to the truth in unexpected moments of clarity', Lady Orla answered. 'Every moment since your birth was about preparing you for two futures: either one where there is eternal peace, or one where the Dark Beings of Ragnarok consume the Worlds and the universe into darkness'.

Haley turned her gaze from the prophetic lake where the mirror of flashing images appeared, to the crystal sphere in its most compelling colour of silver-white. She closed her eyes, shaking her head side-to-side ever so slightly, no longer able to process or think things through with the electrifying sensation of lightning magic distracting her, as it pulsed continuously through her veins. Better yet, she couldn't re-think back to all the phenomenons she accounted: between her birth, the Nebulans' attack, meeting her parents for the first time and Asgard

'I still don't understand why they didn't tell me', Haley pointed out. 'Didn't they think I had a right to know?'

'As Darius and Antoinette clarified, it was for your own protection', Lady Orla explained. 'It was the hardest decision they ever had to make, sending you away...but they knew it was the right thing to do. Not just for your sake and for the sake of the Nine Realms, but for the sake of the prophecy being very rare also. Had you not relied upon the guidance of Eric and Arianna, and trained yourself through controlling your gifts both spiritually and physically, you would have been discovered sooner...and all hope foretold within the prophecy would have been lost'.

Haley played with her necklace, sensing the cloaking spell fade away. Two reasons...one: it was no longer necessary to keep her hidden, now that Vladimir and the Nebulans know she was alive...and two: if it was true according to Antoinette, her ever-growing powers could overshadow any form of magic. The instantaneous circumstance rocked Haley. Indeed, god blood flowed through her veins. Except for the past eighteen years, she was human in the spiritual sense, something she couldn't simply let go in the blink of an eye.

'What are you thinking, Halena?' Lady Orla asked gently, her eyes filled with hope and worry.

'I...I...' Haley stuttered. 'I...I think I need to get out of here. It's just t-too much...I – I don't think I – I can't handle it right now'. A single tear trickled out of her eye.

Despite her kind smile turning back upside down, Lady Orla seemed to understand. Before she could let the situation become even more overwhelming, Haley started back towards the opening, Lady Orla following four steps behind not uttering another word, probably in case it brought Haley closer to having another breakdown from the amount of secrets coming from pretty much every single person she encountered and every area of nine environments she was still unaccustomed with, despite the vast process of the All-Knowledge. Most of all, she did not know the first thing about being a princess.

It did not matter what they say, Haley thought. This was a decision she had to make alone. No interferences from others…and no letting a supposedly inescapable prophecy affect that decision.

CHAPTER 11: MESSAGE FROM THE LORD OF NEBULA

Haley avoided everyone, only exchanging a minimum number of words. They shouldn't blame her for needing time to process all this. But they seriously believed that she was The One, destined to vanquish the evil beings threatening to bring about the Second Ragnarok; her uncle Vladimir being one of these people consumed by the dark magic passed down from his mother, shedding any light magic forever. Recalling that fact gave Haley the shivers, the same feeling she felt when within the presence of dark magic.

It had only been seven days: the amount of time that passed since she arrived and officially met her parents, and the amount that passed since, much to Haley's shock, she learnt about the ancient prophecy through Lady Orla. Yes, she inherited the powers of the thunder god and had been trying to embrace them, but she never imagined she would be part of some unbreakable prophecy. She was not cut out for this, and who knows if she ever would be? She still had yet to accept the supposed warrior princess within her...and from the attack there was a flash of her, according to Lady Orla.

Upon hearing about this brand new information, Haley took a small step back mentally creating her own substantial ultimatum: everyone, including her parents, needed to gain her full trust just as much as she needed to find acceptance towards her ancestral heritage.

Desperate for more time alone, Haley climbed out of bed and changed into a simple blue dress with a matching over-the-shoulder robe while listening to her music box melody, before sneaking past the guards and any early morning palace residents and headed down to the lagoons, with a book Keilantra lent to her, *The Anthology of Yggdrasil*, to familiarize herself more with the cultures the Nine Realms represented. She took an interest in one traditional universal event, the Festival of Starlight, which according to Darius and Antoinette occurs once every two years to pay tribute to their ancestors. There were even records of astronomical events from scholars' subscribed journals. Perhaps the Cosmos Beings, even though highly advanced and intelligent, were very much like the humans than expected, Haley thought. Perhaps she could enlighten some of them about her own experiences once everything settled down...

Haley closed the book after reading an account on the first downfall and rebirth of the Cosmos over a hundred times. Letting out a low sigh, she turned her eyes to the crystallised, turquoise blue lagoons shining against the warm rising sunlight, watching the colony of hippocampuses and mermaids leap out of the water in perfect sequence. The mermaids greeted Haley with a smile, which she returned, before they dove back under. Haley wished she had a sketchbook with her, so that she could draw this glorious scenery. It would be a perfect addition to her submission portfolio.

The silence broke, when a chipper voice startled Haley.

'Bless my soul! It is true!' the voice bellowed out joyously. 'The Asgardian princess has returned'. The shock of hearing it caused Haley to jump out of her skin and withdraw her Valkyrie dagger, the buried warrior princess reigniting in a brief but quick flash. She looked around in all directions to identify the person.

'Who said that?' she asked in a low call.

'Look up here', the chipper voice called out. Haley did as she was told and followed the voice, which led up to a vine tree of cherry blossom. What she saw amongst the pink flowers startled her even more. It was a squirrel...with black eyes and red-brown fur, and a perfect bushy tail. So unlike the squirrels on Earth, Haley all of a sudden sensed its bond with the magic of Yggdrasil.

She gasped softly. 'You – you can talk?' Haley asked speechless. 'Who...who are you?'

The squirrel let out a laugh. 'Why, of course, being the immortal messenger who greatly evolved since the last Ragnarok', he answered heartily. 'Please allow me to introduce myself...I am Ratatoskr'.

Haley gasped again, upon recognizing the name. '*The* Ratatoskr? The squirrel guardian, who journeys through Yggdrasil to exchange messages?'

'Wow', Ratatoskr rejoiced laughing. 'They weren't lying about that All-Knowledge working its magic on you, princess'.

For goodness sake, Haley thought. If she heard the word *magic* one more time...

'Well, of course', a sudden female sarcastic voice came out of no way, interrupting Haley's frustrated thoughts, loud enough to hear over the flapping of wings. 'Like you were told over a thousand times during the past week'.

Haley shifted her gaze upwards to the bird flying over her, which eventually landed on one of the flower branches. It was the most magnificent eagle she had ever seen, with misty yellow eyes. Her beauty only stood out more with the tips of her brown and gold feathers glowing against the sunlight like a rainbow.

'And you know, I cannot help myself when *The One* is standing right in front of us', Ratatoskr chuckled. The eagle just gave him the death stare like a predator. Only there was difference. There was nothing dangerous about it. It was more...playful. The eagle was not a predator, at least not towards Ratatoskr, who did not cower in fear at all. So essentially a friendly banter like a brother-sister relationship, Haley thought to herself, growing slightly amused by the guess.

'Princess Halena, meet – ', Ratatoskr began.

'Vedrfolnir, the eagle of guidance', Haley interrupted, the magical surge of the All-Knowledge electrocuting her like an electric pulse. 'I know. I read about you in my history studies on Earth'.

'Well, well...you do indeed have an intelligent mind', Vedrfolnir replied, impressed by Haley's unexpected burst of knowledge.

'Call it a fifty-fifty chance that these were my own words and not the words of the All-Knowledge?' Haley pointed out as an answerable question, complete with a nervous laugh.

Before Ratatoskr or Vedrfolnir uttered another word, something else came.

'And you are not forgetting someone else?' a gruff voice suddenly called out, Haley dropping her book in the process and swallowing back another low scream, before moving her gaze back to the sky alerted by a sound: a louder set of flapping wings like the noise of a newly formed hurricane. Haley's scream was not from this creature frightening the life out of her, but from the actuality of her always believing these creatures were non-existent legendary fragments.

It was a dragon. Though it had the appearance of a fully-grown dragon, with orange, scaly wings in shades of gold, its average size could be easily compared to that of a dog. His snout and mouth curved up into a smug smile. Except it was not dangerous at all, unlike the numerous dragons from the books. As if not giving a care in the world, the dragon perched himself in between Ratatoskr and Vedrfolnir nearly knocking them both off the flower branch, its petals tumbling down from the force of the dragon's wings, and landing on Haley's head and robes. Vedrfolnir appeared irritated by the dragon's constant presence, while Ratatoskr just rolled his eyes.

'And of course, the best for the last', Ratatoskr mumbled sarcastically. 'Halena, meet Nidhogg: the guardian of dragons'.

'And the one with the biggest most arrogant tongue in the universe', Vedrfolnir suddenly muttered telepathically, catching Haley off guard as she managed to retain it by an ooze. She couldn't help but laugh on the inside. Another reason for laughing: she never imagined she would, since coming back to Asgard, be meeting the three creatures, who inhabit the immense mythical tree, let alone be talking to them like they were people. The three creatures glanced at her – every olden eye of legend though animal, but human, looking into her sparkling blue eyes. What were they waiting for: a magic showcase? Or more and more All-Knowledge fiesta?

'Umm, no offense...but are you going to just sit there all day, staring at me?' she asked.

Nidhogg's smirk broadened upwards. 'Why not show us, little princess?' he asked rhetorically and winked knowingly. 'Prove to us you are a descendent of the Thunder God?'

Both Ratatoskr and Vedrfolnir looked at him, shocked by his request as much as Haley was.

'For goodness sake, Nidhogg!' Vedrfolnir hissed angrily, annoyed he would ask such a thing.

'What? I want to see her do it', Nidhogg argued. 'Just to prove she is who they say she is'.

Slightly hurt by her statement, Haley took the offensive comment for granted. Was Nidhogg too full of himself to have even noticed her numerous mystical activities for the last eighteen years?

And that was when the bickering started from all three species, quickly getting out of hand to the point where Haley was out of reach in plain sight. Though complete English, the words sounded gibberish through the speedy pace that she could only catch specific words and phrases.

'...always about you, isn't you?'

'…only want to see her actually do something magical…'

'…it's her decision, not yours'.

'…she doesn't look like a descendent of Thunder Boy'.

'…well maybe, if you paid more attention to her activities, instead of just rabbiting on about how you beat your fellow dragon guardians in the tournament over a thousand times!'

Haley rolled her eyes at the never-ending bickering, amused despite finding incredibly annoying. Using this distraction to her advantage, she allowed the protective shield encasing the magic bonded to her blood flow to dissolve entirely. The electrifying current resembling a lightning bolt surged through head to toe, until it journeyed back up reaching her right hand. The power burnt an invisible hole through her skin, only there was no wound, only a sensation. In its place: a ball of purple, then blue, then light blue, then flashing white…a lightning ball, the size of a football, levitating inches above Haley's hand. The animals' bickering only halted the moment the large materialized, awestruck by the intensity of its power. Haley even felt the glowing sparkle in her eye brighten.

'Satisfied now?' she asked, a sudden feisty twinkle in her eye. The lightning ball dematerialized into nothingness, and the protective shield stabilized her magic.

'Well, I'll be damned', Nidhogg said, displaying a gigantic grin. 'And here I thought I was seeing things, ever since the first Aurora Eclipse'.

'Hold up', Haley uttered. 'You're saying you saw what I could do for eighteen years, ever since the first Aurora Eclipse occurred and you pretended not to notice for all these years, so you saw an opportunity to make me look like some sort of idiot in a magic circus show'. A brief tingle of channeling magic threatened to break down the barrier at Haley's little outburst. She calmed herself quickly, unwilling to risk anyone getting hurt, especially Ratatoskr, Vedrfolnir and, as much as she hated to admit it, Nidhogg who snorted.

'What's so funny?' Haley asked, as calmly as possible.

'Just the fact that you were naïve enough to actually fall for it, little princess', he said through his quirky laughter. 'On the bright side, it definitely confirms that you are Thunder Boy's descendent'.

Haley rolled her eyes again, annoyed at his attitude.

'Ignore him, dear', Vedrfolnir advised. 'He is under the impression that he is the best Cosmos Watcher out of the three of us'. Nidhogg's scales flared down, his expression changing from cocky to humiliated within a second.

'Anyway...moving on', Ratatoskr spoke up. 'From what we have witnessed as Nidhogg claimed, you are indeed the descendent of Thor'.

Haley bit her lip, her muscles tightening, troubled by the last set of words.

'You doubt the prophecy, child?' Vedrfolnir said, her wise eyes taking notice of the emotional change Haley sighed and turned back to the lagoons, half-hoping to see more hippocampus colonies.

'It's just...' She paused for a moment. 'I still don't understand why the Gods chose me. Why couldn't it have been someone like Eric or Arianna? Aren't they supposed to be a part of the bloodline, too?'

'Lord Eric and Lady Arianna have more Vanir blood than Asgardian blood within them from your mother's side', Ratatoskr explained. 'Their father...Vladimir, though raised Asgardian, chose to follow in his mother's footsteps, taping into her dark magic, and potentially abandoning the bloodline. They needed it to be a whole Asgardian, not half-blood. With Antoinette being Vanir and Vladimir half Niflheimr, it was impossible for Eric or Arianna to receive Thor's inheritance of his powers...until you came along'.

'My father said Elvira, Vladimir's mother, played a part in him becoming the person that he is, the Lord of Nebula', Haley pointed out. 'Elvira wanted power more than love'.

'That is very true', Vedrfolnir replied back. 'Like Elvira and Vladimir, there are Cosmos Beings who use their gifts for corruption and to gain power over others. At this very moment, the darkness of Ragnarok is seeking out those corrupted Beings to spread fear and death through the universe and to replace those who became extinct'.

Haley did not want to know what horrors lurked within those deadly atmospheric clouds of Ragnarok: the apocalyptic event she researched so many times, all for school history reports. She was afraid. She was not brave like everyone else. Her heart was still more Midgardian than Asgardian too.

'Halena!' a male voice called out. Haley turned: it was Aeolus, handsome in full body armour complete with a sword, Keilantra at his side. She too wore body armour over a midnight blue battle skirt, metal armour armbands coating her wrists and her hair in a delicate fishtail plait. Haley couldn't help but notice the odd change in Aeolus. His cold-hearted arrogance no longer shone on his face. He seemed…concerned. The urgent looks on both his and Keilantra's faces told Haley something has happened or was happening.

'Aeolus? Kelly?' Haley rushed forward, dropping her book on the side and taking another firm grip on her Valkyrie dagger. 'What's going on?'

By this point, Haley didn't even notice Ratatoskr, Vedrfolnir and Nidhogg come down from the flower branches, landing on the concrete riverside wall.

'Prince Aeolus, Lady Keilantra, what on heaven is the matter that is so important than us giving Miss Halena here a history lesson of Yggdrasil's bloodlines?' Nidhogg asked presumptuously.

Haley rolled her eyes, shifting her annoyed gaze in Nidhogg's direction. Does he ever shut up? Haley thought to herself. 'Nidhogg, just let them catch a breather!' she uttered through gritted teeth, despite being shocked by this abrupt outbreak of character as much as Aeolus, Keilantra and the three animals were.

Ignoring the looks, Haley repeated the previous question. 'Aeolus, Kelly…what's wrong?'

Both caught their breath instantly, Aeolus' handsome, intelligent eyes locked with Haley's for a moment, before Keilantra interrupted the silent connection. 'A portal opened unexpectedly in a pathway of Yggdrasil', Keilantra answered.

'What sort of portal?' Haley asked, not liking where this was going at all.

'A portal to Nebula', Aeolus said, angry about saying the last word out loud, due to his possible long-standing grudge. 'A group of Nebulans passed through…' Pause. '…We managed to capture one, and put him in the dungeon, while the other were pulverized. The Nebulan in the cell is refusing to give any information on Vladimir's plans'.

Aeolus halted his speech. Haley tore her glances back and forth between both individuals, guessing there was more of a story about the imprisoned Nebulan. The big pregnant pause only increased Haley's impatience to a whole new level.

'Why isn't he speaking?' she demanded.

'He will not tell us anything…until he has spoken to you in person'.

Mixed emotions ignited inside her like a burning fire. From fear to nostalgia, and then to anger…anger at another shallow mention of Vladimir and the Nebulans – the monstrous creatures who threatened her family and who know how many innocent people in the Cosmos. And she was supposed to be a Cosmo Being herself, so why didn't she sense this particular group of Nebulans coming from a mile away? Why were her magical senses suddenly on mute? It certainly had nothing to do with the invisible protective shield encased around her body. She did not even feel the all-too-familiar coldness crawling underneath her skin, naturally overriding the warm atmosphere.

Suddenly, the world stood still as a vision clouded her mind: a group of six Nebulans opening a portal and a band of Asgardian knights struggling to prevent them from reaching the entrance to the city. The fight ended when the knights pulverized all except one, who seemingly decided to accept defeat; but the sly look in his eyes, with the rest of his face concealed behind a hood and mask, told Haley it was far from over. What was more: why was she only receiving this vision now, when it happened minutes ago?

'I want to see this Nebulan', she blundered out, still processing the past situation.

Keilantra, Ratatoskr, Vedrfolnir and surprisingly, Aeolus and Nidhogg observed her sudden decision in shock, like she was crazy.

'You cannot be serious', Aeolus let out a disbelieving grunt. 'As far as we know, this group of Nebulans came through that portal to kill you on Vladimir's orders. Who knows what mind games the heartless scum in the dungeon could play on you?'

'Do not forget your uncle is the one with vengeance on his plate', Keilantra remind her. 'And you are not his favourite person. He has also become just as powerful as you have'.

Haley's mental memory drive triggered another flash, where she saw a red ball of dark lightning attacking a magical force field…and a lightning strike severely scarring half of Vladimir's face. The only thing she couldn't hear was his voice and she was not sure if she wanted to know what it sounded like, too afraid to question these factors further.

'Look, they know I'm alive, now that the enchantment on my necklace has worn off', Haley argued. 'There's no point in hiding anymore. The Nebulans are the reason I was unable to grow up with the rest of my family. Besides, my family risked their lives for me, since my birth. I owe them so much. Even though I don't fully trust them, they are still my family'.

Haley meant every word. Even the five Cosmos Beings in front of her knew it.

'So, be it', Keilantra said reluctantly, as she silently debated between herself, Aeolus and the three animal guardians through telepathic eye communication. 'But if the Nebulan so much as attempts to harm you, we step in as your protectors. Remember: your magic is still at times unstable when – '

'Triggered by emotion', Haley guessed immediately. 'Deal'.

Aeolus and Keilantra simply nodded, but Haley could tell they were not happy with this decision. They needed to accept this was her choice, her chance to be brave.

The conversation officially terminated, when she dashed off as fast as her dress could carry her legs, glad it did not have a third layered skirt, otherwise she would have felt a burning tingle within minutes. She again reminded herself she was a demi-goddess with strong agility. Aeolus, Keilantra and the three animals were not far behind, occasionally yelling out to her to slow down, but she couldn't not until she found what this Nebulan wanted.

She ran down every open-pillared corridor of the palace, the activation of her memory drive hardwired to direct her to the dungeon. Feeling herself getting closer and closer, Haley projected a protection spell in her mind as a precaution in case the imprisoned Nebulan decided to play mind games on her, as the others predicted.

Darius, Antoinette, Eric and Arianna were already coming through the entrance to the dungeon, the doors shutting behind them.

'Halena, what are you doing down here?' Darius asked, upon noticing her presence.

'Aeolus and Keilantra…informed me that a band of Nebulans came through Yggdrasil and one was captured', Haley answered. 'Is it true?'

All parties sighed, dread on their unreadable expressions.

'I'd like to see the Nebulan you imprisoned', Haley said in pure honesty. She started towards the Celtic-embroidered double door, but all four family members stopped her.

'That is completely unwise', Antoinette proclaimed seriously, as Haley felt her frustration grow up. 'We believe that the Nebulan's request to see you could be seen an opportunity for him to get close enough to you and manipulate or destroy you'.

'Mother speaks wisely, little sister', Eric said. 'Your first experience with the Nebulans has angered even Vladimir himself'.

'Which is why I need to speak this Nebulan, face-to-face', Haley uttered stubbornly, not bothering to notice Aeolus, Keilantra and the animal guardians finally caught up to her. 'To find out more about Vladimir's plans...' She looked in between the four of them. '...And don't say it was my first encounter with the Nebulans, because I know it wasn't'.

Her family seemed gob-smacked by this revelation. Although due to the unreadable expressions they enhanced throughout the conversation, Haley guessed that underneath those, they were already aware of this. But there was still no time to process this further.

'I remember what I did to Vladimir and his Nebulan army, when I was a baby', Haley explained. 'The day of my christening was my first encounter. There's no point in denying it now that I'm beginning to know everything there is to know about the Nine Realms'.

'Your majesties, with all due respect, your daughter is right', Vedrfolnir suddenly stepped forth. 'She has spoken to my fellow guardians and myself. She has been kept in the dark about the nature of her powers and her heritage for all these years. As her sole guardians and her parents, not just her king and queen, you must let her do this'.

A long pause came about. Haley hoped Vedrfolnir's words were enough to convince them.

'Five minutes', her father said sternly, not liking this one bit.

Haley simply nodded.

'I'll take Aeolus and Keilantra with me, but I expect them to wait by the doorway. As you said, the Nebulan needed to see me. If he does try to break out or even attack me, I call for Aeolus and Keilantra'.

Her parents, brother and sister reluctantly agreed with a mirroring nod. The three guardians stayed put, while Haley, Aeolus and Keilantra walked through the now-open doors, Haley ignoring the worried expressions on her family's faces.

Luckily, there were fewer steps down this particular passageway than the spiral staircase. Haley did not bother to count these, her mind being all over the place. The crackling of the flamed torches next to the open based windows on one side showing another beautiful view of Asgard relaxed her ever so slightly, but not enough. This Nebulan held the key to her learning more about her uncle and as much as she hated him for what he did to her family, he too was family and all she felt was pity that he no longer believed in love.

When they finally reached the bottom, Haley studied every rusty cell in the dungeon, the criminals who sat calmly, some of which had a cunning look like they cockily believe they would be out of here in no time. Over her dead body, Haley thought. She turned away, unable to look at their yellowing teeth, dark eyes, and dirty pale skin any further.

'*Three cells down on the right*', Keilantra muttered telepathically. '*Remember: do not let him get inside your head*'.

'*I already projected a concealment charm over my mind*', Haley replied in a whisper. '*I'll be careful, I promise*'. She took a deep breath and began walking down the cold dungeon corridor, ignoring the hooting and wolf-whistling of the prisoners, looking at her like she was a piece of a meat, making her feel uncomfortably nauseous. The only time she saw those looks was only in movies, but witnessing them in real life…she felt like…like a victim.

By the time she walked past the first cell on the right, the strong push and pull of dark magic erupted around her like an invisible volcano. She retained the gasp she became so close to letting out, and continued unable to even stop to think. Haley looked back briefly at Aeolus and Keilantra, who too sensed it, their expressions questioning whether this was indeed a good idea. She slowed down past the second cell, tip-toeing carefully, and rounded the corner to look into the third cell.

The imprisoned Nebulan sat with his back turned to her in meditation form. Like the ones she encountered on the beach, he wore black robes and gloves so Haley could not see the pale skin baring scars and blotches. Either this particular Nebulan did not wish to expose his horrifying features, or he was making it look like Haley was in for some sort of horrifying surprise. Was his appearance completely different compared to the others she encountered?

Haley stood central to the dungeon cell.

'Well, I'm here', Haley uttered sternly. 'You asked for me, so what do you want?'

The Nebulan tilted his head from side to side, his neck clicking as he flashed the muscles.

'You asked for Halena and here I am', Haley repeated, her teeth becoming close to being gritted together as she grew impatient at the Nebulan's silence. 'You called for me for a reason, so what is it you want?'

Pause.

'Well, well...so the young princess who supposedly died of an incurable illness all those years lives', the Nebulan sneered. 'Who would have thought it?'

Haley's chest tightened from her beating heart.

'How were you able to pass through Yggdrasil undetected?' she asked a different question, skipping the first one for a moment.

The Nebulan snorted deeply. 'You do indeed have so many questions, young one', he said.

'Don't change the subject', Haley demanded lowly, holding her ground. 'Just answer the question, and tell me why you're trying to kill me. You're a follower of Nebula...of my uncle, Vladimir. Yes, my parents told me all about him, since I came back to Asgard...told me about the scum like you he created through forbidden rituals. So, stop wasting mine or the whole of this kingdom's time, and tell me what you know!' A deep surge coursed through her veins, the spiritual warrior princess within coming out full force for those brief few seconds.

'Like the Cosmos Beings, the Nebulans were blessed with extraordinary gifts', the Nebulan explained. 'We have the power to give, to create...and to destroy'.

Haley let out a humorless laugh. 'You really think your magic is extraordinary?' she uttered rhetorically. 'That magic...that poisonous magic is the exact power you used to torture innocent people...all on the orders of the corrupted bastard child of a psychopathic witch queen!'

The Nebulan stood slowly, as Haley gestured another glance towards Aeolus and Keilantra who, having sensed the Nebulan's movement, looked ready to withdraw their swords. Haley shook her head and signaled with her hand to mutely tell them to stand down. As she turned back to the hooded creature, a sudden burst of energy swept over her: cold and empty. Aeolus and Keilantra did not appear to have picked up upon it at all.

Before Haley questioned this further, the Nebulan spoke again through telepathy.

'I have just cast a silent shield over the minds of you and I, princess', he sneered. 'Vitally undetectable and strong enough to withstand your own mind barrier...so *no sudden moves, or your precious friends at the entrance will indulge pain far worse, than you imagine'.*

The man was crazy, Haley thought.

'You're bluffing', she pointed out, trying to play along with it. *'You're locked in a magic glass cell. You cannot reach from this distance'.* On that note, she heard a low sizzle like a white-hot iron burning through metal. The smell of melting iron journeyed up Haley's nostrils, turning her brain to mosh for a brief second, before she managed to keep it together again.

'Right, you made your point', Haley uttered telepathically. *'Stop that, or I'm calling Prince Aeolus and Lady Keilantra from over there to apprehend you and use magic to strengthen the prison cell bars to prevent your needs of escaping'.*

'And I already told you that you will be putting your little friends in danger, if they so much as even make a plan of action', the Nebulan replied arrogantly. *'Make your choice, princess'.*

Haley felt she had no other choice. *'Fine'*, she reluctantly agreed.

The prison bars returned to normal, as the Nebulan stopped the telekinetic incantation. Again, Haley checked to make sure that Aeolus and Keilantra were a considerable distance away because even though they looked like they can take care of themselves, Haley did not want them to put their lives on the line at this stage. This was an interrogation, and at least it was slightly less aggressive than the first Nebulan, who was practically on death's door. Turning back to the Nebulan, she observed him lowering his hood. His jet-black hair was mixed with grey, but one odd feature did not add up: he looked tan-coloured for a Nebulan. No signs of blotches or faint scars…

'Do not act so curious, little princess', he hissed. *'See, I am no ordinary Nebulan'.*

Haley's heart pounded heavily. *'I'm sorry?'* she answered back.

'I had hoped to save my true identity as a enjoyable surprise for you', he replied. *'But you have just insulted the memory of Elviva. The one who should have had the throne of Asgard, were it not for the interference of the cowardly High Council…the one who should have passed that onto me…the one whom I should have called…Mother'.*

The last word became a horrifying spectrum of realization, the tone of it and the way the man pronounced it in a vengeful approach.

'You – you're – ', she stuttered, as the man finally turned around. 'You're him'.

'The one and only...niece', he said, turning around with an evil smile. 'Your uncle...your father's brother, Vladimir...Lord of Nebula'.

Haley's shaken state kept rooted to the spot. Something inside her told her not to call for Aeolus and Keilantra, or any guard nearby, and not because of the threat he made to her. Instead, she spent the next few seconds studying her uncle, the man who her parents talked about...the man who abused her mother and siblings. His face served as his trademark, for one side was in tact with a single reddish-brown eye, while the other was disfigured in deep scarring, baring a foggy blind eye. The memory of how he became this way rushed back to Haley, when her single cry created a powerful lightning bolt striking the bad man standing right in front of her.

'You recognize your handy work, I see', Vladimir uttered, pointing out the permanent scarring and blind eye.

Haley swallowed hard, memories of her christening on constant repeat.

'You do indeed have your mother's looks', he sneered. 'The only thing I cannot stand is your eyes: the same eyes which belong to my dear brother...your father...except for that teeny tiny growing sparkle. I am guessing it is a side effect from your powers, passed down to you from the Thunder God'.

Uprising anger began to erupt inside Haley, making her blood boil. 'It's none of your business, at least not anymore', she said firmly, keeping a tight hold of her dagger. 'And I can't say I feel the same way about meeting you'.

'And why do you think that is?' Vladimir asked, challenging her.

'You hurt innocent people who have done absolutely nothing to you', she clarified. 'All Antoinette did was treat you with kindness and respect, and you spat it back in her face, by giving into the darkness Elviva passed onto you. It's a miracle my own brother and sister didn't follow, thanks to the teachings they received and Darius'.

'Because of my father's secrecy, I forged my own path', Vladimir answered. 'Antoinette would not accept my choice. I even asked her to join me bringing Eric and Arianna with her, but she refused. She turned her back on me, by falling into the arms of my own brother'.

'She told me she was in love with my father, while she was with you', Haley explained. 'She didn't realize it, until she spoke to him about her marriage troubles'.

Vladimir eyed her, making Haley uncomfortably sick, due to him having no trace of lightness coursing through his veins. Her parents were right: he abandoned the Asgardian bloodline. He was no longer a Cosmos Being.

They stared each other down in silence for a few more minutes.

'For an absentee princess, who believed her own parents to be dead, your sudden devotion is most intriguing', Vladimir said sarcastically.

Part of what he was saying was true: ever since meeting her parents, Haley felt this devotion, which only grew even in the absence both parties endured. The one thing missing was the earning of Haley's full trust. At this stage of communication, Haley realized Vladimir did not tell her the real reason as to why he came here disguised as a Nebulan.

'Why are you here anyway?' she asked, keen to change the subject.

'Why are you suddenly so loyal to Darius and Antoinette?' Vladimir asked, dodging the question again. 'Surely, you must feel angry at them for giving you up'.

Haley bit her lip and narrowed her eyes, tempted to summon an element capable of perhaps maybe traumatizing Vladimir and prevent him from playing any further cruel games. She was not going to let him twist things round. 'The only reason they gave me up was because they said you were going to kill me', she muttered.

'And yet you still don't trust them', Vladimir replied. 'They told a lot of secrets to your destiny…except one'.

No matter how hard she tried, Haley found that statement unavoidable, especially when she repeated her question through gritted teeth. 'Why…are…you…here?'

Vladimir just gestured an arrogant smile. 'Simple: to deliver a message to you', he sneered.

'And what is this message?' she asked. 'Also, what did you mean when my family told me all their secrets about the bloodline and the Realms, except for one?'

Another pause came about, until Vladimir laughed hollowly. *'Oh, this is good'*, he said in dark amusement. *'Why, my dear niece, this is to do what you need to retrieve, what you need to do to re-forge the object'*.

Haley became close to reaching breaking point, her magical senses almost going into overdrive in the process. A gentle breeze conjured from the wind element transiently penetrated the encased invisible shield Vladimir put around himself and Haley. It touched only them, but no prisoner or guard...not even Aeolus or Keilantra, who looked worried for Haley, but had no idea what was going on, due to her lips not moving. Either that, or they thought Haley was having a staring competition to see if she could force the Nebulan to fear her and her power.

'What are you talking about?' she asked Vladimir. *'What object?'*

'You know...think', he responded, setting another questionable challenge for Haley like an aggressive tutor, pushing her to answer it quick. *'Tell me: which weapon is the only artifact capable of generating lightning, with the ability to a target without missing?'*

The response shook Haley. Realization to the exact precise answer pulsed through the blood in her endless veins...the weapon with one name, and one name only...

'Mjolnir', she breathed out. *'You're talking about Thor's weapon, Mjolnir'*.

Vladimir slow-clapped sarcastically. *'Bravo'*, he said. *'And here is the good part. The part which your precious family did not tell you about...legend has it that only a descendent of the Thunder God can find the hidden pieces and re-forge the weapon'*.

Haley thought she heard the sound of thunder spread across the city above her head, but quickly dismissed it as a metaphorical figment. More and more betrayal arose by another ultimately secluded fact: she, a descendent of a great god, thought she could only do extraordinary things...performing magic. But this new information going out of the mouth of her own uncle, so consumed by hatred, troubled her deeply. She needed to get away from her uncle, and she meant now...

Looking out the corner of her eye, Aeolus and Keilantra still stood neutral. Vladimir's shield obviously did a number on the atmosphere surrounding her and him, it being virtually powerful enough to be undetectable as Vladimir claimed. Haley needed to figure out a way to break it. She began searching the deepest part of her mind, for one small magical essence unaffected by the Nebulan magic. The infrequent twists and turns made her brain look like a maze. All the while, she multi-tasked effectively in the hopes of distracting Vladimir.

'You see…you may think you truly believe my dear brother and my adulteress of a wife created you out of love', he smirked. 'You thought wrong…you were created for a purpose. You are needed to destroy anything that gets in your way'.

'I am nothing like you', she contemplated through mentally gritted teeth, struggling to contain her emotions. 'You're a murderer'.

'Only to those who stand and defy me', he pointed out emotionlessly, forcing Haley to think about the three families and the horrifying pain they suffered during their final moments.

'What about the people from those families you killed?' she asked. 'They had children, possibly no older than five'.

Vladimir was unaffected by the fact, retaining his mental emotionless state. 'They were unimportant', he stated.

Haley's anger only increased further alongside the electrifying jolt of lightning in her veins, disbelieving at his speech. For a despiteful second, she compared his darkened status to Aeolus' current personnel but quickly notified herself of the extensive light magic in his half-Elven blood.

'Unimportant?' she noted. 'Because of you, those children never got the chance to grow up and live their lives! They had friends and family, who are still mourning them to this day, and will stop at nothing to ensure you're prosecuted for all your murderous crimes'.

Haley sensed another mindful smirk formulating inside Vladimir, receiving another cold chill. All of a sudden, the momentary coldness became replaced with warm, pure light: a small, growing fire waiting to be unleashed. She located the unaffected magic. It was a small spark, but she hoped it was enough to counteract the dark magic surrounding her. Haley gathered all her strength, maintaining her posture and eye contact with her uncle, and created an aggrandizing upsurge as it began to channel through her body, slowly dissolving the encased Nebulan magic.

She smiled on the inside at the accomplishment; relieved Vladimir did not seem to sense it.

'I killed them, because they stood against me', Vladimir proclaimed, smirking as if he was expecting Haley's anger to reach breaking point. She was not going to let that happen. All she had to do was fool him in some way. *'They stood against me, because they betrayed me just like your precious family'.*

'You're wrong', she said. *'They stood against you, because they believed Darius to be a far better ruler than you ever will be...because they hated the monster you became, after you abandoned the Asgardian bloodline and began to favour the darkness!'* She hoped that that was enough to make her fake anger convincing to Vladimir.

'I can feel your anger', he hissed with a grin, showing off his pearly white teeth. *'You look like you need a teacher. Allow me to show your true power. You can be anything...be anyone, aside from the pretty, little princess in fancy dresses. With your power and my teachings, you will be invincible'.*

He must be completely out of his mind, Haley thought. Why on earth would he even think she would be persuaded to join him, and betray everyone she loved in the process? Did he not threaten to destroy her, if she was considered to be a big threat to him and his Nebulan inhabitants? Haley thought about the answer to that moment: when he said he would destroy her, did he actually mean kill her, or corrupt her?

Feeling the overriding enchantment become stronger, Haley guessed that now was her chance to alert Aeolus and Keilantra.

'Well, I guess there is only one thing I can do', she said, clenching her fists ready to strike.

'And what is that?' Vladimir asked.

'This!' Haley finally spoke through her own mouth, and pushed the force of the magic with all her might. The sonic wave was so strong, that the entire dungeon would have likely caved in. Haley stood neutral, being the vessel of the wave, but it knocked Vladimir back against the wall taking him by surprise, and broke down the force field he conjured up.

'He's here!' she shouted out to Aeolus and Keilantra. 'The Nebulan is Vladimir!'

Both switched to action mode, rushing forward at the name they solemnly wished they never heard again. As they came rounded the corner of the prison cell, they grew more antagonized at his presence. Aeolus twirled his sword in his hand and stepped forth to finish him while he was down: when all of a sudden, a sparkling red lightning ball stroke him in the chest, burning a hole in his armour plate. Haley's eyes widened: if Vladimir hit him in the same spot, he would be dealt a fatal blow straight through the heart, which, as much as she hated to admit it, terrified her. While Keilantra distracted Vladimir with her rainbow fireballs, Haley ran over to Aeolus kneeling beside him.

'Aeolus, are you alight?' she asked frantically, her hand almost touching his exposed skin inside the armour hole, half-wishing she could listen and feel his warm heartbeat.

Aeolus breathed deeply. 'I'll live', he answered. 'Besides, I've had worse'.

Haley checked on Keilantra, observing her actions. Judging by the slow movement coming about, she was growing weaker from the more energy she was using against Vladimir's magic. He was far too powerful for her to handle it alone.

Aeolus tried to pull himself up, but the still-burning metal on his chest touched his skin, as he let a low grunt of pain. Haley saw the edges left a near second-degree burn. Seeing the wound made her feel sick, with the skin peeling off and the redness of clear blisters and dried blood. She hated seeing Aeolus in pain. She needed to do something…

'Hold still, okay?' she said, gently removing his hand from his chest.

Aeolus eyed her oddly.

'Trust me: I know what to do', she answered, before he could ask how she would be able to heal him. Very carefully, she placed her hand over the wound, closed her eyes and began channeling energy directly towards it, envisioning herself in the exact same pain while thinking about the positive emotions: love, friendship, happiness…any emotion she could think of. Until a white light left her hand tracing against every cornered edge of Aeolus' wound, both individuals watching the wound stitch itself back together. Before either processed this, a loud thump against concrete alerted them when they saw Keilantra being thrown to the wall and collapsing beside them, too exhausted to continue. Vladimir had a deadly look of accomplishment, his dark ego ignited in his eyes – the man Haley's mother once knew and loved, the man her father grew up with was too far gone to return to the light, zero hope and no way back. A larger lightning ball materialized in his hands.

Haley immediately took out her Valkyrie dagger.

Reigniting her warrior princess fire, Haley scrambled to her feet shielding Aeolus and Keilantra, the lightning ball colliding with the dagger. A mesmerizing, yet impossible occurrence happened: the dark magic became absorbed into the blade, in glowing pure blue light, Haley's arms and hands shaking upon contact.

She stood her ground, until the noises and light died down, the only remaining sound being that of another shock wave. The walls and ground shook the walls and ground like an earthquake. Half of Asgard must have felt that, Haley thought.

The prisoners all held onto the bars of their cells, sticking half their heads out eager to take a closer look, their mouths in O shapes, their sick expressions as animal-like as ever. That deliberately turned her stomach over again.

Haley looked towards Vladimir, shocked at how a small dagger defected an unavoidable attack.

'BROTHER!' Darius's voice suddenly yelled out. At the entry staircase, her parents and siblings came down the stairs with the knights, weapons and magic at the ready. As Haley hopefully expected him to surrender, all Vladimir gestured was a slight without-a-care-in-the-world smile, before throwing down a freshly concealed smoke bomb, forcing everyone to shield their eyes and get down. As soon as it died down, all looked up: Vladimir was nowhere in sight.

Except no utmost silence filled the dense air, as the only chilling presence left of Vladimir was his voice, booming through the walls, menacing and dark.

'*You are brave and valiant, my sweet niece*', he said threateningly. '*My accomplices mentioned you were powerful, but never has an attack of that magnitude been blocked by a dagger so delicately small, previously belonging to a Valkyrie*'.

Haley took it as a sarcastic compliment, every word unappreciative.

'*It was truly a delight to meet you*', he continued. '*But I sense there is too much lightness overlapping your darkness. Therefore, you are indeed a dangerous threat to me, other Dark Beings and Ragnarok himself. You have tried my patience and killed some of my finest warriors*'

Her heart came close to jumping out of her throat.

'What exactly do you want then?' she asked, somehow knowing there was more to this.

'Halena, no!' Darius commanded.

Haley ignored him, awaiting Vladimir's response.

'*This is my message and my challenge to you*', he finally answered. '*In five days time, your home-worlds will face catastrophic consequences. Their souls are the perfect feeding product for Ragnarok to restore its strength. The only way you can save them is if you find what you are looking for: Thor's weapon; and face me at the location of my choice. During those five days, I expect you to find it – for it is only you that can revive its original form. So, Princess Halena, do you accept the challenge?'*

Every overly leveled expectation from throughout her life became overpowered yet again by another one of Vladimir's vile, but veiled threat, containing a challenge like it was some sort of super difficult game to play, one she was trying to figure out without instruction cards which are yet to be revealed. Without a specific answer brewing, Haley turned to her family, who too shared and faced the same appreciation-filled dilemma. How was she going to prepare herself for this?

Left no other choice, there was only one thing she could do...and that was to accept Vladimir's challenge, no matter what she faced during the course of it.

'I do', she said reluctantly. 'I accept – as long as you promise not to harm anyone or anything during the course of this challenge. Those are my terms'.

The pause that followed tormented Haley for a split few seconds, before Vladimir responded.

'I accept your terms', he said. *'No Nebulan will attack the Nine Realms for five days...Oh, and dear brother...please ensure her training at its fullest. You wouldn't want her to die on you'.*

Haley's father's facial muscles tensed up, as he struggled to retain his anger towards Vladimir's mockery. His creepy evil laugh echoed throughout the entire dungeon, dying down until the only sounds that were left were the howling of the prisoners and the light breeze, which swept past everyone's ears. After a momentary lapse of taking in the incurring situation, Haley turned to her family who were now worriedly furious about her impulsive decision.

'I had no choice', Haley pointed out, sensing the question coming up. 'He was going to hurt Aeolus and Keilantra, and anyone else close to me, if I didn't cooperate'.

'Accepting a fight with the Lord of Nebula is suicide!' Darius implied. 'Halena, your mother and I have already told you what Vladimir is capable of!'

'I needed to know what he wanted', Haley argued. 'I didn't expect it to actually be Vladimir'.

'Halena, you need to reconsider what Vladimir just offered', Antoinette practically begged. 'Your curiosity is going to get you killed'.

A tiny emotional twinge triggered within Haley's soul, the response from both parents becoming the near cause of the magical siphoning. 'You're only saying that, because you think I'm still too unprepared', she clarified.

All sighed, as they thought of a way to make her understand.

'It is not that we do not think you are ready, Halena', Darius explained. 'It is that my brother has become one of the dangerous beings in the Cosmos. Like you, he has been drawing his power through means of emotions. You are light…he and his followers are darkness'.

She hated being compared to him at this very moment, despite only just receiving an unexpected formal introduction, one so full of hate and anguish, and the constant dark energy journeying through his veins, like perhaps every other Cosmos Being in Yggdrasil. But it was half a truth: she used her powers to create things so beautiful, but there was a dark side to it – one which involved killing living things.

The twinge crawled all over her as if a spider crawled up and down her so quickly.

'Then tell me this', Haley demanded slightly. 'How can I be prepared, when you yourselves can't be honest about my heritage?'

Everyone acknowledged the sudden clarification with puzzled expressions, obvious they were unable to listen on the conversation between Haley and Vladimir, because of his dark shield.

'Vladimir said some things about what I have to seek to face him', she said grievously. 'Something you couldn't be bothered to tell me about; and I had to find out through him!'

'What things?' Arianna questioned.

'When were you going to tell me about Thor's weapon?' Haley asked.

The decisive silence filling the tense air notified Haley that this was something her family could no longer hid from her.

They entered another meditation state to communicate with each other telepathically out of earshot from Haley.

'Halena', Darius said. 'We are taking you to the High Council of the Nine Realms'.

CHAPTER 12: THE HIGH COUNCIL OF THE NINE REALMS

When her parents said they were taking her to the High Council of the Nine Realms, she never imagined it being back in the Hall of Glaosheim. Not to mention the eccentric impossibility that many people came so quickly within the half-hour her parents gave her to freshen up. Then again, they were Cosmos Beings after all, Haley thought. Their abilities were beyond that of the average human. A part of her wished this emergency council meeting would be located in a private area, in an amicable environment, not this immensely lively extravaganza.

A large round table stood in the centre of the hall, the triquetra symbol woodblock-printed in the dead middle, and at least fifty chairs positioned around it. Haley thought back to a legendary time, where a king created a round table. No head of the table: every person who sat around it established equal status. Maybe this particular table was exactly the same? Haley stood in deep astonishment, observing the people waiting to be seated: the Cosmos Beings of the Realms. Asgardians, Vanir Beings, Jotuns, Muspellrs, Niflheirs, Mer-People, elves and dwarves – all of whom stood before her; as if they stepped out from an old fairytale.

Haley first spotted Aeolus amongst the crowd in deep conversation with a woman and a young man two or three years older than him, immediately guessing they were his mother and brother. A twinge of sadness surged through her, the moment they made brief eye contact, giving each other only a small smile, knowing there was one person missing: his father, King Elwood.

As for the rest of the Cosmos races, an utmost number of them were purely human; though virtually every thorough feature was inhuman, Haley sensing every magical pulse in their blood. She became engaged in the initial struggle of processing all this, after eyeing up the groups from Jotunheim and Muspelheim, and the three to four-foot-tall dwarves from Svartalfheim a second time. Having read stories about them, Haley expected even the Jotuns and Muspells to be actual *giants*, towering several feet above the rest. Instead here they were: at almost equal height with the vast majority. The five from Muspelheim included a man with his son and daughter – Haley assumed were the king, prince and princess – and two knights in reddish-bronze armour. The king and the son too wore armour and robes, only more like ceremonial royalty than the moderate knight. Both men had auburn hair and excellent brown eyes, in red. The daughter looked like someone who stepped out of a perfume fragrance commercial advert. Well, with her attractive beauty and a quarter of the noblemen in the room becoming drawn to her, that was something to put into perspective. The girl bore a flirtatious smile, greeting noblemen as she twirled her shining auburn-highlighted hair, and her eyes, the same colour as her father and brother sparkled in accomplished desire. The sequined gems on her shimming red and gold dress flickered against the candle and torchlight.

The Jotuns – the queen, her son and three knights – had hair as dark as twilight and inky-blue eyes, in a glimmering mix of black. The queen wore a contrasting midnight blue silk dress in opposition to her exquisite pale-skinned beauty, her hairstyle a crowned braid. Her son was a pale-faced, but a very good-looking young man of around twenty-one. He wore pure grayish-silver armour, like the three knights, complete with a midnight blue robe and a sword baring a rare blue diamond, and ancient runic symbols on either side.

Before Haley pondered over the elves and dwarves, Angela opened the telepathic line of communication. '*Your parents are asking for you, Miss Halena*', she stated as any handmaiden would professionally. Haley quickly spotted her standing next to them, giving her a light, but silent wave and a sweet smile.

Haley moved to walk around the table, trying her best to ignore the forty to fifty gazes locked upon her very presence. Mutters occurred between various royal individuals, while others stood in silence, their mouths uncharacteristically hanging open unable to believe their eyes. Haley's parents were stood at the far end near five main council thrones, with three people she did not recognize; and Keilantra, Eric and Arianna, Lady Orla and Lady Serena.

'Ah, Halena', Darius said, the moment they noticed her coming closer. 'There are some people we would like you to meet, before we get started'. She assumed he was referring to the three people, who were close to turning around to face her. Antoinette gestured them to do so.

'Halena, meet my older brother and your uncle, King Alexander of Vanaheim', she introduced the man first.

Unlike her evil uncle, this uncle had a kindness and sense of honour. Similar to Antoinette, King Alexander's hair was the same shade of colour: a fair dark brown, with indigo eyes. He looked like he was possibly in his late thirties, about four years older than Antoinette. He wore a green velvet cloak and brownish robes, held by a black belt.

'There is no need for formalities, dear sister', Alexander said placing an affectionate, brotherly hand on Antoinette's arm, with a friendly smile. 'She is family after all...Halena, it is so good to see you. The last time I saw you, you were this small'. He expressed with his hands the highlighted size of a four-month-old baby. At least he had a good sense of humour, Haley thought, half-smiling.

'Pleasure to meet you too...King Alexander', she uttered shyly, as the memory drive inside her head clouded over her in a momentary lapse.

'This is my wife and queen, Elena: your aunt, and my daughter, Princess Henrietta', Alexander said, as Haley turned her sight moving towards the woman and the girl: her own aunt and cousin.

The Vanir Queen Elena was fairly beautiful. She had highlighted brunette hair, and calm blue-green eyes with a dash of gold – another presumed condition of heterochromia iridium, like Serena. The embellished boeidce dress she wore was designed from gold and silver embroidered silk. Another key pointer: her and Alexander's daughter, Haley's cousin was, despite only fourteen years old, mature at quite a young age, but still as lovely as her mother with free-flowing brown hair and similar green eyes. Henrietta's halter-neck royal gown had mix of turquoise and gold. On her petite head was a golden tiara, structured with green crystals resembled as summer leaves, like the kind from the Ancient Renaissance back on Earth.

'Hello. Nice to meet you', she muttered nervously, as another memory trigger came about. She mentally pushed herself to hold back revealing that she remembered a vague time, where Alexander and Elena presented her with a gift, before she went to Earth.

'Welcome home, Halena', Elena replied, smiling warmly.

'It is very nice to meet you, cousin', Henrietta said, sounding older than fourteen. 'My parents have told me so much about you'.

'I see you are wearing the ring we gave you', Elena pointed out, nodding to Haley's finger.

Haley's eyes shifted her eyes down to the ring, finally recognizing it as the gift, one of the three unusual gifts she received on her birthday.

'Oh, umm, thank you', she said timidly, running her finger over the blue garnet gem. 'Forged from a burning star, I take it?'

Alexander and Elena, even Henrietta, appeared startled by the short little revelation, the second those deliberate words impulsively slipped out of Haley's mouth.

'Apparently, my memories are more advanced, according to Eric and Arianna', she explained. 'My first experience of it was when the Aurora Eclipse appeared and further enhanced my abilities. Hence why I remember being given this ring'.

'I see', Alexander said, clearly impressed. 'Your mother mentioned to us your knowledgeable complexion around the Cosmos, but who would have thought you would also be born with a highly advanced memory?'

Haley's eyes narrowed at this point. 'Why?' she asked out of curiosity. 'Doesn't every Cosmos Being have the same thing with their memory?'

'In the time of the gods, yes', Alexander answered. 'But centuries have passed since the first Ragnarok. As a result of it, that power became too limited to master. Yes, it is one of our greatest gifts but none of us have a major amount of magic to such a cause...Until you came along, Halena'.

Unable to blink, Haley reached to touch the triquetra pendant around her neck, biting her lip.

'So, what you're saying is that I'm the first Cosmos Being in centuries to acquire this power from the Gods, not just through my ancestor?' she stated wondrously.

Alexander nodded, mirroring a smile.

'Wow', she uttered under her breath, as the others observed her trying to process all this revelation. Aside from the caution, Haley spotted light amusement between them the moment she laughed, as if it was the sweetest thing they ever heard during this potentially dark time, perhaps pointing to her being the supposed symbol of hope to all races.

A secondary set of footsteps alerted Haley to a presence; made purely of nature magic. She determined the species seconds before she looked up: elves. One particular elven presence became firstly known to her, making her heart flutter in warmth, easing the weight Vladimir's encounter left on her shoulders. Aeolus stood among a small group of elves and half-elves, two of whom he stood close to, Haley guessing they were his mother and older brother. Only difference to Aeolus: a change of armour after the ordeal Vladimir caused by the generated fireball.

'Hello again, Halena', Aeolus greeted her politely, by far in minimal zero emotion, seemingly colliding with the light magic embedded inside him.

'Hello, Aeolus', Haley replied, her eyes shifting to the spot where the near-fatal fireball struck him. 'Umm, how's your wound? I hope I passed on enough healing magic'.

'It healed excessively, thanks to you', he smiled tightly.

'Comes from being a descendent of the Thunder God, I guess', Haley said, shrugging her shoulders.

'Indeed it does', the woman of pure, ethereal beauty next to him spoke with a kindly smile. She was a cross between an elf and another species with emerald green eyes, shining as if they were the actual gem, matching her open-sleeved, shadow elven gown. On her gracefully curled hair journeying down to her waist was a silver forest leave circlet. Haley knew what this woman's name was before she said it, but kept her mouth shut to avoid more All-Knowledge hocus pocus.

'It is truly a blessing and miracle to see you again, Halena, and alive and well', she said, the kindly smile forever plastered on her face as if she was a beautiful marble statue brought to life. 'I am Lady Amara, the First Lady Elf and former queen of Alfheim'. And then turned towards the young man next to her. 'This is my eldest son, Silas: the Elven King of Alfheim'.

Silas was as handsome as his younger brother, with green eyes like Amara, and light brown shoulder-length hair. He wore sky blue robes, held by a dark brown belt, and black boots. A significant form of royal greeting occurred, when Silas reached for Haley's hand.

'As a fellow Cosmos Being, it is a true honour to meet you at last', Silas said, planting a polite but gentle kiss on her hand.

Haley formulated a friendly smile at the same time trying to prophesize how many more royal greetings she would be getting in the potential future.

'Thank you', she uttered.

On the inside, Haley mentally pinched herself, casually ignoring the lingering glances her parents shifted toward the exchanges between the peoples of the other Realms.

'I'm really sorry about your father, and husband', she said, remembering what happened to Aeolus and his family all those years ago, involving his father.

'We are grateful for your compassionate heart and spirit', Lady Amara proclaimed sadly, her eyes clenching slightly as she seemingly flashed back to the day of King Elwood's death. 'He was and will always be the love of my life. So, I thank you for your kind words'.

Haley nodded. Silas and Lady Amara returned it in equality. Aeolus only gave a small gesture of a nod, maintaining the same emotionless statue he had since Haley first laid eyes on him. Must be nice to not feel anything, Haley thought. But he did not and could not fool her in any way whatsoever. He may have this ability to convince people that his soul was encased in a capacity of darkness he did not ever want to leave, but the magic within was still as cloudless as the sun, moon and stars, much like his good heart underneath that dark blanket.

'Elwood would have loved to have seen you, standing here, Princess Halena', Lady Amara continued. 'He and your father were very close, as children, like brothers'.

That statement touched Haley's heart. 'I probably would have liked to have met him as well', she replied. 'From what I heard, he was a good man to my family'.

'Yes', Amara replied thoughtfully. 'Yes, he was'.

The sound of a staff hitting the concrete floor caught everyone's attention.

'To your seats, please', Darius announced, already standing one of the main thrones. Unsure of what to do, Haley simply looked out for Eric and Arianna who thankfully stood across from some dwarves, two to three feet away. They headed towards the main thrones, Haley saying a quick kind gesture of nice-meeting-you to Silas and Amara, before following them as gracefully as possible. She impulsively sneaked a secondary glance at Aeolus, who returned it in a handsome, but intimidating manner. Haley swore she saw another small smile form across his tightened face. She turned away embarrassed, blushing. The emotion escalated, as the electrical change of thunder and lightning came close to being unleashed. Calming herself, Haley walked to her empty seat, the only place unfilled. Everyone else: all seated, eyes as wondrous as when Haley first entered the hall.

Haley casually took her seat, smoothening her dress. A small glimpse of glowing white light delicately shone in her veins, but she covered it with both hands out of sight from everyone's all-seeing eyes. None of this repressed the nerves towards the upcoming duration of this emergency council meeting: her first one, her very first council meeting…

Everyone's voices switched to mute, when a moment's silence filled the air.

'Loyal friends of the Cosmos', Darius greeted every individual equally. 'My queen and I welcome you to this emergency meeting of the High Council of the Nine Realms. We apologize for this being of short notice, but unfortunately under these substantial circumstances, it cannot wait'.

'As you are surely aware, a week ago, our family received a miracle. Our beloved daughter, heir and princess, Halena finally returned to us after eighteen years in hiding'.

Everyone's eyes shifted towards Haley yet again, igniting her magic like the birth of a new flame on a candlestick, the tension forging itself around her soul and body.

'But less than two hours ago, a shadow was cast over the city', Darius continued. 'We managed to capture a Nebulan, who supposedly and willingly surrendered to us after penetrating the shield along a hidden pathway within Yggdrasil'.

Low murmurs broke the atmosphere, as the Cosmos Beings entered an exchange of silent words, raising questions.

'My Lord, how is that even possible? Only an Asgardian or any other Cosmos Being from the Nine Realms has the power to penetrate or forge a shield around a hidden pathway', a woman with long white hair, separated from Haley by Arianna clarified. She was beautiful, with twinkling pale blue eyes, like long-distance stars. Her long, majestic dress was a mix of dark and pale blue against the off-white material holding it together. The young seventeen-year-old boy sat next to her, Haley guessed him being the woman's son, had similar-coloured hair, excluding the shining green eyes. His robes were purely silk, and a black shimmering cloak.

'Halena, may I introduce Nyssa, Queen of Niflheim and her son, Prince Occasso', Darius said.

The woman presented herself with a kind smile in Haley's direction. 'Forgive me, Halena for not introducing myself earlier – it is a true honour'.

Haley smiled timidly, uttering nothing.

'Now, I understand we have more pressing matters to discuss', Darius reminded the two and everyone else, who was searching for the precise moment to make introductions. 'Every Cosmos Being does indeed wield that power to ensure the protection of the Nine Realms, but this was no accident. This Nebulan was no Nebulan'.

Individuals grew apprehensive, Haley coming in connection with their every emotion. She knew what was going to happen next.

Several leaned in closer.

'It was Vladimir', Darius said, the cruel name pouring off the tip of his tongue like it was a poison he was struggling to withdraw to prevent entering his nervous system.

A huge uproar occurred between all the people, seconds after Vladimir's name reached their ears. The shock of it nearly knocked Haley out of her chair, herself never seeing, hearing or feeling anything like this, especially on a high council of royalty. Every member, excluding herself, her siblings and parents, scrambled to their feet, exchanging constant words back and forth, all complete gibberish through talking over one another.

'How will we be able to protect the Nine Realms, with that murdering scumbag looking over our shoulders?' one asked.

'We should have killed him, when we had the chance', the prince of Muspelheim blundered out, slaming his clenched fist on the table so hard that it shook underneath Haley's hands. His fist glowed a slight red-orange, fire threatening to come through. Was his power channeled by anger? Haley would never know, while knowing nothing about the various other Cosmos Beings.

'Nowhere is safe. It has not been for the past eighteen years. Not even our own children are safe', the dark-blue haired, pale skinned queen of Jotunheim shouted out desperately, again reminding Haley of the brutally murdered families who had children.

'We dispatch all our finest men. Take the fight to the Nebulan scum!' a First Knight of Alfheim recommended determinedly. Every knight around the table shouted in sync, in agreement with the Elven First Knight's term. More agreeing and disagreeing came about, as others of military background tried to think up an alternative solution, one that didn't mean war. The overwhelming stress drew Haley closer to having a panic attack, her magic equal to its growth. She spotted a glowing upsurge of lightning emerging from her clenched fist, the threat of a potentially deadly wave billowing. Breathing heavily, she turned to Antoinette with pleading eyes. Antoinette thankfully noticed her helplessness at control.

Through obvious telepathy, she informed Darius of Haley's symptom.

'Silence!' he yelled out. Everyone stopped their debate immediately, turning their direct attention to him. 'Every Nebulan we have encountered for the past eighteen years has abilities proven by the Lady Orla to be unpredictable. Vladimir, however: I thought with him being a former Asgardian, every move he makes across Yggdrasil would be made detectable to us. To plan ahead for a likely confrontation. But I was wrong. We were wrong. Vladimir has become more powerful and unpredictable as every Nebulan on that god-forsaken wasteland of a world he created'.

Eyes blinked twice.

'So what do you suggest we do?' the Muspel King asked. Like his son, he too had reddish-brown hair with eyes the exact same shade, and similar robes.

Darius and Antoinette glanced at one another.

'While Vladmir was captured, he…' Antoinette spoke out, before pausing, unable to bear reminiscing the unfolded encounter. 'He demanded to speak to Halena'.

Haley cast her eyes down to her fidgeting hands.

'His reasons: he wanted to be absolutely sure she was The One', Antoinette continued. 'And because Halena desired to know more about her heritage'. Haley shifted her gaze towards Antoinette, who grew reluctant. 'He also spoke of Mjolnir'.

A long pause took place. No uproar thank goodness, Haley thought, but the low muttering only made the council atmosphere more intense.

'Sister, I thought Mjolnir was hidden in separate locations', Alexander pointed out.

'It was and still is', Antoinette answered.

Haley searched their minds back and forth, checking she heard it right.

'I'm sorry I'm not following', she addressed all family and council members. 'What do you mean: Mjolnir was hidden in separate locations?'

Darius let out a deep sigh, and in sheer reluctance wavered his hand around, mentally conjuring up an incantation. A stream of silver light materialized in his hand, floating some inches above the table. All council members watched, but their expressions said it all: this was a story they were informed about numerous times throughout royal studies or during past council meetings. After a moment, the light manipulated itself into the projection of a king on his deathbed, three cloaked women stood at his bedside, performing some form of ritual.

'Lady Orla foretold the story of how the Lord of Thunder died and the Bloodline Ritual he, the Norns and High Council performed to you', Darius said rhetorically, ensuring Haley was up to date with some aspects.

'Yes', Haley answered. 'That his spirit merged with the bloodline so his descendent would inherit his power'.

Darius nodded in agreement. 'This is another part of the story you do not yet know', he added.

Her parents shifted their glances to Lady Orla, granting her their absolute permission to tell this staggering story. She stood gracefully to her feet and raised her hand up at the projection, animating the images of people as the Lord of Thunder disappeared.

'This is the part we did not yet tell you, young Halena', Lady Orla explained. 'Despite the Bloodline Ritual and the peaceful time, the Norns knew Ragnarok would one day return'.

'When the Thunder God passed to Vahalla and to the stars, the Norns took Mjolnir'. A reflection of an ancient magic hammer appeared with the three hooded women surrounding it. 'And they split it into three separate pieces'.

Haley watched the hammer split into three, flying off to three different locations on a newly materialized mapped-out structure, which she recognized instantly.

'It looks like the pieces are within Yggdrasil', she guessed.

'That is correct, Halena', Lady Orla said, impressed by Haley's quick thinking through the power of the All-Knowledge. 'And do you know where these locations are?' She manipulated the images, enlarging the three pinpointed spots, which sat a considerable distance away from one another. Haley stood up to study it more closely, ignoring everyone's intrigued gazes at her intense focus. Her heart thumped at her amazed recognition.

'The locations are the Three Wells of Yggdrasil', she concluded after a minute's silence.

'Yes', Lady Orla replied back.

Haley blinked twice. 'All this time…and not once did Vladimir suspect', she uttered in awe.

'Vladmir always had his suspicions about the legend', Arianna answered. 'Through his obsession and rise for power, he searched through the library books for information, even secretly tortured people who knew of the legend's reality, but none gave him a single detail'.

'The pieces are still hidden, and that is all he knows', Eric added.

Haley felt a sense of relief. Who knows what Vladimir would do with Mjolnir, if he ever got his slimy claws on it?

'And he will never be able to wield it', Lady Orla said, as Haley cast her eyes back to her. 'As Thor's living heir and The One, Halena, it falls to you to find the pieces and re-forge Mjolnir to its original form'.

With raised eyebrows, Haley looked back at the projection a lump in her throat. She felt sick to this stomach having this new bearing weighed on her shoulders, as she realized something was off about all three locations.

'If I'm the one who's supposed to re-forge Mjolnir, why did I have this strange feeling there is a catch?' Haley questioned. Out of her corner of her eye, both her parents and her siblings pursed their lips in minimal fear.

'What is it?' Haley asked again. 'What aren't you telling me?'

The silence became torture, until Darius finally changed it into a split projection of three golden stones, each with one woman stood before it.

'The Norns transformed each piece into a Thunderstone: a powerful gem always worshipped as a shooting star or meteorite, according to your legends', he explained. 'They then concealed the Thunderstone under a protection enchantment, and hid each piece inside a well: Urd, Hvergelmir and Mimir'.

'Okay, I get that', Haley assumed. 'But what else is there? What is it I need to do?'

She was right: what more was there to know? What was the connection?

And there her parents go again with the same pursing lips action.

'The Lord of Thunder also ensured that the pieces were only to be retrieved by his descendent', Lady Orla explained in their place. 'So, three challenges were created: one at each location',

'Challenges?' Haley repeated questioningly.

'The people call it…The Trials of Thor', Darius said.

The title rang a bell. Haley became dazed in deep thought at the recognizable words, remembering how she read about it in an article from a history magazine, under the very same thing. One particular section: enriched stories about trials for gods and goddesses to test their strengths and weaknesses. Was this what this was going to be like her? It terrified her all the same.

'Thor decreed that these Trials would be created to test his descendant's strength and ability and prove their worthiness as his heir', Lady Orla continued.

'Are they...dangerous?' Haley asked, her voice trembling.

'I am afraid that is an answer we do not know, Halena. Only the ones who created the Trials are aware of what occurs during these tasks: Thor and the three Norns. But should you accept, his spirit within you will serve as your instinctive guide'.

Haley bit her lip. How was she supposed to prepare herself for these Trials, when no one could prevent with any more information on what to expect? The only four people who seem to know a lot more about these Trials were not even her own family. One was a god, her own ancestor, who was now died. The other three: guardians of three sacred wells drawn out of a legendary story...

'Are you alright, Halena?' Elena asked, concerned. Everyone else's expressions displayed the same emotion.

'I just need to get some fresh air', Haley said, pushing her seat back. She politely excused herself.

Avoiding the stares, Haley walked towards the balcony, out into the warm air.

Despite the gentle breeze and warmth of the sun touching her skin, everything buzzed in her head like a swarm of bees. Everything she learnt: every lie, every brand new piece of knowledge began to overwhelm her mind, in sync with her struggling to regain control of her magic. The white lightning in her veins glowed at a slow extent against the sunlight. Tears rolled out of Haley's eyes, not from upset, but from fear. Fear that she was not ready for such dangers in who knows what lies ahead. Realizing her abilities were now at a near-uncontrollable rate, she managed to calm down entering a meditation mode, and her flashing veins changed back into normal pulsing veins.

'Halena?' her mother called out from behind her gently, causing her to quickly wipe away her tears. 'Please try to understand that your father and I did not tell you about the Trials, because we too did not know what awaited in them. All we wanted was to protect you'.

Haley managed to turn around to face Antoinette, who had the same compassionate look of wisdom in her eyes.

'Why tell me now?' she asked. 'Why wait until now at this meeting to tell me? I understand I have to re-forge the hammer as Thor's heir, but this…' She took a deep breath. '…Coming to terms with the fact that I have magic and of royal blood still hasn't fully sunk in, but now knowing I have to go through these potentially dangerous Trials to prove I am worthy, I – I'm not sure how I can handle that either way'.

Her mother caressed Haley's cheeks, the warmth touching Haley's heart.

'We were to tell you by the summer solstice', Antoinette explained. 'It was Vladimir's original plan to strike Asgard, but when he discovered you were alive, he changed his plans'.

'And I accepted his terms on the condition that he won't harm anyone', Haley pointed out. 'At the same time, thinking finding Mjolnir would be like an ordinary treasure hunt'.

'It was a naïve decision, yes, but your heart was in the right place', Antoinette proclaimed. 'You also made it, because you want to protect the people you know and love. That is your greatest trait'.

'But why keep this a secret from me as well?' Haley asked again.

Antoinette lowered her hands to take Haley's.

'Because your father and I have always expressed our fears of losing our children', she proclaimed. 'Including you'.

Haley squeezed her mother's hands. 'I know, and believe me when I say that I share the same fear; but like I said: I can take care of myself. I just…I just don't know what to do'.

'It is your decision whether or not to do the Trials of Thor. If you do, you will be saving millions of lives and securing a bright future. If not, Vladimir along with other Dark Beings could bring Ragnarok back'.

Haley's thoughts spread, as she reflected on two separate futures: one where there was pure light and peace, the other involving darkness. She could not allow innocent people to face the wrath of Dark Beings, but at the same time she expressed fear at failing to protect them. What if she couldn't do it? What if something goes wrong?

'Can I have a few minutes to decide?' she asked.

Antoinette gave an understanding smile. 'Of course, my darling', she replied. 'I will give you a moment. Come back in, when you have made your decision'.

Haley nodded and watched as her mother headed back to the council table to keep them informed.

Half an hour went by, when she stepped back into the hall out of the warm sunlight, only stopping to look up at the sky where Antoinette created the Sky Mirror to reveal Nebula, effectively praying to the Gods they weren't watching. And then at the magnificent city: Thor's city, her soon-to-be city, if it ever came to that. Swallowing hard, Haley stood tall and walked back to the round table of council members. Everyone was engaged in deep discussion, out of earshot from Haley, possibly about what to do if she did not accept the challenges; or if she could face Vladimir without the use of Mjolnir. Sensing Haley's approach, curiosity filled all, as they anxiously awaited her decision.

'I've been thinking about what you said to me', she said more to her family than the rest of the council. 'The truth is: I am scared. I'm scared of controlling my power and losing control…I'm scared of failing, and most of all…I am even scared of my own uncle, the person he has become. At the same time, I am still having trouble accepting that I'm a princess, and a demi-goddess'.

Haley paused. The council members mirrored each other's expressions, eyes of deep interest, except for two of the dwarves, who were scribbling down some notes on pieces of parchment.

She had yet to give the final part of her opinionated conclusion.

'But I also realize that you need me just as much as I need you', Haley continued. 'I can't stand by and watch innocent people die. I have decided…that I am going to do these Trials. I am going to the Wells of Yggdrasil to find the thunderstones of Mjolnir'.

Mixed emotion intensified between the council members. Alexander, Elena and Henrietta smiled tentatively, hopeful her decision was an inspiring first step. The rest of the council retained the same glances of wonder, while some dwarves were as mute as a bunch of mice. Either they lost their ability to speak, or they were as grumpy as one of the seven dwarves. Putting that to one side, Haley became aware she just made sure her first real and foremost decision, as a princess born in the cosmic universe. Question was: what was her next move? How would she be able to prepare with five days on the clock, as Vladimir requested? Who was going to mentor her through these advanced extraterrestrial teachings of magic? Purity shone her parents and siblings' eyes, so pure that they reached the realization that

Haley was a woman making her own decisions. But it also looked as if they read her mind, picking up on the questions like they were sent through a telegram.

'Very well, Halena', Darius said. 'You may go on this quest, but you will need a group of companions to accompany you'.

'Companions?' she questioned through raised eyebrows.

'You will need to select a group of warriors with cosmic abilities, capable of helping you withstand whatever lies within all three tasks', Antoinette explained. 'Like every Cosmos Being, you can sense their powers. We too witnessed your ability to manipulate the elements of the Thunder God. As you were also born under both the most powerful thunderstorm and the first Aurora Eclipse in centuries, you have the rare gift to call upon its lights, should you choose'.

Haley thought back to her birth and eighteenth birthday. Both days where the same Aurora Eclipse took place: one of the greatest astronomical discovery in history. There was most definitely a connection about it, but she never could quite put her finger on it up until now. Could she really pull off a power like this – calling upon the actual Aurora Eclipse? Would she be able to seek out the great ancestral spirits now bound to its lights? The only way she can find out was on this mission.

'I guess it explains why I felt a connection to the Aurora Eclipse in the real world and my dreams', Haley pointed out. 'I'll try it out, when I'm ready. For now, I want to choose my companions'.

'As you wish, daughter', Antoinette said. 'Make your choices wisely'.

Haley took that into consideration, observing the people around her, mentally evaluating their strengths and weaknesses through the channeled sensations of their cosmic powers. All equaled to her, but some were unpredictable, unable to likely withstand whatever lies within each task. She set those aside, like arranging a table of groups, until she settled on five names.

'I have decided', Haley eventually said. 'Everyone has powers practically useful for any task, but I'm choosing the people who have already shared their own experiences on the Nebulans, and also because their powers equal with my own in order to succeed. So, I chose…Eric, Arianna, Keilantra, Aeolus…and Angela'.

Eric, Arianna, Keilantra and Aeolus slowly stood honorably grateful for Haley to allow them to be her companions; but then came low murmuring on all areas of the council table, obviously surprised that Haley would choose a servant girl as a companion. Even Angela felt the same, as Haley sensed the emotion despite her standing a foot away from her chair.

'Forgive me, Halena', the dwarf king said. 'I understand your choices for companions, and I am sure the council would agree...but why a handmaiden? What did she have to help you on this seemingly perilous journey?' In other words, he meant why Haley would select a person of lower class. Haley read the dwarf king. She saw surprise and kindness...and disturbed confusion. Maybe the royals did not understand equality as much as she does from living on Earth. Perhaps she should one day when all was settled tell stories to the citizens and their children about the royal families, and how they greet the crowds of people as equals.

'A wise person once said they believed in equality in all things', Haley said in accordance to her igniting princess wisdom. 'Angela told me stories about the Asgardian culture and the other realms. I see her as a friend now, more than a handmaiden. Not only that, but I sensed she had magic'.

Angela blushed at Haley's sudden complimentary. Seeing as she grew up in a lower-class family, she did not know what to expect from being the first handmaiden of a long-lost princess. Haley felt a twinge of guilt take over from her impulse.

'It is alright, Angela', Antoinette addressed her kindly.

Angela sighed, taking a breath before speaking.

'I am a healer', Angela answered timidly. 'The magic was passed down to me through my mother, upon death but I refused to use it out of fear of it changing me'.

'No Asgardian or any other Cosmos Being should fear their magic', Lady Orla said to her. 'Halena feared her magic all due to her unfamiliarity of the Odinson Bloodline. It was not until her early childhood that she began to notice she was not human, but through the guidance of Eric and Arianna, she accepted her magic was a part of her as she was a part of it'.

Part of that was true, Haley thought. All the magic tricks during her childhood, counting the snow twisters, animal avatars conjured by lightning, thunderstorms in stressful situations and sonic vibrations so powerful that it would set objects and people flying to scattered destinations...

Haley turned back to Angela.

'Angela, you're a healer', she said. 'I sensed it's strong enough to heal anything fatal including poisonous wounds and bites. Believe me, when I say it will be proven useful for these tasks: for you, myself, Eric, Arianna, Keilantra and Aeolus'.

Angela appeared amazed by Haley's quick adaptation to the Asgardian life, though Haley deep down felt differently, due to missing her last eighteen years of humanity. But she still struggled to process Haley's recommendation of her as a companion. Haley awaited her answer, ignoring the fierce electricity of blood pulsing through her veins at a fierce speed. Why couldn't it just activate when she was in a dangerous situation, or better yet when she was on the verge of an adrenaline rush?

'Alright', Angela finally said, inspiring belief and hope shining on her cheeks. 'I will help you…if it is no trouble for your Majesties'. She gestured towards Darius and Antoinette, who looked on proudly at Haley's emerging wisdom.

'Very well', Darius announced, before turning to the rest of the council. 'High Council, Princess Halena will be accompanied on her quest to search for the Thunderstones by Lord Eric, Lady Arianna, Prince Aeolus, Lady Keilantra and Angela'.

CHAPTER 13: THE BIFROST

Plaguing nightmares clouded Haley's mind, following the High Council meeting. With five days to go until the battle with Vladimir, Haley's parents agreed she would be given half a day of training as soon as the council meeting ended, to prepare herself both mentally and physically for the journey ahead, under the observing eye of her group of companions: Eric, Arianna, Keilantra, Aeolus and Angela. One: they had weaponry skills, which exceeded her expectations, after witnessing it during training. And two: she saw them as equals with the same goal to bring peace to the universe; particularly in Angela, who had a magical ability of healing.

They pushed her far and beyond as she advanced quickly in her abilities; all down to the training she also undertook on Earth. Thankfully, the black belt in karate too paid off, she thought. But was it just that, or the warrior demi-goddess inside her? Despite the initial strength she experienced during her childhood, there were never any other likewise moments since. Another psychological problem: Haley still struggled to master the mystical side of her battle training. Her magic at times played up, when her trainers sensed her doubtful, lingering thoughts towards her destiny. They pushed her further and further, until a sudden burst of energy, closely resembling that of the sonic wave from that fateful night on the beach, knocked them back, enhancing her guilt. Everyone dismissed it as a natural reaction, but Haley believed it to be potentially uncontrollable.

'The least they can do is just accept that I was sorry for hurting them', Haley told Angela, who styled her hair back into a fishtail plait, preparing her for the journey ahead. Angela already had her travelling gear on, her hair clipped back to perfection. Haley, on the other hand, sat at the dressing table listening to the soft melody of her music box, the Tree of Life twirled elegantly around in a circle, while waiting for her armour to arrive.

'They are warriors, my lady', Angela said with a sympathetic smile. 'They show no weakness to any enemy, or let their guard down. On the battlefield, they conquer all fear. You too are a warrior, Halena. I have seen you in action. You are also equal to the Lord of Thunder himself'.

'Everyone seems to believe so, but I'm still torn', Haley doubtfully proclaimed. 'I don't even know why I accepted this quest. It felt like my heart was in the right place, but my head kept telling to go in the opposite direction to walk away from this entire ordeal'.

Keilantra, stood in neutral at the bedroom entrance in her own travel armour.

'Haley, know that you are free to make your own choices', she said. 'Despite being unable to walk away from the prophecy, this quest was your decision because you know it is a part of your destiny'.

Haley sighed. The music continued playing on a ceaseless loop. She touched the triquetra necklace catching a glimpse of the silver crystal glimmering against the sunlight. In her recent dreams, the symbols appeared multiple times: an everlasting connection to all Nine Worlds. What was it really about the necklace? It was not just a personal connection. It was something else. Haley kept it to herself, unable to question it further especially to the others. She would have find out on her own.

'You are ready, Miss Halena', Angela said, finishing up the fishtail plait and placing a navy-blue embroidered robe with long sleeves over her shoulders. Haley stood, the cloak falling over the black legging trousers and boots. She headed over to the floor mirror and became awestruck by the unrecognizable person staring back at her. It was like her identity as Haley Freeman was fading away into a dim candlelight and Princess Halena emerged from a blooming burst of re-born flames.

A knock at the door swirled the three girls around. It opened and in came Eric and Arianna. They too were travelling armour with similar robes, each armed with weaponry: Eric a set of katana swords and a dagger, and Arianna a bow and arrow set in a blue and gold quiver.

'It is time, sister', Arianna said.

Haley's heart flipped over. The time went by so fast she failed to notice, due to her formulating a list of logical methods and solutions on how to conquer the Trials. Stepping away from her reflection, Haley eyed up her Valkyrie dagger. It could be a proven choice of weapon, she thought. If any Nebulan or another monster attacked, the blade was magically designed to deflect the incursion and send it straight back to them.

'Alright', Haley turned to the others, placing the dagger inside the pocket of her robe and reaching for the across-the-shoulder bag, containing the essentials for a long journey: water, medicine and extra food. 'Let's go'.

The horse-ride luckily provided an extra twenty minutes of freedom, holding onto the shreds of humanity until Haley stepped through the Bifrost's portal. Gullfaxi galloped in sync with Eric and Arianna's horses, as Haley stroked him contently feeling the magical bond between them. They were right about the ancient horses sensing the power the person inherits from its previous owner.

Although the sun was still rising, the pale-blue sky was growing brighter with the planets' visibility becoming obvious. Earth was the closest. As she gazed up at the blue and green planet, Haley thought about her friends down there. James, Emilie, Matthew…everyone she knew since she lived in Cornwall, probably getting on with their everyday lives, now that their memories of their horrific encounter with the Nebulans were wiped clean. Only problem was that making contact to reassure them she was safe would be of the utmost difficulty: one, though Asgard was a city of advanced species, they were also ancient; and two, after what happened, Haley could not risk putting them in danger again. They cannot know her true identity.

As the Bifrost came in sight, Haley stared down at the ground, not at Gullfaxi's silver hooves, but at the multi-coloured matter reflecting off the stone-gray concrete. Well, considering they were technically and literally walking along the rainbow, she thought. The smell of ocean water travelled up her nose, the waves moving swiftly backwards and forwards.

The horse halted. Haley looked ahead

There at the very end stood a marble archway, towering above the broken edges, damaged from a past war while the main archway remained untouched. In its place – a large rock glistening like water washing up on rocks. The triquetra sign was curved into it and along the top surface of the archway crystallized to closely represent the rainbow bridge, whatever structure it truly was. From legends, it was the rainbow's colours seen spreading across the sky after a rainfall. Darius, Antoinette, Lady Orla, Serena, Aeolus, Lady Amara and Silas stood at the entrance leading into nowhere, except the eternal day and night of the universe. There was another person awaiting their arrival – the current gatekeeper of the Bifrost, and a direct descendent of the god, Heimdall. This man retained the bearing of an honourable man, alongside the appearance of thirty years or slightly older, with his young handsome face and golden-brown hair and wise, but unreadable eyes, leaving Haley wondering how he truly felt on the inside. Did he have a life before he became the gatekeeper? That was a good question. Due to all the time spent guarding the gateway, according to Lady Orla, Haley couldn't shake the feeling that the isolation affected him in some conceivable way.

'My Lord and Lady', Keilantra greeted Darius and Antoinette next to the rest, turning to Lady Orla. 'Mother…Princess Halena is ready'.

Haley's parents cradled other's hands, in close-to-matching robes: her mother in a royal blue open-sleeved dress and wrap, her father in noble armour and a royal blue robe. Both bore anxious expressions towards this being Haley's first quest since discovering she was a princess. They probably thought it was too soon for her to do something big. But there was no time for extra training, especially with Vladimir's threatening deadline weighing down on people's shoulders.

'Halena, allow me to introduce Optimus', Lady Orla gestured at the man. 'Guardian of the Nine Realms, gatekeeper of the Bifrost and descendent of Heimdall, the All-Seeing God'.

'It is truly a great pleasure to meet you at last, Miss Halena', he greeted Haley politely. 'My king and queen requested for you to be watched over by my All-Watching Eye, passed down from my ancestor, Heimdall. He was an honourable and loyal man of servitude to the Nine Realms; and as my sworn oath, I hope to continue that legacy and be of service to you in any way that I can'.

'Thanks…Optimus', Haley replied, expressing nervous gratitude.

He gestured a small smile. 'You have your father's honour and your mother's kindness, My Lady. And the spirit of the Thunder God flourishes within you'.

Haley nodded, visibly surprised yet again by that one statement about the Thunder God's soul now merged with hers, and perhaps the entire bloodline.

'Halena', Antoinette greeted her, stepping forth alongside Darius, their arms and hands interlinked. She took a hold of Haley's hand. 'I sincerely hope you made the right choice to reach this accomplishment'.

'You are absolutely sure you are ready for this?' Darius asked, concern in his eyes as Haley predicted for both of them. She questioned the same thing during those tiringly endless training hours. Could she have learnt the advanced basics in preparation, if there was more time? Would she be able to go a long way to protect the people she cared about? If she answered that two weeks ago, it would have been *no*. Now, the answer seemed fairly straight forward, so she simply replied with a confirming nod. For the first time in her life, Haley felt ready for something extremer than surfing and karate, despite the complicated emotions crawling over her like tiny insects. That secondary feeling only increased her determination to succeed.

'Hello, Halena', Aeolus said, a slight smile quickly as it appeared dissolving back into the hard-shipped posture. In Haley's mind, she sensed more light magic than before, since meeting him, no matter how he tried to deny it. She only saw flashes of his good heart – greeting Haley politely and offering her friendly advice during training.

'Hi, Aeolus', Haley replied. Their eyes connected with one another: Haley's sparkling blue eyes with Aeolus' dark, intense eyes. Warmth brewed between them, leaving a bruise like a burning rock. Were these feelings she had towards him something stronger than a warm, but unsteady friendship?

Haley snapped out of the crushing-on-a-boy-trance, to greet Lady Amara and Silas. 'Lady Amara…Silas', she greeted with a small nod. 'Silas, you're not in Alfheim?'

'I left my second royal advisor, Lord Derek, in charge until Mother and I returned', he replied. 'We decided to come to the Bifrost and wish you, Aeolus and your fellow companions good luck on your quest'.

'Well…thank you', she uttered shakily.

'You are welcome', Lady Amara said. 'Everyone has faith in you'.

Haley raised her eyebrows. 'Everyone? Really?' she asked in disbelief.

'Yes. Since they learnt about you and the prophecy, they believe you were born as a symbol of hope to the Cosmos', Lady Amara proclaimed.

'I hope they're right', was all Haley could say due to everything remaining unwritten due to not knowing what was going to happen, depending on the two possible futures Lady Orla predicted.

'Where are Alexander, Elena and Henrietta?' Haley asked after her other family members.

'They send their apologies for being unable to see you as well, daughter', Antoinette explained. 'My brother and sister-in-law need to prepare their armies in the event of a Nebulan invasion, while Henrietta at her age still has school to attend to, along with her training to be a warrior'.

Haley nodded understandably.

'However, they brought forth something for you to help on your mission', Darius said. With a wave of his hand, something appeared out of nowhere: a pair of iron gauntlets. They were shining silver, beaming against the pale yellow sunlight streaks slowly breaking through the white clouds. Haley watched in deep awe, as they floated towards her. She held her arms out to them, feeling the power surge they generated within the metal. As soon as they wrapped around her wrists, white sparks began to radiate around each gauntlet.

'Jarngreipr: the iron gloves of the Thunder God', Darius pronounced, Haley knowing what they were before he identified them. 'Like Mjolnir, they generate the thunder and lightning element. Not nearly as powerful, but enough to take down an enemy.'

Haley ran her hands over the Jarngreipr, admiring the smooth surface of the silver metal, amazed at how well they fit around her arms; also considering they once belonged to a god who was ten times larger and stronger. It was all too surreal.

'I too bring something as well as, Halena', Serena said, holding out to Haley. It looked like a long leather belt, only the triquetra symbol at the front, with two runic inspirations: one on each side of it.

'Megingjord?' Haley asked, unable to believe her eyes at another piece of myth held out to her. 'The power-belt?'

'Yes', Serena confirmed to her the gods entrusted the Mermaid Clan with this item: to protect it from the eyes and hands of our enemies. Do you know what these words on the belt mean?' Silas and Aeolus helped straighten the belt out for clear observation. Haley ran her fingertips over the elegantly carved writing. It was runic, but very ancient Celtic, which she could easily translate.

'One side says, *"He benefits from the mighty belt"*', she claimed. 'The other: *"He girded himself with his belt of strength, and his divine strength grew"*'.

Serena, a knowing twinkle in her eyes, mirrored Haley's. As the belt suddenly wrapped itself around Haley's waist, a power surge erupted inside her, like it made her a hundred times stronger.

'What was that I just felt?' she asked, confused.

'That belt was originally worn by Thor himself', she explained. 'It was designed to increase his god strength and any other individual, who is chosen to wear the belt temporarily. As long as you wear it, Halena, you will be granted the strength of a god'.

'But aren't I practically a god anyway, because of the bloodline?'

'Despite the small moments of strength, and due to your time on Earth, you are technically a cross between human and god. 'Once Mjolnir is restored, your god strength will become permanent and the belt will not be required'.

The last part created a void: an impulsive urge for Haley to test this theoretical action out, but another side told her it could be a danger to herself. Luckily, everyone was keen to continue with their historical stories of anything else they wished to present to her before the quest.

'Halena', Silas said. 'King Aodhan of Muspelheim sends his sincere apologies for being unable to present his tribute. However, Prince Alcan and Princess Kalama requested I deliver the artifact'.

Something large and circular materialized, out of thin air: a golden shield. Its metallic architecture was of majestic perfection in shining molten gold, the pressed design of the son coming in sequence with the moon in the forthcoming formation of an eclipse.

'This is Svalinn', Silas exclaimed, placing it in Haley's hands. 'Forged before the Sun's fires and blessed with its powers, it will protect you and anyone, withstanding any mystical attack'.

Haley studied the shield, unable to process touching another piece of mythological history. The story of the shield placed before Sol's chariot literally lay in the palms of her hands. The metal felt warm to the touch: as warm as the summer sun, it having been forged within its solar flares. Eyeing the engraved Norse inscription around the sun imprint, Haley couldn't help but read it aloud.

'In front of the sun does Svalinn stand, the shield for the shining god, mountains and seas would be set in flames, if it fell from before the sea', she uttered wondrously. 'It's more beautiful than the drawings I saw in the books'.

A flowing flashdrive containing the information and illustrations about Svalinn traversed along every path of Haley's brain. Every picture of every version in Norse Mythology left her wondering whether other artifacts she studied were indeed like the ones of potentially physical essence.

'There is one more thing, Halena', Lady Orla said. 'Svalinn may be a powerful tool to use in battle, but that does not mean you do not need a blade for combat defence'.

Reaching into her robe, she presented the most beautiful sword to lay eyes upon, so beautiful that it reminded Haley of a certain sword destined to belong to a great king. Although Haley guessed it as being thousands of years old, its appearance looked like it was recently forged judging by the pure shining silver. The helm was red and gold entwined metallic laced, the base an upside-down crescent moon. Despite shining against the sun, the runic letters carved into the sword shone brighter on an eternal loop.

'This sword is Angurvadal, forged by the Fire and Frost Giants', Lady Orla explained. 'After the First War of Ragnarok, the High Council entrusted it to my people and enchanted it so that no treacherous man would ever find it and use it for evil purposes'.

Haley did not want to imagine what it would have happened if a Nebulan or an evil being from across the universe got their hands on the sword. If it were truly a special sword, they highly likely would find a way to work their way around.

'I remember this sword coming up in my history class', she said. 'According to the legend, the sword glows in time of peace or when there's danger. Is that still true?'

'Yes', Lady Orla answered. 'It is of Fire and Frost Giant make. Once the sword reached completion, they combined their powers of fire and ice, blessing the sword with their magic. The runes will glow either red or pure silver. Red means war or danger is close by; silver, as it is right now, means peace. The silver also glows brighter as a sign that day or night is drawing in'.

Seeing the white brightness of the Runic letters in contrast to the sword's actual silver put Haley's mind to rest for the time being. So far, she sensed no indication of an incoming attack. Either Vladimir was indeed following through with their agreement, or he was playing the trickster with her and everyone else. Haley placed Svalinn on her shoulders, and shakily reached out to take the sword. She admired its beauty for a moment, before attaching it to Megingjord, taking a deep breath signaling she was ready despite the sickening feeling in her stomach.

'Daughter', Darius said. 'Remember: the first Well to reach is the Well of Urd across the Dark Sea, east of Asgard; the second the Well of Hvergelmir in Niflheim;

and the third the Well of Mimir located close to the border between Jotunheim and Midgard'.

Haley mentally produced a map of Yggdrasil, showing every corner and pathway leading to another World. It looked like a map from medieval times more than an astronomical map, unlike the ones, which came up in the astrophysics module in her science class. Her father mentioned Earth being Jotunheim's border. Maybe once all this mess involving Vladimir was cleared up, she could drop onto Earth and check in on her friends there?

'I understand', Haley said.

Her parents wished her and the others luck, and hugged her, Eric and Arianna, praying all three would come back safe and sound, much like Haley did over the last transformative week. Allowing them and the others to step aside, Haley, Eric, Arianna, Keilantra, Aeolus and Angela stepped forth to the gateway of the Bifrost, when Optimus spoke.

'Once you have completed each task and retrieved a thunderstone, call upon me through the heavens and the Bifrost's portal will open for you; and take you to your desired destination', he exclaimed, as if he was Heimdall himself, and not Heimdall's descendent.

Haley nodded, secretly wishing she went on that writing program, Eric and Arianna mentioned when erasing her friends' memories. She glanced at the gateway of nothingness, waiting for something to happen.

Sure enough, Optimus thrust his sword into a stone, only becoming visible upon direct contact. A rainbow ripple of energy hummed and unleashed a medium breeze. Both the rock and sword glowed in white, as a multi-coloured veil suddenly appeared gracefully swirled like water. The veil was blank at first, but then came a multiple bunch of images, continuously disappearing and reappearing again. From what Haley saw within the timed two to three second mark between the images, they were gateways to the Realms and other locations within Yggdrasil.

'In order to step through the Bifrost, all you need to do is think of the place, and your mind and thought of that place will be sent to my own mind', Optimus clarified, talking Haley through the process of mystical travel. Haley thought of both the Dark Sea and the Well of Urd. It was like a blank sheet of paper, as she could not see what the location actually looked like in reality. Could it be something to do the magic cast around the Trials, that every detail she had yet to know, much to her frustration, had to still remain a dire mystery until she faced whatever was part of each task?

'Good luck, Halena', Optimus said.

Haley became careful not to break her concentration on the destination.

'Stay safe, our dearest Halena', Antoinette uttered, her voice close to breaking. 'Eric, Arianna and the rest of you: guide and protect her'.

'May the Gods be with you', Lady Orla encouraged.

'We pray for a success on this quest', Lady Amara said, as Silas declared the gesture.

All good luck messages nearly brought on another overwhelming factor, against the special royal-blood attention Haley felt towards the gestures.

Haley held back all the overpowering emotions, alongside her emerging magic, as the final sequence of the bridge transportation began.

The energy ripple circulated repeatedly around the rock and towards the sword. It entered the triquetra glowing bright in white, the remainder of the magical swirls slithering like water vapour up to the crystallized version on the archway, merging itself with the Celtic pattern inside it. The gateway's veil began to change dramatically. Its illuminating whiteness grew against the colour matter along the edges of the bridge. Haley felt a surge of adrenaline, suddenly feeling ready for action. As the others stepped through the veil into the opening of the universe, Haley hesitated at expecting the unexpected.

What was truly on the outside of that veil, despite the showcase of projection images of the Realms? Eventually, she found the courage to step through the veil.

CHAPTER 14: THE DARK SEA

One minute, Haley was floating. The next, she was flying or better yet falling at unbelievable speed like riding on a rollarcoaster. Funny thing was that you would expect intense motion sickness, when hovering in mid-air, drifting on rough waters or travelling at a large percentage of light speed. Haley did not experience anything whatsoever. Perhaps it was thanks to her godly enhanced DNA. The only time she truly suffered motion sickness was when she went on a weekend trip to Alton Towers, where she threw up just seconds after getting off the ride. Haley peered at Eric, Arianna, Aeolus, Keilantra and Angela. They retained pure focus on the destination they envisaged. Well, they journeyed across Yggdrasil hundreds of thousands times, Haley thought.

Then, just when it got to a point where the freefalling wouldn't stop, Haley's feet touched down firmly onto hard ground. She opened her eyes, almost stumbling off the rocky edge of the blackened beach she now stood on, were it not for Aeolus' arm, interlocking with hers to avoid serious injury.

'Watch your footing, princess', he advised. 'The storm is strong enough to take you into the nowhere of the Sea'.

'Storm?' she questioned, realizing she had not yet seen in the landscape in front of her.

The first thing to hit her was the strong wind, combined with the sea salt stinging her skin. Through her almost closed eyes, the entire ocean was a blackened blue and rough as a ferocious monster waiting to burst out of the waters. There was indeed a storm. Nothing like the storm Haley unintentionally caused: it resembled a super-cell hurricane, the dark gray clouds swirling, and lightning spirals circulating it in a timed sequence. No stars or moons were visible at all.

'Is this the Dark Sea?' Haley asked, coughing slightly at the metallic taste of seawater touching her tongue. Keilantra noticed this and conjured up a force field, protecting them from the storm.

'Yes', she answered.

Haley narrowed her eyes at the dark swirling clouds, hoping at least a part of them would fade away so that she could be provided one small glimpse of the sun or an island.

Nothing at all…

'What's on the other side of the storm?' Haley asked.

'Not on the other side, Halena…but inside the storm', Eric answered.

Haley raised her eyebrows and swallowed deeply.

'The Well of Urd is located on a small island, concealed by the storm', Arianna explained. 'No Being has made it across not since the dying Thunder God and his followers, who were granted safe passage to deliver one of the three thunderstones to the Norn of Destiny'.

'I recognize this storm from one of my paintings at home', Haley remembered from her stash of entry paintings for university. 'I guess now I know why I did it'.

From dreams to visions to memories, every painting in her stash had a reason, which led her to this stage.

Haley tried to envision how the storm calmed down thousands of years ago. Perhaps she had the power to do so? She focused on the hurricane, pushing past the force field's magic, but nothing happened. Whatever this was, it had to be the handiwork of the Norns.

Suddenly, Haley's super-senses kicked in indicating another supernatural presence, just as Angurvadal's runic letters glowed red signaling danger close by.

'Lower the shield at the front', Haley demanded, as she picked up a large rock.

Shocked and confused like the others, Keilantra did as she asked and produced an opening large enough for one or two people to step through, were it not for a dangerous never-ending hurricane realm getting in the way. Haley threw the rock as hard and as far as she could into the water. Nothing occurred for the first ten seconds, until suddenly something green and scaly broke through the surface. There were at least four of them at around a hundred feet in length, chomping away at the water with their razor sharp teeth, confusing the rock as a source of prey. Their eyes were bright orange like a predator.

'Ormes', Aeolus pointed out. 'Sea serpents: the descended offspring of Jormungardr'.

'The serpent Thor battled?' Haley clarified. 'The one who according to legend roams the Earth's oceans?'

'After Jormungardr was slain by the Thunder God, his off-spring fled', Aeolus accounted to Haley. 'Banished from Midgard and robbed of their power to travel through the underwater paths of Yggdrasil, they managed to reach the Dark Sea, somehow sensing and knowing Thor would be delivering the thunderstone. However, to prevent further loss, the Norn offered them an ultimatum: they will not harm them or anyone of their kind, if they agree to patrol the waters of the Dark Sea and protect the thunderstone'.

'Is this the first challenge: to find a way past Jormungardr's children?' Haley asked.

'Possibly. But as foretold, none of us, including you, Halena, know what to expect during these Trials', Eric answered. After a short while, the Ormes eventually gave up on trying to find the imposed prey Haley tossed to them, and dove back under into the sea's dark dwellings.

'Is there a way around the storm?' Haley asked, trying to spot any extra pieces of land or an opening in the clouds in hopes of avoiding the flesh-eating reptiles roaming the water beneath them.

There was still nothing.

'The entire storm is eternally circulated around the island', Angela said. 'It seems the only way to reach the Well is to find a way across the sea, past the Ormes and through the storm'.

Haley gulped, but could not swallow. Fear pulsed through her veins, as she stared at the rough ocean water, awaiting another outburst from the serpents.

Until a reckless but intelligent idea formed in her head.

Looking around from top to bottom, left to right, Haley searched a certain something to make out of something: the very thing that sparkled her love for water sports. Sure enough, she spotted a lonesome tree root between a crack in the rocks. It was close to its first stage of rotting away, but perhaps. Haley raised her hand over it, and focused on the one object it would become out of its intact bark. She felt her eyes glowing in sparkles, as the root became to change shape. The others watched in deep awe at what was happening. The root's rotting patches returned to its original healthy form, and it grew as if growing into a tree. Instead, gold dust encased it like a cocoon. The scale changed, growing larger and flatter in size, transforming its wonders-of-nature brand into an object you would buy or rent at a beach shop.

'A surfboard?' Arianna asked.

'It's a big surf out there, thanks to that endless storm', Haley said, gesturing her head towards the dark cyclone clouds. 'Like you said, the only way to reach the Well is to cross the Dark Sea. We can't go around and the Bifrost would be impossible to transport us there'.

'Therefore, this is the best option I can think of'. She turned to Keilantra, with a small boost of confidence. 'What do you think, Kelly?'

Keilantra appraised a devised type of road map in response to this being a true likelihood. Everyone else mentally clarified amongst themselves what Haley impended upon them. Another thing: when did she get so wise in just weeks after learning her identity? Well, Haley repeatedly asked herself that same question since her feet touched the universe.

'It seems she makes a logical point', Keilantra agreed. 'I too experienced this sport mortals call surfing. Having spent a majority of my life in ocean water, it is the best course of action to cross the potentially perilous surge, as you see before you'. Imitating the same incantation as Haley, Keilantra too created a surfboard from another lonely blackened root hanging off the beach edge.

She then turned to Eric and Arianna.

'With your permission, my Lord Eric and Lady Arianna, I wish to accompany Halena'.

Eric and Arianna appreciated Keilantra's determined spirit. Haley saw that in their eyes.

'Very well', Eric said reluctantly. 'If your theory is correct and with the right timing, your presence should go unnoticed by the Ormes'.

'As a precaution, we highly recommend you keep your weaponry on you', Arianna added. 'Especially your sword in case you are alerted to danger'.

'I will go, too', Angela volunteered. 'You will need my healing powers in case, not just your ability to heal. Who knows what devastating consequences await out there?'

Eric and Arianna silently agreed with a corresponding nod, and conjured up another surfboard for Angela, considering she did not hold that ability to do so herself. Haley smiled slightly. Angela was slowly becoming more friend than handmaiden to her, and she hoped nothing would happen to her along the way. She needed her as much as she needed the others, and not just for the healing factor.

First thing's first though, Haley thought. Eric specified the crossing of the Dark Sea to be at the right probable moment, so Haley long-handedly scoured for any Orme sightings, but the ocean's darkness blocked off her power. This was a call of manual work, in other words: the same agility she used to home in on their location. Picking up another larger rock, Haley huddled it into the ocean as hard as she could, white lightning elevating off her fingertips. It travelled further than the last one, much to Haley's surprise.

Ten seconds passed again, until the Ormes suddenly broke to the surface again blindly searching for decoy prey. Haley started counting. One…two…three…four…five…six…seven – they stopped chomping – eight…nine…ten…eleven – they began to dive back under one by one – twelve…thirteen…fourteen…fifteen.

And they were gone.

'It takes them fifteen seconds to attack any sudden movement within their range', Haley assumed.

'In which case, we will need to use that amount of time to catch the waves', Keilantra added.

A deafening clap of thunder resounded around the obscure hurricane, startling everyone, except Haley. Like she half-expected it to occur more than the last flashes, and much like most of the other occurrences throughout her life. Her connection to every cloudburst or elemental incident held a direct connection to the Odinson Bloodline. Deep down, she was still too eager to find more about the Bloodline and her gifts. Hopefully, when this was finished and done with…and if she and everyone make it out of this alive.

'Well, here goes nothing', Haley uttered, nervously shrugging her shoulders as she pursed her lips together while trying to defuse the apprehension. Directing her attention back to the stormy ocean, she removed her chest-plate armour, boots and cloak, while Keilantra and Angela did the same. The rocks felt cold to her bare feet, wet from the continuous storm-strucken waves, which were theoretically powerful enough to form a tsunami. Only a possibility, Haley thought to herself, praying that did not happen, or they were going to fall into the deep dark abyss of Hel.

'Good luck, my lady', Aeolus said, giving her shoulder a reassuring, but gentle squeeze. 'I sincerely hope you, Keilantra and Angela come back safely'.

Again, Haley saw a strong glimpse of the light conquering his brooding darkness. His hand felt like a desirable fire, soaring all around her. Why did this feeling emerge, whenever she was around Aeolus? She only met him weeks ago, and they only really talked at training sessions. At least it was just polite conversation; otherwise she would be losing the plot blushing over his charming handsomeness.

'Thanks, Aeolus', was all she managed to get out, before turning Eric and Arianna. 'We will be back as soon as we can'.

Haley stepped closer to the beach edge, her toes hanging off ever so slightly, coming into small contact with the foamed white of the waves, crashing into the rocks. Her wariness came promptly, as she gazed repetitively at the dark, stormy landscape. In exactly a hundred yards, a thunderstone laid safely guarded inside one of these ancient Wells, only ever touched by the Gods and only mystically sacred to humanity.

There were no more loose rocks lying around. Maybe the cracked surfaces were dense enough to break pieces off? Clenching her fist, Haley gained the genetic energy she inherited, homing in yet imagining how her own ancestor tapped into his own strength. Although still a blur, it was there like the continuous sparkle in her eyes which became in sync with it, almost as if the Thunder God was standing right there, transferring more of his power. Haley wondered for a split second whether it was her own power or the power of Megingjord. Sensing it at a moderate peck, Haley pounded her fist into the rock, breaking into half a dozen pieces, astonishingly shocked like the numerous times she manifested superhuman strength. Thankfully, those times were out of the public eye. But now that she was somewhere where people were just like her…

Only problem was a part of her still longed to remain human for as long as possible, that part being indecisive about fully letting it go, keeping in touch with the memories of her Earth friends. Everyone in the Cosmos were seemingly seeing it as a distraction, most of them having had no or minimal contact with humans for thousands of years. Now here she was, about to take a perilous journey by surfing across a treacherous ocean into a freshly concealing storm.

Haley picked up another rock.

'We throw one at the same time', she suggested. 'Perhaps that would buy us triple the time?'

Taking that in agreement, Keilantra and Angela too grabbed a broken rock. As the shield dissolved, they were soon met by the salty sensation of the Dark Sea, and the rainfall hitting their skin like millions of tiny pebbles. Luckily, neither inhabited an acidic substance otherwise they would have been burnt to death, to the point of being decomposed into nothing, invisible beneath the blackened rock.

'Be careful, sister', Eric and Arianna said together.

Haley nodded, evasive on turning around to see their worried eyes.

'On the count of three', Haley told both girls. 'One…two…three!'

All three girls threw the rocks hard, Haley producing three additional small lightning bolts out of her left unused hand toward them. It provided extra force for the rocks to travel more distance away from the land.

Haley silently prayed for a worthy outcome on her theory.

Ten seconds later, the Ormes resurfaced at the spot the rocks hit.

This was it.

'Now!' Haley shouted, jumping flat into the water climbing onto her surfboard, Keilantra and Angela following in pursuit.

The cold water tingled Haley's skin, producing goose bumps. Thankfully, not ice cold – but cold enough to drop a body temperature if in it fully for too long. Haley couldn't care less about that minor aberration, after only beginning the first Trial. She started paddling, harder than the normal pace she went through the past years of surfing, duck-diving under several large, violent waves with Keilantra and Angela following her every move. For someone who had hardly seen Earth or experienced its cultures, Angela was natural. Bright side: Haley could not wait to see her catch some waves, where it was not in the middle of a gigantic, never-ending hurricane.

Eventually, Haley sensed a larger wave forming on their right-hand side. Haley, Keilantra and Angela changed direction so the noses of their surfboards were facing the swirling dark clouds. The Ormes still gnawed at the water, but it was only a matter of time before they became aware of their presence. Catching to the wave, Haley paddled harder and harder. Until she finally gathered enough energy to stand on her own two feet. She soared like a free bird on the water, but somehow it felt eccentric in contempt of it being the Dark Sea. Like she wasn't the one controlling her flawless moves…but something else dragging her along. Haley recapped on Markus' story about the spirits of Aegir and Ran roaming in the waters of the Nine Realms. Despite not always believing in life after death, but if what she thought of was true – well, she did not know anymore.

Suddenly, Haley let out a gasp, her eyes widening as her magical senses built up. She took her eyes off the water, looking down at Angurvadal: its runes glowed red. Danger! Haley hadn't realized the time limit was up too, until she spotted a section of the water shimmering…close to Angela!

'Angela! On your left!' Haley shouted out, but too late. Angela was already in the water, her board in broken pieces as the large Orme dove back underneath.

Haley and Keilantra ceased their surfing, noticing the colony of Ormes slowly beginning to circle the terrified Angela.

'*Do not make any sudden movement, Angela*', Keilantra instructed her through telepathy.

In all honesty, Haley wondered whether her sister was out of her mind. But nevertheless, it was the only real conceptual action, if someone encountered a dangerous predator, stalking its prey; and it only took a minute to stay silently still, until boredom drove the predator away.

Haley quickly opened up her own telepathic connection.

'*We have to do something*', she pleaded to Keilantra, fighting every intention to break through the Ormes' circle to get to Angela. But witnessing their predatory traits from afar made it an impossible revelation. They swam too close together. In sheer impatience, she watched Keilantra seemingly calculating the Ormes' rhythmical movements. Angela maintained her floatation in the same quiet manner. She only had healing powers – no defensive magic making Haley five times more scared for her new friend.

'*I have a plan. Wait for my signal*', Keilantra commanded, and she jumped head first into the water before Haley had a chance to ask.

Haley struggled to process her best friend's bold but reckless course of action. What was her plan? Swim up to the Ormes and ask them nicely to leave Angela alone? No way, she would end up being their next meal anyway. All Haley could at this stage was wait for whatever signal Keilantra interpreted.

Two minutes passed, and Haley started to really worry if her best friend drowned. Until she remembered that Keilantra was half-mermaid, meaning she had a swimming speed hundred times faster than a human being, meaning she could hold her breath underwater for a considerable amount of time: minutes or maybe even hours. The lingering vanished at the sighting of gigantic, erupting water swirls. It only grew larger in size like a small maelstrom. Only difference was that it glowed in rainbow colours, liquefying against the swirls. Fire and water, blending together like allies on the battlefield. Haley just bore witness to the first epic potential of Keilantra's rainbow fire. Who knows what other tricks and turns she possessed? The fire continued to manipulate into various shapes and forms, including mermaids with titans, and eleven other unknown figures of intelligent beauty, with watery hair of silk rushing in to assist.

Aegir, Ran and their nine daughters!

Haley envisioned them in slow motion. Aegir and Ran's spiritual forms briefly turned their heads in her direction. Her sparkling blue eyes met their misty blue, matching the bondage of water around their bodies. A knowing twinkle of hope differently mirrored, but there was something else, as Haley eyed Aegir and Ran held refusing to let go: love. A love so strong that it reminded her of the story of Mani and the Valkyrie, Raven; and their powerful unbreakable love, which created the Aurora Eclipse in the first place.

Haley broke eye contact from them. Something rose up from the maelstrom's centre: it was Keilantra. Her entire body shone like a multi-flare, the lenses in her eyes blazed in colours changing every three seconds, and her hands burst into the same flames she demonstrated to Haley. Keilantra didn't wince or scream in excruciating pain especially while defying gravity. The fire she produced illuminated like the rainbow, snaking itself around at a faster pace.

What Keilantra was doing seemed to be working. The Ormes became too distracted by Aegir, Ran and their water nymphs, and Keilantra that they began to ignore Angela entirely. Arrows and small blades, Haley noticed, struck several; she looked back at the beach. Eric, Arianna and Aeolus were attempting to create a secondary distraction, while Haley entered lifeguard mode.

'Go now, Halena!' Keilantra yelled telepathically.

Another wave began to form with such luck. Haley jumped down flat on her stomach and paddled hard. As the fast current carried her, she stood up and swerved up and over the stormy sea's incoming waves, heading towards Angela. Her heart thumped in her chest. With the speed she was going, there was no way she was going to reach Angela if one or two Ormes end up turning around, not unless she created momentum. Haley directed her eyes to the eternal storm clouds above, the spirit of the Thunder God channeling through her blood. Her eyes blazed in white. Her hand suddenly glowed and a lightning bolt materialized out of a singular thin streak of light, coming down from the heavens. During those few seconds, it felt like holding a sword or magic staff, amazing Haley. Not once during that time limit and like Keilantra did she experience a painful episode. She waved the lightning around to the back of her surfboard, driving it into its edge. The power created a stronger current, speeding the surf up, and dragged Haley along.

'*Angela, get ready to grab on!*' Haley shouted through telepathy, remembering her father's words about the belt around her waist. If she activated it, it would increase her strength to god strength.

Maybe the lightning surge in her blood alongside Thor's bonded spirit was enough to charge it up. Only one-way to find out, Haley thought, for Angela's sake during these mere minutes of freedom from the monstrous children of Jormungand. Haley concentrated hard, placing her hand on the buckle. Breaking down her mind barrier, and with the assistance of the All-Knowledge, multiple images of the Thunder God passed through as she imagined the power of his own durability merging with her own strength. Suddenly, a burst of flashing energy emerged from her palm touching Megingjord like a white-hot torch. The magic broke through her armour, entering her bloodstream. It felt like she was being given an upgrade. Like she became branded by the strength of a thousand men. Her focus reaching its peak, Haley swept over another large wave and tilted downward towards Angela, reaching her arm out ready to grab her. Angela's hand gripped her tightly, and with a quick, but shocking energetic move, swung her up onto the board behind her.

'Are you okay, Angela?' Haley asked quickly, as she surfed back towards the swirling hurricane on the dark horizon.

'Yes', Angela answered shakily. 'Thank you'.

'Hold onto me'. Angela did as she said, keeping a firm grip on the belt around Haley's waist. As the two girls surfed back in the hurricane's direction, Haley opened up her telepathy to Keilantra.

'*Kelly, I've got her! We need to move now!*' she shouted out, watching as Keilantra threw rainbow fireballs at leaping Ormes. Aegir and Ran's deities pulled other of her concealed line of view.

Quickly alerted, Keilantra conjured up one more fireball and threw it right into a Orme's eye. All Haley could think was bullseye, like a daring version of darts with sea serpents as the target. The Orme hissed and shrieked in pain, before disappearing under the water. Keilantra dived back into the water, leaping out like a dolphin. She was half-mermaid after all, Haley thought.

The closer they got, the louder the super-cell cyclone got: so much louder that Haley's own eardrums could end up being damaged. This task was not over, until they reached that island behind that fog. Haley heard Angela throwing daggers at approaching Ormes, who now became aware of their presence, in an attempt to slow them down with Keilantra hurdling out more fireballs.

Except this momentary diversion spelled trouble for Haley...What she failed to notice was the swirling water right in her path, and a ferocious and very angry Orme abruptly bolting out, sneering its sharp fangs and long pink tongue. Haley and Angela hastily dodged its attack. But not fast enough for Haley: one of its long front fangs struck her left shoulder, its tip piercing her skin deeply! It hurt far worse than the rock that scratched her. Haley gritted her teeth trying to surpass the pain, before withdrawing Angurvadal and slicing off the end of the Orme's tail. Purple blood submerged with the ocean, and coated Haley's sword.

Haley all of a sudden felt peculiar. The wound on her shoulder did not heal itself. It was burning through her entire body. Dizziness clouded her line of view at the approaching storm...she was too blind to see where she was going. A wave of cold disabled herself and her power.

The last thing she heard was Keilantra and Angela calling her name...

CHAPTER 15: THE WELL OF URD

Haley was falling through the dark abyss into the unknown, entering a realm of despair, nowhere close to heaven. Only a brewing darkness breaking free from a prison it longed to leave with a vengeance at its fingertips.

Until the darkness magically transformed into pure light, and she was thrust backwards to the world of living, when two voices were the first things she heard.

'Was it enough?' one voice sounded scared for her.

'We can only hope', another voice answered. 'The healing process is working, but slowly. All we can do is wait until the substance is fully out of her system.

The second thing Haley felt was sand. Soft sand. She clenched it, relieved to be on land. Her eyes were still closed, taking in the beautiful sounds of nature: birds twittering, waves sweeping up on the edge of the beach; and the gentle, calm breeze of pure warmth touching her skin. It was just enough to stop her still-spinning head.

After a long moment, Haley finally woke.

Through her blurry vision, she spotted two pairs of eyes above her. Coldness still stuck to her skin, a mixture of seawater and feverish sweat. Whatever happened to her on the Dark Sea, it can't have been good. Blinking, her vision quickly cleared. The eyes were fortunately Keilantra and Angela's. Blue and green shining in utter worry at the focal point over the aftermath…

'Halena, thank goodness', Keilantra sighed in relief. 'We were so worried'.

Haley tried to sit up, but the quicker she did the worse the small hint of pain became.

'What happened?' she asked nervously, trying to sit up.

The dizziness threatened to control again.

'Sit up slowly, Miss Halena', Angela said, placing her hands on her shoulder and arm to assist her. 'Your body is still healing from the venom the Orme passed through your system'.

'Venom?' she asked, feeling like she was going to be sick.

'The Ormes' poison is very powerful', Keilantra explained. 'One strike into the heart or any other internal organ in the body, and the victim would have been dead in seconds. You were struck on the shoulder, meaning its effects would have been at its deadliest within one or two hours'. The words sounded factually cautious, but there was still that worrying strain in their tone of voice. If Haley died in the field at the hands of an enemy as worse as an Orme or a Nebulan, how would Keilantra and Angela break the news to not just Eric and Arianna, but her parents as well?

All it took to prevent this was the power of healing, but to Haley, it was strangely more than that. Fate. A fate tied to her destiny and her place in the Odinson Bloodline, as a Cosmos Being and a child and princess of the Nine Realms. But why did Haley's body not heal itself entirely? She slowly turned her head slowly to the shoulder, where the fang struck her. Angela's healing power combined with her own most definitely worked, riding her body of the toxic venom. Only a scar remained. Haley ran her finger delicately over it. It was smooth. Still sore and red, but smooth; all blood washed away from the water.

'How?' she mumbled.

'Poisonous bites leave scars', Angela said, while checking her over for any more injuries. 'You will carry it for the rest of your life'.

Haley became dazed in thought. She always recognized the good and bad sides of having scars. A lot of scars were the horrific results of brutal torture both psychologically and physically. But there was another side even good. Scars are left as a sign of an accomplishment or completion of something extraordinary.

She found the courage to stand with some assistance from Angels and Keilantra, to look around at their current location: the central part of the hurricane…the eye of the storm.

The thundery eye-wall of cloud in the distance was taken over by a series of rainbows and pure sunlight, from the opening above. Warm like spring and summer, it was so calm and sunny, with clear, blue sky that the stars of the universe shone brightly against it and the planets provided full view, like on Asgard. A flock of birds flew around joyously, their sounds like music to Haley's ears. The ocean now was so purely blue, that Haley could easily see dolphins and hippocampuses swimming around, possibly patrolling the perimeter of the island the three girls stood on.

Speaking of island…

Haley turned around observantly in all angles of view and direction. Eric and Arianna were right about one thing in the First Trial: she had indeed landed herself on a remote island which funny enough was on her planned-out bucket list before all these supernatural events occurred. The island looked like the ideal location for an escape route away from complicated problems, with its range of evergreen forest trees, and fresh leaves and flowers. That was until Haley spotted the misty gateway, leading into a circular courtyard of concrete stone.

'The Well of Urd lies beyond the gateway', Keilantra said

Haley nodded and swallowed hard, nerves hitting her like a rock.

'What is it, Miss Halena?' Angela asked.

'All these years...' Haley muttered, pausing on that last word. '...I believed the Wells of Yggdrasil were a legend, a children's story. It's just so surreal'.

And to think a part of an all-powerful weapon laid beyond the gateway, Haley thought.

'Well, if it helps, I too heard many tales from my mother', Angela replied, offering some reassurance. 'Like you, this is my first time seeing a Well but it was just as I imagined'.

Haley raised her eyes at Angela.

'My mother foretold to me a story about the Well of Urd being based on a beautiful island of eternal spring and summer', Angela explained. 'She mentioned nothing about the Trials, her too having zero knowledge of what to expect'.

Haley pursed her lips, taking in this piece of information.

'Come, the Norn of Destiny awaits', Keilantra eventually said, breaking the momentary silence.

Gulping again and letting out a deep breath, Haley gravitated herself towards the gateway. As she edged closer, a sudden energy surge similar to the Aurora Eclipse came forth but unlike anything she felt to date. Like it knew her, like she too knew it despite only knowing about the Odinson Bloodline. That or thanks to the All-Knowledge, Haley guessed. This...this was an ancient magic, most likely over three thousand years old: the exact time of the aftermath of the First Ragnarok, and the Gods' deaths. Every step she took was when the vibrant intensity of the magic grew, drawing her further in.

Until finally she reached the gateway's edge, her toes touching the mist. She did not feel any water vapour. This was no normal mist. Haley's heart pumped harder. What if this entrance was not what it seemed? What if it was a ruse to lure some god-forsaken wasteland, not to the Well? What if Vladimir and the Nebulans found all three Wells and destroyed the Thunderstones, or worse stolen them to use Mjolnir for darker deeds?

Finding all these theories overwhelming, Haley's focus shifted towards the temptation of turning around and never look back. But she remembered not half a hour ago, she just crossed a stormy ocean inhabited by venomous Ormes. A flashback of what happened when that Orme's fang struck kept her rooted to the spot, gazing into the misty-protected courtyard. And the second reason: if she ran away now, she would be walking away from the deal she made with Vladimir. Most of all, with five days to complete this mission, she would be walking away from her place in the Odinson Bloodline. It was an act of cowardice, walking away. This quest was brave and honourable, and one of her many chances to come to prove she was not afraid; that she could do this.

Now or never, as they all say…

After much coaxing from Keilantra and Angela, Haley stepped through the gateway.

Walking through the thin mist, Haley expected the feeling of walking through the silhouette of a ghost, where deathly coldness swept and crawled upon her skin. There was nothing of the sort; only relief towards the fact that the courtyard was not an illusion; and the gateway did not teleport her, Keilantra and Angela to an unknown place.

Haley's mouth briefly hung open, her eyes unblinking in utter fascination.

Two stone statues guarded the courtyard's archway she, Keilantra and Angela just walked through. They were ancient knights, each baring a crest of the World's Tree. Haley looked at the floor. It was partially grey concrete, tufts of grass growing through. Around most parts, there was some elevating bluish-white mist, mixed with the yellow sunlight. Not far off from where she stood, three thirteen-foot standing stones were positioned like a fragmentary ring around a fountain in the ground. The farthest one had the triquetra sign carved into it – it being the symbol of destiny, Haley thought knowledgeably. In the very centre of the fountain, Haley spied a giant tree trunk of running water. It towered high up into the sky, into the heavens, concealed only by a range of white cloud. Haley traced back to when Lady Orla took her to the Lake of Prophecy and she commemorated three tunnels made up of waterfalls leading somewhere.

The Wells…

Looking beyond, Haley caught sight of something. They were not alone. A fourth person was here. Someone easily spotted amongst the standing stone, observing and protecting every corner of the Well. As they edged closer, the person became clearer.

A woman.

She wore a long, white gown; the sleeves separate from her petite shoulders, but hanging off her arms. Her hair was a long, silky white blonde styled into a crowned pattern braid at the back.

Haley, Keilantra and Angela stopped within four feet of the woman.

'Welcome, young Cosmo Beings of Yggdrasil', the woman said welcomingly in a calm, angelic voice as sweet as a melody.

Haley was unsure how to greet the woman. She pursed her lips, thinking long and hard.

'Umm, my name is Haley, I mean…Halena', she stuttered. 'Daughter of…of Darius and Antoinette of Asgard and descendent of the Thunder God, Thor'.

'I know who you are', the woman answered elegantly turning around to face them.

Her beauty shone like stars, her skin so pale that she must have avoided many years without the sun; although there was only a small hint of rosy colour on her cheeks. Her misty blue eyes were filled with curious fascination and endless wisdom. The smile on her face let Haley know that she was not an enemy to them.

'I and my sisters have been awaiting your arrival and return for a long time', she said. 'I am the Norn of Destiny: guardian of the Well of Urd'.

'Then, you know why we're here', Haley interpreted in response. She hoped that didn't sound too forceful, in spite of time being of the essence. Luckily, all the Norn did was inside.

'You seek the Thunderstones', she said. 'The three fragments of Mjolnir, the mighty weapon of your ancestor'.

'It is the best possible hope of stopping Vladimir, my uncle', Haley explained, hesitantly saying his name as it fell off the tip of her tongue.

The Norn's expression maintained the unreadable conversion to the point that Haley was unable to feel what she was feeling, or think what she was thinking. All she did was put her petite hands together, seemingly processing this.

'As you know, myself and my Norn sisters hold the power to observe and control the destinies of the Cosmos Beings', she explained. 'Even the Gods themselves. But your uncle, Lord Vladimir, former prince of Asgard: his destiny has become entwined with the returning Ragnarok'.

Haley had come to the conclusion that this Ragnarok was more than just a legendary comic being. It was a harbinger of evil. But in what form? She did not want to know, but at the same time she needed to know.

'Vladimir forced me into making a deal with him', Haley recapped her encounter in the Asgardian dungeons, as the Norn of Destiny listened.

'From what you described, Vladimir has grown more ruthless and cruel during all those years since his creation of Nebula and alliance with Ragnarok', she proclaimed. 'Nebula is one of many vessels, with a power source capable of bringing back Ragnarok. Like your Earth's core being the force of the gravitational shield protecting humanity from extinction. As for the deal you made with him, Halena…although it was by seemingly negotiable terms, I express fear towards the possibility of Vladimir not following through one of the terms. The Nebulans the Cosmos Beings have faced in the past are non-negotiable'.

'So, that would mean him harming my family or thousands of innocent people, while I do the Trials', Haley guessed, her heart sinking. 'Believe me: I felt nothing but darkness in my uncle. No humanity whatsoever. It's like the man my parents once knew died upon his corruption'. All Keilantra and Angela did was stand in silence, letting Haley do the talking, inside being surprised by Haley's sudden growing strength and determination.

'Plus, since the dungeons, I too have had this sinking feeling that Vladimir won't follow through with the agreement, too', Haley continued. She was right. Ever since they journeyed through the Bifrost, despite the intense motion sickness, her mind went all over the place. What if Nebulans came out of no way, coming through the gateway, blocking their paths to the Wells? Was Vladimir really that far gone, yet it was clearly declared that he was beyond redemption?

Keilantra came forth.

'She is right, my lady', she said. 'Vladimir is now pawn to Ragnarok and one of many to unleash it, as you say. Halena, being Thor's sole heir, is the only one capable of seeking out the thunderstones of Mjolnir'.

'I need your help', Haley pleaded ever so slightly. 'We need your help'.

The Norn took some time to process the newfound information, like it was being uploaded on to a psychic hard drive. Did every single Cosmos Being enter a meditation state to consider the best possible options? Like those Nebulans who played judge, jury and executioner to Haley. On Earth, there was the odd research done on computers, taking notes or reviewing the outcomes from a meeting.

'First of all, I congratulate you on succeeding in the First Trial, distant daughter of Thor', the Norn finally said with a proud smile. In spite of almost getting eaten by poisonous sea snakes, Haley thought sarcastically. 'You have grown stronger over the years, Princess Halena. As the Norn of Destiny and follower of the Thunder God, I am now your servant and guardian'.

'Thanks', Haley replied instinctively.

'What you seek lies safely sealed within the Well of Urd', the Norn continued, directing everyone's attention to the Well. It looked more like a crater than a well, with the Tree's giant root going down and down into the tumbling unknown. Haley couldn't help but look down. It had to be more than three to four hundred feet down, as the water on the root and around the crater-well led somewhere.

'So, how do I get the stone to the surface?' Haley asked. She hoped the others helped her with this one dilemma, but they remained thoughtless.

'Do either of you know?' she asked in deep concern. They shook their heads.

'It is too concealed within the Well to determine the best way', Keilantra concluded. 'This is beyond even my own abilities'.

'I'm afraid I have no magic other than healing', Angela uttered apologetically.

Haley turned back to the Norn. 'Surely, you must know', she implied, hopeful she would possess such knowledge being the guardian of a sacred well.

Through her timeless beauty, the Norn displayed the same unreadable expression.

'I am afraid not', she said. 'My sisters and I hold the power to seal the thunderstones and transform them into entrapped stars, but since then our duty was to guard them. None of us planned to research ways to break the enchantments. Only you can do this, Halena'.

Now, she was back to square one. Haley rounded her eyes homing in on every circular edge of the Well, even watching and listening to the white waterfall coming down from Yggdrasil's trunk root to calm her senses. In Haley's opinion, everything leading up to this stage became a needle in a haystack. Everything in this chamber was now a treasure hunt. She brought to mind the numerous Easter egg hunts and birthday party games. Those were simple. This was a challenge. If the thunderstone was sealed securely in a magic treasure chest, there had to be a key to opening it.

Iron or mystical.

If she was truly the thunder god's descendent, she should know.

Out of no way, something light and beautiful triggered Haley's senses. It went through a range of blue and green, indigo and white; lighting up like the sun and moon, flashing like lightning. Warmth touched Haley's chest, not just esoterically but palpably. She reached up and realized the magic source came from the crystal in the centre of the triquetra charm on her necklace. The light reflected through the sun, like diamonds until light-streams flowed out: an aurora. Haley was definitely not the one doing this. The necklace had a mind of its own.

Keilantra, Angela and the Norn watched in awe, as the aurora flaked its way down into the Well, probably all the way to the very bottom. Until a subsidiary whiteness slowly burst through, breaking up a billion tiny little pieces, all of which elevated in mid air above the Well, also surrounding Haley, Keilantra, Angela and the Norn.

Haley blinked multiple times at its finished product she couldn't help but produce a small smile.

'How did you do that, Halena?' the Norn asked, still starstruck.

'I-I don't know', Haley answered speechlessly. 'The crystal in my necklace did all the work for me. None of this was my own magic. Somewhere, it has a connection to the Well, and possibly the other two Wells'.

The Norn walked around, closely examining the specs of light floating around, twinkling. A minute later, realization dawned upon her.

'Do you know what they are, Halena?' she asked.

Haley recognized the twinkling pattern from anywhere. From all the times she spent on the beach house balcony, gazing through her telescope, all those patterns she recorded for her school homework or for personal reasons was safely stored in the back of her mind.

'Stars', she answered, still too captivated by the pure projection.

'Yes...A perfect reflection of the universe around us. That crystal in your necklace is one, charged with the power of an Aurora, and one of the many reasons why you are connected to the Aurora Eclipse'.

Haley examined each and every one of the mix of sparkling blue, orange, yellow and white displayed from an up-close perspective, as if looking through an invisible telescope. She spotted the Milky Way, the Pole Star and Sirius. Everything about it was all too extraordinary. Everything down to the star lores and constellations of cherished mythical stories. The star-struck moment vanished, when Haley's necklace glowed again along with a significant blue star that began to grow in size, its intense brightness luminous enough to blind any one in close range. Suddenly, it exploded into an energy surge, causing Haley and the others, minus the Norn who appeared relatively familiar to exploding or dying stars, to shield their eyes. Haley was almost tempted to use the Svalinn, it being powerful enough to withstand dominant attacks. Perhaps it could block a supernova? A minute or two went by, until the starlight eventually died down. Haley opened her eyes, along with Keilantra and Angela. She transfixed her focus on the spot where the blue star exploded. Haley expected stardust tumbling down the ground, glittering like grains of sand. Nothing, except what was in its place.

A large crystallized stone.

As it floated slowly towards her, Haley could just make out the shape of something inside: a piece of something.

'This is the thunderstone, isn't it?' she asked, avoiding the temptation of reaching out to touch it.

'One of the three', the Norn of Destiny answered. 'Encased in a powerful crystallized casket, which can only be opened by Thor or his descendent, a piece of Mjolnir lies within'.

At that moment, Haley's entire body ignited, the surge of lightning coursing through her, until her eyes glowed white, and the lightning touched her necklace. The triquetra became hot to the touch, but none of that affected her due to whatever trance she went under. Everything inside caused the universe to stand still. As the triquetra glowed, its reflective pattern touched the crystallized stone, it too glowing. The stone slowly cracked like pure glass, streams of light fighting to break through. Until finally the light broke the stone apart, its pieces disappearing into thin air. Something else floated in its place: a hammer handle.

With nervous hesitation, Haley reached for it feeling drawn to it, as Keilantra, Angela and the Norn observed her actions. The moment her hand made contact with the handle, lightning ignited in Haley's palm. Its millions of sparks temporarily coated the handle before dying down, recognizing her as a descendent of the Thunder God.

'The handle of Mjolnir', the Norn whispered in deep astonishment. 'It senses Thor's spirit within you, Halena. His rekindled power is what is needed to reawaken each piece'.

Haley turned it ninety degrees, admiring it even more, from the metallic shining wood to the golden runic letters on its front. *May The One be blessed with the power of Mjolnir,* was what it said. Haley treated the handle like a very valuable artifact for a museum display, like a sword withdrawn from a stone. Everything was turning into a big epic moment of hope. Haley saw it in the Norn's eyes, as she looked between her and the handle.

'It is beautiful', Haley uttered. 'I didn't think it was possible. To actually be holding a piece of Mjolnir'. It got to the point where she let out a low, disbelieving giggle. 'It's just incredible'.

'Now, it is yours', the Norn said.

Haley slowly, but hesitantly, attached the handle to Megingjord, all the surreal emotions going round and round in her head. She turned to the Norn.

'Thank you...my lady', she said gratefully.

The Norn nodded, before saying, 'You are welcome, young Halena. Well done for completing the First Trial. I have faith that you will do the same for the next two'.

Haley pursed her lips, dreading the thought of thinking about them. Like the First Trial, she did not know what to expect. Well, they say the more levels you complete, the harder the game gets. This was only three, and definitely not like an Olympic game or sporting event. Now that the Norn mentioned the next two, Haley looked back to the archway entrance and then from the continuous hurrlance to its calm eye.

'So, how do we get out of here?' she asked. 'Because I'm not sure I want to swim back across'.

She blushed out of fear of enduring another potentially unpredictable encounter with man-eating Ormes, which could be proven problematic.

The Norn just laughed lightly, her eyes compassionate.

'I think I know someone who can help', she said as she looked up the trunk of Yggdrasil, and whistling a soft tune. Haley too looked up at the very top of the trunk, which appeared to have no top due to the foggy effects of the storm's eyes and warm, orange sunlight.

Through the fog, Haley spotted a silhouette of something flying towards them. It must have taken under a minute for this something to receive the Norn of Destiny's call. The creature broke through, its wings as strong as wind. Haley instinctively gripped the helm of Angurvadil, watching the something land in front of them.

Annoyingly enough, she recognized him instantly.

'Nidhogg?' she said, raising one eyebrow in annoyance, but also at his changed appearance. He was not the same small dragon she met by the lagoons, and who pretended to not know of the extent of her gifts. Only baring the same orange scales and eyes, he was now twice as large at forty feet, his neck at the leveled eye contact with a Cosmos Being.

'Long time no see, little princess. You miss me?' he greeted her cockily. Could he be any more annoying with his inflicting ego?

'Of course not', Haley unwillingly said, rolling her eyes. 'I just didn't expect you to be...larger'.

Keilantra and Angela smiled in amusement.

'One fun fact about me: unlike most dragons, *I* have the ability to change my appearance, even my own size', Nidhogg said, before showing off the ability. His scales morphed like a chameleon, and he shrunk to the size of an ant, and back up from dog size to horse size, and to a full-size dragon.

'Impressed?' he asked pompously, winking his cat-like eye.

Haley felt creeped out by that. Nidhogg was such a presumptuous show-off, thinking he was all high and mighty, as Vedrfolnir and Ratatoskr clarified.

'That is enough making a show of yourself, Nidhogg', the Norn called out impatiently. 'Need I remind you that I called you down here for a reason'.

Relief hit Haley when the Norn stepped in, otherwise she probably would have gone full demi-goddess of thunder.

'Are you saying the only way out is flying?' she asked the Norn.

'Yes', the Norn answered. 'You see him as an arrogant dragon, but he is one of the best flyers of his kind'. At that moment, Nidhogg stood proudly taken by the Norn's compliment, even though it wasn't meant to be a compliment judging by her low tone. It was more of a force-out fact.

'*Probably why he was chosen to be a guardian in the first place*', Keilantra suddenly muttered telepathically, causing Haley and Angela to laugh briefly.

Haley's eyes shifted between Nidhogg and the storm's eye. Compared to its farthest outside, the atmosphere above was so calm, like viewing the clear sky during an airplane journey in the day. She wished she could stay on this island forever. Everything on it was a pure reminder of the beach in Summerfield. Her home…where all her friends were getting on with their lives after the memory wipe. Hopefully, it was enough to keep them off of Nebula's raider.

'*Are you sure about this?*' Haley asked Keilantra and Angela telepathically, blocking out the words from the Norn and Nidhogg with her mind barrier.

'*As much as even I hate to admit it,*' Angela started out, '*Nidhogg is our best chance to get back across the Dark Sea*'.

'*And I too can't deny that he is useful in his own way, when he is not showing off*', Keilantra said. '*And as the Norn claimed, he is a skilled flyer*'

Not to mention an arrogant pig, Haley thought to herself out of telepathic earshot.

Much to her own reluctance, she saw the honesty in their eyes. Both Keilantra and Angela displayed positive and negative opinions on Nidhogg's part, but that was only because, unlike her, they must have had their own substantial encounters with Nidhogg and the other two guardians.

She just sighed, and said, 'Fine. Nidhogg, you may…take us back across the Dark Sea'.

Nidhogg grinned in response, his sharp pearly-white teeth on display. 'And I look forward to doing so, little princess', he said excitedly. He lowered himself down, providing allowance for the girls to climb on.

Again, Haley rolled her eyes struggling to hold back a small smile at Nidhogg's charming excitement: a side of him she did not see since meeting him. Maybe he wasn't bad so after all? She shrugged her shoulders at the thought.

Keilantra and Angela walked towards him to climb. Haley lingered behind and turned back to the Norn.

'I do have one question', she said.

The Norn produced an understanding glance, awaiting whatever it was Haley was about to ask.

'You said you could see the destinies of every Cosmos Being in the universe, including the Gods', Haley began. 'Does that mean you see the future of my destiny as well?'

A pause occurred between herself and the Norn.

'Your destiny is unpredictable', she answered. 'As Lady Orla foretold, we saw peace and brightness in your future…but there was a separate future of darkness, if you should fail. You are a very powerful descendent of the thunder god, Halena. Fearless and strong'.

'But do you believe I can do it? Do you believe I can prevent the next Ragnarok?'

The Norn cast her misty blue eyes around the chamber, before shifting her gaze back to Haley.

'Unfortunately, it is not my place to say', she said. 'But yes: from what I too witnessed in the eighteen years of your growth, you are The One destined to bring peace to the Nine Realms once again. The only thing I will say is that I hope you are successful in your quest'.

Slightly more satisfied with her answer, Haley said, 'Thank you…for what you did for us'.

'May the Gods be with you, distant daughter of Thor', she said, bowing her head.

Haley returned the nod and headed to Nidhogg, and climbed on his back behind Angela. As soon as she was on his rough-scaled back, Nidhogg began to flap his wings in a ready-for-action mode. Haley, Keilantra and Angela took a tight hold of the spikes on his back. Before they knew it, they were up in the air heading towards the swirling eye's opening, as the Norn vanished into the developing mist.

Chapter 16: The Well of Hvergelmir

Along the way, Haley impulsively developed this distinctive premonition that Nidhogg would perform unexpected twists and turns while she, Keilantra and Angela clung on for dear life. Him being the show off that he was, Haley thought. Nothing of the sort happened, much to her relief, but she held onto the dragon spike tightly in case.

They were now flying through the cloudy fog created by the hurricane. As they descended lower like a plane reaching its destination, the sun's orange rays slowly faded away. It was not until they made it past the fog that Haley noticed a change in the Dark Sea. Although it was still dangerously rough, it was not as violent as it was before, but the forever presence of the Ormes roaming its waters made Haley's skin crawl. The lower they got, the cleaner the blackened rocky beach became. Eric, Arianna and Aeolus stood in the same spot, where Haley, Keilantra and Angela took off surfing.

'Thank the Gods you are alright', Eric said, as soon as they landed and called off Nidhogg

Arianna brought Haley into a sisterly hug, while Aeolus made eye contact with Haley from behind and gave her a small smile and his eyes softened: a sign that underneath his hardship, he too was relieved. Haley returned the smile, finding at least some comfort in his presence.

'Well, looks like my work here is done for the time being', Nidhogg said grinning, potentially halting the little reunion.

Haley shook her head, just smiling slightly. 'Thank you, Nidhogg', she replied.

Keilantra and Angela replied with the same gratitude.

'If you need me, just whistle', Nidhogg said, winking at Haley. With that, he opened his wings and took flight, disappearing again into the thickened cloud. When Haley turned back to Eric, Arianna and Aeolus, she assumed from the looks on their faces they had some questions about what happened during the first Trial.

She first showed them the scar the Orme left on her shoulder, their eyes briefly widening at the thought of being close to death.

'Each trial must come with a price', Eric clarified.

Haley silently agreed, knowing she may expect something similar or more dangerous in the two yet to come. Without hesitation, she filled them in with the rest of the details about the island, the Norn of Destiny, the miniature Aurora Eclipse channeled by the crystal in her pendant, and the first piece of Mjolnir which was thankfully still safety attached to Megingjord. She detached it for Eric, Arianna and Aeolus to receive a better look.

'All that time, you did not know the Aurora Crystal in your necklace was the key to unlocking a thunderstone?' Arianna asked.

'No, nothing of the sort', Haley said, still in deep awe at the repeated flash of the Aurora Eclipse's cosmic replica. 'As I said, the crystal somehow knew that that thunderstone contained a piece of Mjolnir'. As she finished that sentence, Haley thought back to her time at school where she studied the Northern Lights in her science and history classes. 'Unless...', she said thoughtfully.

'What is it, Halena?' Eric asked.

'My history teacher on Earth mentioned the Native American legend about the tribe's spirits living on in the Aurora Borealis', Haley proclaimed. 'What if that happened to Thor and the Gods? They all became bonded to the Aurora Eclipse, and the crystal identified the thunderstone through Thor's spirit'.

Everyone considered this information of great importance.

'It is a possible theory', Aeolus answered this time, clearly recalling what Haley told him on the horse-ride to Vandalla in an attempt to get through to the kind boy she was told about.

Haley ran her finger over the Aurora Crystal. How something small demonstrated such extraordinary power became added to her list of curiosities. A low thundery rumble in the distance caught everyone's attention.

'We should take shelter', Eric recommended. 'We have until dawn, which is when the storm next calms'. Haley figured it was a four to five hour window between each storm sequence. Unpredictable, but cunning, both like and unlike the numerous weather forecasts back on Earth.

'That cave over there', Angela pointed out a large opening in the transparent mist, with water dripping as fast as an actual waterfall. As rain and hail started coming down, Haley and the rest of her company legged it to the cave. They were inside within seconds. Everyone either leaned against the rocky cave wall, catching their breath. Haley, on the other hand, stood at the edge of the cave entrance, staring in deep content at the storm. To think she, the descendent of the thunder god, found her way through a violent hurricane with a supposed no end…well, it was all too surreal.

'You should eat and rest', Aeolus suggested, as he used his cosmic elements ability to conjure up a campfire.

Haley knew she needed rest after the day she just had – the storm gave that to her. Only something inside her told her that she needed to keep going at an unstoppable pace, no rest required. As Lady Orla said, Mjolnir needed to be reforged and her biggest worry at this second was wasting time, before Vladimir carried out his threats. Eric said the storm would calm at the break of dawn, but what time of day was it at this moment? She hadn't thought about it, because she was preoccupied with not being eaten alive. She looked at Angurvadal, remembering it also glowed silver when day or night drew closer. Middle of the evening, Haley guessed thoughtfully.

Four days and a half left – all she could do was hope that the Nine Realms and her friends, and new family remained untouched at her request.

Reluctantly, Haley tore her eyes away from the storm and went over to the warm fire, setting down Angurvadal, Svalnn and the handle of Mjolnir. She wondrously examined the handle over and over again, still taken aback by a fragment of legend. Although released from its cage, the question was how she was going to reattach it to the other pieces once recovered. The low growl of her stomach put the questions off. She looked in her bag to see what supplies she received: sleeping blankets, medicine, bottled water, grapes, vegetable greens and honeyed bread. As Haley took a bite of the bread, its sweetness made her mouth water as much as the fruit of Asgard, serving her emerging hunger. Her brother unwrapped something brown paper: venison. As soon as it touched the dancing fire, Haley's hunger returned as the delicious smell travelled up her nostrils.

Once the meat was ready about four minutes later, Haley and the others sat on their set blankets, and eat in silence. It tasted good with the bread and greens Keilantra and Angela put together, that Haley ate it ever so slowly to indulge the flavor.

'So, which well is closest from here then?' Haley asked, feeling the need to not only break the hungry silence.

Aeolus cleared his throat, setting down his copper bowl and placing his hands together.

'That would be the Well of Hvergelmir', Aeolus answered. He appeared fascinated by her determination, but she brushed it off to retain her focus.

'It's where the liquid from the antlers of Eikpyrinir flow, isn't it?' Haley guessed intelligently.

'Only few amounts enter the numerous rivers, which lead to a Realm', Aeolus proclaimed. 'But ever since the Trials of Thor were created, it changed'.

'Changed?' she repeated the last word worriedly. 'In what way?'

'Have you ever wondered why they call it the Kettle Well, Halena?' Keilantra was the one to ask the next question.

'According to the Norse Legends, Hvergelmir means *bubbling, boiling spring*', Haley intelligently answered, but it was not until the last three words that a secondary theory came to mind, which terrified her in a sickening form, just picturing it. 'Do you mean to say that the Norns enchanted the Well's waters to boil people to death?'

'As we said, it is a theory but a high possibility', Arianna retaliated.

'That's just awful', Haley pointed out, worried she may survive that fate if she failed.

The loud rumble of thunder in the distance was bringing the discussion. Rain and hail came down harder and faster, like tiny pebbles hitting solid stone, even distracting Haley from the speculative circumstances of the second Trial. Outside the cave, she looked to the east past the concealing rainfall: the furthest distance…the predicted location of the Well of Hvergelmir.

'We're going to Niflheim', she said in a matter-of-fact tone, knowing full well that it was the truth. For some reason, it excited her even more that she was going to see another one of the Nine Realms, settling the sickening rhythm of her heartbeat.

'Queen Nyssa awaits our arrival at first light', Kelantria replied. 'She knows the Norn, who guards the Well'. For a split second, Haley wondered for how long, remembering Queen Nyssa's ice-cold beauty, but with a heart of golden warmth.

'You should get some sleep, Halena', Arianna said as everyone else wrapped themselves in their set of blankets. The storm was at its worst height, sending out cold chills through the mild air. All Haley could do was curl up into a ball, in her camp bedding desperately trying to keep warm; hoping and praying the storm would indeed calm as Eric defined earlier.

Her mind drifted back and forth, wondering what her uncle was actually doing. Probably preparing his armies for war, Haley thought with such dread that it made her blood boil. She did not want to imagine the suffering all the people endured since Nebula's creation, let alone Vladmir's psychopathic nature. As Lady Orla predicted, she saw two futures: one of darkness, one of purity and light. Haley concentrated as hard as she could on the light future, filled with love, happiness and beauty; stopping her powers from overloading them-selves again.

It worked like a charm.

Sleep followed soon after, with dreams of stars shining as brightly as the moon and the sun. Even her recurring dream of flying through the stars in her blue and gold dress returned to her.

*

Haley lost count of the sleeping hours she endured, when she jolted awake and looked outside the cave. As Eric predicted, outside was the calm before the storm, the only sounds that of the lightly crashing waves of the Dark Sea against the rocks and the gentle breeze. No thunder whatsoever. Rubbing her eyes, she saw the others were already awake, sharpening their weapons and packing up ready for the journey to Niflheim.

'How long was I asleep for?' Haley asked, standing up to pack.

'Seven hours', Arianna answered. 'Now that the storm has calmed, we should be able to call upon Optimus to open the gateway to Niflheim'.

This whole time, Haley's thoughts were all over the place.

Since being told there were numerous pathways with Yggdrasil, after even her uncle's breach of one, she was under the impression that there was a hidden shortcut to Niflheim around the area of the cave they stood in. Haley recalled her parents and Lady Orla's clear instructions: as soon as one Trial was complete, call upon the gatekeeper of the Bifrost. She just nodded, keeping her nerving thoughts at bay, avoiding asking any further questions unless it was absolutely necessary. As a precaution, Haley carefully placed the handle of Mjolnir into her sack covering it with her blankets like a fragile museum artifact. Svalinn lay across her back, while she attached the glowing silver rune Angurvdal to the buckle of Megingjord.

While the others packed up, Haley couldn't help but walk over to Aeolus who was stood at the opening of the cave, dazed in thought, his expression in its usual unreadable state; though Haley was no fool to notice the growth of the sparkling warm in his eyes.

'I never got to say you did well, Halena', he said, upon sensing her presence. The closer she came to him, the stronger the fiery current between became. Was this love she was feeling, or just a mutual attraction?

'Thank you', she replied with a small smile, blushing at the sound of his deep, strong voice. 'And thank you…for helping me, Keilantra and Angela while we were crossing the Dark Sea'.

He just shrugged. 'I did my duty as any prince would'.

She did not know whether to be grateful at the fact that he was truly protecting her, or annoyed that he dismissed it as a matter of duty. Knights have a duty as much as a prince or nobleman would, but Haley felt this was different. She swore she saw a look of concern on his face, the moment the Orme struck her shoulder.

'Still, it's good to know I have someone like you to look out for me', she simply said.

Aeolus turned his gaze towards her.

'Also, all five of us are a team now. We need to look out for one another, with this being my…destiny', Haley continued.

'Yet you still seem doubtful of the prophecy, my lady', he pointed out.

Damn these complicated emotions! Haley thought to herself. Was this connection between herself and Aeolus becoming more entwined?

She sighed deeply, looking at the sky hoping to see at least one or two stars to provide her some comfort. 'Since I was a baby, I lived a normal life despite having these powers. It was hard for me to keep them hidden from my friends. Worst of all, I was afraid of what they would think of me if I ever exposed myself in my uncontrollable state'.

'Uncontrollable state?' Aeolus questioned.

'Every day, something would emerge inside me triggered by emotion…notably fear. It was so strong that I struggled to control it at times'.

Her eyes locked with Aeolus's brown eyes. In a changed state, he appeared sympathetic towards Haley upon her recalling of the old and latest emerging of her powers.

'Yet somehow, you were able to do so while you were out there on the Dark Sea', he implied it as a foreseeable circumstance. 'You saw Angela was in danger, and you needed to control your power to help her. You were born for this. It is in your blood'.

Hearing the truth in Aeolus' voice made Haley a bit better. She found herself in a similar situation compared to the violent beach incident, except both encounters were unexpected. There was no planning ahead – plans changed. She saw the people she loved and cared for in danger, and her first instinct was to protect. The moment she then made eye contact with Aeolus, they held each other's gaze for the longest minute possible. Although there was no hand touching, Haley felt warmth surrounding him, the walls around his broken heart over his father's death breaking down, his eyes softening at her compassion. She felt it, like they were the only two people standing there in the face of the incoming dangers ahead.

'We're ready to go, Halena', Eric called out, breaking the connecting silence between them much to both parties' reluctance. Haley could easily tell Aeolus did not want their communication to end, feeling he was enjoying her company, finding it nice to have someone to talk to, aside from his brother and mother. Like she was the only person able to reach out to him.

The grudging wall he displayed towards Vladimir returned, and he turned away from Haley who appeared saddened that he would do such a thing. What else could she do to help him find peace and accept his father's death? If only he was here, so she could talk to him and ask what she could do, even if it was his spirit…

Right now, Haley needed to focus on the remaining trials.

She and the others headed outside. Much to Haley's relief, all she saw was a mixture of grey and white clouds to the same swirling fashion as when they first arrived, only less violent against the mini tsunamis of the Dark Sea. There was no sign of any movement below either. Haley assumed the Ormes entered temporary hibernation, at least until the next sound brought them to the surface.

'Optimus, open the gateway to Niflheim!' Eric called out to the heavens. Haley followed the direction of his gaze. Every corner and area of the sky maintained its grey status for a short period of time, until one section began to change. Bright light broke through like the sun, alongside the all-too-familiar lights of the rainbow bridge: a message saying that Optimus answered to the call. He was a descendent of an All-Seeing God after all, Haley thought to herself.

Formulated into a stream of light, a portal materialized right in front of them similar to the images the Bifrost presented before they were transported to the Dark Sea. On the other side, there was only fog. Misty blue fog and mist, so cold that one travelled through each of Haley's body. Through the fog, Haley spotted a silhouette of what appeared to be a frozen lake and waterfall, a set of buildings stood at the very top. While the others stepped through accordingly, Haley held back through minor hesitance that she failed to notice Aeolus held back too.

'Are you alright, my lady?' he asked with shallow concern, much to Haley's surprise.

'I don't know', she said honestly, as she glanced at the mist where Eric, Arianna, Keilantra and Angela disappeared. 'I don't know how I feel at this point'.

Despite the brief feigning of ignorance, Aeolus presented the aspects in sync with her emotions, understanding her all the same.

'Hold my hand', he offered as he held it out to her. 'Do not be afraid'.

Haley did as he said. The moment their hands touched, the warmth returned to him reignited against her lightning power. A powerful sensation as strong as what she felt for him – fire and lightning in connection, but locked in loving amenity between two individuals. Deep down, Haley felt grateful to Aeolus, providing her with help in overcoming her fear of what was on the other side. Again, was this love? Haley was not sure. All her life, she only knew parental and sibling love.

Her mental inquisition came to an infinite end, when she and Aeolus stepped through the looking glass-like gateway, Haley tightening her hold on Aeolus' hand never letting go. Unlike when it first opened, the chill of Niflheim was colder. It was a only good job Haley was wearing robes appropriate for this climate change, otherwise she would have frozen to death in minutes, and worst of all, seconds.

As soon as they were in the presence of Eric, Arianna, Keilantra and Angela, who stood waiting on the frosty grass of a misty meadow, Aeolus let go of Haley's hand retaining his soldier status, much to her discouragement and in spite of the small smile he kept glued in his face for a few more seconds.

'This is Niflheim', he eventually said. Luckily, The only necessary distraction provided for Haley was Niflheim itself.

The Realm of snow and ice bore a relating resemblance to places like Antarctica or Iceland, except the only real different was that it was a more magical winter wonderland. All Haley could think about was how beautiful the sight was, so beautiful that a flashback of her twirling around the snow, controlling the snowflakes became a constant reminder. Unlike the Dark Sea, the atmosphere was peaceful with its surrounding snow kissed mountains and frozen waterfalls. As for the sky – Haley was beyond glad to see it crystal clear with the billions of sparkling stars and the all-too-obvious sighting of the Aurora Borealis without the lunar eclipse, its lights dancing above the highest mountain peak. Haley felt the continuous sparkle in her eyes grow, as she stared like a day-dreamer at the mesmerizing view.

Were all the other Realms this beautiful? Haley thought to herself. Her question became another answer, when she spotted bushes of blue roses in eternal bloom, the petals shining like the stars. She walked up to one and sniffed it, the smell as fresh as the start of spring. Everything in this part of Yggdrasil looked or felt like a pleasant winter evening, particularly with the purple, blue and orange sunset feature on the farthest horizon behind the mountains; mixed together like on a paint palette. The perfect time for people to relax after a hard day's work, Haley wished for herself. Another thing she wondered was the sudden time difference. When they left the Dark Sea behind, it was the break of dawn. Now, it was a cross between day and night. Was that what it was? So many frustrating theories about Niflheim's natural habitat – it was hard to pick just one.

What was the most disheartening was none of the others an inch, since their feet touched the frosty grass. They were waiting for something or someone. But right now, Haley wanted to remain glued to her spot, admiring the Northern Light's reflective colours and Niflheim's beauty, while waiting for something else to leave her in deep astonishment as her heart skipped three beats every five seconds. If only she had a digital camera to take a picture, but at the same time she remembered she had a photographic memory.

'What exactly are we waiting for? Haley asked the others, hoping at least one of them would provide her with a reasonable answer for their still-as-a-statue mode. In the end, she did not need one after all. A minute later, a figure emerged from the mist at the edge of the frozen lake. One in particular Haley recognized.

'Queen Nyssa', she blundered out softly. The queen of Niflheim from the High Council: she was wearing a sky blue embroidered flow dress, which was long sleeved. Her white hair flowed freely, now beautifully curled – as radiant as the sky itself. The design of her crown was elegantly made up of blue and white crystals, embroidered to pure silver metal.

'Welcome, Halena', Nyssa greeted her, gesturing a gorgeous smile. 'And welcome: Lord and Lady Eric and Arianna, Lady Keilantra, Prince Aeolus and Angela'. They returned their greeting with a small bow or curtsey.

'You will be pleased to know I received your mother and father's message regarding the completion of the First Trial', she continued, addressing it more to Haley. 'I congratulate you on your victory. If there is anything you need now that you are grated safe passage, please speak your minds'.

Haley returned the smile, before asking politely.

'We're now looking for the Well of Hvergelmir', she explained. 'It is located somewhere on Niflheim, but even I have no idea where. As queen of Niflheim, I was wondering if you knew?'

Pause.

'Time is of the essence', she uttered shyly. 'We have only four days until Vladimir plots a possible attack and until then, I have to find two more pieces of Mjolnir'.

Nyssa pursed her lips in an understanding manner. 'Your agenda is also your motivation, young Halena', she answered. 'You have grown stronger since our first meeting, as strong as the Thunder God himself. As a guardian of the Nine Realms, it is also my sworn duty to protect not just my kingdom, but you and your family as well'.

'So you know where the Well is?' Haley asked.

'Yes. I do. Please follow me', Nyssa smiled angelically. She motioned them towards the far lake in front of them, as frozen as solid rock. Haley, Eric, Arianna, Keilantra, Aeolus and Angela followed. Every step Haley took felt heavy, the icy grass crunching beneath her boots, keeping a firm grip on her sword prepared for anything. She wondered what other creatures inhabited Niflheim – she only knew Beings like Nyssa and her son, Occasso who seemingly controlled ice and snow.

Haley and the rest of the company halted at the lake's edge. For the first time since crossing Niflhem's borders, Haley got a proper look at it. Every corner, edge and fraction of surrounding was covered in purely solid blue ice, making it impossible to see the discoloured water beneath – all down to the night sky; and the lights reflecting off the ice's top. The only areas not frozen were eleven rivers of free flowing fresh water.

The moment it dawned upon Haley, Nyssa spoke.

'This is Lake Elivagar', she explained, before turning to Haley kindly. 'As you now possess the All-Knowledge, I assume you know what it means in the English language.

'Ice-waves', Haley answered wondrously. 'The rivers existed even at the start of the Nine Realms, as the original source of Yggdrasil, going by the name of Ginnungagap'.

'Exactly', Nyssa said, impressed by the effects of the All-Knowledge. 'Each river has a name: Svol, Gunnthra, Ejorm, Fimdulthal, Slidr, Hrid, Sylgr, Ylgr, Vid, Leiptr and Gjoll'

'I thought Ginnungagap was a primordial void', Haley pointed out. 'In the legends, people of different cultures believed it was the true Big Bang theory'.

'Like the Sola System, the Nine Realms were created from the very same energy and ancient magic from the Gods', Nyssa proclaimed. 'To this day, the Earthlings still believe your theory is to be the most classical theory to study. They are a very intelligent species that their concepts regarding the universe are still carried through from generation to generation. As for Ginnungagap, it still remains an unknown void but maintains a north and south side like a map or compass'.

Haley looked into Nyssa's electric blue eyes. 'You're referring to Niflheim and Muspelheim being the north and the south, aren't you?'

Nyssa simply nodded towards the rivers. Confused, Haley was not sure what she should be looking at. All she saw was ice and rushing water – until she used her advance vision to look closely at each river, eventually coming across faint white steam in the air like evaporating water heading back up to be condensed by the sky.

'Does each river lead to Muspelheim then?' Haley asked. 'I read that it does so'.

'Elivagar is the natural source for travelling water, both hot and cold', Nyssa replied. 'When it rains here in Niflheim, it freezes upon direct contact with the ice and snow. Over time, it evaporates itself and condenses into the rivers, thanks to the heat of Muspelheim. There is also a separate water chamber for our supply'.

'The Well of Hvergelmir', Haley guessed. She wondered whether the lake itself was the actual Well. If it was, how was she supposed to locate the second piece? Will her necklace carry out the same method, as it unexpectedly did at the Well of Urd? Well, they always say expect the unexpected, Haley thought.

'What you seek lies behind the Falls of Elivagar', Nyssa answered, gesturing to the frozen falls. 'However, only a descendent of the Thunder God or a Being unaffected by the ice element can make it across the lake alive'.

'Why not anyone else?' Haley asked, despite dreading the answer that was coming.

As she thought of it, Nyssa waved her hand, blue dusts animating itself above the ice surface much like the magical projection at the High Council. The humanoid figures re-enacted a battle against what appeared to be a dragons. That was only the first worst thing to be killed by in this kind of environment; the second worst thing showed itself directly: any skin contact with the ice, and the warriors who did not possess ice element magic froze to death in seconds, horrifying Haley. Everyone else seemed familiar with this story presentation, but underneath their skin they were just as edgy as Haley was.

She herself possessed ice in her genetic structure, remembering the ice ball from ocean water; but seeing this distinctive re-enactment did not, would not take the edge off of the nauseating feeling in the pit of her stomach. Haley gulped deeply, but her throat tightened and not from the brisk coldness of Niflheim.

The silence broke, when Aeolus spoke once the animation vanished.

'I volunteer to accompany Halena', he said without a moment's beat. 'As prince and protector of Alfheim, and possessor of the Seven Cosmic Elements of the Universe, she will stand a better chance of getting across the lake without a doubt'.

Haley laughed sarcastically on the inside, while she remained deeply touched by Aeolus' selfless volunteering. Duty or not: he was a man of true honour, and whether he wished to admit it or not, he did care about her, his family and the people of the Nine Realms. The ice cube act was never going to work around her. According to the projection, it was going to take more than a descendent of Thor to get across the lake as Nyssa implicated.

Unfortunately, she couldn't help but worry.

'Are you absolutely sure?' she impulsively asked. 'I mean, what if something bad happens to you? As you've seen from that replay, all those warriors died'.

'Only because they did not have the power to control ice', Aeolus reminded her, obviously hoping to decrease Haley's doubtfulness. 'I control seven elements. That is more than enough'. He was a cross between confident and overconfident at this point. Haley saw it in his eyes. Those years of mourning his father took a toll on his life, with the whole pushing-people-away-but-not-neglecting-his-duty. He was stronger…tougher.

Maybe Haley should be too, if she tried harder?

'I just can't help but think', she uttered. 'I mean, look at what happened when Vladimir attacked us in the dungeon, or when I almost died from Orme poisoning. After the First Trial, I realize now that the rest isn't going to be easy'.

Arianna took Haley's hand in sisterly comfort. 'Sister', Arianna said. 'It is alright to be afraid of not succeeding. But know this: you are stronger than you believe. You even stood firm in front of Vladimir, in spite of the danger he possesses'.

What caused it anyway? Adrenaline or warrior princess? She asked herself that questions multiple times already, since that intense encounter. Now that Haley thought about it more and more, Arianna was right about that specific factor: despite her fear, she kept a leveled head and stayed calm, pushing aside Vladimir's mind games, providing aberration. If she could do that, alongside combatting poisonous sea monsters, then maybe…maybe from what she saw, there was a chance.

'Alright, let's do this', Haley said to Aeolus, gaining a small confidence boost.

Aeolus nodded, before saying, 'One more thing'.

With a wave of his hand and a mute incantation, streams of blue sparkling light materialized flowing its way towards Haley's feet, another complementary recall of Lady Orla's magic identifying Haley's genetic structure at the Lake of Prophecy. She felt like she grew another two inches, until she lifted one foot and saw what became magically attached to her boots: skating blades. They shone like diamonds with the Northern Lights reflecting off the silver metal.

Haley stood in amazement, gesturing over Aeolus' handiwork. He too wore matching blades of the same craftsmanship, which made each set look like they were brand new.

'Those dragons you saw will be alerted to your presence, the second you step onto the ice', Aeolus warned.

Her heart hammering against her rib cage, Haley gave an understanding nod. The frozen waterfall was yards away. If what she saw from the projection were precisely accurate, if the ice dragons and obstacles were not a part of this, it would have been a piece of cake. Except it was nothing of the sort. These ice dragons were going to do everything in their power to prevent her and Aeolus from making it across.

This was it...she was about to begin the Second Trial.

Everyone else, including Nyssa wished her luck. Eric, Arianna and Angela readied their weapons, Haley sensing the channeling of their powers for extra assistance.

In Haley's eyes, the lake looked as beautiful as a winter wonderland that she almost wished she did not have to ice skate across. What if the ice wasn't thick enough? What if the ice element of her powers was not enough to withstand the curse the Norns placed upon it to protect the Well of Hvergelmir? One look at Aeolus told Haley there was no going back.

Unable to hesitate a second longer, she and Aeolus leapt off the ground with all their strength, landing on the ice; and began skating straight the waterfall. Hope coursed through Haley's blood as she counted in seconds due to the creatures and obstacles not showing up right away. Were they like the Ormes, who emerged ten to fifteen seconds upon hearing seconds?

She mentally spoke it too soon, when something underneath caught their attention. At first, it appeared black and circular like a giant fish was moments away from bursting out of the water.

Haley did not know, but Aeolus did. 'Split!' he shouted out.

On those words, Haley moved right while he moved left. As they did, a giant pillar of ice erupted out of the spot growing until it towered ten to twenty feet above them. Unprepared for this level of magnitude, Haley unlocked all her super-senses and re-activated Megingjord. Numerous icicle towers burst out, blocking their re-evaluated pathways. Three were near impossible to avoid – until Haley unleashed a bolt of lightning through Jarngreipr, creating a powerful shockwave. The ice shattered into thousands of pieces. First, came claws; then legs and black eyes of darkness; and lastly, wings.

Dragons...ice dragons!

The very ones Nyssa spoke about...what Haley saw in the horrifying re-enactment of those warriors, who froze instantly and disintegrated into nothingness. There were ten dragons. They roared and screeched like sneering predators. Their eyes were so black, that it was difficult to identify their current emotion at first. As they screeched and spread their wings, Haley realized it was out of anger at being disturbed from their three-thousand-year-old migration. What eventually happened that day, when the second piece was delivered to the Well, which stood now at fifty years away? Was it Thor's idea to include ice dragons in the Trials, or did the Norns request it?

Haley's focus returned. Time stood still, as she and Aeolus halted their skating after taking out more ice pillars with Aeolus' help from the fire element of the Cosmic Seven; and Angurvadal which cut through the larger ice blocks smoothly clean, before formulating into another dragon. Ten became fifteen. Fifteen cunningly intelligent ice dragons. They swarmed directly above their heads, circulating around like a giant hive of bees. Suddenly, Haley spotted one larger dragon with a crowned head, leading them: it could only be the queen, Haley thought.

'I think I know what we have to do', Haley told Aeolus, gripping Angurvadal and readying Svalinn. 'We have to kill the queen'.

Aeolus looked at her, like she was crazy. Haley on the other hand made sure the others heard everything through their enhanced super-hearing.

'A honey bee colony has a queen, called a gyne', Haley explained. 'She is the leader of the hive, which means she is *the mother of most, if not all of the bees*, as the people on Earth say: the only adult which the younger bees will follow and protect'.

'Meaning?' Aeolus asked.

The Queen Dragon led the smaller dragons higher and higher. It won't be long until they reached swan-dive mode, meaning they needed to act quickly; in less than a minute.

'What if these dragons are the same? They follow no one, but the Queen Dragon', Haley continued. 'So if we kill her, the hive will be called off and destroyed'.

Aeolus observed the dragons' seemingly unchangeable sequence. At his own realization, Haley took it as a sign that this was indeed the right course of action. 'We lead them towards the waterfall and strike with our combined powers', he suggested.

Sensing the others agreeing with the plan, Haley nodded in agreement. Making eye contact with the Queen Dragon sent chills down her spine. The blackness bore a close resemblance of emptiness: no emotional heart whatsoever, for these particular dragons were not flesh and blood. Only soulless moving ice statues, created like they were genetically engineered. As they eyed up the Queen Dragon, Haley and Aeolus watched as she broke her current flight pattern, while the smaller dragons circulate around them. True to the prediction, she swan-dived her wings pulled flat back from the force of an upward breeze; and unleashed a ring of blue fire towards them.

As quick as a lightning bolt, Haley and Aeolus launched into defense mode, Haley using Svalinn to protect herself and Aeolus. The bluebell flames contacted with the metallic gold. As it did, the sun shield dramatically glowed bright yellow like the real sun. Heat radiated from Haley's fingertips to her toes, as the fire spread all over its circumference close to overflowing like water on a disc, potentially re-enacting a scientist's theory about the Earth being flat. Slowly, the force brought Haley and Aeolus to their knees, both gripping the shield providing combined strength.

Everything about this first attack, much to Haley's dawning realization, was a stalling tactic, meaning the Queen Dragon as intelligent and cunning as she was continued to breath fire while continuing to swan-dive towards them; meaning the second she stops gasping out fire was the moment she intentionally strikes with her razor-sharp teeth.

Haley prayed Svalinn was powerful enough to withstand this upcoming secondary attack, otherwise she and Aeolus were toast; and no one else in the Nine Realms would stand a chance against Vladimir and the Nebulans. For an abrupt minute, she thought back to her uncle's plans. She knew he wanted to destroy her and her family as some kind of follower to Ragnarok; but she couldn't help but think there was something more to this, other then being so driven by hatred and jealousy – like he was seeking something else that was not Mjolnir.

What was it?

There was no time for answers, while in between life and death at this stage of the Second Trial. Haley needed to stop the Queen Dragon from killing them. At that moment, the fire stopped. The dragon was closing in, ready to devour them!

'Aeolus, down!' Haley shouted out. He did as she said, getting down in a crouching position on one knee, shielding himself. With all her strength, Haley struck the Queen Dragon full force with Svalinn, sending her hurdling along the thick ice. The minor impact cracked her crowned head, leaving her disorientated; you would think it was a mild concussion.

Unfortunately, it was not enough to kill her. It only made her ten times angrier, more determined to stop them from reaching the Well of Hvergelmir.

'We need to move now!' Haley yelled.

As instantly as she said it, Aeolus grabbed her hand and threw up another fireball, distracting the dragon colony. Haley looked back towards the lakeside. Using her rainbow fire ability, Keilantra generated combatant dragons against the ice dragons, reminding Haley of her mystical lightning phoenixes. While the secondary distractions were carried out, Haley and Aeolus skated off hand-in-hand, their moves in sync with one another. To Haley, everything happened in slow motion. Her heart stopped. She looked at Aeolus, star-struck by how close she was to him at this intense moment. Even in the face of life and death, his protective warmth kept her calm and focused. They were so close to the waterfall, that Haley sensed two things: the strong power of the Well behind the ice, and the ice dragons closing in on them. Haley glanced over her shoulder: they were so close she felt their breath on her face. She and Aeolus skated fast and hard, until they came to a skidded stop in the front of the falls, to face the Queen Dragon and her little minions.

'*Unleash your power when I do*', Aeolus instructed telepathically. All Haley could do was nod again, too speechless to think straight, everything she experienced since stepping through the Niflheim gateway processing her brain at a slow pace. Here she was: relying on Aeolus to guide her, protect her. It was a good think he was born with the Seven Cosmic Elements of the Universe – that was his speciality, a big pinch-yourself moment from what she witnessed so far.

'*Now!*' Aeolus finally yelled out in her head. Fire glowed in the palms of his hands, the heat increasing that it felt like you would melt. Haley was unaffected. Instead, she looked to the sky, her eyes glowing an intense white. Dark clouds appeared, rumbling like an angry God reborn; sparks of electricity hit her eardrums as they travelled to her fingertips. As both fire and lightning reached their peak, Haley and Aeolus sent each cosmic element towards the blue gem on the Queen Dragon's crowned head like a sideway funnel of a tornado.

Her painful screeches formed the temptation for Haley to withdraw. She had heard enough screams in the past, it was too difficult to handle. The more she thought about it, the stronger the temptation became; putting her focus off balance. As the gem glowed and cracked, the dragons too followed. Then, came an explosion and scattering ice blocks coming down like meteors; Haley using Svalinn to shield Aeolus and herself from further injury. And nothingness…the dragons were gone.

Haley let out a breath of relief at the worst being over.

'Fire melts ice, lightning destroys', she guessed, as the ice blocks dissolved beneath the frozen lake, disappearing entirely.

Aeolus responded with a small, but incredulous snigger. 'But combined together, they can withstand anything', he said emotionlessly. Unbelievably, it became an incredulous situation for Haley, due to the fact that he was so quick to put up his little emotion shield. One was for sure: he laughed. Only slightly; and it sounded sweet like the boy she was told about.

Maybe she should give him another pep talk, when this was over.

She thought she heard the rushing of water close by, and it wasn't either river. Seeing the others did not help, as the mist returned to the lake concealing from view. Haley hoped they saw they made to the other side. For now, time to find the source of the water sound, she thought. Haley and Aeolus turned around: it was the waterfall. Only no water was breaking through the thickened ice. A stream of magic liquid emerged from nowhere, burning through a section of ice, revealing a gateway into a cavern; the water-like substance continuously swirling. Through it, Haley spotted the silhouette of a woman wearing a white gown with familiar separate sleeves. Her light brown hair was tied up in a crowned braid. This could only be the Norn of the Well of Hvergelmir, her back facing them in the exact same position as the Norn of Destiny; in front of the same three thirteen foot tall standing stones in a ring.

'Well…here goes nothing', Haley uttered, before stepping through alongside Aeolus.

Hardly any coldness filled the cave, compared to the outside, like it was an average autumn temperature. The only chill in the air passed through the circular opening in the cave ceiling, with a tree root of Yggdrasil reaching up to the skies from the endless bottom of an identical water crater. The walls glistened like diamonds. Haley placed her hand on it: cold to the touch. Each wall bore cave drawings etched in: warriors battling, a dying king surrounded by his loved ones, and a map of Yggdrasil.

'Princess Halena', the woman said, turning around. She was shockingly identical to the Norn of Destiny: the same star-shining, pale-skinned beauty with rosy cheeks and misty blue eyes. They had to be triplet sisters, she thought.

'Welcome to the Well of Hvergelmir', she introduced herself politely 'I am Vethandi, sister of Urdr and Skuld'.

Haley nodded shyly.

'My sister, Urdr informed me of your arrival', Vethandi replied. 'Congratulations on completing the first two Trials. Both you and Prince Aeolus demonstrated true courage against the Queen Dragon and her ice dragons we created'.

'So it was you who created them?' Haley questioned, her voice sounding accusing. She couldn't help herself, even though it was for a good reason: to prevent their enemies from setting foot on either Well.

'Those warriors Queen Nyssa showed you were enemies and monsters from thousands of years ago', Vethandi explained. 'Somehow, they received word from scouts that a powerful treasure laid hidden in the Well around the time Lord Thor was fatally wounded by Jormungardr. My sisters and I created these ice dragons and cursed Lake Elivagar, only allowing those who control or withstand ice. As you are a distant daughter of Thor, born with weather manipulation, and Prince Aeolus controls the Seven Cosmic Elements of the Universe, the curse did not affect you or him'.

'Will the ice dragons be brought back to life?' Haley asked out of curiosity.

Vethandi smiled and shook her head. 'No. Now that the Trial is completed, the curse will also be lifted once the second piece of Mjolnir is freed from the Well'.

Well, that was good news. Now that she had knowledge of how to unlock the secrets of Yggdrasil, Haley stepped towards the Well. She shifted a quick glance through the cave opening in the ceiling. Like Urdr's Well, a root of Yggdrasil towered to the misty heavens as the Northern Lights danced in a forever sequence. Elivagar's waters fell into the crater of the unknown, presumably travelling to the other Realms, along with the water tumbling down the tree root.

'Do you know how to retrieve the piece?' Vethandi asked.

Haley sighed, looking down into the crater. 'Yes', she said, touching her necklace. 'I do'.

At that point, the Aurora Crystal on her triquetra necklace glowed. Luckily, Haley was prepared this time: being more prepared, she allowed the streams to journey down the bottomless crater. Eventually, the same white light exploded upwards and everywhere into billions of tiny stars. A reflection of the heavens, as Urdr implicated, this location replica of the universe featured the very stars above, and the manifestation of the Aurora Borealis.

'Incredible', Vethandi whispered by Haley's newly found magical talent.

Every star constellation was so beautiful, that Haley wished she could spend long hours studying the ones she had not yet identified, but she couldn't. All she could do right now was keep it locked away in her photographic memory drive for safekeeping.

'Do you see it yet?' Aeolus asked, breaking his own silence. On the last word, Haley's necklace glowed as a familiar blue star edged closer. A brief surge of energy filled the entire atmosphere around Niflheim: the curse was broken, Haley felt it as much as Vethandi felt it.

'Yeah', she uttered out, remaining captivated by the star, as it exploded and released the thunderstone. Inside Haley, the lightning surge touched every vein in her blood. As her eyes glowed white, the triquetra's pattern embedded the crystallized stone. After a brief pause, it cracked as light streams burst through. The pieces were replaced by a certain piece of something: a sliver leafed vine rod. Pure and ancient – but baring the appearance of something recently manufactured by a blacksmith. The dwarves must have gone a long way to ensure Mjolnir's power prevailed any probable damage.

Reaching for it, Haley ran her fingers over the silver. It was smooth like a pebble, with a mirrored reflection of the Northern Lights, like a decoration on a mantelpiece. 'I never knew Mjolnir had this part of it', Haley pointed out.

'Why do you say that, dear?' Vethandi asked curiously.

'On Earth, each drawing of the hammer is different', Haley replied. 'At the time of the Vikings, the people wore iron pendants called Mjolnir amulets. I guess they saw it as a sign of wisdom, like the Cosmos Beings shooting stars'.

'Hmmm…a very interesting fact. Your knowledge is truly astonishing, young one'.

Haley shrugged her shoulders. 'People have been saying that every time, long before the…All-Knowledge affected me'.

'That is what makes you special', Vethandi said. 'Aside from your inherited powers, your intelligent mind is the most precious thing to be gifted with. It will serve as the perfect advantage against your uncle and Ragnarok'.

'Did you know?' Haley asked. 'That I would be able to complete the Trial? You're the Norn of the present, which means you see every occurrence or event currently happening'.

'I saw two potential presents', Vethandi answered honestly. 'You evaluated your actions as I saw it happen. Even as we speak, I continue to watch every happening across all Nine Realms'. It was startling how she clarified that. After all, there were trillions of souls in Yggdrasil, it would be hard to keep an eye on them all at once – unless you are someone like Optimus or Vethandi.

Now that Haley had her answer, she thanked Vethandi for her hospitality, before turning to Aeolus to let him know she was ready to return the other side of the lake. As they headed back towards the waterfall opening, Haley turned back to Vethandi who still bore the same intriguing expression since meeting her. Only one more thing shining in her beautiful misty eyes...

Hope.

CHAPTER 17: THE DREAM

Despite Haley's own protest, Nyssa insisted that she, Eric, Arianna, Keilantra, Aeolus and Angela stayed one night to recover from the journey so far. The reason for Haley's protest: it was coming up to three and a half days, until Vladimir and his Nebulans showed their faces again.

After several hours of settling into their rooms – each architecturally designed from ice crystal – Haley changed into an elegant sky blue halter neck dress, as her assigned handmaiden, Lyla, with aqua blue eyes and light blonde hair styled her hair into a side fishtail plait. In contempt of her nerves, Haley felt a small buzz of excitement inside her: much to her shocking surprise, Aeolus volunteered to escort her to dinner. Either he was indeed doing this as her protector, or he truly did care about her enough, clearly having a change of heart about his cold attitude.

There was a knock at the door. He was here – Haley sensed his power.

'Could you get the door please, Lyla?' she asked politely, as she checked her makeup and hair. Lyla, as quiet as she was, looked astounded by Haley's actions. According to her, most noblewomen just sit there all poker face waiting for the moment the servant says they are ready, the thought of which made Haley want to burst out laughing, as she imagined it.

'Of course, Miss Halena', Lyla eventually said with a smile on her pale, pretty face; and went to answer the door. It was indeed Aeolus – handsome as ever, in blue robes, black boots and a gold belt with his sword attached.

'You look lovely, my lady', he said. Although he once again retained the same emotionless state at this moment, it was nice for a change to receive a compliment from him.

'Thank you', Haley replied, blushing with a nervous smile.

Like a real gentleman, he offered his arm out to her, which she apprehensively took. As they stepped out into the crystallised hall, Haley's legs slowly started to turn to jelly, like pins and needles came about so suddenly. She felt like she was drowning with no means of escape, until Aeolus gently tightened the interlock between their arms. Thanks to this specific action, Haley felt safer.

'You know I never thanked you before', she said as they descended down the ice glass grand staircase.

'For what?' Aeolus asked questioningly.

'For saving my life for the third time', she replied.

Aeolus raised one eyebrow.

'Aside from what happened on the lake, you saved my life twice', she pointed out gratefully, turning things around. 'When we were riding out to Valhalla, Keilantra told me about the first two times you saved me – that's something else I have to thank you for'.

He simply shrugged his shoulders, looking at the floor. 'It was nothing really', he uttered. 'Besides, Keilantra talks too much anyway'.

Haley laughed on the inside. At least they agreed Keilantra had the biggest mouth - well, when it comes to gossiping at least.

'True', she agreed. 'But I'm glad she did. Otherwise, how would I know who my rescuer was if you didn't tell me it was you?'

'I appreciate your kindness, my lady', he replied. 'But it was just me who strives to protect. Your family and other Cosmos Beings willingly agreed this sworn duty to protect you'.

Inside, Haley was driven by an urge to plead with him to let go of his agonizing anger at least for a few hours. At the same time, she sympathized him knowing Vladimir was the ultimate cause of his pain. Bringing nothing but death and hurt to families like his...killing their parents, or known close relatives for sport: that was a line crossing over to the point of no return.

'Still, you did a good thing, duty or not; because you have a good heart', she finally said. 'It's okay to feel anger. Believe me: I understand'. She was trying as hard as possible to reach out, to connect with him. He was so close to regaining even a fraction of his humanity. The warmth, the light...and love for the people. Haley felt it. He could not deny it.

Haley waited for a response.

Nothing came. She reluctantly let it at that – she needed to find another way to convince him to feel something rather than anger. Worse case scenario was it consuming him.

The open pillars of the grand staircase they walked past revealed the breezy but beautiful frosty Realm, snowflakes coming down gracefully. Three landed in her open palm, and she twirled them into the formation of a perfect twister, multiplying into identical flakes – like she did when she was a little girl. Through the pillars, she saw the people, including the children, of Niflheim ice-skating on another nearby frozen lake, throwing blue and white sparks of magic.

'I never realized how beautiful Niflheim is, when it snows like this', Haley said to Aeolus in a small by happy tone, as she watched the Northern lights through the thickened snowflakes. Compared to Earth snowfalls, Niflheim was different: graceful and fluid. Buried underneath a blanket of soft snow, illuminating against an eternal Aurora. Quiet, but cheerful like Earth…

'Yes, I suppose it is', he replied. Haley felt him smiling on the inside, despite his attempt to mask it with his hard demeanor.

At the bottom of the staircase, the ice glass double doors opened automatically, leading into the dining hall of Niflheim's palace. The entire structure exhibited a similarity to one created by an ice princess. Mesmerizing – crystallized out of pure ice down to the very last detail. Only the dining hall was different: crystallized out of ice and enchanting lights, like an imprint of the Aurora Eclipse. In the centre was an ice crystal round table, with a print of the triquetra sign in the middle, much like the one at Glaosheim – meaning the other Realms held the same kind of table, only made out of a different material or element in accordance to their natural habitat. A vase of pure blue roses stood in the triquetra's midpoint. Candles were lit in bluebell flames, with plates of delicious food: boiled vegetables, salad, bread and fish. The domed window above revealed a spectacular view of the stars and the Aurora.

Eric, Arianna and Keilantra too were all dressed up. Keeping things simple, Angela just wore a perfect lilac silk dress, half her hair clipped back. She looked different in a good way. It suited her.

The guards opened the doors a second time, and in walked Nyssa escorted by her son, Prince Occasso. Both look majestic in their sky blue and silver wear, a possible trademark of Niflehim's royal household. Nyssa's dress was out of this world, fitting perfectly around her figure. Its magically embedded sparkles on the silk glowed in sync with her eyes. Her hair was half down, now a crowned braid wavering around her silver tiara of snowflakes and blue sapphires.

'Good evening: Halena, Aeolus, Eric, Arianna, Keilantra and Angela', Nyssa greeted them all.

Everyone returned the greeting.

'You remember my son, Prince Occasso'.

Of seventeen years, Occasso had flawless, young pale skin from forever exposure of Niflheim's atmosphere. Through eye contact with him, Haley saw he definitely inherited his mother's benevolent good nature, baring a charming smile. His robes were embroidered in white Celtic patterns.

'It is good to see you all again', Occasso said with a charming smile. 'You too, Halena'.

Haley returned the smile. 'Nice to see you again too, and meet you in person'. His gaze appeared to hold with hers a second longer, before Haley shifted her eyes down to the floor, tightened her hold around Aeolus' arm. Following that instinct, Aeolus led her to one of the eight chairs set around the table. Haley thought she saw jealousy in his eyes towards Occasso, but she brushed it off. It was just a friendly greeting, nothing more.

As soon as everyone was seated, wine and water magically filled the glasses by their food plates. Fruity red wine, Haley guessed by the scent. She took a small sip – mixed berries, sweeter than juice – before eyeing the food in front of her. Judging by the sight and smell, the fish was roasted sea bass, crispy with herbs and spices making Haley's mouth water. The moment she tasted it, her hunger surpassed at every bite.

'Thank you…for letting us stay, Your Highness', Haley said, breaking apart a deep discussion between Eric, Arianna, Nyssa and Occasso, regarding the prophecy.

'There is no need for thanks or formalities', Nyssa replied sweetly. 'Know that you are always welcome'. She made it sound like Haley was a guest of honour, much to her own discomfort. At least one side of that statement allowed her some normalcy.

'Thanks. Your kingdom is very beautiful', she complimented, as the Aurora illuminated the entire hall through the stain glass window dome. The artwork was made up of nine circular stars – the Nine realms, including the Earth, as if seen as stars through a telescope.

'It is nothing like you ever seen before, is it not?' Occasso guessed.

'You could say that', Haley answered, shrugging her shoulders. 'Some parts of Earth don't get much snow, because of the climate we live in'.

'Unlike your Earth, our Realm was created from ice caused by the creation of the universe', Nyssa explained. 'Once the supernova died down, everything divided: rocks, stars, elements – everything. The Nine Realms formed like the Solar System. Niflheim and Muspelheim were the first to be formed being the north and the south. In the process, Ymir – the ancestor of all giants – was born'.

Learning about Yggdrasil's cosmological history increased Haley's knowledgeable excitement, temporarily fracturing her worry towards the Third Trial. Every word spoken became embedded in her soul, touching it like the permanent scar on her shoulder, and the cloud birthmark on her collarbone.

'Ymir was the god of all gods', Haley stated knowingly.

'All Cosmos Beings are direct descendants, including generations of distant relatives through multiple bloodlines', Nyssa implied. 'Notably cousins'.

'Wasn't Ymir born from venom that was drawn from the rivers of Elivagar Lake?' Haley questioned.

'He was indeed. When Ginnungagap came during the Big Bang, he was born. After the Nine Realms formed, he made a willing sacrifice to create Earth: his flesh for grass, his blood for ocean and rivers, his bones for mountains, his hair for trees, his brains for clouds and his skull for the heavens'.

Haley seemed shell-shocked, but in sheer fascination. 'Are you saying Ymir is God himself? The creator of mankind?'

'In a way, yes', Nyssa confirmed. 'You're a believer of God?'

Haley answered, 'Yes, in a way. Through His teachings, I believe in truth and having faith in others, and the world around me both spiritually and physically.

'Then, you have your answer. Ymir and God are one and the same'.

Her heart warming, Haley smiled thoughtfully.

*

Dinner was finished in minutes, which was when Nyssa insisted only Haley joined her for a walk through the palace. The crystallization of the architecture was absolutely breathtaking, that it felt like Haley stepped into the page of a children's fairytale. Excluding the fabric cushions, candle-stands and tapestries, everything shone like a star – a rare crystal. Every time they passed a window, the Aurora illuminated through, lighting up the entire hallway. Haley's dress flowed gracefully in sequence (Nyssa went through a lot of trouble to ensure her guest-of-honour wardrobe was ready).

One particular tapestry showed a clear view of Yggdrasil, the circles of imagery highlighting what Realm was supposed to look like. What really caught Haley's eye the most was the one single painting on the wall. It was a painting of Nyssa, holding her infant son, and a king: her husband. He displayed extraordinary handsomeness, standing noble and strong. In his hand was a sword, which he held up to symbolize his kinghood. Nyssa's beauty in the beauty was as inspiringly majestic as she looked to the present day, that Haley found it difficult to compare to even the blue roses of Niflheim.

'Is that your husband?' Haley asked out of interest.

'Yes', Nyssa answered. 'Goliath was the love of my life. From the moment we met, I was constantly drawn to him. We ruled the kingdom with love, kindness and loyalty'. She sighed sadly. 'After we had our son, he died in battle'

Haley gasped lightly. 'I'm so sorry', she said with deep sympathy. 'How old was Occasso?'

'Eight months old', Nyssa answered.

The exact age Haley was when she was spent away…unlike her, Occasso never knew his father but he must look up to his legacy from what Nyssa told him. Haley's heart sank.

'I will always love him', Nyssa reassured her. 'He lives on in my son, and we will remember him'.

Finding it too painful to talk about her husband further, Nyssa then changed the subject back to their discussion of the Cosmos.

'Every version, every answer I am sure you have come to an understanding tells a different story on how the Universe began, and the ordering of the Cosmos – ' Nyssa continued, her voice as angelic as her together hands, before Haley's interruption occurred.

'They called it a cosmogonic myth', she implicated. 'Scientists, even philosophers studied the universe through models speculating its born nature. One of which was the Big Bang'.

Haley stopped herself, trying to keep her power of the All-Knowledge under control. It couldn't pick a relevant time to take effect, could it? Haley thought. A powerful form of magic affecting her in ways she never thought possible, until she woke up for the first time in Asgard: when she had her first teaser of it. Oddly enough, Nyssa didn't show any signs of annoyance towards Haley's uncontrollable interruption. Instead, she was clearly fascinated by this revelation like nothing she had ever seen before upfront.

'Your wisdom and knowledge never goes amiss, my dear', Nyssa continued. 'It seems you harbor vast expertise of the universe from all cultures'.

'Notably the Norse and Celtic culture', Haley was quick to point out. 'You know, before all this, I researched into my ancestry. No record at all – until I stepped through the Bifrost for the first time. That was when the first effects of the All-Knowledge came about. All that time, I thought it was because I studied hard at school'.

'Your mother and father said you exceeded at highly advanced levels, even beyond people of your year. It is a part of who you are – being a Cosmos Being'.

Like aliens, Haley thought amusingly. As hard as she tried, she couldn't dismiss off that one thing. How could she, when it was a seemingly memorable reminiscence, like everything else in her past?

All these learning curves made her heart beat fast and right now, it was in sequence with the electrical current of magic embedded in her veins. It was like a permanent scar on her soul, without an ability to heal – Haley touched the scar on her shoulder briefly upon that thought. At the same time, the memories of her powers were beautiful memories stored insider her mind. Haley developed a small smile, as she flashed back on those moments, in the process realizing all she felt then was…freedom. An escape from the outside world, a world where she did not fit in despite looking like a human girl – where she had to hide her true identity, her supernatural self.

'Are you alright, Halena?' Nyssa asked out of concern, noticing how quiet Haley became.

'Yeah, I guess', Haley muttered. 'It's just…the Norn at the Well of Hvergelmir, Vethandi spoke of what Lady Orla said: that there were two possible futures after the Second Ragnarok'.

Nyssa narrowed her eyes to listen further.

'There are apparently other Dark Beings out there', Haley continued, as they walked onto a nearby balcony facing the Aurora-kissed mountains and the now-liberated Lake Elivagar. 'Ragnarok chose these Dark Beings, because they are true evil with no way back to the light, just like Vladimir. Yet I feel there's more to this, like they're searching for something. If I don't stop them, the universe could become nothingness'.

'And you never spoke of these concerns to your family?' Nyssa asked.

'No', Haley answered, playing with her necklace. 'Only because it's just a feeling. I look around to find that something, but nothing comes to mind. Everything's all jumbled up, like a jigsaw puzzle I can't solve. I even doubted the prophecy at first'.

'It is not a terrible thing finding out you don't have all the answers, my dear', Nyssa said with a comforting smile. 'Even now, you are still seeking answers after eighteen years in hiding. Maybe you will find what you seek once you have retrieved Mjolnir?'

And what then? Haley thought out of earshot from Nyssa's telepathy. Should she go back to living a normal life, or take her place as primary heir to Asgard's throne? She had this destiny to fulfill, but will it also involve restoring some sense of normalcy to her former human self: the one side she was beginning to miss terribly.

'I'm not going to lie. Being human…it seemed so easy, despite discovering my powers. I felt normal. I could do normal things and be equal to every other person I am, was close to', Haley said honestly.

Nyssa simply smiled. 'Almost every other Cosmos Being is more human than you realize', she proclaimed. Her eyes spoke the truth. Humanity existed in all the Cosmos Beings she met or encountered so far. In a funny way, Haley half-expected even the descendents of the Muspel Fire Giants – especially Aardham, Alcan and Kalama – as violent as Surtr himself, who played a major part in the original events of the First Ragnarok: a sworn enemy of the Asgardians. She only met them briefly, but she couldn't help but wonder whether they worshipped Surtr still and only tolerated Asgard, because they shared the same enemy. Then again, they were the ones who were entrusted with Svalinn.

'All, except one', Haley uttered, looking at the spot in the sky where the dark shades of Nebula appeared. 'For some reason, I pity my uncle. Despite everything he's done, I can't help but feel that way'.

'There is nothing wrong with feeling that way, Halena', a voice said behind them. It was Arianna, with Eric and Aeolus. Haley assumed Angela, Keilantra and Occasso went off to bed. 'But you also need to know that Vladimir is somewhat destined to follow this path of darkness'.

Haley became racked with guilt over talking about their former father in the most sympathetic way possible, behind their backs. What was wrong with her? Haley thought to herself. Maybe she was still trying to see if there was still any good in him: that he could still change his destiny, that he was a man worth saving? By channelling his hatred, betrayal and jealousy, he created Nebula. Worst of all, it only made a unique natural food source to unleash the Second Ragnarok, freeing it from hibernation.

'I'm sorry', she mumbled, shifting her shameful gaze to the ground. 'Believe me: I know how much you hate and loathe him. My emotions are all over the place. Since that day of the beach, everything changed. Everything happened so fast'.

'You have always tried to see the good in people, sister', Eric calmed her babbling. 'You show kindness and compassion in the face of the darkest hours...but Vladimir is now a bad person. Thanks to Elvira's influence, he longs for power and control. The dark magic has poisoned his mind completely and his obsession thrives'.

Haley nodded, understanding their reasons and her own reasons.

'It has been a long day for all of you', Nyssa said. 'I would suggest you take as much rest as you can for the rest of your journey'. She took Halena's hand. 'Halena, you are strong just like your mother and father. It has been an honour getting to know you properly in person'.

'Thank you', Haley replied politely.

'Aeolus will escort you back to your room. I must take my leave for the evening', Nyssa said, before moving to leave. 'Have a good night'.

With that, Nyssa left the balcony and turned right down the long corridor. Haley and the other walked in silence the other way. She peered through the numerous pillars and windows they walked by. The skies still bore an exact copy of the galaxies across the universe, shining in mixtures of blue, midnight blue, purple and pink, combined with the Aurora Eclipse, which unexpectedly appeared like in Vahalla. Along the way, Haley was tempted to tell Eric, Arianna and the others about her theory of Dark Being searching for something, which did not just involve destroying the Nine Realms. The only reason she held it back was because she could not reveal anything of the sort until she actually confirmed it.

The second Eric and Arianna were in their rooms, Haley was alone with Aeolus again. Nerves hit her. Aeolus' expression remained unreadable, but the hold he had on her arm was gentle and warm. It became clear to Haley that their friendship was somewhat growing from the weeks of knowing each other.

'Aeolus, can I ask you a question?' Haley asked, as they edged closer to her bedroom. Hopefully, she can use that small amount of time to reach out to him. 'And please answer honestly'.

He nodded.

'Do you believe in love?' she asked, blushing at the question. 'I mean I'm starting to believe in it, after hearing those stories about how my parents fought to be together. Well, let's just say it is borderline epic'.

The way Haley described her parents' love story left Aeolus touched: the details of how they met, fell in love despite Antoinette's marriage, how they conceived Haley, and adopted out of love.

'For my own parents, it was love at first sight', Aeolus said with a hint of sadness. It was painful having to talk about his father, even for him. No wonder he was in this emotionless state for long. 'Seeing them together, I learnt love is a special feeling with a powerful force'.

'Yet you don't seem to want to reach out to it', Haley burst out quietly. Realizing her mistake, she anxiously awaited an angered lecture from him to counteract his mourning, moving her down to the future as they faced each other at the door.

'Since my father's death, I became trapped and conflicted', Aeolus finally answered. 'The truth is: I do not want to feel that, because I fear if I do, something bad will happen to my mother and brother. They are the only family I've got'.

'That's why you push people away, isn't it?' Haley questioned. 'Because of what happened to your father…look, I know it's none of my business. I'm just trying to understand you, to figure you out. Ever since you saved me and we officially met, you had this flickering light, which has not yet extinguished. It's like you're holding on to the small part of you that feels'.

Aeolus' eyes softened slightly, which Haley took as a good sign.

'I hated the Nebulans, especially Vladimir, for causing my family so much grief', he continued. 'My mother was heartbroken over his death, that she stepped down from the throne, allowing Silas to ascend. I refused to get close to anyone, because of what happened'.

'You still save people though', Haley said hopefully. 'It's a part of who you are, how you used to be. You do it, because you still care'.

'It is a reminder of being human, I guess', Aeolus said, shrugging his shoulders and blinking multiple times. 'I do not want what happened to my father, to happen the people I care about'.

Haley reached out for his hand, in an attempt to comfort him. A warm fire connected with their contact to one another. It was beautiful, yet thrilling, touching Haley's heart. As they locked eyes, Haley became more drawn in – like she felt whatever she was feeling could become something more. For a while, she forgot where she was. She stood in a peaceful land with Aeolus as the only person for company. Aeolus' eyes softened some more, but at the same time he was fighting the urge to let it in – all the complicated and uncomplicated emotions he held for a long time, since his father's death. As Haley imagined, he was like a book of unreadable words; but he could become readable if he let someone in.

'Anyway', he eventually said, sighing and withdrawing his hand. 'You should probably get some sleep…my lady. It's been a long few days, and you need to rest if you wish to complete the final trial'.

Haley pressed the fingers of the hand she placed in Aeolus' hand, against the other – disappointed to the fact that he shut himself down again. Reluctantly, a nod was the only reply Haley could give. Hearing what he said in the subject change left her emotionally drained, wondering whether she should just give up trying to help him.

'Goodnight, Aeolus', she finally managed to say, before turning her back on the small guilt-ridden expression on his face. She pressed her forehead against the hardwood, her frustration building on the numerous things buzzing around in her head: the prophecy, the final Trial, Vladimir and the Nebulans, her family, her feelings for Aeolus – everything that overwhelmed her to the point of unleashing a lightning surge across the sky. She tried so hard not to let tears fill her eyes, having dealt with enough of that all her life.

All it took Haley was a vague moment to calm down, so that she could change into a white nightgown Lyla left for her on the armchair, by the balcony doors of her bedroom. As she wiped away a single tear at the refusal to not cry, she came across something laid out on her bed: a single blue rose. Confused as to how it got there, Haley eyed it more closely. It was beautiful, glowing continuously, reminding her of a certain enchanted rose. Haley smelt it – as fresh as spring. Next to it laid a small parchment, with a note. The writing was unfamiliar, but in very neat italics. With shaking hands, Haley picked up the note to read:

As bright as your beauty is this rose. Please understand I do indeed feel something for you, Halena. I am just not very good at expressing my feelings. I have not done it in a long time, until you came along. You have a warm light within you. Never forget that.

Sweet dreams,
Aeolus

Haley gasped on that single name: Aeolus. Everything word touched her to the core. He did feel something. No matter how hard he tried to hide it, the emotions surged through him like a storm. She wanted so badly to leave this room, and run into his arms to tell him how she felt – how it was so easy, so peaceful to be around one another. But she couldn't, at least not until all this was eventually over. As she re-read the letter, she smiled slightly. It was the first time she received something partially romantic. Sure, there was the odd crush here and there, but this was different. Her heart soared, her eyes shone brightly, and she had that strange sickening feeling in her stomach.

There was hope for Aeolus. Much like there was hope to save the universe from destruction: to save everyone from the pain, suffering and darkness.

Letting out a massive yawn, forgetting how tried she was, Haley collapsed onto the soft bed, facing the window showing the Aurora Eclipse in the endless sky, its beauty shining against the sparkle in her eyes.

The sight eased her, until she eventually fell asleep.

Haley entered her world of dreams. Unfortunately, it was far from that. What she thought was going to be a peaceful sleep was the complete opposite. Danger lurked in the darkness. She opened her eyes, looking at her surroundings in a foreboding fashion.

It was so dark, the only light being the moon, illuminating through the thick clouds of a cosmic storm on a bloody battlefield. Corpses laid spread out, cold and lifeless. Haley nervously edged closer. Her eyes widened, her knees buckled. She let out a shocked gasp, placing her hand over her mouth, when she realized who the bodies belonged to: her mother, her father, Eric, Arianna, Keilantra, Aeolus, Angela, Orla, Alexander, Elena, Henrietta, Matthew, James, Emilie – everyone she cared about, everyone she regarded as family all dead.

Tears of loss and anger streamed down Haley's face.

As she looked up, four lone dark figures were approaching her menacingly. Their walk caused Haley to tremble violently from head to toe. Everything seemed so real. She tried to call upon the lightning, but something in the darkened cosmic storm prevented it from doing so. All she saw was a giant shadowy face, consuming the universe; consuming Yggdrasil.

She felt powerless. Paralyzed in the sense of fear. She couldn't bear to look at her loved ones' lifeless eyes any longer. She needed to find a way out of this horror.

Haley looked around some more. Everything was darkened with the cosmic storm above, that she didn't notice a fifth dark figure behind her. From the evil eyes and smile to the partially pale skin, they could only belong to one person: Vladimir. He and the faceless figures surrounded Haley. She wanted nothing more than to move from the spot she was super-glued to, but her legs were too numb to take immediate action. She didn't even have her Valkyrie dagger to defend herself.

As she eyed up Vladimir, one of the figures grabbed Haley's arm. Haley yelped in pain at the humanoid person's strong hold, their long nails piercing her exposed skin drawing blood. Her horror increased, when she saw the scratches were not healing.

Her healing power was gone too.

Nausea passed through her, feeling the bones underneath the person's blotched skin. Haley tried desperately to break free, but the strength of the person\s hold on her grew stronger. Soon, the other figures grabbed both her arms, preventing her from escaping. As Haley gazed defenselessly at Vladimir, he started laughing maniacally; his arrogant, ruthless ego glimmering in his eyes. There he stood right in her face, his cold breath crawling through every inch of Haley's body.

'You have lost, niece', he sneered mockingly in sickening amusement. 'You were not strong enough to beat me…them…Nebula…or Ragnarok. We have taken everyone you loved'. He then reached into the inside pocket of his robe and pulled out a sharp dagger. 'Now, I am going to take your life'.

Frightened, Haley's eyes widened. No one was around to protect her this time. She looked from her parents and siblings to her friends, ending on Aeolus, hoping at least one of them would return to life. No movement came. Haley wiggled with all her strength, but the humanoid figures' grips tightened, as she tried to take drastic action for her escape. She cried out in more pain, as more blood drew from the nails and claws. What if she bled to death?

Her heart pounded achingly against her chest. Vladimir's horrifying smile widened, like he could hear Haley's fearful heartbeat – like he was planning to collect it as treasure, as a horrific reminder of having defeated Haley. Hoping to not think about her impending death, Haley thought about the happier times in her life, with her friends and family: her birthdays, meeting her parents at long last, her short time with Aeolus despite his emotionless state – everything she cherished.

As bravely as she could, Haley locked eyes with Vladimir. He raised his dagger and struck.

She let out a scream.

Except it was not her bloodcurdling scream, which drew her out of the nightmare…

CHAPTER 18: THE WELL OF MIMIR

It was a loud explosion and a shout.

Keilantra.

'Halena!' she shouted. As Haley's eyes popped open, a bolt of lightning shot across the sky, hitting the highest mountain peak. The door opened and in came Keilantra. She was back in her armour and travel wear, which meant what was happening couldn't be a good sign. 'You need to get dressed right now!'

'Why? What's going on?' she asked, as she scrambled out of bed to change and grab her gear. Keilantra's expression was a reflection of her frightened gaze. 'Keilantra, you're scaring me'.

'The Nebulans broke through Niflheim's south border', she explained. 'Vladimir is leading them. Eric, Arianna, Aeolus and Angela are outside, fending them off alongside Nyssa, Occasso and the knights of Niflheim. We need to go right now'.

The mention of Vladimir caused Haley to become increasingly haunted by that horrible nightmare, worried that what was happening was going to happen in accordance to it. Her blood raced. This was an unprepared attack: a way of possibly provoking Haley and everyone else, who hated Vladimir for choosing darkness over light. He was out for blood.

Haley didn't even have enough time to process the situation, when Keilantra practically dragged out into the debris filled hall. Shards of ice crystals lay strewn across the floor from the ongoing explosions the Nebulans caused with their incredible power. Going around it wouldn't have been a problem, if not for the group of Nebulans heading towards them.

Sighting Haley seemed to have unleashed their brewing hunger to destroy her, as Vladimir proclaimed.

'Halena, be ready for anything', Keilantra cautioned Haley, as she morphed her hands through illuminating rainbow fire. Haley unsheathed Angurvadal and readied Svalinn. One of the Nebulans sent a dark fireball hurdling towards, so deadly that it vaporized the artifacts still in tact. Remembering her sword skill from karate, Haley swung Angurvadal up and over, splitting the fireball in two. More fireballs came along afterwards. While Keilantra destroyed some with her rainbow fire, Haley performed the same technique.

It was not until the thirtieth fireball disappeared, that the Nebulans agreed mentally enough was enough. Reading each other's minds enabled them to conjure up a single fireball. Within moments, they became one – in a larger fireball. More powerful, more deadlier. The way they stood next to one another served as a reminder to Haley of when the dark figures in the dream grabbed her and Vladimir's striking blade, glistening with her blood. Their poisonous presence became more unwelcome. Knowing her family and friends out there in danger, Haley's anger built. As the fireball reached its peak, it surmounted towards them, Keilantra knowing her own fire was not strong enough to stop it.

That was until Haley stepped in its line of path, with Svalinn. The impact was a vigorous force of nature, heating up the golden metal, which burnt Haley's fingertips. From the looks of it, even with Keilantra's assistance, it was going to take a lot more than the sun shield to stop this kind of Nebulan attack. Haley activated Megingjord, recovering her strength.

'What are you doing?' Keilantra asked through her gritted teeth.

Haley refused to answer, in the case of losing focus. She clenched her fist, trying to channel the lightning surge inside her. Its journey ended when it touched one of the Jarngreipr gloves. It glowed brightly, and with her activated god strength, she pushed mightily forward. Svalinn contacted with Jarngreipr. As they did, something else happened: the combined power sent forth a shock wave destroying the fireball, and sending the Nebulans flying back outside into the unknown – a similar attack from the beach, Haley thought as she recalled that shocking moment.

'Come on!' Haley shouted out at Keilantra. The two girls headed down the grand staircase. Through the open pillars, Haley could clearly see the ongoing battle. At the very front were Eric, Arianna and Aeolus, fighting off the advancing Nebulans. She couldn't yet see or sense Vladimir, which made her more worried. Wherever he was, it wasn't going to be a pretty picture.

Along the way, they fought off more Nebulans until they made it through the open front doors of the palace. Nyssa's knights were now on the verge of being on the losing side, as Haley noticed the intense struggle to withstand each attack. She remembered the day of her christening. The forcefield created by the Mermaid Clan was not strong to stop Vladimir's attacks, breaking down at every impact of the repeating fireballs.

Using Jarngreipr, Haley unleashed a wave of lightning vaporizing the advancing Nebulans who spotted her, but more kept coming through a portal: a gateway to Nebula. Haley only caught a glimpse of the barren wasteland on the other side – bare, dark and abandoned, except for the dead trees and blackened castle stood stubbornly proud underneath an endless cosmic storm of blackholes and eclipses. All of which were so filled with evil and rage, probably channeling towards the Nebulans to enhance their abilities, providing them an advantage. No matter how hard Haley tried, even increasing the density generation of lightning, they just kept coming.

'*Give up, niece*', her uncle's cunning voice opened her telepathy, chilling. '*Even with that power-belt around your waist, your strength is no match for my Nebulan army. More will keep coming, until there is nothing left*'.

Haley refused to give up. She was so caught up in the battle, that she didn't realize her anger and rage was building.

'*You are strong and fearless, yet here you are – fueled by rage. The kind I was fueled with, when I discovered who my mother was, what my true destiny was.*

'*I'm nothing like you*', Haley whispered angrily. '*You've murdered too many innocent people*'. Again, another flashback of the nightmare passed through her mind.

He laughed on the other end.

'*What did you have?*' he asked mockingly. '*One where you would hide away in fear – where people would not accept or understand you? Face it, Halena: you have lived with so many lies, you were too blinded by your need to self-control to see the truth*'.

'*The only thing I understand is that I know who my family is*', Haley answered, attacking more Nebulans, struggling to control her rage. '*And unlike you, they protect each other and the Nine Realms*'.

'*Yet you cannot admit you love them*', Vladimir uttered. '*Face it: you are still in denial, that you cannot fully embrace your power. You only use it for battle purposes or to keep your mind in check*'.

'*Shut up*', Haley shouted through mental gritted teeth. As her lightning power intensified, storm clouds came over Niflheim.

Haley needed to shut out Vladimir!

'Since your birth, you have become a serious threat', Vladimir sneered. *'Because of that, you will soon be annihilated, along with my dear brother, my traitorous wife and children, the rest of your family, and your precious Aeolus.*

That was the last straw. Now, Haley couldn't think straight, blacking out from the outside world momentarily.

'SHUT UP!' she finally yelled out loud. As that happened, a huge burst of energy escaped her entire body, igniting it in a cocoon entrapment. It was so electrifyingly bright, changing into an enormous shock wave, which hurdled its way towards the approaching Nebulans, pushing them back as the lightning bolts disintegrated them into dust.

Breathing heavily, Haley stood in shock at her loss of control. She was still too angry to concentrate. Vladimir drove her too over the edge…she couldn't move, not one inch, or see and think straight; until Eric, Arianna, Aeolus, Angela and Keilantra reached her.

'You need to go now!' Nyssa called out, as she and Occasso summoned their ice power fending off more Nebulans.

'What?' Haley asked in disbelief. 'We can't! We have to stop Vladimir!' Her rage started re-emerging, driven by an unexpected desire to hunt down Vladimir and stop him once and for all – with or without Mjolnir.

The other ignored her request.

'Open the Bifrost now, Optimus!' Arianna called out to the heavens. The brightly-lit gateway of the Bifrost opened within seconds.

In the struggled to rush back into battle, Haley was being dragged backwards by Aeolus, his strength equal to hers. As they stepped through the gateway, Vladimir stepped through the small crowed of Nebulans, an accomplished smile the opposite reflection of Haley's vengeful gaze.

Within a minute, Haley, Eric, Arianna, Keilantra, Aeolus and Angela landed on concrete. The Bifrost's gateway faded away, clearing away any dust formulated. Worry and fear for Nyssa, Occasso and the people of Niflheim, and anger towards Vladimir clouded Haley's focus. They were back there fighting for their lives, while they practically force her to retreat and complete her mission, instead of staying behind to help.

Recalling what happened made Haley ten times angrier. Her predicted premonition came true, and she thought it was her own paranoia. Her uncle went back on his word and attacked one of the Nine Realms, putting more innocent lives at risk. That nightmare she had was clearly a message from him, a glimpse into a possible dark future, should she fail. Vladimir and four other unknown faceless people holding her down for torture and sport, until she could no longer breathe: the adrenaline kicking in…it only caused her lightning power to almost reach overloading level again. What was her uncle trying to do: make her believe she was weak…that she was not cut out to be a princess of the Cosmos…that her power was an abomination?

How she wished to remain human without supernatural beings or magic. All this happened so fast, she barely had time to process all of it. Only problem was that the powers of the Thunder God were bonded to her flesh, blood and bone. She was branded with it, like an unbreakable spell. If Haley stopped using her magic, would her heart and soul revert back to being more human than Asgardian? She remembered Nyssa's words about humanity and Cosmos Beings being one and the same, in terms of showing emotion towards others.

Haley looked back at where the gateway was, sadness and anger in her eyes, praying for Niflheim's survival and wanting nothing more than to put her uncle to the ground. As she opened her mouth to call upon Optimus again, Eric and Arianna stopped her.

'Halena, you…we cannot get back', Eric said regrettably.

Haley turned to them, angry tears threatening to pour from her eyes.

'What?' Haley questioned, her fury close to breaking point that the lightning current visibly shone through her veins. 'All those people could be dying, probably unable to take on Vladimir and the Nebulans. He went back on his word, that he wouldn't hurt anyone'.

'Likely to speed up your mission', Arianna said in an attempt to calm Haley.

'I can't just stand here, knowing that Nyssa, her son and their people could die', Haley shouted out, her eyes slowly glowing white as thunder rumbled above. 'I wanted to help them – to do something'. And by something, she meant more than fighting off Nebulans. Healing and tending to the wounded, she thought. Like when she healed Aeolus's chest wood during the brief battle with Vladimir that day in the dungeon.

'You can help them by finding the last piece of Mjolnir', Arianna answered back. Haley opened her mouth in an attempt to argue back, but she couldn't – at least not while she was at breaking point. 'Your mission is important, especially to Nyssa and her people. Even they know that'.

Despite wanting nothing more than to follow the same agenda – to go back to Niflheim – they were right. Haley needed to finish the last Trial, before Vladimir does something more devastating and destructive.

'But Vladimir has to pay for what he has done', she said unexpectedly, igniting her inner warrior princess fire. A naïve but too bold move at this stage, the others seemed to think, but they held back their words, not wishing to upset Haley even more.

'He will', Eric reassured. 'He will answer for his crimes, and our family will get justice. However, he is one of many who follow Ragnarok, one of many who could bring it back. We might need him alive for answers. Do you understand, Halena?'

It was the truth. How else would they find out more about the Second Ragnarok, if he were dead?

After much coaxing, Haley reluctantly nodded in agreement through tear-filled eyes. The thunder and lightning ceased its course through her five-breath count. In the end, she retained her level head. And while she did this Trial, she would continue to pray for Niflheim's survival. Haley became quite fond of Nyssa and her son in their welcoming committee, as they educated her more on Niflheim's history.

Haley looked around. They were standing on a part of a pathway, leading through a gateway very much like the one at the Well of Urd, opposed by large amounts of thick fog. Through it, Haley made out the silhouette of Yggdrasil's giant tree root, but also something else. On her left, she saw some mountains reaching the heavens like Mount Everest. Where they were standing must be the border between Jotunheim and Midgard, from what Haley recalled through her teachings of Norse Mythology. There was a blizzard at the highest peak, only deadly to those who were not Jotunheim-born. Yet she couldn't see any features of Earth whatsoever – maybe the passageway was hidden?

Haley caught sight of something in the front of the gateway: a stone sculpture of an ancient face. A man. His eyes were shut tight, his lips pursed together perfectly, within his late fifties according to the small wrinkles. It was such exquisite work by whatever artist sculptured it. Underneath it was a Norse inspiration: *the rememberer, the wise one.*

To Haley, it rang a bell, but she couldn't put her finger on it, not with her head still fragile. She reached out to touch the stone face. It was smooth like marble, with every detail captured perfectly.

Suddenly –

'If you are quite finished', the face spoke, his eyes popping open revealing intelligent pure blue – they were surprisingly filled with wisdom. His features moved like he was an animating puppet. Shocked, Haley and the others jumped out of their skin. Did that face just talk? As if Haley's day didn't feel bad already even with all things supernatural: besides, the last thing she needed right now was to deal with another adrenaline rush to trigger her power.

She paused her thoughts. Was this stone face friend or foe?

Only one way to find out, Haley thought.

'What...umm....who are you?' she asked speechlessly.

The man arched his eyebrow, like Haley was some sort of idiot to ask something of that kind, but brushed it off

'Why, my dear child', the man eventually said. 'I am Mimir'.

Eventually, the feelings of recognition took its toll on Haley. '*The* Mimir?' she asked, like a die-hard fan, her anger all but vanished.

'The one and only', he answered back. 'And you are the young princess I have heard so much about: the descendent of Lord Thor himself'.

'But...how are you still...you know, breathing?' Haley tried choosing her words carefully, but it was difficult considering the fact that she was now talking to a live object. Instantly, she regretted those words worried it was an insult to Mimir's supposed legacy.

Instead, he let out a low laugh.

'You are a curious one, Halena', he said. 'I am afraid I cannot answer that question for you. You see, this is a part of the Third Trial'.

Confused at first, it quickly faded when Haley understood what he was talking about. 'I have to guess the answer, about what really happened during the Aesir-Vanir War?' In a way, it was a relief that she didn't have to do anything too extreme, compared to the last two Trials. 'Is that why the All-Knowledge was blocked out?'

Mimir simply nodded.

'Out of a number of campaigned tasks, the Norns and the majority agreed this was within their particular interest', he answered. 'This is the only place in Yggdrasil, where the All-Knowledge does not take effect. Some like yourself barely have knowledge of what really happened during the time of the war'.

'Well…I only know it ended when the Aesir and Vanir tribes agreed to a peace treaty', Haley pointed out. She briefly studied the war at school, but only knew Mimir by name. If only the All-Knowledge worked…how she wished she knew.

'That is true. Except there are three stories about the outcomes of the war, one of which you correctly identified with the treaty. However, there is more it that means the eye'. A ball of light materialized above Mimir, splitting into three. As the whiteness faded, in its place came three images moving like short films on a continuous loop. 'My question to you, Halena is this: which story do you believe to be true?'

Haley gulped deeply. 'What happens if I answer wrongly?' she asked, worried what consequences could await. It only increased, when Mimir refused to answer.

'The clues are in the mirrors', he simply stated.

Eric, Arianna, Keilantra, Aeolus and Angela all mirrored Haley's wondrous, but openly confused look. At the same time, Haley wondered whether to trust Mimir. Her first instinct was to follow through with his instructions, but the second instinct was to find an alternative way to get the Well. If she didn't do the Trial, then no last piece of Mjolnir…no peace or preventing of this Second Ragnarok, if it comes to it. None of the others helped with their skeptical expressions, except for small flickers, which told Haley they knew which image it was. They figured it out before her.

Now, it was up to her to think what they thought; to choose carefully. Otherwise face whatever consequences could come about – from the Norns, the Gods or even Mimir himself by their decree from thousands of years. Every imaged sequence in the looking mirrors each bore an accurate storytelling, true to all the myths regarding the Aesir-Vanir war.

Question was: which one was real and which two were not? They held the fate of the entire universe. Was there something within one mirror, which played an important part in the war's climax? All Haley saw were different playbacks with alternative endings. Each displayed a good possible outcome.

Minutes passed, until a newly formed realization shone in Haley's eyes, as Mimir patiently awaited her answer. The image she was drawn to the most was the left one. During the sequence, the battle was forging with the Asgardians in their gold and silver armour, the Vanirs in silver and green. Whatever the conflict was which led to this war, Haley never knew the answer. And to think her mother was a former Vanir turned Asgardian upon marriage. She watched, as Odin beheaded Mimir whose face turned to stone as he was now. Every move the armies demonstrated was more self-defense strategy than vengeful murder – Haley knew from all her training. Almost every warrior wanting so badly for this war to end…thinking the exact same thing brought the next setting into motion. Like a meteorite crashing into the Earth, a star fell from the sky. The fighting halted at the last possible minute, as the armies retreated out of its line of sight at the last possible moment.

A blinding light erupted out of the crater, dividing into five. They shone like stars for a split second, until the light faded revealing something: crystals. As the scene played out, Haley watched as all warriors became fixated on the crystals. What was so special about them? Was it what drove them to stop the war and negotiate a treaty in favor of these crystals? All was a guess, but Haley knew she needed to try, in order to be given passage through Mimir's gateway to the Well.

'The look on your face tells me you have your answer', Mimir pointed out. It seemed he observed her thinking as well.

She nodded. 'As the fighting continued, a star exploded and crashed onto Vanaheim', she recounted the repeating event. 'The resulting explosion formed a crater and starlight broke into five separate pieces. They became crystals. For whatever it was, these crystals were the key to the ending of the Aesir-Vanir War. Something about them bonded not just Vanaheim and Asgard together, but the rest of the Realms together'.

It was the wild guess, but a very good one. Even Eric and Arianna thought so too, as well as Keilantra, Angela and Aeolus who were in agreement; for they too observed the scene. Could the same be said for Mimir though? At first, his face reverted back to being unreadable until –

'Ha!' he let out a small joyful laugh. 'I believe you have done it, Princess. What you saw in this particular mirror is the true event, which led to the ending of the war, sparing more lives from being lost'.

Mission accomplished then…

Except Haley couldn't help but wonder even more, captivated by the crystals.

'But what's so special about these crystals?' she asked. 'What have they got to do with the Nine Realms? Wait…does it have something to do with the prophecy I'm in?'

Mimir sighed. 'That I cannot answer', he said apologetically. 'You must never ask too many questions in relation to your destiny. It is something you need to figure out by your self'.

In other words, it was another missing piece of the jigsaw puzzle…like a missing word in a sentence. A mystery behind the story: an undiscovered story until now. Something Haley knew nothing about. Out of the many theoretical stories about the Aesir-Vanir War, this was quite something. Maybe Lady Orla knew something? But at that very thought, she remembered Mimir's words. She needed to figure this out herself: fill in the missing gap about these five crystals, and find out if they were intertwined with her destiny.

Hoping not to misjudge, Haley concealed her disappointment.

'As protector of this Well, I hereby grant your safe passage through', Mimir said.

Haley felt thankful, although one more question brewed in her mind. 'Just out of curiosity, what would have happened if I answered wrongly?' she asked.

'Those who answer wrongly, those who have little god blood in them, are turned to dust', he answered without hesitation, much to the annoyance of the others, who silently demanded he didn't answer. 'Those who are born a god become like me'.

Haley appeared shocked by this utmost fate. The only difference was that Mimir bore no ill grudge nor did he wish to seek vengeance against Odin. This was his destiny. He knew it, and the gods knew it. Yet the thought of it terrified Haley, spending an eternity as an ever-watching statue, that her own guilt got the better of her. Why did she have the one to answer correctly, when others couldn't and they suffered for it? She looked around the grass, remembering the ones who died were taken by the slow chilling wind through dust. Combined with the anger she was still feeling toward Vladimir, thinking about it almost triggered her magic. At a random pace, a small wave of electricity pulsed through her, and quickly went away.

'Halena?' Aeolus asked out of concern, placing his hand on her shoulder. His comforting touches made Haley remember the blue rose he left for her, which she placed impulsively inside her travel bag during Niflheim's violent commotion. She hoped its beauty was as eternal as they say, because she did not want to open up the bag to find the smooth petals fallen and dying. In fact, what she secretly wished to do was thank Aeolus. It meant a lot after that small moment they shared. Despite his denial, there was a connection. He was just afraid to get close to someone after that happened with his own family.

'I'm fine', Haley eventually mumbled, before thanking Mimir for his assuming help.

Mimir gave one last smile, before reverting back to his original state – temporary life as a statue.

A few seconds later, Haley looked beyond him towards the gateway. Oddly enough, despite Jotunheim's cold air and Earth's salty ocean breeze, the archway was decorated in vines and flowers growing endlessly around and across its marble stone. What looked like oranges also grew along the emerald green vines.

'They're the vines of Mimameidr', Keilantra explained.

'Mimir's tree', Haley whispered. 'The fruit helps with fertility, right?

'Mimir was also a god of fertility', Keilantra answered. 'Alongside Freyja, they both worked out a way to bless women with the highest possibilities of conceiving a child of their blood'.

Haley gazed at the vines in wonder. 'They're beautiful, like they were untouched, unharmed'.

'That is the greatest quality about them, princess', Aeolus proclaimed. 'They cannot be harmed'. With a wave of his sword, he slashed at a section. As quickly as the vine browned to dust, a new vine grew in the exact spot where they came.

'Unharmed by fire and metal', Haley muttered wondrously, as fresh pink and purple flowers blossomed like the archway leading to a hidden garden.

'Well…let's go', Haley eventually spoke out. 'We need to find the last piece'.

Everyone else nodded, showing how much he or she appreciated her spirit, but Haley felt the emotional concern over her anger towards Vladimir. Her head became all jumbled up. She wanted him imprisoned, but at the same time, she wanted him dead. Being imprisoned would only intensify his fueling vengeance, yet death on him would be a cold-blooded act – unable to escape or take back. She could be on the verge of losing herself, but she wouldn't care, so long his reign of terror made the chances of Ragnarok returning slimmer; and everyone she cared was safe.

As they stepped through the vine archway, the dense air changed to the scent of fresh flowers, the gentle sound of a familiar waterfall coming down the trunk of Yggdrasil. Like Urd and Hvergelmir, it too towered up to the heavens, concealed by white cloud. Three stone pillars, one of which bore the triquetra sign, stood protectively around the open Well.

The Well of Mimir...

It became all too surreal, this being the last Well, the last part of the third Trial. Haley saw even Eric and Arianna were affected by it. Once, they told or heard stories about the Wells themselves. Keilantra and Aeolus, on the other hand – well, they looked like they knew about the natural structure of this Well. Like Keilantra knew enough about the Dark Sea to conjure up an intense power with her rainbow fire and mermaid genetic structure.

Directly in front of them was a young woman in a white silk robe. As magic dust flowed around her, flowers grew through the concrete, unleashing a natural beauty, similar to the Well of Urd's island but unlike the Well of Hvergelmir's ice chamber.

Upon sensing their presence, the woman halted her handiwork.

'You have come a long way, distant daughter of Thor', she uttered. Haley sensed her smiling, as the Norn slowly stood up.

'Are you Skuld?' Haley asked as politely as possible.

'Indeed, I am', she answered, as she lowered the hood of her robe over her white gown, revealing her timeless beauty, identical to her sisters. 'Skuld: guardian of the Well of Mimir, sister of Vethandi and Urdr; and former member of the Valkyrie Tribe'.

'You're a Valkyrie?' Haley asked in surprise.

'Half Valkyrie', Skuld corrected her. 'Myself and my sisters. Our mother found love in an ancient, formidable, but fearless warrior, who fought alongside Odin himself. After they eloped, we were conceived. Unfortunately, shortly after the birth some months later, we lost our parents to Ragnarok'.

Haley's heart sank at the horrific event, which cast numerous lives.

'I'm so sorry', she said compassionately. 'Urdr and Vethandi never mentioned it'.

'We never do, and never did after', Skuld explained, a hint of sadness in her eyes. 'It was too painful for the three of us'.

They must have been very young, Haley thought. To lose a parent at an early age – well, it was almost sheer comparison to how she herself believed she lost her own parents. A ripple of guilt surged through, as Haley finally had them while others didn't.

'I see you hold a dagger, crafted by the original Valkyrie', Skuld gestured the shining blade, attached to Haley's belt.

'The original Valkyrie?' Haley questioned with a raised eyebrow, as she touched the dagger. 'You mean Raven? Mani's lover?'

'Yes, that is exactly who I am referring', Skuld answered. 'Upon becoming one with the stars, she ensured her most treasured possession would be presented to someone equally as worthy and strong'.

Haley blinked twice, thinking back to her birthday, when she received it.

'Why me though?' she asked.

Skuld simply smiled.

'My dear', Skuld replied, approaching Haley. 'You are a child, born of all the Nine Realms: the first in centuries to wield great power, passed down by the Thunder God and his people. It is only fitting that with that power, you can wield that very dagger'

Questions about the one simple, yet special dagger buzzed around in Haley's head. Until she remembered it was designed to block even Vladimir's Nebulan attacks, as she herself could with the powers of Thor. What did this mean for her? Did she have Valkyrie blood in her too? If she had the time, Haley would be tempting to find out more. She looked at the Well. Like the others, it too closely resembled a crater leading down the centre of nothingness. Somewhere down there was the last piece of Mjolnir.

'I can see from your change of behavior that time is of the essence', Skuld spoke again.

Haley wondered how she knew, until she guessed it a second beforehand: Skuld was the Norn who foresaw the future, like Urdr saw the past and Vethandi saw the present. She edged closer to the Well, drawn to the intense of that of the hidden thunderstone, but also something incredibly different. Focusing hard, Haley tried to reach for the Aurora Crystal's magic on her necklace but nothing came out, leaving her in deep wonderment.

'Why do I get the feeling that this Well needs something more than the magic of an Aurora?' Haley asked.

'Are you familiar with one of the legends of this very Well?' Skuld questioned her.

Haley looked down into the crater again. 'One legend said that the waters of Mimir's Well contains wisdom, and that Odin sacrificed one of his eyes to it for a drink'. The last few words gestured a small stutter at the realization. 'Are you saying I need to sacrifice something?'

Saying that crawled down every edge of Haley's skin, her senses tightening with worry and anguish. Odin sacrificed his own eye, keeping it true to the legend; but what if the term was now a divergent situation for Haley? What if Eric, Arianna, Keilantra, Aeolus or Angela needed to sacrifice themselves, in order to fulfill the end of this quest? From the looks on their faces, whatever the price was, they were willing to pay it gladly.

'Odin sacrificed his own eye to be blessed with pure wisdom, by drinking the water of Mimir's Well', Skull proclaimed. 'And for all reasons that are good…Now that the Well is the stored alcove of the last third of the thunderstones, divided from Mjolnir's displacement, it now falls to you to grant the Well something'.

Haley thought long and hard, hopeful that neither of the others would step forth as a human sacrifice. There had to be something else…something deep within her, or a part of her.

'My blood', she finally answered. 'The magic in my blood – what happens if I chose that?'

Skuld sighed, wondering whether it was the right decision. 'Then, one part of your power will no longer be a part of you. You will lose it forever'.

'I'll do it'.

'Halena, are you sure that is necessary?' Eric asked. 'Skuld said you will lose a third of your powers, meaning you will no longer have it, when you need the most'.

'If it means saving the innocent lives across the universe, then yes: I'm prepared to make that one simple sacrifice', Haley answered determinedly. 'I'm a descendent of the thunder god, so the power I will need the most is my lightning power'.

After silent debating with the others, they agreed.

Haley took a few more steps closer to the Well's crate opening, looking down into it. It was so dark, like the other two – a bottomless pit. Withdrawing her Valkyrie dagger, Haley let out a slow, deep breath, praying nothing bad would happen once she drew some of her blood. As the sharp silver blade ran across the palm of her hand, a white light emerged through the drawn wound. She gently squeezed her hand to draw the blood out, at least half the amount to fill a mug. For a second, Haley felt light-headed like a power being drained from her lifeforce; and a burst of wind swirled around her, untouched by Skuld, Eric, Arianna, Keilantra, Aeolus and Angela. Once the light faded and her wound healed, leaving a small scar, it stopped. Haley reached deep within herself. Her power was the same, but different; like a piece of herself missing. She definitely still had the lightning element, which she was thankful for, it being a requirement for Mjolnir. Yet the other elements – ice, water and wind – seemed unreachable. She couldn't identify which one was taken.

'Halena?' Keilantra lightly touched her shoulder.

'I'm fine', Haley said. 'I just feel…different. Something is missing, like a jigsaw'.

Meaning it worked, Haley thought, much to her secretive sadness at the loss of an elemental power. At the same time, it was a relief meaning she could put even Matthew, Emilie or James in danger. She did not want to know how they would react with her being *not normal.*

'The amount of blood you sacrificed from your body permanently removed a part of your power, except your lightning power', Skuld explained. 'Because of your god heritage, that is the only part bound to you for the remainder of your life'.

Haley bit her lip at the price she paid. At least it did not involve death. She would not survive losing someone else she cared about, especially if it was indirectly by her own hand, or by their own choice. Would they have volunteered? Keilantra and Angela, or even Eric, Arianna or Aeolus? All of them watched over her: protected her. Eric and Arianna watched her grow up, practically raised her, taught her to control her powers; and Keilantra came along, being a great friend…so did Angela, who had shown through her awkward shyness her loyalty.

And then there was Aeolus. Haley saw light in his eyes, which she was drawn to from the moment she laid eyes on him. He saved her life three times. He was a savior, a guardian angel, a good person who got lost along the way; a broken man who witnessed death face-to-face when his father fell. Now, she had these incredibly intense feelings for him, afraid to express out of fear of him losing himself. Yet that moment they shared on Niflheim that was the first time she actually saw the real him, the boy he was before he lost his father.

The sky darkened, as the Aurora Borealis came in sequence with the glowing crystal on Haley's necklace. As the moon moved swiftly in front of the sun, the Aurora streams exited both the crystal and the sky making their way down into the crater; and the bursting light erupted upward and around everyone. It faded in seconds, revealing the structure of the star-filled universe.

'I see it', Haley finally said, as an exploding star unveiled the crystallized thunderstone.

Haley's eyes turned white, the lightning electrocuting her veins. The sensation was ten times stronger as if it in turn sensed its brother pieces, stored in Haley's bag. As the triquetra sign reflected through, the crystallized stone cracked into a dozen pieces rapidly consumed by any remaining light. In its place was...an axe-head. Entirely of iron metal, it was not as heavy as Haley thought once she held with two hands, but very sharp around the edges. One side displayed an engraved version of a painting, like the one Haley saw back into the High Council hall on Asgard: the thunder god on a mountain in battle, as the people worshipped and respected him, grateful for his heroic protection.

'Mjolnir's axe-head', Skuld whispered out loud. 'Now it is yours, distant daughter of Thor'.

Hearing that sentence got Haley thinking. She reached into her bag and retrieved the iron vine leave rod and handle, laying them carefully onto the ground next to the axe-head.

'What are you doing?' Angela asked.

'Mjolnir needs to be reforged', Haley explained. 'As I'm an apparent descendent of the Thunder God, what if I used my lightning power to draw the pieces together?'

'Hmm...' Skuld murmured thoughtfully. 'It is a distinctive possibility, but worth a try'.

'Remember, sister: concentrate. Focus', Arianna said.

The exact words even her own mother and father would say, Haley thought.

She wished they were here.

Haley reached deep within herself, finding her lightning element. Pushing past reality, transforming into a moment of clarity; a symbol of hope – pure peace right around the corner...Haley hovered her hands over the pieces of Mjolnir. Feeling the power emerge, she along with the others shielded their eyes from the white, sparkling brightness. So intense it was, it could have easily vaporized them, if they were a hundred percent human.

The light faded. Haley eagerly opened her eyes.

Disappointingly, the pieces remained, as they were – detached parts. Haley tried again, with every ounce of strength she had before feeling the lightheadedness return from using too much energy.

Nothing.

'I don't understand', she said. 'I thought it would work'.

'Maybe there's another piece we do not yet know about', Keilantra clarified between everyone, initially directing it to Skuld.

'Mjolnir is simply a vessel for channeling lightning', she answered. 'How to bring it together: we do not know, not even my own sisters'.

Frustrated, the temptation to let go built up, to allow those quiet and depressive feelings to take control.

'So I let him win?' Haley asked herself. 'Give up? Vladimir is the reason I am in this mess in the first place! I should have known better than to come here! I'm not cut out for this at all! I can't control my magic! I can't reforge Mjolnir! I wish I were never a princess! I wish I never found out who I was!'

Lightning electrified her hand, as she slammed into the stone floor.

In the heat of her anger and the storm surge inside her, Haley instantly regretted her words. Never has she displayed such incredible fury until now, when her fist hit the floor causing it to shake and crack like a minor earthquake about to create a crust displacement. Eventually, Haley calmed down after some long seconds passed. She couldn't fight back the tears in her now darkened eyes. She let them stream down. The hand she used to hit the floor was grazed with open wounds of fresh, glistening blood, which healed quickly; but did not shake away the painful guilt Haley was feeling both physically and mentally.

Her courage was floating away from her body and soul along an endless river. Hopelessness took over. She let them down: her family, her friends, Aeolus…everyone.

Worst of all…she let herself down.

'*Halena*', the gentle voices of her parents broke through the mind barriers.

Haley gasped.

'M…mother? F…father?' she uttered out loud. She realized it was the very first time she called Antoinette and Darius those names. It was strange, yet heartwarming. Even in her lowly, darkest hour, her parents' voices provided a soothing comfort.

'*Never doubt yourself or your abilities, daughter*', her father's voice came through.

Haley's tears were fiercer now, her mind in dubious doubt with the dark memories of the nightmare from the previous night as a constant reminder.

Her eyes filled with pain and worry.

'How am I supposed to feel then?' she asked, ignoring the others' astonishing glares. 'Everywhere I go, people get hurt. The pain I feel: it's a clear indication that I can't reforge Mjolnir. Vladimir was right. I am weak: a weak, defenseless little girl, living in denial, fueled by rage over what he had done'.

'*Halena, know that you are nothing like him*', Antoinette whispered gently. '*You are different. Everything you presented from your birth to the Trials of Thor, is sole proof that you are worthy and stronger than he will ever be. Your strength is inspiring to all Cosmos Beings across the universe*'.

'*Then tell me: what do I do?*' Haley asked. '*My lightning power wasn't enough to bring the pieces together*'.

'*Because there is more to this process that meets the eye*', Darius admitted. '*You need to believe this is your destiny, that something more will come of this. You are as strong and fearless as a lioness, and gentle and beautiful as a rose. All you have to do is embrace it*'.

'*What do you mean?*' Haley asked.

'*Well, we –* ' A sudden new set of footsteps cut off the communication.

An Asgardian knight.

'My lord and lady, Vladimir has relied his Nebulan army', he informed them. *'They are about to breach the city border'.*

Silence fell at the reality about to unfold. Haley's five days were up. One way or another, she was to face Vladimir. But could she truly do so without Mjolnir? Suddenly, a bang severed the telepathic connection between herself and her connection. She tried calling out to them, but she was in much pain from the invisible force hitting her repeatedly, doubling her over in pain. Everyone's voices were withdrawn, like she all of a sudden became deaf in two seconds.

The dark fragments of nightmares and haunting memories became one and the same. Haley saw Asgard slowly falling to ruin, knights fighting off Nebulans, as the skies darkened. Then, came another place, a place Haley thought she would never see.

Earth!

Haley's body went rigid. her eyes glowed white yet again, rolling back. At that moment, she realized she was having an intertwined vision of Asgard, Earth and Nebula. Every shadow fought against one another on both fronts; the civilans took cover from the oncoming attacks. Breaking the hold the vision had on her, Haley gasped. A lightning bolt came down from the sky.

'It's not just Asgard', Haley blundered out. 'The Nebulans have gone back to Earth! They're going to kill anyone in their path!' She half-hoped that with enough motivation, the pieces of Mjolnir would come together, but they still lay there like rocks.

Living in her own denial dramatically changed to the reminder of who and what she was. She had to fight: with or without Mjolnir. In spite of her channeling fear and anger, she had no choice but to intervene. This time, there was no escape, no nonsense, no turning back…Whatever Vladimir had planned for her, it was not going to be good. Not to herself, not to the Nine Realms – all living in fear with the return of Ragnarok. What frightened Haley more were the other faceless followers, as foreseen in her nightmare, all coming together into a unity which would cost the lives of millions, including Haley's family.

Haley gathered up the pieces of Mjolnir and placed them in her bag, careful not to damage the eternal blue rose Aeolus gave her – it warmed her heart, knowing he really felt something for the first time in a long while. It gave her strength. The initial eye contact with Aeolus provided further confirmation.

Remembering the situation, Haley struggled to focus.

'So, what do we do?' she asked, looking at the others for guidance. 'I can't just go to all three places. Vladimir could be at either one of them'.

'Halena is right', Eric answered. 'Vladimir has the capability of mind manipulation, meaning he could be in one place, but is actually somewhere else'.

'Are you saying Vladimir will try to trick Halena, while she tries to figure out where he is?' Skuld asked.

'Yes', Eric replied. 'I am afraid so'.

'If my sisters and I knew more about that kind of power...' Skuld uttered thoughtfully.

Haley bit her lip.

Vladimir was feared among many and, judging by her voice tone, Skuld too. Haley assumed to her being the younger sister, and Urdr and Verdrandi were the ones to protect her, like a complete parallel to what Eric and Arianna did for Haley. What if she herself wasn't strong enough? What if she was not a worthy enough princess of the Cosmos? Looking back on everything, Haley always justified her strength coming from her powers. Yet, protecting the ones she cared about was her top priority emotionally not physically. That was what love was. Vladimir knew nothing of the word.

She spotted Vladimir in all three places, menacing as ever; an arrogant smirk as evil as the first time they met. Something was off though. Amongst of the terrifying screams and wars, every proportion looked deceiving but real, especially with Vladimir appearing at random. Like Mimir's looking-glass-type mirrors.

'*Find where I really are, niece*', Vladimir's voice sneered telepathically. Haley's anger built up, knowing how far he had gone: taking drastic measures no matter how violent or cruel to draw her out. All of it was for the wrong reasons, Haley thought.

'*Your heart is racing*', he smirked. Haley felt it, wishing she increased her mind barrier's strength, but the concealed worry of overwhelming herself ceased it. '*Your five days are up. Congratulations – you have found Mjolnir's pieces. Yet I still feel your anger and fear. If you are too afraid to face me, then you will watch as both your homes die. They...will...burn with you, and the return of Ragnarok will fulfilled*'.

That couldn't happen, Haley thought.

'You sent that vision as a way to trigger my fear', she uttered telepathically, struggling to hold back the dominating sensation.

'I see it as my way of fun', Vladimir answered in sickening amusement. *'You have seen it: the premonition of Ragnarok's Five Followers'*.

So that was what they were, Haley guessed. Followers like the four horsemen of the apocalypse – but why were there five, instead of four? Haley did not have time to process this, not when she still had Vladimir's request to fulfill.

'Where will I find you?' she asked, shifting the gaze back to the vision. On Asgard, she watched as her mother assisted the infirmary alongside Amara, Elena, Lady Orla, Serena and Henrietta. Her father, Alexander, Silas and everyone else she met from the Asgardian armies relied their best warriors, fighting alongside other species of the Realms.

'Name the one place where you find peace', Vladimir spoke in riddle. The Earth vision: the one that frightened Haley the most – everyone she practically knew or grew up were defenseless, running for their lives. No Nebulan performed any form of deadly attack, much to her own surprise, just had their way of casting fear. Her childhood home and world, facing deadly destrutction...

'Optimus, open the gateway to Earth!' Halena called out. The all-too-familiar rainbow light materialized, opening up the blue and green of Earth: the clifftops of Summerfield.

'Halena, what is going on?' Arianna asked out of worry.

'The visions are reflections of doubt', Haley answered. 'Vladimir created them to challenge me to make a choice. He said, *Name the one place where you find peace*. He knows I go to the hills of Summerfield, whenever I needed to think; where I use my powers freely with no one around. It's where I need to go'.

Eric and Arianna became scared for her. The others simply questioned whether this was truly the best course of action to take.

'If I don't show, he'll kill everyone I care about', Haley pointed out underneath her stubbornness. 'I have no choice'.

'But if you go, you'll not only be at risk of losing control, but also at exposing yourself to James, Matthew, Emilie and everyone else you know', Eric pointed out.

'I know the risks', Haley argued back. 'I'm aware of the lack of control'.

'But without Mjolnir – ' Skuld started before being cut off by Haley.

'It frustrates me that my own lightning power was not enough to restore it', she said, fighting against the cosmic storm surge with all her inner strength. 'The only thing I can rely on right now is Angurvadal'.

As the pause occurred, Haley hoped it was enough to prove she was right. Her stomach did a backward somersault.

'I will go with Halena', Aeolus volunteered, stepping forward. 'It is my sworn duty to protect you from harm, princess'.

Haley's heartbeat accelerated. She looked into Aeolus' eyes, feeling the bond between them. Whatever his reasons are, he gave a pretty good one; she just hoped his reasons were not to take on Vladimir by himself. Enough grief had been cast upon his family; Alfheim and most importantly Amara and Silas do not need to lose anymore.

'Me too', Keilantra said next. 'I cannot leave my best friend to take all the glory, can I?'

Haley produced a light smile at Keilantra's need to stand by her, like she did since they were fourteen years old; since they became lab partners in their science class.

'Me as well', Angela volunteered.

'No, Angela', Haley said, placing her hand. 'You're more than likely to be needed on Asgard'.

'But my lady, your friends are human', she answered with worry. Haley knew exactly what she meant. While she and the rest of the Nine Realms were practically of god blood, most of the humanity did not have the capability to block out these deadly cosmic attacks. An explosion jumped Haley out of her skin. Sand and leaves spread everywhere; buildings collapsed; and roads opened up one hundred sink holes with black holes in formation.

'Angela, you're needed on Asgard', Haley repeated. 'I'm on Earth. And don't forget: my ancestor was also the god of healing. I even healed Aeolus'. She gave a nod towards Aeolus, who seemed to smile gratefully at the memory.

'I never knew that', Angela responded.

'And it's a story I will tell you, when this is over. That's a promise. I was once told that Cosmos Beings are just as human as Migardians. So, they need me now more than ever'.

Inside, Haley pinched herself at the sudden wisdom in her voice. It was such an odd feeling that it felt like every part of her body melted.

After a long moment of hesitation, Angela reluctantly agreed with a nod.

'Little sister', Arianna said as she pulled Haley into a tight hug. 'Please be careful: Mother, Father, Eric and I cannot risk losing you again'. Tears filled the sisters' eyes at their goodbye. Eric joined the hug afterwards.

'Never underestimate Vladimir', he said. 'But also...give the bastard what he deserves'.

Haley nodded curtly, wondering whether that meant death or imprisonment. Ignoring it, she turned to Skuld who smiled angelically.

'You are a very strong and compassionate young woman, Princess Halena', she said. 'May the spirit of Thor and the gods be with you for guidance'.

Haley held the bag on her back, where the pieces of Mjolnir laid, hoping to feel at least some fragment of power come at them full force; at least on that statement. If she could sense, then the spirits of the gods in the air, sky, ground and water should sense it.

Nothing came. Only a silent prayer – otherwise the fight with Vladimir was all for nothing.

'Tell...' Haley began to say to Eric and Arianna. '...Tell our parents that I'll do my best'.

Her brother and sister gave their word to pass on the message. Honour shone in their eyes – one of their many specialties taught by Darius, the father who raised them, their true father. To think they were almost victims of corruption influenced by the bloodline of their biological father...now, here they stood: honourable Asgardian warriors of love and compassion.

'Time to go, Halena', Aeolus said as more explosions sounded through the gateway, followed by fearful screams. Haley wished she could go back in time to just after the first dream, and change the history she wrote through her vocal words and actions; to when she went surfing with Keilantra on a normal day without unintentional power surges; one normal day where the alternative outcome was different. That outcome being: she forgot everything about the dream like most people do, and she continued to leave as normal life as possible. But the one question raised more truth in all things eventful: what if dreams chose you?

After a long moment of hesitation, Haley reluctantly took Aeolus' hand and Keilantra's. All three turned back to the others, Haley thinking the exact same thing they were: was this the last time they see each other? As she, Aeolus and Keilantra, edged closer to the Bifrost opening, Haley wondered about Darius and Antoinette. They were worried sick, not just for her, but Eric and Arianna.

'*Be strong, daughter*', they said telepathically. Haley tried to respond, but all that came out was a low, hoarse sound.

Instead, she opposed a quick gaze at Angurvadal. Its red glow was brighter than ever, as bright as the original silver, due to the impending danger.

This was a fight to the death.

CHAPTER 19: THE FOURTH PIECE

As they stepped through the Bifrost, Haley, Aeolus and Keilantra held onto each other tightly. At first, the rainbow bridge's brightness circulated around them, like a tornado with mixtures of dust, levitating them through open air; until they touched the sand of Summerfield's beaches, or as Haley called it, *the place where it all began.*

The place where she finds freedom and peace…

The battle had not been going on for long. Although the Nebulans were not killing anyone directly, they were forcing them to cower in fear. Despite the humans' memories being wiped previously, having to experience these monstrous creatures a second time – Haley didn't know how to answer that to herself. The Nebulans were the predators, stalking and scaring her friends: their targets, their prey. And when they select their target, the hunt was on! And a hunt it was indeed – for Haley watched in horror, as James, Emilie, Matthew and everyone else she knew scrambled on the wet sand, as several Nebulans advanced upon them slowly. Other Asgardians and species fended some off, at the same time erasing any memory of the battle.

Without thinking, Haley charged forward before Aeolus and Keilantra could stop her. A reckless move on Haley's part…but she needed to be just that, if it meant saving innocent lives. Her own anger flourished alongside the formed thunderclouds above: her own army, her ally. As she sprinted, the storm inside her grew stronger. Like a super-charged soldier, Haley unsheathed Angurvadal and Svalinn, dealing a clean but compelling blow, blocking the Nebulans' methodical attacks; one of which almost killed Emilie, if not for Haley.

Suddenly, the last standing Nebulan sent a deadly black and purple fireball towards James, Emilie and Matthew, who were covered in cuts and bruises. Everything happened in slow motion – Haley reached the realization that she was risking exposure once she came face-to-face with them, not as Haley Freeman, but as Asgardian Princess Halena: descendent of Thor.

Left with no other option, Haley pulled out her Valkyrie dagger and held it in defence position as she moved in front of them. Flashes of what happened between her and Vladimir in the dungeon crossed her mind, the moment the fireball hit the powerful silver blade. Both powers equally matched, until the energy streamed to Jarngreipr. The tingling vibration shocked Haley; and an energy force exploded outwards, sending the Nebulan flying high into obvilion.

Haley felt lightheaded afterwards from the large amount of energy. If she was going to face Vladimir, she needed to save her strength.

'Haley?' Emilie's shocked voice came from. Unwillingly, Haley turned towards them. Silence filled between them from the ongoing battle, Haley feeling guilty at keeping her secret for so long. Now that they knew in the worst way possible, there was no going back. The way they looked at her like someone they no longer recognized increased Haley's guilty conscience.

'You need to get out of here right now', she said, trying to set the record straight, with no time to explain.

'Haley, what's going on?' Matthew asked in shock over the explosions. 'What happened to you? And what was that you just did?'

Haley pursed her lips. The whole playing-twenty-questions-during-a-battle was taking its toll. Knowing they were looking for answers she couldn't give without endangering them made the situation ten times harder to avoid.

'Look, I'll explain later', Haley lied. It was a false promise, for she knew their memories would be wiped again once this was all over. 'For now, you need to get off this beach right now. It's too dangerous to stay here'.

'But those...those things', Emilie began to ask, her voice trembling. 'What are they?'

'All I can say is they want me dead', was all Haley could give. 'I'll be fine, but you need to go now'.

'But Haley...' James started to speak.

'Go!' Haley shouted, her eyes glowing white in her frustration. The three took three steps back from her small outburst. They were afraid of her, just as they were afraid of the Nebulans; and Haley knew it. What would they decide, now that they knew? Yes, their memories would be erased again, but what if over time something triggers a flash? That was what worried Haley. They would be put in even more danger, because of her.

Thankfully, the outburst was enough for them to give into her demands. Keilantra was lucky enough to close by to gesture them into the right direction, protecting them at all costs. She and Aeolus took down more Nebulans than Haley could count. Once they were over the hills and out of sight, Haley let out a breath of relief, which was quickly short-lived at the sighting of a dark hooded figure with his back turned to her. Haley gripped her sword, knowing whom it was before he turned and lowered his hood.

Haley's heart flipped. For the very first time, she was scared, terrified she was going to lose. All this for some prophecy, Haley thought – at least her old self did. This new side had to prove she was not some damsel-in-distress, especially to her scar-faced uncle.

'Finally brave enough to show your face, niece', Vladimir smirked, twirling his dark blade. 'I hope you like the way I rearranged your former home'. He and Haley circled each other cunningly, as Haley struggled to keep her anger under control upon seeing the numerous houses in flames. Thankfully, no one was in them. Haley sensed their living souls beyond the hills, in the safety of the Asgardian knights.

'No comment I see', he continued sarcastically. 'How disappointing'.

As much as Haley hated to think it, she really wanted to squeeze the life out of him even though he was still technically family.

'Once Ragnarok returns, your worlds will soon face extinction', he replied, his smile broadening. 'And you and your family will watch it all happen'.

That was the last straw. Haley's dominating anger reached its peak, as she lost all sense of reality and focus. She charged forward, her sword rose ready to strike. As she opened an attack, Vladimir swiftly blocked it, smiling in amusement. He pushed her back, her feet skidding against the sand. Haley would have regained her full balance, if Vladimir didn't send a dark fireball towards her that she knocked back with the Valkyrie dagger. Soon enough, they were engaged in direct combat, sword-to-sword, magic-to-magic. Flashes of Haley's christening passed by, seeing Alexander, Darius and Aeolus and Silas' father, Elwood battling three on one. They were closely matched, but Vladimir appeared stronger. Haley saw that, even as she summoned lightning balls, which Vladimir easily deflected unaffected by its electrifying power, and transformed it into another dark fireball; and sent towards Haley. She only managed to block it at the last minute, but the impact brought her to her knees. She recovered quickly.

As she staggered to her feet, Vladimir's sword suddenly collided with Svalinn sending her back down again. Haley toppled backwards, but she didn't back down from the attacks. At the tenth hit, Vladimir decided enough was enough. In one split second, he snatched the shield away, which twisted Haley's arm painfully, and threw it one side. Her uncontrollable relapse caused Haley to attempt to fight back with Angurvadal aggressively but she missed, giving Vladimir the opening he needed to punch Haley in the mouth.

Haley quickly wiped the blood away from her bottom lip.

'Indeed, you are quite the fighter, Asgardian Princess', Vladimir said mockingly. 'But let's see you fight back without Svalinn, shall we?' Another fireball came her way, which required both blades to block it. The watching crowd noticed what was happening, but were too preoccupied to observe further. Haley spotted Aeolus taking down three Nebulans on his own. Unfortunately for him, their three-time strength together was deliberately crumpling his: it was only a matter of time. And it was in that moment that Haley realized she couldn't lose Aeolus, not yet, not when he just started regaining his humanity.

Throwing a high kick to Vladimir's chest, she rolled around him, temporarily subduing him with a deep gash in the right leg. When she forced her fist hard onto the ground, her body and soul became her weapon. The earth opened and shook, like a fault-line shifting, and right in the pathway of the three Nebulans who came so close to killing Aeolus, if they didn't fall through the hole; and engulfed into nothingness. Aeolus's eyes followed the direction of the crack. Their gazes locked, relief that the other was safe and alive. There he was: the boy who cares about those who matter.

The moment was cut short, when Vladimir grabbed by the hair, tossing her to the ground. Out of the corner of her eye, Haley spotted Aeolus and Keilantra trying to get past the Nebulans to help her, but to no avail. On her failed attempt to stab Vladimir with her Valkyrie dagger, the next thing she knew was being flung fifty feet through the air toward the grassy clifftops. Thank heavens for her demi-god strength and Megingjord, she thought to herself. But that did not stop her from bleeding or enduring multiple fractures from her collision with the now crumbling rocks.

All Haley could do was lie there in a dizzy episode, trying to recover at least one small ounce of strength; one that would be enough to take away the pain. Through her blind vision, she could sense Vladimir's demonic, fast-approaching presence. Blood trickled down her face. She surveyed her side, touching it with her hand. Judging by the brief twisted grimace of pain, Haley broke four ribs. They were healing slowly, which meant not enough time until Vladimir dealt his climaxing blow.

Breathing heavily through the surpassing pain, Haley only got as far as on one knee but she was still in a dire condition. In sequence came the distressing thunderclouds, as they did when she almost drowned that day. Now would have been a good time for Mjolnir to reform, but no immediate power elevated the three pieces on the ground next to the blue rose. Haley's heart broke at her fading strength and rapid heartbeat: her strength for the lack of energy for Mjolnir, and her heart for the gift Aeolus gave her. Guilt sickened her through her harsh, ragged breaths: what would he say?

The small, stir-crazy moment was interrupted by a something. Darkness surrounded her like a cage, the second Vladimir's prevailing latency became known.

Luckily for Haley, he did not deliver a brutal blow right away. Instead, he encircled her while observing every part of the sand dune clearing.

'Do you recognize this land…dear niece?' he asked with a low sneer. Vengeance trickled down his tongue. The dawning realization sickened Haley, even the grass forever touched by dust and water crawled demonically across every corner of her skin. This spot, the very spot she laid was the exact same spot; where she killed that group of Nebulans from the first encounter, their frozen remains melted and disintegrated to the ground.

'This is the final resting place of my comrades…my finest warriors', he said as he turned with a mocking, emotionless look. 'Where you murdered them'.

Haley pushed past her heavy breathing. Despite knowing it was for good intentions to take a life in self-defense, she didn't want to hear that word ever again.

'They…they were…hurting…innocent…people', she stuttered. 'My friends…and my brother…and sister…'

'They were unimportant', he answered back, which angered Haley.

'Unimportant?' she said rhetorically, holding Angurvadal which surprisingly remained in her hand. 'They were…your children…your flesh and blood…' All that was delivered back was a hard slap, sending her back to the ground.

'They are no longer my children!' Vladimir yelled in her face. 'I offered them, even your precious mother, the chance to join me, to embrace my power; if not for my brother's pitiful interference. He stole my wife and children; and I will return the favour by taking away his beloved daughter…you'.

A sudden kick in the abdomen knocked the wind out of Haley, striking such a blow that she slowly began to bleed internally. Whatever happened during the Trials, Vladimir sure as hell became stronger. In pure remembrance, Haley touched the grass thinking back to the battle strategy she performed on that day. The Nebulans froze upon direct contact with water, and were shattered by lightning. What if that was enough to stop Vladimir? Using the ounce of strength she recovered, Haley reached within seeking out both water and ice.

But the only element she could find out of the two: water. Panicking, Haley searched again and again. On the tenth try, she attained the incurring awareness: the third trial required a sacrifice in order to obtain Mjolnir's last piece, and her sacrifice was a loss of one part of her power, just like Odin sacrificed his own eye.

Her ice element…

She cast her eyes down to the ground in defeat.

'You lost one gift I see', Vladimir simulated. 'A simple but stupid thing to sacrifice…especially when you needed it to conquer impending death – after your death, no one will question my legacy or power. When you are gone, no one will stop my master Ragnarok from returning'.

He grabbed her by the hair, dragging her across the ground, before punching her hard, opening a bleeding wound on her cheek.

This time, Haley gave up.

She no longer had the strength to fight back now…and probably never would…

Lifting her head lightly through the pain, Haley looked back at the beach. She horrifyingly saw Keilantra, Aeolus and the Cosmos Beings were shifting toward the losing side against the Nebulans. In desperation, the humans went for the hills for cover. There was nothing she could do. It was only a matter of time, before death took her. All she could do was send a silent prayer to the heavens, a message for Ratatoskr to pass between Vedrofolnir and Nidhogg, so that it was delivered to each and every one of the Realms highlighting her failure to stop her uncle, hoping someone else would carry out her mission…

Unconsciousness took her…her spirit fading…

*

Haley's eyes opened. First thing she saw was white fluffy clouds and blue sky, a sweet breeze filling the air. She looked down: replacing her armour was a blue and gold gown – the exact same one from her dream of flying across the stars of the universe. Only this time was different: where she was looked different. The hills and destroyed houses surrounding the beach were gone. Slowly standing up, Haley also quickly realized she was bare-foot. Either she was having a nervous breakdown, or this was a clear sign of spiritual grace towards the after-life. Was that where she was? Has she really gone to heaven? The clouds were like the ocean: foamed waves of pure white, light and cool to the touch; as Haley dipped her foot. She felt air, a gentle breeze. She was standing on a mountain, blended with patches of snow and fresh grass, the sun reflecting through the brilliant blue sky. The universe shone through dramatically, like she was on Mount Olympus.

Soon after, Haley sensed a presence. And not a Cosmos Being or a Nebulan: this was more…magical. A godly presence, powerful and equal to her own status as a demi-goddess…

'Halena, heir and princess of Asgard', a man's low, deep voice sounded behind her, echoing all around the mountain area.

Haley turned around. There stood a man in possible mid-forties, baring shoulder-length greying bronze hair and wise sparkling blue eyes, much like Haley's. He wore battle armour with a velvet red robe.

'Distant daughter of mine', he said with a smile.

Haley gasped. 'You're – you're my ancestor', she responded, frowning. 'Thor'.

He nodded and gestured his hands as confirmation.

'Where exactly am I?' she asked. 'What is this place?'

'Where do you think we are?' Thor asked in return. 'Does this particular mountaintop not look familiar?'

Haley looked around more times than she should, until it eventually dawned upon her.

'This is the mountaintop from that painting in Glaosheimr's Hall', she answered in amazement. 'But why am I here?'

'What is the last thing you remember, distant daughter?' Thor asked.

Haley played every blurred picture back, right to the point she collapsed. 'I was fighting my uncle, Vladimir, and...' Shock came about. 'I was too weak to fight back. I-I wasn't strong enough to defeat him.

Pause.

'Am – am I dead?' she asked, looking down at the gown she was wearing.

'If that is what you choose', was all Thor answered back with. His charm and wisdom was intriguing, like an ageless book that had been here since the dawn of time.

'I don't understand', Haley clarified.

'All your life, you have been preparing for this', he sighed. 'Yet you still seem to be fighting fire with fire'.

'I thought I could fight Vladimir even without Mjolnir', Haley argued back in a stubborn, light tone out of respect for the God of Thunder. 'But I don't know if I can now'.

'You are willing to give up so easily', Thor uttered thoughtfully. 'That is not what a true heir of mine does. That is why you are trapped in the Realm of the Afterlife...because you do not fully believe in your full potential as my heir'.

Haley bit her lip.

'But I accepted who I really am. I accepted that I'm not fully human. What I don't understand is why my lack of belief and the loss of one part of my power are the two reasons why I am so weak, so helpless to stop this'.

Fighting back tears, Haley gestured towards whatever was underneath the clouds. She prayed it was Earth, meaning she wished she could see what was going on down there: whether Aeolus and Keilantra made it out of there alive, stopped Vladimir and took her body to honour and grant to God in heaven of earth. They say heaven is a place on earth. Maybe that was where her still-beating heart truly laid. Another part hoped it was also Asgard. Her family: her parents, her brother and sister – what must they be thinking right now?

'Not fully, my dear', Thor replied back. 'Now, come. Walk with me'.

He held his hand out to her. Haley looked at it for a moment, wondering whether to trust this legend she read numerous times in the hundreds of Norse Mythology books she checked out tirelessly from local libraries. Hesitantly, she took it feeling her lightning power coordinate with his: one and the same on different levels. They walked over to the only plant on the mountain: a tree of golden brown bark and emerald green leaves. Haley reached up to touch one of them. Unlike Earth's leaves, these were softer, more smoother.

'This tree is a representation of life itself', Thor explained. 'It is a living, breathing replica of Yggdrasil: a symbol of hope and beauty. Hope that those who pass through Vahalla find peace in the afterlife'.

'What does this have to do with me though?' Haley asked, catching on the idea.

'Like the tree, you have grown into a symbol of hope, Halena', Thor proclaimed. 'Not only were you born with my power of thunder and lightning, you were born with the power to heal and bring peace to the Nine Realms'.

'The prophecy said The One would unite the Realms into a new golden age', she recalled thoughtfully. 'But I've been doubtful about it lately. Why's that?'

Thor sighed deeply. 'Maybe it is because you are afraid'.

'Afraid?' she asked. 'I'm not afraid of my own uncle'.

'You are afraid to face the reality right in front of you', he corrected quickly. 'You have your doubts, yes; but since finding out who you truly are, you finally have the chance to embrace it'.

Haley looked between the tree, Thor and the entire cloudy landscape view. One part of her wanted to go back and stop Vladimir, but at the same time, she wanted to accept defeat. However, if she did, then she was giving up any chance of stopping Vladimir, Ragnarok and other Dark Beings.

'My life…I prepared for something which I did not know at the time', Haley proclaimed. 'But I don't know how to fully embrace it. If I can't reforge Mjolnir, then who am I?'

'My dear, there is a reason why you cannot reforge Mjolnir', Thor answered, his eyes shining with hope she would listen, which Haley came to do. 'The missing piece'.

'There's another piece?' Haley asked. 'What is it then? Tell me'.

'Your determination is inspiring, much like my father and his father before him', he continued. 'I too used that to my own strength, to protect the innocent and the Nine Realms. There is but one way to recover this piece'.

Every word sounded like a piece of a riddle. Haley's nerves tensed up, as she thought this through carefully. Her confused feelings were causing her brain to become flooded with hundreds more unanswered questions.

'What do I need to do?' she asked simply. 'Like I said, I don't know if I can stop my own uncle'.

'In order to defeat him, you must let in the one thing you value the most', Thor answered. 'Look deep within you. Find the one thing that matters, the one thing your uncle does not have…and Mjolnir will come to you, alive and reborn'.

Haley thought long and hard.

Here she was with her ancestor on top of potentially the most beautiful mountain in the world, depicting on what world that actually was.

In her memory drive, Haley saw how every day served a challenge; how almost each moment was spent hiding herself from the world. Protecting herself from her powers; from losing control: it was a struggle. Yet there was more. They were connected…her creating lightning phoenixes, her family watching her in wonderment, her twirling around in snowflakes; the connection between her and Aeolus; her friendship with Keilantra…the happiest memories leading one thing and one thing only.

'I think I know…like you do', Haley uttered wondrously to Thor. 'But will it be enough to stop what is coming?'

'Do you truly believe it…right at this moment, distant daughter?' he asked her

All the sacrifices her family made for her served as a restoration of hope and meaning. If the Cosmos Beings believed in it and the Gods believed in, then –

'Yes…I do', Haley answered back honestly.

'Then, return to the battle. Fight for the Realms, fight for all that is good in the universe', he encouraged. 'Take up Mjolnir…and fight!'

*

An energy jolt shocked Haley, like she was being resuscitated. Every cell in her entire body became electrified. Something formed inside her; something re-awakening for the first time in a long time, as her wounds fully healed. Her eyes glowed more intensely now, and the lightning in her veins bore foreseeable visibility. Stars shone through, stars of hope and beauty. Beautiful, was her first thought, much like looking through the telescope. The moment was over, when Haley reached hard ground: the same spot where she came close to death.

'Thank you, Thor', she uttered in silent telepathy to the stars. He was with her now in this moment, his spirit fully bound to hers. This was the moment where she knew she was strong enough to fight back; to stop Vladimir.

Through the strongest white intensity of her eyes, Vladimir raised his dagger ready to stab her heart. Haley was quicker this time, evaluating his movement before it came about. She threw the most powerful high kick, like lightning, sending him flying backwards over a nearby hill. While he attempted to recover from the unexpected attack, Haley sensed something else glowing: her necklace. Never had it glimmered this brightly, especially when the crystal detached itself from the triquetra charm. The crystal twinkled vibrantly in the colours of the Aurora Eclipse, which much to Haley's surprise appeared in the sky, becoming one with the thunderstorm. Something else changed about the crystal, hovering directly above the pieces of Mjolnir. Its glow intensified, drawing the pieces together like an electromagnet. Once they were close enough, the light exploded, much like the exploding stars from the thunderstones, engulfing Haley and the entire surrounding atmosphere.

As the light died down, the crystal returned its original spot around Haley's neck. Wonderment overtook Haley's emotions. Out of her own doing, Thor's hammer re-forged from her newly-found hope, faith and belief. She reached out to grasp it, knowing this was her destiny to wield a weapon of such great power having no equal to any other weapon forged. Upon contact, Haley's own power and Mjolnir became one, as if Thor's voice was telling her the hammer was hers now; to take it. The lightning inside her, now fully visible, escaped her veins and surged all around her, as the sky darkened and thunder rumbled more violently.

This was nothing to do with anger. It was acceptance…to fight, to protect, like her ancestors before her.

Vladimir emerged from over the hill, taken aback in anger by his failed accomplishment to destroy Haley, surprised by her sudden recovery. Once again, he let his arrogant ego cloud his judgment. Even the battle on the beach came to a pregnant pause. Haley sought out Keilantra and Aeolus from bird's eye view – both stood proudly, watching their friend embrace her newfound power. This was the truth. She was not going to run anymore, or look away. She hoped Darius, Antoinette, Eric, Arianna and everyone else she came to know witnessed this from the clouds above.

No more hiding…

'How?' Vladimir asked, eyes widened in shock and fury against his disfigured face., keeping his sword at the ready.

Haley grasped Mjolnir tightly, ready to use it.

'Because I have something worth fighting for', she said contently. 'Something you will never have again'.

Vladimir's anger was building up again.

'Love', Haley continued with that one simple word.

Their eyes locked, as Vladimir made the first move. He did not want to hear that word ever again. A black fireball blasted out of his hand, but Haley sensed it coming before it formed. Swinging Mjolnir over, she struck the fireball splitting it into a dozen harmless fires as Mjolnir's metal vibrated underneath her. Not only had it heightened her powers, but it heightened her warrior flexes.

'Love is what makes them weak!' Vladimir shrieked out, sending out more numerous fireballs towards Haley, which she destroyed single-handedly without so much of a scratch on her exposed skin. Eventually, two weapons collided creating a shock wave, bringing them face-to-face.

'It's what makes them strong', Haley clarified through gritted teeth. 'It's what they choose to believe in: to master what they are born with. Something I learnt all this time…'

Images continued to flood her mind: the memories she treasure without fully realizing. The love for her family was one of the most beautiful moments she could have experienced. They gave her strength. With it, Haley managed to push Vladimir away from her.

'As my father once said…' Haley said with a small smirk, as she watched the gauntlets engulfed in lightning, alongside Mjolnir. '…you, Vladimir: my uncle, know nothing about love. You never have…and you never will'.

Vladimir's eyes flared brightly in fury, his veins popping. The fire he conjured up was one so powerful, that it could cause death the second it touched someone's skin. Haley reached inside her to check for the one thing she needed to combat this: her water element. It was back, stronger: flowing around like a tidal wave waiting to burst out.

All she needed was the right possible moment to strike.

'I will not be defeated by my own niece again!' Vladimir shouted out.

As the fireball began to make its way towards Haley, she twirled Mjolnir around directing it towards the ocean. Sure enough, a large wave generated by the lightning snaked its way upward to her, circulating around her like a whirlpool.

Flashes passed through: from her transforming a mini whirlpool of ocean-water into ice, thinking it was the most beautiful, yet extraordinary out-of-this-world object to create; to when she transformed three tiny raindrops into a single, larger wave and froze a bunch of Nebulans.

If every element she inherited became more enhanced, then maybe with the ice element…it was a vigorous possibility.

At the best-timed moment, Haley sent the wave hurdling towards Vladimir who in turn attempted to block with his dark shield. Both energies connected once again, the all-out epic battle slowly reaching the climax that could determine each other's fate. Who lives? Who dies? Haley gripped Mjolnir with both hands, trying to channel more power. The metal shuddered under her hand, when the light-headed sickness started to emerge slowly. A small drop of blood came out of Haley's nose. She was using too much energy, as she was warned numerous times…

But she didn't care…she needed to finish this battle once and for all!

Pushing past her sickness, Haley channeled as much as ice, water and lightning toward Mjolnir as possible. It was working. In the conflict for both sides to control, Haley's combination of all three elements made their way towards the struggling Vladimir. Much to his own shock, his shield did not match the same strength Haley's newest shield. It came closer and closer, until finally –

Both sides exploded!

Every element evaporated or vanished into nothingness. Dust and sand elevated all around, before clearing. Breathing heavily through her fading vision, Haley saw what she accomplished: her uncle frozen like an ice statue, in a state of shock…the only movement in his eyes.

'It's done', she whispered, in a tiny smile. Darkness followed, as she collapsed to her knees still holding onto Mjolnir.

Thor's voice rang in her ears saying she did all Realms proud.

Chapter 20: One of Five

Haley awoke slowly, her vision still blurred. The only thing she saw were a bunch of figures, watching over her. Blinking twice, it finally cleared. It was everyone: Darius, Antoinette, Eric, Arianna, Aeolus, Keilantra, Angela; even Alexander, Elena and Henrietta. All of whom stood there in sheer worry waiting for her to wake up.

'Halena', her mother cried, tears filling her eyes. 'Thank goodness you are awake. We were so worried'.

Out of the corner of her eye, Haley saw she was in the infirmary. Like every other room inside Asgard's palace, it was huge with its familiar golden brown-bricked pillars and tall windows towering up to the domed ceiling, the warm sunlight pouring in. Some of the many single beds were taken from warriors, injured during the co-ordinating battles on both worlds.

Her parents each hugged her, relieved she was alive. Haley returned each one, this time without hesitation. Everyone else joined in, even Aeolus, who displayed such tenderness that Haley's heart soared. His humanity was back at long last.

'How are you feeling, daughter?' Darius asked.

Haley placed her hand on her head, which still pounded like a drum ever so slightly.

'Like I've been hit by a massive truck', she muttered, trying to lighten the mood.

Everyone else seemed to have felt the same way. Aside from the obvious cuts and bruises on most of them, there was also exhaustion from tiresome hours of battling and helping treat the wounded.

'Wait...so what happened...after I passed out?' Haley eventually asked. 'What happened to Vladimir? Is everyone on Earth okay?' Her voice turned to worry. 'What about Nyssa?'

'James, Matthew, Emilie and everyone else', Arianna stated. '...They are all safe, thanks to the memory wipe, and the town has been returned to exactly the way it was'.

'Queen Nyssa and the rest of Niflheim are still alive, but many lost their lives', Eric proclaimed. 'Those who died will receive a place amongst the stars for their selfless sacrifice.

Haley felt like she could breathe again, staying strong by withholding her tears. Yet she felt sad for Nyssa and her people, wondering whether this was something they would ever recover from like they did with the First Ragnarok.

'As for Vladimir...he'll live', Darius uttered. It always amazed Haley at how tough her father was to keep the anguishing anger he felt towards his half-brother.

'I am sorry', Haley said shamefully.

'What for, Halena?' her father asked.

Haley bit her lip, her eyes shy as she fidgeted with the bed-sheet covering her nightdress.

'I know there was an open chance for me to...kill him', she muttered under her breath, a single teardrop leaving her eye, which she quickly brushed away. 'But I just couldn't bring myself to do it in the end'.

'Do not ever be sorry for compassion, Halena', Antoinette said comfortingly. 'It shows you are strong enough to let someone live, despite all the awful things they...have done...to hurt people'. The beats had Haley guessing that her mother too thought back to the times Vladimir hurt. He was her first love, but in the end he chose darkness over love.

'When I passed out...' Haley started. '...I saw my ancestor, Thor'.

This time, everyone's eyes shone in sheer wonderment.

'What was it like?' Aeolus asked.

'It was amazing, like I was having a dream, outside the body', she continued. 'He was the reason I was able to re-forge Mjolnir in the first time. He told me not to be afraid – that was the only way I could let that power in. If it wasn't for him, I probably wouldn't be here right now'.

'Love – that was what he told you let in', Eric guessed.

Haley just nodded.

'It was the most beautiful thing I ever felt', she said, smiling thoughtfully. 'Without it, I would continue to be surrounded by darkness'.

Not only her love for her family all around her, but also Aeolus as well, she thought to herself. Since she became drawn to his intelligent, brown eyes, the warmth and comfort he gave only made the feeling stronger: his simple acts of kindness through his cold demeanor. Every second she spent with Aeolus since that first meeting, when she was only a baby, felt like a simple moment of clarity, much like meeting her parents for the first time. The hole in her heart, the missing jigsaw puzzle piece, healed, her world completed. Like a shield, it kept her safe, protected and calm.

But then came the dark side of Haley's thoughts. The heavy chained events physically and emotionally drained her, as she suddenly craved for more answers about the recent occurrences.

'There's more', Haley said, touching her necklace. 'This Aurora Crystal: there's something more to it. Eric, Arianna, Angela and Aeolus: all four of you saw what happened at the Wells, when the stars became the thunderstones. This crystal called out to them. When I remembered the memories filled with love and joy, the crystal activated to re-forge Mjolnir'.

At her bedside, Mjolnir stood tall like any normal axe except for the low hum of thunder ringing silently through Haley's ears, but out of complete earshot from the others.

'What exactly did you feel, Halena, when this happened?' Alexander asked knowingly.

'I felt purity…this balance between light and darkness, life and death', Haley answered honestly. 'Why do you ask?"

Alexander looked between Darius and Antoinette, who nodded permission to whatever this substantial unveils was; and then back to his wife and daughter, before rushing out in a dash.

Confusion washed over Haley.

'What was that all about?' she asked, while everyone else seemed to understand Alexander's actions immediately. Wherever he went, Haley had a guess that the obvious choice was the Oracle, Lady Orla. Only she would she know something about the crystal around Haley's neck. Another thought crossed Haley's mind: was it to do with the five crystals she saw in the visional windows at Mimir's Well?

'What about Vladimir? Where is he?' she asked.

Her parents, or pretty much, everyone were entirely reluctant to answer that question. Haley came close to getting down on her knees to guilt them, were it not for her father eventually answering.

'He is being held in the dungeons for the time being', he said. 'His powers were temporarily compromised, so he won't be able to use them, or draw power from Nebula'.

'What happened to Nebula then?' Haley asked out of curiosity.

'Both Aesir and Vanir tribes combined their energies to leave Nebula in a dormant state', Elena replied. 'Any surviving Nebulans will be imprisoned and sentenced in accordance to the laws of the Nine Realms'.

'So what will Vladimir's sentence be?' Haley asked.

Darius sighed, unable to speak, clearly thinking about the brother he grew up with, the brother he lost in the dark side of his power.

'Your father and I called an emergency meeting with the High Council', Antoinette exclaimed.

'Despite all he had done, he is still my brother and it will sadden me even more if I was to have him executed', Darius continued. 'So it was decided that he will be given a life imprisonment in the Realm of Chaos'.

Haley's eyes narrowed.

'After the First Ragnarok, the Gods created this Realm which remains unknown and undiscovered from Earth's legends', he continued. 'A world of endless nightmares for the cruel, it was designed to act as a prison stronghold, supposedly inescapable for murderers and criminals, who dare stand against the Gods and the Nine Realms'.

Darius was right: no matter what he had done, he was still a part of Haley's family whether he or Haley liked it or not. Killing him would be the most dishonourable thing to do. She learnt that through the guidance of the Gods.

'May I...see him?' Haley asked, as much as she dreaded to do so.

Everyone thought this to be extreme. They won the battle and the threat was compromised, but what more could there possibly be for him to bring further strain? Haley was not about to let that happen without getting what she needed to say out of her system.

'Halena, even without his powers, he will try to torment you much like he did the first time round', Aeolus said worrisomely. Even though his humanity returned, there was that momentary lapse of rage hibernating inside him.

No matter what, Haley was insistent.

'There are still some things I need to say to him', she answered. 'I won't get the chance to if he's trapped on another Realm'.

'Shouldn't you wait until my father gets back though, Halena?" Henrietta asked. Haley saw it in her eyes: wisdom. The most mature trait, even for a fourteen year old, Haley thought. No doubt, her cousin would make a fine queen someday.

'As I said, I'm done with all this waiting around for more answers', Haley said, lifting herself out of bed. Aeolus was there to make sure she didn't sway from another dizzy spell.

'I need to speak to him', she repeated to Darius and Antoinette. They suffered as much as Eric and Arianna, made sacrifices for her, and just because they understood Vladimir's mysterious motives doesn't mean they did fully. Especially after what Haley speculated to Nyssa on Niflheim...and Mimir's looking glass of the Aesir-Vanir War.

'At least take someone with you', Darius instructed to her.

'No', Haley said with more insistence. 'I want to do this alone'.

With one more look at Aeolus, she was out the door, hoping and praying no guards would follow her on her parents' orders.

Thankfully, no one came.

The familiar walk to the dungeons was no walk in the park like before, but it was easier without the feeling of dark magic coming off every corner of the stone walls. First time round, Haley thought that her uncle was an actual Nebulan with some sense of honour who willingly surrendered. But they were just as ruthless as he was, even more so when she walked past them in their cells. They hissed and growled like wild animals, and threatened her despite all their powers being neutralized. Unable to be reminded of all the evil deeds, Haley dared not look at them – all of whom created soully out of the dark magic flowing through Vladimir's veins. The very dark magic passed down from his mother, Elvira who too could have likely been a follower of Ragnarok, before the duty was passed down to him upon death.

What answers he would give, the answers she would get. As Haley rounded the corner of the last cell, no dark surge erupted invisibly in a bubble. Thank the Gods, she thought. There she saw him, hands on his back, turned to her, baring a calm, collected posture; much to her own surprise. Aeolus' reminder passed through: he would not attempt to attack without his powers, but whatever words were going to come out of his mouth, it would be nothing but poison.

As Vladimir turned around, his expression unreadable, the daunting silence replaced the Nebulans' shouts. He and Haley stared each other down for under a minute.

'You should have killed me when you had the chance, niece', Vladimir scolded. Even without his powers, he deemed her weak. Haley, on the other hand, was relieved that he couldn't create a barrier to block out their conversation this time.

'Death would have been too kind, uncle', Haley replied back, shrugging her shoulders. 'In the end, it was my choice to let you live. Killing someone in cold blood: that's not who I am. Just because you've done so many horrible things doesn't change the fact that you are still my father's brother'.

'Half-brother', Vladimir hissed.

'And my mother's my first love', Haley continued, dodging the interruption. 'You could have chosen to a different path, followed the same path as my father did'.

Vladimir let out a low, disbelieving laugh, curving his lip.

'Instead, you chose to follow in Elvira's footsteps. That was why my mother turned to my father. You became a vessel of nothingness: no love or compassion whatsoever; someone who spent his time obsessing over destroying so many innocent lives, and worlds under Ragnarok's bidding. If Antoinette didn't, she would've shared a piece of your own darkness, controlling her: even Eric and Arianna.

'Your mother...betrayed me. In doing so', he argued. 'My brother and my children betrayed me. In doing so, I stopped ignoring my destiny. I embraced it'.

'The only reason you chose that path is because you became consumed by the fact that your true identity was kept a secret from you', Haley fought back firmly. 'All my father did was try to help you. You knew damn well that all that lying was to protect you. Something I have come to terms during the weeks gone'.

A long pause endured, Haley's shocking wisdom still and perhaps always surprising, even to Vladimir and his fellow Nebulans in the cells next to or in front of him. All these years, they believed her to be dead, while some saw her as a simple girl with a collective range of interests, like every other human doing the normal things any human would, not a Cosmos Being; someone with minimal experience of the Nine Realms. Haley was glad to have proven them wrong in the slightest. Too bad they were too self-absorbed to fully see that, she thought. They underestimated her, like she underestimated them

Another lesson learnt…

All the while, Vladimir's posture changed. He slowly walked around, a prisoner in waiting, dazed in thought; too prideful to even think about his sentence. Haley wondered whether a part of his power remained untouched from the Asgardians' neutralizing magic. She couldn't help but notice a difference within him, compared to the last time. His eyes were tired and withdrawn from the world, but still menacing. Was it Haley's words that were slowly driving him down into a deep, dark pit of shame, or a side effect from the magic: weakening him to the point of no return?

'I admit I am amazed by your sudden loyalty to your mother and father', he finally spoke out lowly. 'Yet you did not fully answer my question back then: why so sudden?'

Once again, it felt like testing beyond her limits: one simple question, which could bare a simple answer. All this time, Haley realized it was the most difficult until now.

'Even though I couldn't see them', she answered. 'I could hear them. Their words were a comforting element: the perfect ingredient, like an antidote needed to help me control my powers. Every now and then, they sent messages in my dreams. Despite not knowing them or getting to grow up around, I know now, thanks to my ancestor, that everything they did for me was out of love'.

'Despite all the secrets?' he asked in amusement. It sounded more rhetoric than directed fully to her. Everyone had secrets, even Haley. She hid herself from the world, hid her powers from everyone she cared about because she was afraid of hurting them when she couldn't control it. She remembered James, Emilie and Matthew – their faces forever embedded in her mind. Even if she explained her true nature, even if their memories were not erased a second time; they would not accept her. In time, she would have accepted that: as an act of sacrifice, a sacrifice of friendship.

Haley ignored Vladimir's rhetoric question.

'Tell me this: what were you really after then?' she asked.

Vladimir looked at her in confusion.

'I saw it in your eyes', she continued, crossing her arms together. 'The need for discovery, the search for something: it must be so important, even to Ragnarok, to have caused you to turn your back on family'.

Haley eagerly waited for Vladimir to break the silence next. What exactly was he planning in the first place, aside from trying to kill her? He identified himself as a follower of Ragnarok, but what about the other four she saw in the past vision at Mimir's Well? Who were they? Were they after the same goals as Vladimir? Did it involve a deadly fate, or just an endless, slaughtering war of pure hatred and anger?

'You really have no idea, do you?' he asked, letting out a low laugh, the other Nebulans watching in amusement

'About what?' Haley asked. She hoped the All-Knowledge answered that for her, but nothing came.

'About why I chose this path, about why I created my friends in all these cells', Vladimir replied arrogantly.

'Why?'

Pause.

'Why not ask the Oracle, Lady Orla? I am sure she will provide you with some more accurate insight', Vladimir said.

Haley rubbed her wrist, hiding the electric current, which almost became visible again. She couldn't handle any more secrets, no more meaningless questions and answers...she needed closure to the circumstances of this mission: to defeat the perilous darkness of Ragnarok, if she was able to get to that point.

As she turned to leave, the Nebulans started laughing as Vladimir spoke again.

'If you think the Realm of Chaos will hold me and my fellow comrades, you are wrong', he said, Haley feeling his evil smile, which sent creepy crawls up and down her skin. 'We will escape and free Ragnarok, niece; and our world and its glory will restored'.

'ALL HAIL NEBULA! ALL HAIL NEBULA!' he and the Nebulans yelled out. Unable to take anymore, Haley rushed out of there as the guards raced to the cells bashing the Nebulans' fingers on the bars in an attempt to shut them up. As she ran, Haley breathed heavily. Everything was a mess again: her uncle's sentencing was the next day, and he pretty much confirmed more information at her mission. It was just unwritten – unwritten due to the fact that she still didn't know what was going to happen next.

*

When Vladimir's sentencing came about, Haley half-expected it to take place in Forseti's hall, Glitnir, it being the hall of law and justice. Instead, here she was back in the mer-people's caverns, standing beside her mother, father, Eric, Arianna, Alexander, Elena, Henrietta, Serena, Keilantra, Aeolus, Silas, Amara and Angela. Even Queen Nyssa with her son came along, having come forward as witnesses. Vladimir and the Nebulans were in chains, levitated above the water against a blood-red sunset outside. She saw her mother hold her father's hand, a glimpse of sadness in his eyes at the loss of the brother he grew up with, now a vessel of darkness and power.

Storm clouds, which were not Haley's doing, swirled like a violent hurricane, opening an eye in the centre, blackened. Eerie screams and voices demanding to be released filled the air. That was not a good sound, Haley thought, especially for prisoners who were imprisoned in this supposedly horrifying place for who knows how many years. She would much rather have her mother use her Sky Mirror for her to see the other Worlds in Yggdrasil and appreciate their beauty. Worry swirled within: Vladimir swore he would escape, that this place would not hold him for long. He and the Nebulans would find a way out either way.

On her right, Aeolus took a hold of her hand. Her unexpectedly developed feelings for him and his humanity made her feel alive, a perfect attempt to take her mind off this ordeal. She too provided comfort for him and Silas, who stood close to his brother and held his mother's hand, knowing this was partial closure and indefinite justice for Elwood.

She and everyone else watched as Vladimir and the Nebulans carried up by the vortex. Up above, knights on flying horses closed it up, the sky returning to normal, much to Haley's own relief. Everyone started departing, except for Haley, who held back because of Vladimir's revelation.

'Halena?' her mother asked.

Haley looked towards Lady Orla, who too was curious about why she remained.

'I need to know something', she said. 'I need you to be honest as well'.

Lady Orla simply nodded. 'I know what you are going to ask, Halena', she answered.

'You do?' Haley asked.

'While you went to speak with your uncle, King Alexander came to me', Lady Orla continued. 'He mentioned something about there being more to the Aurora Crystal around your neck that meets the eye'.

Haley nodded.

'And that you saw a vision of the truth behind the aftermath of the Aesir-Vanir War'.

'Yes'.

Lady Orla sighed.

'That crystal…' She gestured to the necklace, as Haley ran her finger over it. '…It is one of five very rare crystals, created by the Gods. The Aurora Crystal is designed to give life to anything mystical, it being a reflection of the Aurora Borealis: a spiritual reincarnation of passing on a second life.'.

Haley was taken aback by this revelation. Everyone else remained insecure, as if it was not possible something like this existed. That would explain why she was able to release Mjolnir's pieces from the thunderstones, why she was able to finally re-forge it at the best possible moment.

'I don't understand', she eventually uttered. 'What does this have to do with the prophecy?'

'The crystals are a balance of life itself', Alexander explained. 'Your mother and I were told this story by our fathers when we were children. They said if and when there were a time where Ragnarok would return again, these crystals are the symbols of hope in ensuring that it does not happen again'.

'Vladimir was after this, wasn't he?' she asked, turning to her parents, showing them her necklace. 'It was what he was looking for from the moment he discovered his relation to Elvira'.

'We did not realize it, until the Aurora Eclipse awakened the Aurora Crystal from its dormant state', Darius explained. 'Until it sensed your greatness towards your destiny, Halena, with you being Thor's heir to Mjolnir'.

'Five crystals and the Followers of Ragnarok', Haley reached the realization. 'They plan to use them to awaken Ragnarok'.

'That was why you needed Mjolnir', Lady Orla proclaimed. 'Without it, you will not be able to find these crystals. If Vladimir had gotten his hands on it, the other followers would have sensed and made it their own mission to find the other four, and join them together to form their unity and unleash Ragnarok'.

'So where are they now?' Haley asked, directing it towards both these crystals and the followers she spotted in her vision. 'In that dream I had, it was more than a dream. It was a vision of what happen if I fail. I'm scared of that happening'.

Lady Orla turned toward the sky, looking at the open universe.

'They are out there somewhere amongst the stars', she answered. 'As princess of Asgard and heir to the throne, it is your destiny to find them. Find them and unite the Nine Realms. Defeat Ragnarok and lead us into a golden age'.

Haley gulped. Everyone else looked at her.

'How long will it be before Ragnarok returns?' she asked.

'Only if they get the crystals can they create such horror', Darius answered. 'Right now, you are the keeper of the Aurora Crystal. You must guard it with your life'.

'It is your choice, daughter', her mother continued, caressing Haley's cheeks. 'You are bound to the prophecy and everything you learnt over the weeks'.

'We will help you in any way we can, Halena'. Antoinette squeezed Haley's hands. 'You are our greatest love, a savior of the Nine Realms. We and the Gods will guide you through this'.

Love shone in everyone's eyes, especially Aeolus. Haley mirrored it through her conflicting belief. She looked up at the sky, wondering whether Thor was watching over her. He said she did the Nine Realms proud, defeating her own uncle: the first follower of Ragnarok. Now that she knew there was more to her quest, that there were enemies possibly searching for these crystals at this very second, it was now a more concerning factor to deal with. Yet the future was blank like a canvas, which only she could paint in time.

They were right: it was too late to turn back the clock now, and pretend these experiences never happened. Lady Orla and her family: they all were right.

This was only the beginning for Haley. The prophecy, her destiny: everything was beginning to fall into place.

This was her new life, her mission. She was now Halena Thora Antoinette: princess of Asgard and destined savior of Yggdrasil.

Printed in Great Britain
by Amazon